BLACK FLAG

Best wishes

Jake Morris

Jake Morris

Published in 2014 by FeedARead Publishing

Copyright ©Jake Morris

A CIP catalogue record for this title is available from the British Library.

This is a work of fiction. Names, characters, places and incidents are the products of the author's imagination or are used fictitiously. Any resemblance to actual events, locales, or persons, living or dead, is entirely coincidental.

To

The homeless ones, the noiseless dead

(Siegfried Sassoon)

ONE

Owen Gallagher had spent the morning praying for death. It was the relentlessness of it: the pain spiking through his body, the ebb and flow of unforgiving nausea, the sucking and dumping of mental flotsam borne on a sea of agonies. Even his hair seemed to hurt. Then there was the noise, the bright light, the smell, the shouting, the shoving and the sheer dreadfulness of the human condition writ large.

As he stepped inside off the street, he heard a woman's voice.

'Where were you last night?'

That was a good question. He had other last-night-related questions himself – like how he'd woken up in Kennington next to a woman with a broken alarm clock – but he wouldn't be attempting any answers until a drink had been had.

'You said you would take me dancing.'

Gallagher fished around in the murky pool of his recent memory but caught nothing.

'You always disappoint,' said Eve, with a pout so French that it managed to be accusing and alluring in equal measure.

'It's been said before, but never by anyone nearly as beautiful as you.'

Eve moved towards the counter to hide a smile that was threatening to shimmy across her lips. 'Glass or bottle?'

The bar was just off Charing Cross Road. Gallagher moved to his usual table in the corner, with a view of the door, to settle into the comforting late morning light.

'We'll start with a glass, I think.'

It was a good vantage point for watching unobserved as London went by outside the window. Reaching into his pocket, he pulled out a book still in its paper bag and placed his coat over the back of the chair. As he sat down, Eve placed a glass of chilled Alsace Pinot Noir on the table – followed by the bottle. Gallagher was about to speak but the young woman gave him a wink and walked away.

Might as well be drunk as be as we are, he thought.

The menu of various meat and cheese platters held no interest for him, but it would be pleasant enough to while away a couple of hours as the lunchtime crowd came and went. He would watch Eve wiggle between the tables, read his book, sip his wine and wave his hangover goodbye in a thoroughly civilised manner.

Within two sips another customer entered and ordered coffee. A figure blocked the light in which Gallagher was reading.

'Do you mind if I join you?' asked the shadow.

'Are the empty tables not to your liking?' Gallagher answered without glancing up.

'That's no way to welcome an old friend, Owen.'

'I think that would be pushing things, don't you?'

'The camaraderie of brothers in arms?'

'Too long ago – another life, in fact.' Gallagher put down his book and finally looked up at the man in the suit grinning down at him.

'A cheery hello for your guardian angel?'

'What do you want, Bannerman?'

'Jesus, Gallagher, you're a miserable bastard. I come bearing gifts, well, a job actually – interested?'

'Sit down then and try to use one word when ten won't do.'

'Kind of you, I think I shall,' said Bannerman. He held out his immaculate trench coat to Eve who was hovering nearby. Her friend Claire prepared his coffee.

'How did you know I was here? Actually, don't answer that.'

'I was surprised you weren't watching the door as I came in.'

'I saw you turn the corner and cross the road.'

'Very observant, that's what I like about you Owen. Ha! You look a picture. A good night was it?'

'I have no idea. What have you got for me?'

'Just a find and a fix. Not worth putting an Alpha team on it, so I thought I'd farm it out to you. Good book?'

Bannerman nodded his thanks to Eve as she placed his coffee down.

Gallagher pushed his book across the table.

'Ah, Richard Harris, the hell-raising thespian,' said Bannerman, turning the pages of the biography. 'Here's a good quote: "I often sit back and think I wish I'd done that and find out later I already have." Is he a role-model of yours, Owen?'

'Please, be my guest,' said Gallagher, leaning back in his chair to watch Bannerman read the book's cover blurb.

'So, who do you want me to watch?' Gallagher asked. Claire had started to flash cutlery noisily, sending fresh agonies through him. Eve was absent-mindedly polishing glasses at the bar.

'All in good time. I think I'll join you.'

Bannerman called for an empty glass and Gallagher saw his afternoon disappear before it could begin.

* * *

On his last day in Baghdad Tom Edwards had made the short journey from the team's compound, listening to banter directed at him across the radio by colleagues yet to finish their security contracts in Iraq. At the airport, he'd wished his friend Gus well. They'd arranged to meet in London for a quiet beer – to be followed by ten louder ones. Then Gus was gone and another tour was finished, next stop Africa.

Now Tom was worried. Gus had telephoned and left him a message via the firm's operations centre in Johannesburg. Tom had been on a security detail down in Cape Town for a few days. The message was that four of their old six-man team in Iraq had been killed in the last week. They hadn't lost a single man in two years. There was no mention of how they'd died. Of the originals on the contract, only he and Gus were now left alive.

Gus had said he'd call again regarding funeral arrangements in the UK. The message had been taken five days ago but there was no record of a return call. Gus had said something else at the end of his message: 'Jack is the wrong way up.'

A South African colleague had delivered a hand-written note containing the message's details and had placed it on Tom's bed ready for his return. Tom stood looking at it, his mind racing. He placed the note back on the bed and peeled off his equipment. As he removed his clothes, he read the note again. Trying to take in the fact that Gary, Martin, Chalky and Joe were dead, he walked to the shower in the en-suite bathroom.

He allowed the water to wash over him, clearing away the dust and the dirt. He felt a surge of emotion and punched the tiled wall. Then he turned, sliding down the tiles, to sit as the cleansing heat of the water rushed over his head.

With a towel wrapped around his waist, he lay on his bed and stared up at the ceiling. The note was in a scrunched-up ball on the floor to his right. Jack was the Union Flag, the Union Jack. Most people were unaware that there was a right way and a wrong way to fly it. An advert at Waterloo Station in London had been taken down some years before with much embarrassment, after a major media company had attempted some positive public relations by backing 'our boys' in Afghanistan. The problem was that the Union Jack they'd placed above the caption was upside down. Arseholes.

Traditionally, as all British service personnel knew, if you were approaching a garrison or outpost and the flag was upside down then there was something wrong – it was a distress signal, a warning. And it was a good one at that, because no one else in the area would notice – like most of the British public. So whatever it was, it was serious. And whatever it was, this was a warning for Tom to go careful, to watch his back.

* * *

Gallagher moved under a glowering sky along Upper St Martin's Lane to his flat a short walk away from Le Lion Rouge, where he'd left Bannerman to settle the bill. He passed the sundial monument and headed into Shorts Gardens three minutes after the rain began bouncing off the pavement, but was soaked before he reached the top of the steps to Seven Dials Court.

Having disabled the alarm, he looked back along the hallway at his wet footsteps and threw his sodden coat at the hooks behind the door. It hit the rack and fell in a heavy heap on to the letters he had stepped over a moment before.

The room he walked into could have been described as moderately spacious for central London, had it not contained so many books and so much clutter. There was a vintage brown leather sofa of such distressed demeanour that it wouldn't have looked out of place in a trendy bar or a shop selling overpriced sweaters and boat shoes to the middle classes. An armchair of the same age and colour was its constant companion and the two sat contentedly across from each other, as they had done for many years. An Edwardian mantel clock ticked through the slow minutes, chimed the quarter hours with a melancholy bong and the hours loudly with – ironically, Gallagher thought – no consideration regarding the time of day or night.

He hated that clock. He hated it and its obsessive marking out of minutes and mortality. But the clock, like almost

11

everything in the room, had been Uncle Edwin's and although Gallagher had arranged the transformation of the rest of the flat since it had been left to him four years before, he'd left this room exactly as Edwin had known it. He liked the fact that the old boy still seemed to inhabit the space in some way, an absent presence between the artefacts collected during a life centred on the West End for over half a century. Edwin had been the black sheep of the family. Gallagher smiled in remembrance as he flicked on a standard lamp in the corner.

The envelope that Bannerman had given him at the bar was wet but the contents were held in a black plastic zip folder, which Gallagher emptied on to the small desk on the far side of the room. When he switched on the desk lamp the first thing to be illuminated was the face of a young woman under a woolly hat. The picture had been taken by a police photographer at a demonstration in London. The woman in the picture was smiling, while sticking two fingers up at the rank of riot-shielded officers in front of her. Gallagher paused for a moment to consider this seemingly carefree figure flanked by angry protesters with scarves pulled up over their faces, hats and baseball caps pulled firmly down.

Gallagher sat and began to sift through the various papers and pictures contained in the file. First he found a printout from the Police National Computer detailing a couple of cautions for public order offences and a dropped charge of affray.

Next was a newspaper clipping that possibly explained the dropped charge. It described a court victory for compensation against the Metropolitan Police. The pay-out seemed proportionate to the injuries that the awarding judge had deemed proven to have been inflicted by 'over-zealous and fatigued' officers of the law in an incident a street away from the main route of a march.

A photograph taken in a police custody suite showed the same woman two years later. The image was clearer this time. Her black hair was below shoulder length in this shot and her blue eyes pierced the lens with what seemed like good-humoured defiance. There was no record of any action being taken against her, nor anything relating to why she'd been detained.

The last photograph in the pile was similar to the first one. The woman was visible in a crowd of protesters some months later. In this one she was just another 'known face' in a crowd dotted with, no doubt, long-term subversives at a student demonstration.

The only other document for Gallagher to read was a Student Records Form from City University. Back in the day, there might have been a file created by 'F' Branch (counter-subversion) an inch thick but priorities had changed. Documenting the lives of left-wing crusties had given way to a massive investment of resources focused on counter-terrorism. Not to worry though, thought Gallagher: Connie Edwards, born 14th of March; aged 28; student, School of Social Sciences, City University, London; studying for a PhD in International Politics. Address: 271 Dagnall Road, SE15. How hard could it be? He'd almost be embarrassed to take MI5's money. Almost.

* * *

Connie Edwards reached out to silence the alarm that shrilled her awake, only to remember that it was several feet away. She had placed it on the other side of the cabin the night before, to ensure an early arrival at the British Library. Bagging your favourite seat in the reading room was part of the research ritual, after all.

Throwing back the duvet, she stretched out the pain in her shoulder and massaged the ache in her left wrist. The little skylight above showed a rectangle of blue, promising a pleasant day ahead rather than the incessant rain of recent weeks – although she would be cloistered in the still hush of a book-lined room for most of it.

Connie left her robe hanging on the back of the cabin door and padded into the galley. There was a slight chill in the air but it wasn't too cold. The tingle on her skin felt good. She arched her back and yawned before blowing out the match

14

that had lit the gas. She loved living aboard and was sure she'd buy her own boat one day; in the meantime, her godfather's gift of rent-free accommodation for the year was more than welcome.

As she waited for the kettle to boil, she heard voices greeting each other out in the canal basin. She craned her neck, looking to the left through the window over the small sink and saw Tony pushing his bike in a circle as he checked the brakes. The widower would be off for his usual morning ride along the towpaths of Regent's Canal.

Stirring her coffee with one hand Connie opened the top section of the window with the other to let in the cool morning air, just as Tony's legs and wheels came into view.

Tony crouched.

'Ah, Connie,' he said, holding the bike's cross bar with his left hand as he fixed a bicycle clip to his right ankle. 'A beautiful crisp morning and a great day to be one of the Hackney Boat People.'

Tony's conversational gambits were rather limited, but she liked to play along. 'Kingsland Basin is a very salubrious address, don't you know,' Connie replied, laughing.

'That's right. You wouldn't want to live in one of those poncy new developments, would you?'

As he looked up from placing his trouser leg in the clip, Connie saw the blush spread rapidly across the man's face. Poor old Tony: Connie berated herself for her thoughtlessness – she hadn't meant to shock him, it was just the way she was. It wasn't the first time he'd seen her in some form of undress, but he'd never been greeted by quite so much of her at once. She moved closer to the sink unit to spare some of his blushes and half crossed her arms across her breasts as she held the coffee mug in front of her.

'Sorry Tony, I forget.'

The father of three grown-up daughters closed his mouth. He fumbled with the clip again. 'So, any news from that brother of yours? Still out in Iraq earning his crust?' Tony was an ex-paratrooper like her brother, and the two had met briefly on one of Tom's short visits.

'Not lately. He's moved to a short-term contract in Africa. I heard from him when he arrived, but he must be busy,' she replied, trying to give Tony an exit. 'Maybe tomorrow.'

'Yeah, tomorrow, I'm sure. Take care, Connie,' Tony said, with a friendly roll of his eyes.

As he moved away, pushing his bike towards the main path, Connie placed the mug down, turned around and leant back against the sink. She bit her lip and went in search of her mobile phone. She found it on the small bookcase and took it to the equally small table in the narrow boat's sitting area. With her forearms flat upon the wood, she held the phone in a triangle between her fingers and thumbs.

This wasn't like Tom, not like him at all. There was a phone call once a week or so. If not, he'd have told her in

16

advance that he wouldn't be able to contact her. The only time he hadn't been able to and three weeks had elapsed, one of the other lads had called. Occasionally, he'd even write — if he was holed up somewhere with little else to do — telling her about the local landscape, wildlife and people, sharing some of the cleaner jokes flying between the men. If something had happened the company would have called her: she was his Next of Kin. She knew better than to call the head office in London. But it wasn't like him to go so long without making contact. She was his only family and he hers.

'Where are you, Tom?' she asked aloud. Perhaps she was being silly. It hadn't really been that long. He'd been to all sorts of places on security contracts in the last few years and he'd always managed to keep in touch. He must be busy. He'd tell her off for worrying, for nagging. She wouldn't mention it when he called.

* * *

Gallagher was back at Le Lion Rouge. It was early evening, a few days after his meeting with Bannerman. He needed a couple of hours to take stock of the unfolding situation. Actually, he needed to work out why the situation wasn't unfolding at all. In truth, he needed red wine and some ambient noise in which to think.

He'd been out walking for hours, eschewing the joys of London's public transport system, on what had been a pleasant, if cool, sunny day. That was something at least. The city seemed a brighter, happier place in the sunshine. Another bonus was that Eve and Claire were nowhere to be seen, so he wouldn't need to be charming. The girls always took their day off together. Monsieur Moreau was holding the fort until the other girls on the staff arrived for the evening shift. His business partner Monsieur Laroche, Eve's uncle, would no doubt appear before long for a glass or two and a chat.

Moreau and Laroche were an old-fashioned kind of business double act. They had arrived from France in the early eighties, set up shop and became part of the fabric of the area. However, the choice of name for their establishment was a prime example of how they were generally taking the piss.

It wouldn't be busy. Even if it was, Moreau would shrug his way through his customer-facing interactions at a Gallic pace and with an understated belligerence cultivated over three decades or so of living in London.

Gallagher went back to taking stock. The address in SE15 was a non-starter. To be more accurate, it was a newsagent's shop. There was the possibility of a post-handling service or a personal arrangement with the owner, but he hadn't seen anything that confirmed either and he couldn't very well ask in case it was the latter. He'd staked the place out for a few hours at a time, but no joy. Not surprising really, he needed a more disciplined approach. He wasn't just going to get lucky on this one.

Bannerman had called, as promised, but had drawn blanks too: no council tax records for Ms C. Edwards in any of the Greater London boroughs; no driving licence details held at the Driver and Vehicle Licensing Agency; nothing held by internet service providers. There was a university email account, but it had never been accessed. Her library card had the same address as her student record, obviously. There was no listing with Directory Enquiries; no mobile telephone contract and no record of a registered 'pay as you go' phone; no National Health Service interactions recorded in the last four years; no bank accounts in her name; no social security benefits claimed; no National Insurance or tax records held by the Revenue for years. Nothing. Bannerman hadn't had time to talk.

Gallagher had done the usual internet searches but found nothing on Facebook or via Google. No listing on the Register of Electors, either. A PhD Politics student not registered to vote: that was more than a bit odd. Connie Edwards was, as they say, well and truly 'off-grid.'

He had spent more than a few hours around City University, hoping that she'd take her lunch in Northampton Square with other students, or that he'd see her coming from the bus stops on the main road. Then he'd made a tentative attempt to look around for any postgraduate hangouts, with no luck. Gallagher hadn't gone to university. He'd wanted to get away, to earn his own living, to live his own life on his own terms. The army had given him that opportunity.

He'd made his way into the Social Sciences Building across the road in Whiskin Street but was pounced upon by a bored administrator in the main building's entrance: a woman who could differentiate between students and non-students with a studied ease. At the reception desk he quickly explained that he'd just popped in to look for a friend. The gatekeeper was a female dragon in her early fifties, her scales hardened by years of deflecting idiotic questions fielded by baffled undergraduates. She'd given him short shrift and mocked him for assuming that a PhD student would be in the vicinity of a university building on a daily, or even monthly, basis. She would, of course, be happy to take a message if it was a serious matter – if he'd just give his name and show some form of identification. He'd played the bumbling fool well enough for her not to be alarmed and then made a tactical withdrawal.

Gallagher looked towards the door as four braying suits walked in off the street to disturb Monsieur Moreau's own stocktake. The first chinless wonder attempted some one-way *bonhomie*. When that elicited a quizzical look from Moreau and embarrassed chuckles from Chinless Wonders

20

Two, Three and Four, Number One slapped his palms on the counter and called for 'the finest wines available to humanity.' It was his best Richard E. Grant impression. He was very proud of it.

Gallagher eased back in his seat and folded his arms.

Monsieur Moreau put down his pen. 'Gentlemen, what is it that you want?'

This seemed to confuse his new customers, but Number Three stepped bravely forward and declared 'Beaujolais!'

'Yes,' said Number One. 'Two bottles of your best Beaujolais, Monsieur.'

Moreau shrugged. 'We do not sell Beaujolais, Monsieur.'

'You mean you've run out,' Number Three suggested.

'I mean we do not sell Beaujolais, Monsieur.' The last two words echoed with a weary disdain.

'And you call this a French bar?' said an increasingly discombobulated Number Two.

'Yes,' said Number Four, not wishing to be left out. 'Why not?'

'I do not like Beaujolais,' Moreau answered, straightening a cloth on the counter with both of his large dark hands.

Moreau then sold the men two hideously expensive bottles of red and they removed themselves to the corner farthest from the bar, occasionally catching themselves being too loud beneath the Frenchman's gaze.

Gallagher went back to looking out of the window. A find and a fix: that was the job. Locate the target, fix her to an address, observe and await further instructions. He had a bad feeling about this one. It was going to drag on and he didn't like the jobs that dragged on. That kind of job interfered with his social life. He was going to need some help. He was going to need Harry.

TWO

The following evening, Gallagher took his pint from the bar and selected a booth at the back farthest from the door. It was a classic Victorian boozer in Southwark, full of original period fixtures and fittings: all dark mahogany and etched glass. The early-evening punters were beginning to trickle in, but it was still quiet enough for the bored barmaid to take her time acknowledging new arrivals. Serving him, though, she'd looked twice, the second time as if she were trying to reconstruct the face that didn't quite fit the man to whom she handed the change. There was no embarrassment, just the look of someone who has chanced upon a puzzle and is wondering where to begin.

Taking off his jacket and placing his leather messenger bag on the floor, Gallagher watched as she managed to serve and ignore her next customer simultaneously. Catching himself watching the girl and then the door once too often, he took out the evening newspaper in an attempt to slow his thoughts. He was saved from the depressing column inches bemoaning the state of the economy – interspersed with litanies on the layers of social malaise inflicting 'Broken Britain' – by the sound of Harry Burgess attempting to engage the barmaid in conversation.

Harry came to sit opposite and took the head off his beer. 'Piss off, Granddad? Charming.'

Gallagher caught the girl's eye and was given a view of her stud-pierced tongue framed by a playful scowl.

'I think you might have pulled.'

Gallagher laughed as he and Harry spoke in unison.

'So,' said Harry. 'What's the job?'

'Just a find and fix.' Gallagher pushed a photograph of Connie Edwards across the table.

'Why do Five want her watched? Is she an activist like the last one?' Harry took another sip of beer and then gave Gallagher a pained look. 'She's not a dissident Irish, is she?'

Gallagher shrugged. 'Bannerman wasn't forthcoming. As usual, we'll work on the premise that they want to prove the need for a warrant. Bannerman was most interested in fixing her to an address.'

'Is the target aware?' Harry asked, peering at the photograph. 'She's a looker, that's for certain.'

'I'd say semi-aware. If she's up to something and she's any good, she'll expect some level of occasional surveillance – particularly given her relationship with the police.' He pointed to the police records and the newspaper cutting. 'Anyway, we always work on the expectation that the target is aware.'

'Of course,' said Harry, not looking up. 'But we need to find her first. Any start points?'

Gallagher gazed out across the pub at the nearest customers as he pushed the rest of the photographs and papers towards Harry. A group of men in paint-splattered clothing were drinking quickly and talking loudly. One of the older men gestured for two of the others to make way for a couple in their mid-thirties attempting to move past.

Gallagher looked back at the material he'd given to Harry. 'As you can see, the university and the newsagent's are all we've got so we'll start with them.'

'Two start points, two of us, not ideal coverage,' said Harry, turning his pint glass in his hands. 'An initial follow would be difficult.'

'Did you get hold of Kenny or Ross?' asked Gallagher.

'Nope, Ross's up in Scotland at his sister's wedding. I don't know where Kenny is. It's that time of year. You know what he's like when he starts brooding about Afghanistan, about Mick.'

Gallagher rubbed his temples, elbows on the table. 'Do you think he's gone on a bender?'

'A pound to a penny.'

'Just us then.' Gallagher gathered up the documents into a pile but left Harry with one of the photographs.

'Looks like it,' Harry said, standing up. 'Another beer?'

* * *

At that moment, across London, Sandy Bannerman was sitting in Thames House, the headquarters of the Security Service, MI5. The black lacquered fountain pen he'd been twirling in his fingers clattered on to his desk and brought him back from his thoughts.

He hadn't heard from the glorious Flic Anderson in years. They'd been close at university – granted, not as close as he'd like to have been – but since she'd joined 'the Friends' at MI6 he'd only had occasional and marginal contact. Now, out of the blue, she'd asked a favour.

Of course she'd flattered him by pretending to hope he was well, wishing it hadn't been so long and all kinds of the usual patter – but who cared? It was the marvellous Flic Anderson and he'd wilted beneath her heavenly countenance once again. Well, her voice at least. She hadn't said where she was calling from but she needed a favour, just a small one, for old time's sake. It was an off-the-books job, just a hunch, but it might do both of their careers no harm if she was right. If there was one thing that had Sandy Bannerman standing to attention quicker than thoughts of the lovely Flic and her golden tresses, it was the good of his career – unless it was Flic tearing down the left flank in a university-league hockey match. He let the image fade.

Could he be a dear? It was just a find and a fix, off the record – their little secret. Yes, he was a poppet and they'd have to have dinner soon. All very satisfactory.

When Harry returned from the bar he found that Gallagher had placed another A4 plastic zip folder on the table.

Gallagher thanked him for the pint. 'Right, we start in the morning.'

He took out a map.

'We'll begin together. We'll park here.' He indicated to a street half a mile from the shop. 'You can drive the van with me in the back to here. So I'll have the corner, diagonal to the shop, at six. You can walk back to your car and move it to here.'

He pointed to another junction on the map that would give a view of the newsagent's from the right. 'There's a café opposite the shop between our two positions.'

'Nice one,' said Harry.

'I played the jogger around the area the other day and I think these are the best places for us to be,' Gallagher said, pointing at the map again. 'But you might want to have a tour around on Google Street View when you get home tonight, just to familiarise yourself.'

'Will do.'

'If you have any better ideas we'll discuss it at the RV, but this angle gives me eyes on the main shop door and the side door to the accommodation. The rear exit is accessible through a gate on the same side. There's no entry over the back wall as it's eight feet high and topped with glass and razor wire.'

'So I'll insert you and the van and then act as back up?' Harry asked.

'Yeah, I prepped the van this afternoon. I'll have to be self-sufficient. If I have to move after you've gone there'll be a risk of showing out by climbing out of the back.'

'Gone?'

'I'll keep the shop. At nine you'll be at the university. Sorry, should have asked, are you happy to use your car?'

'It'll fit in well in Peckham. I haven't cleaned it in a fortnight. City University isn't in a particularly swanky area either, so yeah, it'll be fine. These are long shots.'

'We'll need to be lucky,' agreed Gallagher.

Harry laughed. 'We'll need to be more than bloody lucky – we could be sitting there for weeks.'

Gallagher gave a thin smile and pushed an envelope across the table. 'Here are the A-Z refs, postcodes and the rest.'

From his bag, he pulled out a copy of the A-Z Knowledge, the London taxi driver's map of choice. He opened a page and took out a colour photocopy. 'We'll meet here, about three miles away, at 05:15. This will be our RV point. It's got a 24-hour supermarket and service station, so we won't look out of place.'

He passed the photocopy to Harry, who glanced at it and then slotted it into the envelope.

Gallagher leaned back. 'As far as the shop is concerned, if she lives locally, she might use it for milk and newspapers. I've been moving between there and the university for days, which is ridiculous, but we've got nothing else to go on.'

'And Bannerman can't come up with any more than this? How about a mail intercept on the shop?'

'Not how he wants to play it.' Gallagher gave Harry a version of his last conversation with the spook.

Harry rubbed his chin. 'She's a proper little enigma, isn't she?'

Gallagher smiled.

'What?' Harry asked.

'Nothing.'

'I do have a vocabulary, you know. Anyway, Mrs B bought me some of that dictionary bog roll for Father's Day. I learned something every time I...'

Gallagher put out a steadying hand. 'Thanks. I get the picture. Not that it's one I want in my head, but thanks.'

'Just saying,' Harry smirked.

'How's Harry Junior?'

Now it was Harry's turn to lean back and rub his temples. 'He's a little sod, just like I was.'

Gallagher picked up his bag from the floor, gathered his papers into the folder and placed it and the map book inside.

29

'Before we head off,' said Harry, 'you know that I've been volunteering a day or two here and there at Veterans' Aid near Victoria?'

Gallagher nodded as he put on his jacket.

'Well, yesterday, in walks former-Private Mark-bloody-Keane.'

'You're kidding. How was he?'

'OK, I think. Said he was just having a nose around and that he was thinking of volunteering. Just off the coach from visiting his mum. I suggested we all meet up for a beer and a catch up. He seemed chuffed.'

'Absolutely, do you have his number?'

'He'd lost his mobile, probably when he was pissed up. I've never known anyone leave so much stuff in taxis as that lad. I gave him my number and he said he'd drop by soon to arrange something, if he didn't call first. I'm not there that often but I told him to leave a message with whoever's on the front desk.'

'OK, good,' said Gallagher. 'So I'll see you in the morning?'

'Yeah, no worries. But talking about phones, what are we doing for comms on this? Not the usual old shite?'

'Yep, usual covert radio kit – personal set and car set – are yours serviceable?' Gallagher asked, knowing he needn't have bothered.

Harry nodded. 'Checked it all over this afternoon. We could really do with some new stuff, though.'

'Good,' said Gallagher, ignoring the point. 'We'll be too far away to use either once you move, so we'll have to use mobile phones when we move to Phase Two. I know, yeah, I'm going to upgrade the kit.'

Harry shook his head and put on his jacket. Gallagher was always talking about upgrading the comms kit. As they walked to the front of the pub, he returned the two pint glasses to the bar and thanked the barmaid. She gave a curt nod and went back to ignoring a newly-arrived customer who was wiping the condensation off his glasses.

Outside, the rain was falling steadily. Gallagher pulled up his collar as they reached the door and let out a sigh.

Harry chuckled. 'Getting soft in your old age, boss?'

* * *

It was another swelteringly hot day and her shirt began sticking to her back five minutes after she left the air-conditioned building. The woman, codenamed Hariq, was making her way across the Green Zone, the International Zone of Baghdad or, as some called it, 'the Bubble.'

The Green Zone, the ultimate gated community: four square miles of heavily-guarded diplomatic area, surrounded by razor wire, T-Wall defences, Hesco barriers and

31

checkpoints manned by heavily-armed men. It was home to the US, British, Australian and Kuwaiti embassies and a number of private military contractor firms. It also represented the Iraqi government's safe haven – well, it was supposed to. Of course, no one had informed the myriad terrorist groups that were always looking for an opportunity to drive in a car bomb or lob a mortar into the mix.

Following the invasion of Iraq in 2003 the allied forces had set up camp in the remnants of Saddam's court, with its fine palaces, houses, ostentatious archways, wide avenues, the beaches by the River Tigris. But what had begun as feeling like a golden cage had in places turned into a stinking enclosure, strewn with rubbish, machine parts, detritus of all kinds. Its human inhabitants lived a bizarre life in limbo, detached from the world outside. It was strange, she thought, that she was at yet another checkpoint in Iraq with all its dangers and simmering tensions, but this one was to enter a theme park.

Once inside Al-Zawara Park, she passed the amusement rides, the go-cart track and looked up at the huge Ferris wheel slowly turning against an azure sky. Then she headed for the zoo. The zoo had been opened in 1971. It and its inhabitants hadn't fared well during the invasion of 2003 but, due to incredible efforts by various international animal welfare groups and specialists, it now contained more than a thousand animals. As she passed the tiger enclosure she saw her contact standing with his back to her. She passed him on the right and walked on, looking at the crowds, looking for anyone who might be watching. She stopped at various points, doubling back occasionally and completed a circuit of the area before approaching.

'She is magnificent, isn't she?' said the man.

'She's beautiful.'

He smiled, looking her in the eyes. 'Beautiful and dangerous. You are ready?'

The woman codenamed Hariq tensed. 'It's over. The operation is compromised.'

The man dragged on his cigarette and looked back at the female tiger swimming in her pool. 'Nothing is over. It has begun.'

'How did it happen?'

'A contact with a team of British mercenaries on Route Irish.'

She swallowed hard and then took a deep breath. 'He had the key with him.'

'It's gone. We recovered his phone, the bodies, the car and weapons but nothing else.'

Her fist clenched and the urge to cry, barely detectable in her voice, was replaced with a harder edge. 'Say that again.'

'It's gone. We're certain that one of the British has it. We had a back-up car stuck in traffic a few minutes behind him.

They recovered the bodies and searched the car. We've already found some of the mercenaries.'

'You'll be thorough, very thorough?'

'We always are.'

'Make it clean.'

'We always do. Don't worry.'

She turned and leaned back on the enclosure rail, watching the families moving along the pathway. 'You've sent them?'

'They have arrived. Our handler in London will hold them in position. The mission will proceed as planned.'

She controlled her irritation as best she could.

A man with his family in tow gave them, or rather her, a withering look. She was modestly dressed and her hair was covered, but her independent manner clearly offended the Iraqi's sensibilities. Her contact stared the man down as she looked away in the coyest manner that she could muster.

'The operation has begun. There is no turning back. Our masters have made it clear, the operation must succeed. The evidence must lead back to only one source. You understand this.'

'Except that at the moment it might be traced through me. I'm a cut-out, is that it? Am I being set up?'

He stepped back a pace so he could look her in the eyes. His face softened. 'He loved you. We have our orders.'

'He's dead and I'm out on a limb.'

'He was like a brother to me. You know it must be this way. We have our instructions. There can be no official involvement on record. No logistical support from my country, no communications, however secret, must be logged or passed through either of our services or our embassies. Nothing must ever be traced.'

'The operation is compromised.'

'No,' he said, with more iron in his voice than he had intended. 'The operation is not compromised. The key is secure. It is hidden in plain view. The mercenary may have discarded it already. What could he do with it? He would need to know what it opens in order to use it – even if he recognised it as a key in the first place.'

She turned to watch the tiger swimming. 'There's nothing to worry about, is that what you're telling me? I can't say I'm convinced.'

'Her name is Hope,' said the man, gesturing towards the tiger and then dropping his cigarette end to the floor.

'I'm leaving. You'd better hope that we don't meet again anytime soon,' said the woman.

He put his hand around her upper arm, with enough force to keep her attention. She wanted to knock him to the ground, to reiterate her position with her heel on his throat, but they were surrounded by people ambling around the zoo in the late afternoon heat. She pulled away as slowly as she could without drawing attention.

'We will find him. We will find it,' he said.

'Where is he?'

'He left Johannesburg and flew via Doha to Munich on Qatar Airways. Three days later he left Munich and flew to Madrid via Lisboa.'

'And you couldn't pick him up in Munich? I thought you could do anything anywhere.'

'We narrowly missed him. We can't use the organisation's resources as we usually would. There were only two local agents that I could use and they had to travel to get there. I can't deploy a kill team just like that. We think he has friends in Munich; he went to ground as soon as he landed. My agents are in Madrid now.'

'He could be anywhere by now. He could even be back in Britain. He'd better not get that far – do we understand each other?' The woman sighed, turned and rested her chin in her hands, elbows on the rail. The man lit another cigarette and blew the smoke over his right shoulder, away from her.

She turned her face towards him.

'Look around you,' he eventually replied. 'Look at this "zone." Most of the bureaucrats never leave the bubble. They don't know what's going on a mile from the perimeter walls. How can they build peace if they don't know the place in which they are trying to build? Those in charge in Washington, in London, Paris, Berlin, Rome, are going to ensure that our way of life is destroyed. It is up to those of us

36

who have eyes to see, those of us who know the truth, to make sure that doesn't happen.'

The woman codenamed Hariq watched the tiger moving easily through the cool water.

The man placed his hands on the rail. 'You understand.'

She thought for a few moments.

'It'd be too much of a risk to change things now. It'd take too long and we can't afford any mistakes by rushing it or drawing attention. It'll have to go ahead as originally planned.'

'Very wise.'

'Wise? Are you forgetting how long it took to put this into place?'

'Thank you,' he said, ignoring her last comment. 'It is the right thing to do. What will you do now?'

'I'll be in position.'

The man ground his cigarette under his shoe and looked back at the tiger in the pool.

'Once it is done, relax. Take a holiday, swim. We won't meet again.'

* * *

Kenny Collins was disorientated. He lurched into the wall on his left. The music was thumping through his brain, the carpet was sticky underfoot and he could still taste the vomit in the back of his throat. He rested against the wall and downed the double Jack Daniels he'd managed to carry to and from the toilets. Three girls with luminous fake tans giggled their way past him as he heaved himself upright and walked down the corridor under the ultra-violet light. Someone of a similar size was standing at the end of the corridor where the lights were out. The emergency exit sign shone dimly, illuminating the other man standing squarely to Kenny's front. Kenny stepped forward. The other man stepped forward. Kenny stopped. The other man stopped.

Kenny paused for a moment, putting out a steadying hand on the wall. The nausea came in waves and the instinct to survive kicked in. Without fully turning, he threw his glass at the man, heard it smash and threw himself forward down the corridor, throwing a punch at what he thought would be chin-height. The mirror smashed around his fist and Kenny looked at his own reflection, then down at the bloody mess of his hand. He stumbled backwards and began to laugh.

The door to the main bar opened and the full volume of the music followed the bouncer into the corridor. 'I warned you, you prick,' said the big man with the shaved head.

Kenny was still laughing when the bouncer had finished calling for reinforcements on his radio. Kenny raised his hands in supplication and took a step back.

As his two colleagues came through the door, the first bouncer shoved Kenny hard in the chest and piled in with the other two men until Kenny lay on the floor trying to curl into a ball. Another bouncer arrived and Kenny was marched through the throng of dancing clubbers to the front door. He didn't struggle. He didn't fight.

He landed hard on the pavement and looked up the steps at the four men standing, arms crossed, looking down at him. He looked at his bleeding hand and tasted the blood in his mouth. Pushing himself up with his good hand, he got to his knees.

'What was that for?'

The first bouncer cupped a hand to his ear. 'What was that, dickhead? Speak up: we can't hear you.'

Kenny felt the anger surging and the alcoholic-fog began to lift. 'What was that for? I didn't do anything to you.'

'Because you're a pissed-up twat. Now jog on or we'll give you the kicking you deserve.'

Kenny got to his feet and stared at the men. Blue lights lit the road as a police van turned the corner and pulled up a few feet away. Kenny watched as the crew debussed, then turned back to look at the bouncers.

Even though the other three were raining down punches, Kenny had managed to shove the first bouncer back through the doors of the club. The dozen or so onlookers were being moved back by a couple of police officers while the rest ran up the steps. The police report later described how Kenny had moved with incredible speed up the club steps with clear intent to cause bodily harm to one or more of the door staff. It took the three upright bouncers and four policemen to pull Kenny away from his chosen target and back down the steps to the pavement.

Subdued and cuffed, he was led to the van.

'You going to behave yourself?' asked the officer to his left.

'Yeah,' said Kenny, 'I've had enough for one night.'

'Right, well we're going to get you down the station where you can sleep it off. We'll sort this mess out in the morning when you've sobered up.'

The back door of the van was opened and Kenny saw the cage. 'No,' he said quietly.

'Come on, mate. We haven't got all night.'

'No.'

'All right, Sam,' the first officer said to his colleague holding Kenny's other arm. 'Let's have him in.'

They pulled him forward, gripping harder around his upper arms. Kenny kicked up his legs, pushing off the rear bumper, causing the two officers to step backwards to steady him. He lowered his head and then threw it back as the man on his left attempted to reassert control. Kenny heard the policeman's nose break and then threw his head forwards diagonally to the right, head butting the other man, cracking his cheek bone.

'No! Fucking no!'

40

A baton hit him squarely in the back of the knees. He'd lost count of the fists and boots by the time he'd been dumped on the floor of the cage. The door was slammed shut.

* * *

Tom Edwards was sitting in the semi-dark lounge at the front of the ferry. The ship pitched up on the dark sea and he felt his stomach lift and fall with the swell. He pulled the jacket that he was using as a blanket up over his shoulder, to stop the chill at his neck. As he tried to find a more comfortable angle in the seat, a baby woke at the back of the lounge, started to cry and then thought better of it. Quiet descended again and the dozen passengers dotted around the room went back to dozing.

Tom had contacted Baghdad, only to find that Gus had been abducted three days after the message had been left with the colleague in South Africa. They'd found Gus dead by the side of the road two hours before Tom's call. Confusion reigned. Gus had been beaten to a pulp and shot in the head. Apart from that, no one was able to tell Tom anything. Of the original team, he was now the only one left alive.

He'd taken a flight from Johannesburg via Doha to Munich the next day. His boss had understood and signed off his

41

contract. It was an inconvenience but they'd all lost mates. Five in quick succession was likely to put a bloke off his game.

After arriving in Germany, Tom had spent a couple of days lying low with an old comrade. Duncan Barnes had been with him in basic training and they'd joined the same battalion, but he'd left the Parachute Regiment after three years to join the French Foreign Legion. Now he worked for a German millionaire as a security advisor.

Barney had a cabin in the forested foothills of the Bavarian Alps and they'd done some drinking and fishing. Tom hadn't burdened his friend with his worries – just said that he was a bit burnt out and needed a recharge. Barney had been glad of the chance to get up into the mountains and not have to speak German all day. He'd offered Tom a job. Tom had to decline. There was a mess to get out of before he could consider his next career move – not that that was the reason he gave. Barney left the offer open and they'd polished off a bottle of whisky.

From Munich Tom had flown to Madrid, with a seven-hour stopover in Lisbon. Then he'd taken a train from Madrid to Santander, where he'd caught the ferry to Plymouth. The crossing was twenty hours. He glanced at his watch. He'd be back in the UK in another fifteen.

What Tom had not done was call Connie. He felt bad about that, but something was wrong. Until he could work out what it was, he could be putting her in danger. Better that she thought he was out in the Bush or raving it up in nightclubs and nagged him about it later, than have her involved in whatever this might be.

There must be a connection. He was on someone's radar and whoever it was didn't seem to have difficulty getting things done. But whose bloody radar was he on? Why? Of course, it was possible that it was an unlucky coincidence. What were the odds? Jack was definitely upside down.

He'd feel safer once he was back in the UK. He'd go to ground, visit friends in Aldershot and Colchester. He'd put some feelers out – quietly. He could make it up to Connie later.

THREE

Blackness: a heavy suffocating blackness weighing down a consciousness racing with fear. And cold: the cold of the night-sweat. And silence: silence punctuated by a rapid heartbeat pounding in a paralysed body. Control the breathing. Look for clues in the darkness. Listen. Move slowly. Legs moving, keep it slow. Arms responding. No sudden movements. Eyes scanning the darkness. A chink of light. Up in one swift movement. Go to the light.

Bollocks.

'Are you OK?' a tired voice asked.

'Yep,' said Harry, feeling foolish, lying on the floor.

'You're not wearing your false leg, you silly sod.'

'Thanks. I worked that out when my face hit the floor.'

'Where did you think you were off to?'

'I was dreaming I was in the 100 metres final,' he lied. 'Go back to sleep.'

'Silly sod,' said Lynne Burgess, turning over.

* * *

Gallagher stared into the darkness. It was 03:10, exactly five minutes before his alarm was due to go off. After a quick shower, he dressed in the light of his bedside lamp. He

44

placed a nylon shoulder holster over his t-shirt, into which he eased a thin covert radio so it nestled comfortably under his left arm. He pinned the inductor tab containing a microphone on to the shirt near his collarbone. Also connected to the radio was another cable with a thumb-operated pressel switch. He threaded this down through his trousers and up through a hole in his pocket.

He could now operate his communications system without notice. A small leather pouch held a flesh-coloured earpiece, which he put in his other pocket having checked that the 'wax trap' was clean and that there were two spare batteries in the holder. Then he put on a sweatshirt. He switched off the bedside lamp and walked out into the hallway.

In the kitchen, Gallagher checked the equipment that he'd laid out on the table the night before. He wrapped a digital camera in a waterproof jacket and placed it into a holdall. In with this and its two other lenses went a pair of binoculars, maps, a Sat Nav and a first aid kit. He checked that the digital voice recorder on his mobile phone had full memory, that the phone was fully charged and checked the bag for a notebook and pencil. He took a handful of change from a dish on top of the bread bin in case he needed it for parking and checked his wallet for money and his driving licence. Into another section of the bag he placed a police-issue LED torch. There was a heftier Maglite version in the van that gave far more light and doubled as a weapon if things got sticky. Then he checked the side compartment of the holdall where there were several types of spare batteries. Harry would be going through the same checks at his house in Walworth.

Gallagher filled a flask full of coffee and placed it next to the bag, into which he'd placed the sandwiches he'd made the night before. While he was eating a banana, he looked over the photographs of Connie Edwards: an enigma.

He switched off the kitchen light and walked down the hallway to his front door. He stopped, placed the bag and the flask on a table and walked back to a cupboard in the kitchen. From it he took a small thermal-imaging camera and two spare batteries, which he placed in the bag in the hallway. Before opening the door, he checked his reflection in a full-length mirror. He was wearing black work boots, a pair of scruffy jeans, a t-shirt, an old grey sweatshirt and a light-weight dark jacket, over which he'd placed a hi-vis vest.

He pulled the pressel cable back through the hole in his trouser pocket and ran it down his arm, through the jacket's lining and into the left-hand pocket. He could move it if the weather got milder, but he'd be sitting in the van so this was more convenient. He pulled on a woolly hat against the early morning chill, looking like just another bloke heading off to work.

Gallagher activated the house alarm, turned off the hall light and then locked the front door behind him. He walked to the communal cycle shelter on the opposite wall. There were no lights on in any of the other properties in the row. He unlocked his bike and placed his flask in a small pannier to the rear, securing the holdall with bungee cords over the top. As quietly as he could, he unlocked the gate at the top of the steps and carried the bike down to the pavement.

It was a twenty-minute ride to the lock-up garage. He loved being up and about at this time of the morning. And it was a pleasant change not to have a hangover. The streets were quiet, as London paused for a couple of hours between the late-night revels and the early morning bustle. As he approached the area of the lock-up, he took a right turn and rode away from it, doubling back on himself. Back on the main road, he stopped and made a show of adjusting the bike chain. A supermarket delivery truck passed him but there were no other vehicles or people moving through the immediate area. No one else knew about the existence of the lock-up – well, Harry and the lads did, but only them – and that's the way it would stay.

Once inside, he pulled the door down behind him and switched on his torch. He lifted the bike over the top of a van that was parked nose forward and placed the bike at the back of the garage, next to a motorcycle: a black Triumph Speed Triple. There wasn't much room, but Gallagher had fitted a series of cupboards on the back wall. The place was orderly and he knew exactly where everything was, not a thing out of place. He took down a small camera tripod from one of the cupboards.

The van was a blue Ford Transit Connect. He'd chosen blue as it didn't stand out as much as the more official-looking black and although London had more than its fair share of white vans, a white van would often cause a target to look twice in the rear-view mirror to check that it wasn't a police vehicle.

He opened the side door. The back of the van was insulated to offer a degree of soundproofing. On the carpeted floor lay a beanbag. A compartment along the left-hand-side contained empty plastic bottles for urine, a toilet roll, hand-cleaning gel and large zip-bags for excrement: all mod cons.

Next to it was another containing bottled water, foil-wrapped energy food bars, wet wipes and a safety kit: tow rope, space blanket, jump leads, chemical light sticks, a voltage inverter, a portable charger, multi-tool kit, a spade, a can of tyre weld, screen wash, de-icer and scraper and the heavy-duty torch. There was a sleeping bag wedged between the two boxes and a bag that contained a set of running kit, a towel and a spare set of clothes.

The van had an air-vented roof. The rear windows were smoke-tinted glass and there was a two-part blackout curtain a few inches away from the rear doors. All the interior lights had been disabled, as had the lights inside the door panels. The side access door made for ease of entry and exit as an alternative to the rear set. The back was large enough to operate in comfortably and the van small enough to drive into any kind of car park. He made sure that the blackout curtains were closed, placed his bag inside and shut the side door.

He'd checked the fluid levels, the tyre pressures and had filled it with fuel the day before. The tyres were legal, the tax disc in date. Nothing about the van should arouse suspicion. You couldn't do anything about dogs sensing someone in the back and barking, or kids rocking the bloody thing to set off the alarm, but those were occupational hazards. Someone had once tried to break into the van while he'd been hidden in the back, but Harry had spotted the drug-addled scrote and had seen him off, pretending to be the returning owner. They'd had to get out of the area for a day. Just one of those things.

Once he'd driven out of the lock-up, he secured and then double-checked the garage door. The front of the van was partitioned from the back with another pair of blackout curtains, clipped in the middle. Sitting back a couple of feet, it was possible to take good quality photos and video through a small gap without being seen – as long as the rear curtains were drawn to prevent a silhouette.

Before moving off, he checked the glove compartment. There was another torch, three pay-as-you-go mobile phones, a pair of gloves, a can of self-protection spray, a mini A-Z, the spare Sat Nav and two packets of mints.

'I'm turning into such a geek,' he said aloud, driving out on to the main road and heading south of the river.

* * *

When Gallagher reached the rendezvous point Harry was already waiting. He'd been into buy some energy drinks and he looked like he'd need them. Gallagher told him so.

'Not as tired as Mrs B but, yeah, I'm out of practice when it comes to getting up at silly hours dark o'clock.'

'Getting grief?' Gallagher asked.

'No, she's fine. I don't sleep too well, you know how it is. I keep her awake with my tossing. How about you? Still sleep walking to the window?'

'I'm usually waking up, but I move so fast towards the light I only come around properly when I hit the glass.'

'Could be worse, I know of some blokes who wake up outside in their boxers with no idea where they are or how they got there.'

Gallagher nodded. 'All set?'

'Yep. Frequency changes?'

'On the half hour when static and nothing's doing. Switch through on odd numbers and back down the evens.' Gallagher pressed the pressel switch in his pocket. 'Got me?'

'Got you.' Harry's voice was clear in Gallagher's earpiece.

'Do a check on the car set as we move off.'

Harry nodded. 'Right, we'd better get you inserted. Synchronise?'

'It's about twenty past – that do you?'

'So early and yet still so professional,' Harry said, slapping Gallagher on the shoulder. 'Come on then, boss, let's be having you, the war won't win itself.'

Gallagher drove out of the supermarket car park and led the way to their first stop, a few streets away from the newsagent's shop they'd be watching. Once there, Harry left his car – giving Gallagher time to get into the back of the van. There could be no cross-contamination, no contact between him, Gallagher and the van, until Harry returned and drove him away, still in the back.

Harry checked the street for watchers and then walked to Gallagher's vehicle, using the spare key to drive it to its stakeout position. He parked it in the side street to allow the best view for Gallagher and his camera. They didn't speak. Harry checked for signs on the lamp-posts, making sure they'd understood the parking rules. Harry's mate, Keith, couldn't leave his own postcode without getting a ticket – one of those blind spots that people had, but an expensive one. A parking fine wouldn't be ideal but a snooping traffic warden could be a real issue.

As he walked back to his own car, he pressed the switch in his pocket. 'Hotel this is India, radio check, over,' he whispered.

'OK, over.'

'OK, out.'

The most important element on any surveillance job was communication. Like Gallagher, Harry had a more powerful transceiver in his car in addition to the covert radio he was wearing. The switches were wired in to blend with the gear stick and there were microphones in the sun visors. Gallagher's vehicle transceiver also worked remotely in the back of the van. Mrs B had the family car so she didn't much care about Harry fiddling with this one.

He walked back to the grey Mondeo and moved it to his own vantage point down the road. He was careful to line his wheels up with the kerb. Park pretty: don't give anyone anything to notice. Then he got out, checked the street and got back in, sitting in the passenger seat. He locked the doors. Now he was just someone waiting for someone – far less suspicious than sitting watching the world from the driver's side. It was still dark so he'd parked under a lamp-post. The light would bounce off the windows making it harder for the passer-by to see in. Amateurs would park away from the light not realising that this would illuminate the interior of the car.

Gallagher had found a comfortable position on the beanbag, after he'd placed the camera on the tripod and arranged the blackout curtains front and rear. There was no point in holding the bugger for hours on end and it'd help get clearer shots when the time came. If it came. Now we wait, he thought, as he realised he'd left his flask in the bike pannier at the lock-up.

After an hour, Harry informed Gallagher – with some relish – that he was going to camp out in the café diagonal to the shop on the other side of the road.

Gallagher's voice came through the earpiece: '*Bon appétit* – full English?'

Harry smiled and gave two clicks on his pressel: two for yes. Gallagher insisted on using the military protocol rather than the 'one for yes' and 'two for no' employed by civil enforcement agencies.

'Save some for me?' whispered Gallagher.

Harry clicked once for no. Nothing came back and he stopped himself laughing as he walked into the brightly-lit café.

* * *

Connie gathered her papers together on the table in the galley and finished her coffee. It was nine o'clock and she'd spent the last two hours making notes for the meeting with her PhD supervisor later that morning. It was going to be a fine day by the look of things and it would be pleasant to cycle down to Professor Benita O'Sullivan at the university. They often had their progress meetings at the British Library café, where Benita would offer comments on Connie's latest chapter plans or draft pieces of work. Today, however, the academic was in a borrowed office and had asked Connie to meet her there. Benita's office in Whiskin Street was being decorated. She'd be in the building at Northampton Square attending an administrative meeting before leaving for a conference in Leeds.

Connie went to her bedroom and dressed. The meeting was set for 10:30, so she'd have plenty of time to cycle down between Hackney and Shoreditch to Finsbury. Afterwards she'd bring her files back, lock up the bike and travel down to Peckham to check for post and messages. Maybe Tom had managed to drop her a line. Of course, email would make things easier but she no longer had a presence in cyber-space and that was the way she wanted to keep it – for the foreseeable future, anyway. Her tutors and the ladies in the office left messages in her pigeonhole in the department and Benita was happy to call or text. The internet's tentacles could feel into all the areas of life, holding you in place, feeling your every move. She wanted no part of that. As long as she stayed invisible, anonymously on café computers around the city, she could use the Web on her terms. And she liked to receive an envelope with a stamp on it occasionally. She liked to sit and feel the paper that the writer had touched, to see the personality in the handwriting, to see the thoughtful effort of ink and composition.

She locked the cabin doors of the narrow boat and fitted the security bar across them. Then she unlocked the padlock securing her bike to the prow. She eased it to the side, stepped off the boat and pulled the bike on to dry land. Holding the handlebars, she used her free hand to adjust the straps on her rucksack.

Tony was sitting at the front of his boat pulling an inner tube through a bowl of water at his feet. His old but well-maintained bike was upside down on the pontoon, one of the wheels missing. 'Puncture,' he mouthed, stating the obvious.

'Morning, Tony,' Connie called.

'Great day for it,' he called back. 'Whatever "it" is.'

Connie swung her leg and positioned her feet on the pedals, waving at him as she rode slowly away. 'Have a lovely day, Tony.'

'I would,' he grumbled, 'if it weren't for all these yobs leaving broken glass everywhere.'

Connie moved along the towpath down to the bridge and then headed west along Regent's Canal. She loved London's

55

waterways: the river, the canal, the wharves, the docks. The canal had once been an arterial route at the heart of London's industry. Now it was a haven for wildlife, weekend walkers, trendy types using the waterside bars and public spaces and those seeking a more tranquil way to traverse the manic metropolis. Bits of it were grubbier than others and it would be stupid to get complacent about personal safety but, compared to the dangers to cyclists out on the roads, it was relatively safe and definitely blissful, even on a chilly morning like this.

The canal had been constructed between 1812 and 1820, connecting the River Thames at Limehouse in the east to Paddington Basin and the Grand Union Canal eight and a half miles further west. She passed Mandarin Wharf and Kleine Wharf, then the old horse ramps and the warehouses. She rode under the bridge beneath the thundering New North Road, past Sturt's Lock and the Victorian factory chimney, before passing Wenlock Basin and City Road Basin beyond Wharf Road, which marked the boundary between Hackney and Islington. What a morning to be alive, she thought, to be free, to feel her heart beating, her legs moving and her brain fizzing with so many possibilities.

The towpath reached Islington Tunnel, where the narrow boat and bargemen would have 'legged' their craft through by lying down and pushing along the brickwork with their feet. Connie, however, turned up on to Colebrooke Row, lined with its tall Georgian terraced houses, and onwards to the busy City Road. Across the traffic was the Old Red Lion pub and Goswell Street.

She freewheeled right into Friend Street and then pedalled out into St John Street, finally turning left into Spencer Street and Northampton Square.

* * *

Harry was getting bored. It was 11:30 and he'd already eaten the sandwiches that he'd made the night before. He hadn't been hungry – the massive full English in the café had seen to that – he was just bored. That was the nature of the job, just like the army: hurry up and wait, eighty percent boredom, twenty percent excitement – if you were lucky.

But he did it for that twenty percent. The extra money was needed too. His disability pension wasn't bad but Lynne had to work. Luckily, her mother lived down the road and could help with Harry Junior. Gallagher didn't really need the money at all; his uncle's legacy had left him more than comfortable financially. It was a nice little earner for the other lads, Ross and Kenny, but Gallagher didn't tend to chase work so it was never going to be a full-time thing.

Harry flicked through four radio stations before switching it off. He didn't dare read the newspaper that was sitting on the driver's seat and he couldn't face another cup of coffee from the flask lying next to it. He was sick of the energy drinks he'd bought earlier, so he decided to take another stroll, keeping an eye on the Social Sciences building's entrance in Whiskin Street but not getting too close.

The university term was in full swing and the undergraduate population was in residence; however, the area wasn't anywhere near bustling enough to ensure that he was never a lone figure and the car stood out a bit parked where it was. But he hadn't got many options.

Having returned to the car, he saw a security guard – a beer-bellied chap pushing sixty – moving with a slow purpose towards him.

'Here we go,' Harry thought.

'Good morning, sir,' said the man, as Harry lowered his window. 'Can I help you?'

'No, thanks,' answered Harry. 'Just waiting.'

'May I ask what you're waiting for, sir? It's just that I noticed you sitting here earlier and, well, we have to be careful, what with this being a university and all these young students to keep an eye on.'

'I'm here to serve some divorce papers,' said Harry.

The security guard brightened. 'Ah, a private investigator? Who on?'

'You know I can't tell you that. Ex-army, right?'

The man puffed out his chest a little. 'That's right, sir, the Pioneer Corps, twelve years. Yourself, sir?'

'No,' Harry lied. 'But you can always spot an old soldier, can't you?'

'That you can, sir. I suppose you're an ex-bobby. Met Police?'

'Something like that.'

'Say no more, sir. Anyway, I must get on. Good luck.'   -

Harry saw the guard glance back at the car's number plate. He could see the effort of trying to memorize it playing across the man's face. Another twenty minutes would allay any suspicions caused by him driving off now, but he'd been noticed. He'd have to move. He couldn't have gotten a better angle on the entrance but he was too visible, the road layout wouldn't allow anything else. It was just one of those things. There was only one way she could come in or out to reach her department's building, so Harry parked his car on the Northampton Square side of Spencer Street. Perhaps he should have done that from the start. Never underestimate the old soldiers eking out a living in the security business.

He'd been covering the door of the Whiskin Street building since leaving Gallagher and the van and he was pretty sure she hadn't been past him. Bloody students, she was probably still in bed. There was no guarantee she'd be turning up today or tomorrow.

After half an hour of sitting in his passenger seat, he decided to stroll up Northampton Square. He'd keep a weather-eye on the junction opposite, but if she hadn't

59

arrived she wouldn't be leaving immediately, so he'd catch her on the way out if he was unlucky enough to miss her in the next few minutes. He couldn't just sit in the car staring across the road.

He walked along the square, as if he was admiring the architecture. At 12:10 Harry looked up from the A-Z he was pretending to read and saw two women standing at the top of the stairs to the university's main entrance. The older of the two was in her late forties, a striking woman with long dark hair that was beginning to grey a little. She was wearing a flowing floral dress, low-heeled shoes and a turquoise scarf was draped Boho-fashion around her neck. The two women were sharing a joke and the older woman leaned in to kiss the cheeks of the younger – Connie Edwards.

Connie skipped down the steps and waved back at her companion, who returned inside. A lucky hit, but he wouldn't be telling it that way later. Harry took the mobile from his pocket and pressed the speed dial. Gallagher's voice came back to him.

'Yes, Harry.'

Harry angled his body away from the centre of the square. 'That's Echo One foxtrot into Northampton Square.'

'Roger that,' replied Gallagher.

Connie walked across to the railings diagonal to Harry's position and searched for keys in her rucksack's side pocket.

'She's got a push bike,' Harry said, moving back to his car at the most leisurely pace he could manage.

'It's down to you,' said Gallagher. 'I'm too far away to be of any use.'

'Yep,' said Harry, unlocking his car with the remote key fob. He placed his bag and the newspaper on to the passenger seat as Connie rode towards him – then leaned down to open the glove compartment so she wouldn't see his face. 'That's Echo One mobile towards St John Street.' He waited a few moments until she'd passed him before starting the engine. He'd parked facing out of the square and was glad that he had. The car was an automatic, which made operating various bits of kit on the move much easier.

'She's right into St John Street towards St John Avenue and Angel. You're on speaker, my windows are up.'

'Roger that.'

Harry eased into the traffic.

'Echo One right into Friend Street, it's one way.' He looked back at the Sat Nav. 'I'll hope she goes left into Goswell Road and up in my direction. There's no way I can turn around here without a loss.'

'Roger that,' Gallagher replied.

Harry arrived at the traffic lights. 'That's me held at a fresh red.' To his left was Pentonville Road, to his right City Road. A 64-year-old convicted murderer had climbed over the Victorian wall of Pentonville Prison, using a makeshift rope, not so long ago and had managed a few days of liberty before getting caught. Cheeky bastard.

Sitting in the right-hand lane Harry waited for the lights to change and saw Connie cross City Road.

'Eyeball regained, I have Echo One – wait.'

The lights changed and Harry joined the slow moving traffic as he watched Connie disappear again. He turned left into the one-way street – going the right way unlike this young lady's habit – just as Connie put her arm out and manoeuvred through a junction.

'That's Echo One into Colebrooke Terrace. It's one way, she likes to live dangerously. That's me into Duncan Terrace.'

'Roger that.'

Harry turned right and reached a junction.

'That's me unsighted.' Then he noticed the bridge in front of him. 'Wait.'

He pulled over, activating the car's hazard lights and turned off the phone's speaker. The driver coming up behind him beeped an angry horn and gesticulated at Harry, mouthing 'wanker' as he passed close to the side.

'Have a nice day,' said Harry quietly, as he stepped on to the pavement. 'Eyeball regained. That's Echo One east along Regent's Canal: she's riding along the towpath.'

'OK,' said Gallagher. 'Can you follow parallel on the road? You might get lucky.'

Harry was already climbing back into the car, where he flicked the phone back to speaker. He ignored the pain where the prosthetic was rubbing.

'That's me mobile Vincent Terrace.'

Gallagher provided directions from his map book so that Harry could keep looking for a glimpse of Connie to his left without having to repeatedly glance at the Sat Nav. The road bent right into Graham Street taking Harry down alongside City Road Basin and away from the towpath on which Connie was travelling. Within a couple of minutes he was back at another junction with the City Road. The traffic was slow and by the time he'd made his way up Shepherdess Walk, left on to Eagle Wharf, across the New North Road and along Bridport Place to the bridge, she was nowhere to be seen.

He stood on the bridge looking east and then west: nothing. Drivers were beeping at him, parked as he was on double yellow lines, not helping him to keep a low profile.

He lifted the phone to his ear. 'That's a loss. That's a total loss.'

* * *

Bannerman had spent a slow morning wading through yet more preparatory work for a major surveillance operation. There were a number of briefings set for the afternoon that he wasn't particularly looking forward to relating to a forthcoming scientific conference. How he'd ended up with that job he still couldn't fathom.

The Americans were in town, trying to run the show as usual and the Israelis were bleating about a possible Iranian threat against their visiting scientists. The Home Office were panicking about problems that didn't exist and the police were being a pain in the arse about pretty much everything else. He needed some air.

He walked up Millbank and into Victoria Tower Gardens, where he sat on a bench. Big Ben sounded out a solitary bong as he sat listening to Gallagher's number ringing.

Gallagher answered.

'Are you well, Owen? Just thought I'd call and ask for a sit-rep, anything doing?'

'No,' lied Gallagher. 'Nothing to report as yet. I'll keep you posted.'

The line went dead and Bannerman stared out across Westminster feeling the unease – which had been growing at the back of his mind – pitch forwards momentarily, amplified into a flash of indistinct anxiety.

He'd just got time for a sandwich.

* * *

The man who said good morning to the security guard on the gate before walking out into the street opposite Kensington Palace Green was in his early forties. His hair was short and tidy. His jaw was square and his nose had been broken, but he wore it well and thought himself to be the right side of handsome. He was wearing a dark grey tracksuit with an iPod attached to his upper arm. The earphones were in his ears but no music was playing. He jogged down to High Street Kensington Underground Station, slowing to a walk when he was a hundred metres from the entrance.

He went into the station ticket hall, stood back by the map of the underground system and looked at the people who came through to the barriers. He stayed there for a few minutes and then went back out to the street. He jogged eastwards, past the Royal College of Music and Imperial College London; down Queen's Gate, past the Science and Natural History museums, into Queensbury Place; left into Harrington Road and through to the South Kensington station – walking the last hundred metres or so, as before. Anti-surveillance drills and counter-surveillance tactics were second nature, but today he was being more cautious than usual when in London.

From South Kensington he travelled along the Piccadilly Line to Piccadilly Circus, where he joined the Bakerloo Line south to the Elephant and Castle. From here he took the Northern Line to Borough. From there he walked to Guy's

Hospital where he took a black cab through Bermondsey and was dropped at Tower Bridge Business Complex. No one had followed him, of that he was sure. The flat had been arranged by the girl, it was secure. They would be waiting for him, as they had been instructed. He walked north and then eastwards a short distance to his destination: the Kirby Estate adjacent to Southwark Park, off the Jamaica Road.

The door opened.

'I am Mimar,' he said quietly. He was ushered inside by a man in his mid-twenties, who didn't really look his age.

'Where's the other one?'

The young man pointed down the hallway. 'He's through there, watching television.'

The first man's companion was sitting on a sofa in the living room.

'Turn that off and stand up,' Mimar said.

The man did as he was told, but didn't seem particularly concerned by Mimar's presence or authority.

'Which one of you is Ozi?'

'I am,' said the one who'd opened the door.

'So you must be Net,' said Mimar.

'Yes,' answered the man with the TV remote in his hand.

'No,' said Mimar.

'I am Abbas,' said Net.

'Correct.' Mimar looked around the room, waiting for another response.

'And I am Rasul,' said Ozi.

'Better. Now sit down and listen.'

'Do you want tea?' asked Ozi.

Mimar raised his eyebrows but then relaxed. A cup of tea would have been welcome, but there was no way he was going to touch anything in that flat.

'No, thank you.'

'We've been waiting. What's happening? We're running out of food,' said Net.

'There was a delay. Now I am here. I have what you need.' He took a small plastic wallet out of his pocket and let a smaller paper envelope drop on to the coffee table, careful not to touch it. He put the plastic wallet back in his pocket.

'Credit cards: use them to buy food, whatever you need. Draw cash. Go to the cinema, be normal – but no alcohol, do you understand? You are here as students but no drinking, I've read your files. Good boys, quiet boys. Yes?'

They understood.

'You have the cell phones and the other equipment?'

They did. The equipment bags had been expertly hidden in the wall behind the washing machine.

'You have the college cards?'

They did.

'And you know the details of the courses that you are enrolled on?'

They knew the details and they knew they would be long gone before the college would realise that they'd never been to a lecture. They would have new passports before the job was complete and would spend a few days in Ireland when they'd finished, before going home via Europe.

'I will contact you when it is time for the first visit. We will not meet in person again.'

* * *

Bannerman was pissed off. He'd just lost to an oik from the second floor who was six places below him on the squash ladder. It had been his own fault: he hadn't been concentrating. That was because of the other reason, the main reason, he was pissed off.

Flic Anderson had called again. It had started well enough. She'd even asked after his parents and the Labrador that had been dead for ten years; however, he'd had no information to give her and she'd barely managed to mask her annoyance with a show of polite disappointment.

He was in danger of looking like an arse. He was in danger of looking like an arse in front of Flic – the glorious, high-flying, extremely well-connected Flic Anderson – and that pissed him off beyond anything that had pissed him off in a very long time.

* * *

Harry had driven back to Peckham to move Gallagher and the van. They had then driven the two vehicles to the RV point, where they bought coffees in the supermarket café and began to talk through the situation. Gallagher stretched, easing the tension in his shoulders. He placed the A-Z Knowledge map book on the table. Harry turned it, orientating it to the position he'd held on the bridge.

'She could have been going anywhere.'

'True but how many people do you know personally who use canal towpaths in London, Harry?'

'OK, so what are you saying?'

Gallagher looked at the map. 'Let's follow her last known direction – going east.'

Harry ran a finger along the page. 'Bridges, wharves, housing, parks, schools, and a leisure centre, all within minutes of the canal. Like I said, she could have been going anywhere.'

'Stick to the canal, stick with what's immediately adjacent.'

Harry read out the name of anything of potential interest along the canal.

'Then there's Kleine Wharf, Mandarin Wharf, Canalside Studios, Kingsland Basin, Timber Wharf.'

'Wait,' said Gallagher. 'Kingsland?'

'Kingsland Basin, why?'

Gallagher picked up his phone and touched the Google icon. 'Something I remember reading, a while back.'

He typed in a phrase.

'Here it is,' he said, scanning the article and handing the phone to Harry. On the screen was a newspaper lifestyle piece entitled 'Away from the Hackney Main Stream.' The author described the basin as 'home to Hackney's secret narrow boat community.'

Harry glanced up.

'We know she's off-grid. Worth a look?' asked Gallagher.

'Got to be, unless you want to go back and sit outside a newsagent's shop in Peckham for the foreseeable.'

FOUR

By the time Gallagher and Harry had arrived in the vicinity of Kingsland Basin, Connie had dropped off her bike at the boat, had a sandwich and caught the train from Haggerston to Queen's Road Peckham. She'd walked along the High Street, turned right into Dagnall Road and had picked up her post from the newsagent.

Out on the street she scanned left and right and walked back to the busy high street. Finding a telephone box, she stepped inside and opened a small brown envelope. She called the number on the piece of paper contained within and spoke to a man. Then she returned the handset to its cradle and tore the paper and envelope into several pieces – half of which she put in a bin, before crossing the road and placing the remaining pieces in another.

* * *

Gallagher had changed into his running gear. His smartphone was in a holder strapped to his upper arm and he had the earphones in. He jogged up the towpath to the little bridge crossing the entrance to the canal basin. Harry had also taken the steps from Kingsland Road and was now in the part of the basin where the boats were moored. He had a

71

pair of binoculars around his neck, a book sticking out of a map pocket and was taking photographs of any wildlife that happened to pass by.

He looks like a right spotter, thought Gallagher.

Harry made a mental note of what he could see in the basin: the number of boats, properties overlooking the canal, anything that might be of use later. There was a floating allotment garden to one side. An allotment: that was another thing on his wife's list of things he could do with his time. He might as well dig a hole and chuck himself in – he wasn't ready for a flat cap and growing champion runner beans just yet.

A man on a red narrow boat waved hello.

'Nice day,' shouted Tony. 'You looking for birds? The feathered variety, I mean.'

Harry laughed and waved the copy of The Book of British Birds that had been in his pocket. 'Got it in one.'

'Not that there are many of the other type around here, apart from Mary up the top there; Jim's missus, Elaine; Charlie's partner Sarah and our Connie,' said Tony, pointing at another red boat a few feet from Harry.

Good job I'm not a woman-hating serial killer, eh mate? Harry thought. He waved and smiled at the man, then strolled alongside the canal photographing birds in front of points of interest for ten minutes – and anything that landed or flew past Connie's boat in particular.

Once he was back on the road he called Gallagher, who was checking other possible entry points and potential laying-up spots. 'I've lost a life talking to some geezer in the basin, but it was worth it. He confirmed she lives there; the silly old duffer even told me which boat.'

'I know you didn't ask him,' said Gallagher, confused.

'Of course not, you pillock. The bloke decided to have a bit of a conversation; it's just that he did most of the talking.'

'Result,' said Gallagher.

'My thoughts exactly.'

'OK, let's lift off. I'll meet you at Michael's Café in Bethnal Green, the one we used during that job before last Christmas.'

'Half an hour?' asked Harry.

'Yeah, I'll head away up the A10 for a couple of miles and then I'll swing back.'

'OK, I'll come in via Cambridge Heath. The traffic will be murder so you might have to leave my tea in the pot.' Harry hung up.

Gallagher's phone beeped – one missed call. Sandy picked up on the third ring.

'Owen, thanks for calling, any news?'

'We've just fixed her to Kingsland Basin. She lives on a narrow boat in Hackney.'

'How jolly,' said Bannerman. 'Photos?'

'Of the boat, yes – of the target on or near the boat, no.'

73

'Not to worry,' said Bannerman. 'Send over the details this afternoon.'

'Is that it then?' asked Gallagher.

'How are you fixed?'

'Why?'

'Well, if you're at a loose end, it might be helpful to know where she goes over the next few days, who she meets, that sort of thing.'

'A new tasking?'

'Same one, surely?'

'A new tasking, a new fee – and I want Harry's percentage factored in.'

'Ah, the gallant Sergeant Burgess – is he well?' asked Bannerman.

'Tickety-boo. Yes or no?'

'Yes.'

'Good, I'll get on with it then. I'm going to need a couple of residents' parking permits, for the area around Haggerston Station down to Dunston Road.'

'OK. One more thing: I'm sending you some new toys, see what you think. A courier will leave a box with your friend Mr Achtouk at the restaurant. I'll pop the fake permits in the box.'

'Fine, I'll drop by this evening.'

'Have fun,' said Bannerman, ending the call.

* * *

Harry walked into the café fifty minutes later.

'Like I said, the traffic was murder.'

Gallagher told him about the conversation with Bannerman. 'We need to set a trigger for a follow.'

'Covert camera? I noted three options for hiding it by the canal,' Harry said, spooning sugar into his stewed tea. He grimaced at the first sip and indicated to the woman behind the counter to bring another pot.

'Could do. There's a high risk of compromise, though. I've got the kit at home but it might be a faff we don't need, especially as we think we've fixed her to the boat.'

'Fair enough,' said Harry. 'But she's got options on leaving the basin and there's still just the two of us.'

'We need to confirm she's actually living on the boat. If we're back there early tomorrow morning, we'll also be able to see if she takes us anywhere else.'

'She'll probably drag us around the shops half the day.'

'Well Bannerman clearly thinks something's on. We need to keep the momentum and see how it plays out. Maybe a camera would be for the best.'

'It could make life easier.'

'I'm all for that,' said Gallagher. 'Right, we'll insert it in the early hours – you OK with that?'

'Sounds like a plan,' said Harry.

'Tonight, then. I'll plot up in the van a few streets away. You can head home after and meet me back there in the morning.'

'I'll need to nip home now and show Mrs B that I'm not out enjoying myself.'

'Fine, I need to pick up some kit and Bannerman is sending something over to Mr Achtouk.' Gallagher pulled out the map book. 'Meet me here at 01:00?'

'Got it,' said Harry, sipping his tea. 'Mrs B wants some decking in the garden; I'm supposed to go to the DIY place with her in the morning.'

'Take the day off: I'll cover it.'

'Fuck off, Owen.'

* * *

Connie arrived back at Kingsland Basin late in the afternoon. Tony was tending the plants on the roof of his boat. 'Hi Connie, good day?'

'Lovely, thanks. You?'

'Not bad. Are you out on the tiles tonight?'

'I should be so lucky,' she said. 'Note-taking and then an early night, this PhD thesis won't write itself and I've got a pile of books begging to be read.'

'Good girl. See you.'

Connie unlocked the cabin doors, stepped inside and put down her bag. It had been a productive day. Benita had been wonderful, as usual. Tomorrow's meeting was set with the co-ordinator and she'd enjoyed being out and about on a beautiful clear day. She walked into the bedroom and opened a drawer, in which she found a camera. She removed the battery, placed it into a charger and plugged the unit into a socket. But no letter from Tom and still no call, no reply to her text messages. She shouldn't worry. She was worried.

* * *

A few miles to the west of Connie's boat, George Parker was calling one of his many employees.

'Where are you, lazy bollocks?' he asked, swinging his feet off his desk and putting his cigar into the ashtray. 'What the fuck are you still doing in Acton? Get your arse back here in the next hour or I'll kick you to death on arrival. Got it? Good. Now fuck off.'

Surrounded by muppets, it was a wonder anything got done at all. He picked up his brandy and ginger with one hand and the cigar with the other and put his feet back up on the desk. The call he'd had from the woman that afternoon had been an unwelcome surprise. He'd done most things in his criminal career, but he wasn't too keen on kidnapping civilians – messy, too much heat and a long stretch if it all went pear-shaped, which, of course, it often did. Not that he got too close to the messy end of things these days, but still.

The other thing he wasn't happy about was that he had no choice in the matter. He'd supped with the Devil. It'd have to get done or things would get complicated, very complicated and fast. He didn't like having his strings pulled, but they were strings of his own making. Bollocks to it; that was life. He blew a smoke ring into the air and stared at the ceiling. He knew just the lads for the job.

* * *

Gallagher dumped his bag in the hallway of his flat and went to change out of his running gear. Once he'd showered and dressed, he walked down to the Marrakech Restaurant. Mr Achtouk was at the wholesaler but the waiter, Nabil, had been told about the package that Bannerman had sent over. Gallagher had often eaten at the restaurant when he visited Uncle Edwin. Since he'd inherited the flat he'd continued the tradition alone. Mr Achtouk was a good and trusted friend.

Back in the flat, Gallagher opened the box. The parking permits looked real enough, particularly as they'd been produced in a matter of hours. There were also four smartphones in the box, with a selection of headphones and Bluetooth headsets. He took out a printed sheet of instructions. The phones had an application built in that provided a global secure Push-To-Talk system, or PTT. One button set up an instant voice call. It also allowed one-to-one or one-to-many calls, like a radio net. Clever, thought Gallagher. Other pluses were that the phones had state-of-the-art encryption and had an integrated GPS. The PTT system, said the instructions, would run in the background so the phone would function normally. Very Gucci.

He placed the phones to one side – they were charged up and ready to go – and went to his wardrobe, opening the lockable cabinet inside, where he found a covert camera unit that would suit his purposes.

It'd take a couple of hours to watch the area, find a suitable location from the three suggested by Harry and test the equipment. Gallagher went to his desk and pulled out a small laptop from the bottom drawer. The camera would give a live feed once the laptop application was activated. It would also send movement-triggered alerts to his phone via SMS, like the camera he had hidden in his hallway covering the front door of the flat. He'd have to angle the one in the basin so it wouldn't be set off by every passing duck. The cameras were other bits of kit courtesy of Bannerman that Gallagher had forgotten to give back. Well, it was a big company and the government hadn't seemed to have missed the equipment so far.

He took the camera memory card Harry had given him at the café and emailed the details of Connie's location to Bannerman, along with some photographs of the boat and basin.

Gallagher would take up position in the van nearby, where he'd be able to doze and wait; hopefully, she'd stay tucked up in bed for the night. Harry would go home. Bannerman wasn't paying for full-on 24-hour surveillance, so Harry would come back in the morning in case Ms Edwards went walkabout early.

He looked in the fridge. There was some beer, some cheese, some wine and not much else. He didn't bother to check the freezer. The bread bin was empty. In which case, he'd go back downstairs, thank Mr Achtouk and fill up on Moroccan food. He'd have to drink water, sweet tea and coffee, as he was driving later. He found no drinking easier than trying to stay under the legal limit. It was a simple rule not to imbibe any alcohol at all when driving, rather than to try to just have the one. Mr Achtouk would be vocal in his approval.

There was no point trying to get any sleep. There was too much going around in his head and he was sick of staring into the darkness at the bedroom ceiling.

* * *

Ray Carver and Vince North were standing in George Parker's office. Ray was tall and athletically built. His head was shaven to stubble in an attempt to belie a catastrophically receding hairline and he had a prominent scar at the end of his chin – a reminder of the end of a bottle thrust into his face when working the door of one of Parker's rougher nightclubs. Vince was shorter, with collar-length untidy brown hair, jowly features and a bulbous nose. Neither man knew why they were standing on the plush carpet in front of the boss's huge mahogany desk. Parker had been looking at a computer screen since they'd walked in. Vince was sweating more than usual.

'Lads,' said Parker, pushing his chair back. 'I've got a job for you.'

Ray tried not to look relieved.

Vince put his hands in his pockets.

Parker pushed a photograph of Connie across the desk. 'I want you to watch this girl – wipe that smirk off your face, Vince, this is serious. I want you to watch this girl and build up a picture of her movements, patterns and what have you. All right?'

Ray and Vince nodded.

'Have you got an address, boss?' asked Ray.

'Of course I've got a bloody address, how else are you going to watch her? Jesus wept.'

'Sorry, boss.'

Parker thought of his Greek villa and the big pool under the clear skies, resisting the urge to throw something at Ray – Vince's decapitated bonce, for example. He pushed another photograph across the desk.

'She lives on this boat in Kingsland Basin, Hackney.'

Parker stood and, taking the photographs with him, walked around to perch on the front edge of the mahogany. He handed the pictures to Ray.

'When do we start?' asked Vince.

'Tomorrow morning, early. Dave Greene is setting up a house for when we have to lift the bint. Loz has got an A-Z, a Sat Nav and a camera to give you on the way out.'

'A kidnap?'

'A little holiday, Ray,' answered Parker. 'A mutual friend wants her kept safe, out of the way for a while – that all right with you, boy?'

It was.

'What's her name, boss?' asked Vince.

'Why would that be important to you two? I told you to watch her, not serenade the bitch.'

It wasn't important to them, they agreed. Vince thought his arse felt like it was struggling for breath.

Parker moved back to the other side of the desk.

'Right, take the VW van. Keep a low profile and keep me posted. Got it? Good. Now fuck off.'

* * *

Kenny Collins lay in the semi-darkness listening to the shouts from the other cells on the wing. He heard the prison officers pacing the landing, the jangling of keys. He'd been surprised, on his first night, when he'd asked the screw what time 'lights out' was and the screw had pointed to a light switch on the wall, shaking his head as he turned to lock the lump of iron that made the room a cage. The door wouldn't be unlocked again until 08:00. That sound: the sound of the key turning in the old heavy lock and the observation hatch slamming home. He'd felt sick; he still felt sick. He'd wanted to say sorry, to be able to apologise and go home. All he wanted was to hold Leanne, to tell her he'd change, that he'd stop drinking, that he'd stop being an angry dick.

It was never quiet. There was never any peace, no let up to the noise and the stink, or the simmering violence ready to erupt at any moment. He was due in court for sentencing the next morning. It would be a custodial sentence, his lawyer was sure. His army record wasn't going to save him this time; they'd throw the book at him. His previous visits to court, all fighting related, added to charges under Section 47 of the Offences Against the Person Act and Section 89 of the Police Act, among others, could only lead to one outcome.

Gallagher had given him a chance, had given him a way back, a way of earning a crust in the company of men he respected; a chance to get the buzz, to feel the adrenaline on the job, not fighting in pubs and clubs and out on the street – a real and clean buzz, not pissed-up scrapping with other boozing losers just like him. He'd been offered a way of getting back to being happy; a way back to looking at himself in the mirror and not seeing his own disgust; a way back to standing tall and proud; a way back to being useful and worthy of the word 'friend.' He wanted that way back so badly now that tears welled up in his eyes as he stared at the shadows on the ceiling, listening to the shouts and the threats and the jangling keys along the landing.

He just wanted to go home.

* * *

The two brothers, the university security guards Omar and Ibrahim, had played their parts well. The equipment and materials had been brought in over a six-month period and hidden, ready. Now they were guiding Imran and eleven others to the entrance of the roof space. Ibrahim undid the padlock and then moved back to stand at the top of the stairs as they filed past him.

'You'll be warm, at least,' said Omar, shining a torch into the dark void. 'All the main pipes run through here.'

Imran nodded but didn't reply. He and the other eleven had been waiting for the all-clear from the men with the keys, the men who could switch off the cameras and write the fault reports. He motioned for Yasir to enter the space and watched as the man's head torch illuminated large heating and water pipes, electrical ducting and junction boxes.

'Your area is down there at the back,' said Omar.

'I have the plans memorised,' Imran replied. 'Thank you, brother.'

Yasir signalled, turning his head torch off and on twice. Imran waved through Zeeshan, Syed and Salman, Baha, Dekel, Tarif, Mahir, Lufti, Eisa and Cadi, before turning to Omar.

'You've done well. Now lock us in and forget you ever saw us.'

FIVE

The camera insertion had gone well. It had been raining hard, which reduced the visibility of the few people out and about braving the deluge. All but one of the boats in the basin had no lights showing by 02:00 and that one had gone out within the hour.

Harry had kept watch from the shadows, keeping an eye on the towpath, the basin, the entrances and the windows of any flats overlooking the area. They'd both been soaked but the kit was well hidden and worked. Luck was definitely with them that night.

The camera was disguised and secured up a tree. Its infrared LEDs were invisible to the human eye and it was triggered by motion detection. Gallagher had angled it to cover Connie's boat on a shallow diagonal, giving a view of the cabin doors and side windows. He would be able to get digital stills and full colour video. The battery life was pretty good as it wasn't drawing full power all of the time and the waterproof housing could withstand the weather. It had the words 'ENVIRONMENT AGENCY' stencilled down both sides, along with a telephone number to an automated message should anyone discover it in its camouflage and decide to follow it up.

Gallagher had climbed into the van parked up in Lee Street while Harry did a sweep of the surrounding area before going home. Gallagher had then checked the signal and the laptop, before changing into dry clothes. He'd be able to doze for a few hours in the sleeping bag. His only worry was that the wet clothes might cause condensation to form on the windows and draw attention to the van.

Harry arrived at 07:00 and parked two streets away. During his first contact of the day with Gallagher he explained how the coffee he'd just bought was still too hot to drink. Gallagher had ended the call. He was stiff and cold but he could see the funny side – not that he was going to join in with Harry's piss-taking.

It was an hour later when Gallagher could see Connie moving around on the boat via the picture on his screen. Apart from when she went on deck to stretch and wave at a neighbour at 08:47, he saw little of her for most of the morning. At 11:50 he saw her come out again. She placed a rucksack on the deck and started to lock the cabin doors.

Gallagher activated the PTT. 'Standby, standby. That's Echo One foxtrot.'

Harry sat up in his reclined seat, got out of the car and walked around to the driver's side.

Gallagher spoke again. 'She's on foot, no bike, heading down the towpath to the bridge, so she'll probably come up the steps opposite Dunston Road.'

Harry drove his car around the corner just in time to see Connie walk out into the street. 'I have Echo One, north up Kingsland Road. Want me to take?'

'Keep eyes on,' said Gallagher, getting ready to climb out of the van. 'I should see her when she meets Lee Street.'

Harry watched her walk away.

Standing at the side of his van, Gallagher turned and saw Connie walk across the road.

'I've lost eyeball,' said Harry, slowly pulling away from the kerb.

Gallagher turned and put his head back in through the open side door of the van.

'Have Echo One foxtrot my direction – looks like the railway station.' He closed the van door and made his way to the front, out of her line of sight. 'Echo One into the station. I have.'

'I'll have to wait for your next call, unless you want me out on foot,' said Harry.

'No, stay with the car: I'll call you forward when I get an idea of where we're going.'

* * *

dared and followed her into Somers Town, where she knocked on a door on the ground floor of St Anthony's flats. A scruffy-looking man opened the door, checked the area for watchers and let her in.

Gallagher weighed up his options. Standing around might get him some attention and probably the worst kind of attention. To his right was an adventure playground. No good: a lone male hanging around a playground? He'd be battered to death within ten minutes.

A young woman with dreadlocks came from the other direction and entered the same flat that Connie had. Gallagher stood by the health centre on the corner and called Harry, who would be able to plot up by the sports centre in the car and trigger the target away. There was a café nearby that Gallagher could sit in once Harry had arrived.

* * *

rry gave the standby two and a half hours later, having ched eight other people arrive at the flat. Four pairs had ith a ten-minute interval between. Each pair contained ale, one female, all in their mid to late twenties and y dressed – very casually dressed in some cases.

e came out of the flat with a young Asian male, the youngest of the men to leave so far. The man in losed the door behind them. Harry was able to

90

Ray and Vince had arrived in Kingsland Road and turned into Dunston Street – a couple of streets away from where Harry was now parked – shortly after midday. Ray had been out drinking the night before and Vince liked a lie-in given half a chance. Parker would be playing golf or shagging his mistress down in Fulham, so as long as they had something to tell him later they'd be all right.

By the time Ray had told Vince to shut his face or he'd shut it for him, Gallagher had followed Connie from Haggerston to Highbury and Islington and was now in a carriage adjacent to the one she was sitting in on a Victoria Line train heading for Euston.

She got off at Euston and Gallagher called Harry once h᷈ reached the main station concourse, telling him to hea᷈ Eversholt Street. He watched Connie as she ᷈ Eversholt into Grafton Place, which he knew led int᷈ Way. He took a chance and headed right and ther᷈ reached the front of the fire station he saw he᷈ the side street and turn left down the Eʋ᷈ followed at a safe distance and watched as᷈ The Rocket pub. He hung back for a few᷈ stood on the corner by the Novotel. Sʲ᷈ seen.

A couple of minutes later᷈ newsagent's next to the pub ?᷈ from him, down Chalton Stʳ᷈

Hᵃ᷈
waᵗ᷈
left᷈
one ᶰ᷈
casual᷈
Conn᷈
probably᷈
the flat ᷈

6.

watch the couple as they walked the length of Aldenham Street and then turned left into Eversholt Street. Gallagher moved to Phoenix Road and saw them cross it, following them across Euston Road and into Tavistock Square. They went west towards University College London's Bloomsbury campus.

Harry found a side street and parked up. There was no point in taking the car through the West End without a destination, leaving it would be tricky and they might need it at short notice.

Gallagher followed Connie and the young man through the streets surrounding the British Museum. It wasn't difficult as the two made frequent stops.

'What are you doing, Ms Edwards?' he said to himself.

* * *

This particular day had been chosen because there was a huge demonstration planned against government cuts to public services that would be making its way from Little Portland Street, down Regent Street, past Trafalgar Square and into Whitehall. There would be noise, hundreds of people with cameras and the police would be stretched.

Connie and Shafiq had been given an area between Euston and Marylebone, north of Oxford Street. They looked like a young couple out to photograph the sights, often stopping outside the usual London landmarks, at tube stations like Goodge Street, striking poses but not in shot when the pictures were taken.

Walking up Portland Place they looked at several buildings from several angles, including BBC Broadcasting House, the Langham Hotel and a couple of banks. Connie took voice notes on a recorder built into her phone. They walked up past the embassies: the Chinese, Columbian, Kenyan and that of Poland. When they reached Park Crescent, Shafiq went right towards the Central London County Court and then rejoined Connie, who had taken a short detour, at the junction. They continued up the crescent towards the Central London Justice Court.

Connie noticed that Shafiq was sweating.

As they continued to walk slowly along the sweeping Regency terrace he glanced behind him. 'Shit. Don't turn round.'

'What is it?'

'Coppers, in a car. I saw them five minutes ago. I thought they'd gone.'

'Calm down,' she said. 'We're not doing anything illegal.' She could hear the car slowly creeping up behind.

'They can stop us under Section 43. They'll stop me under Section 43 for being a brown-skinned male with a rucksack and a camera – who just happened to be pointing it at a government building when they spotted me.'

'Act normal. They'll drive past: we're just a couple out walking.'

'Connie, they spotted me when I was on my own. I've got an outstanding warrant from Finsbury. I could get sent down.'

'What? And you didn't think it worth mentioning?' Connie said through clenched teeth as the car drew level.

The passenger was holding a transceiver handset, talking to a controller about a call from a high-end clothes shop half a mile away, so the driver got out.

'Afternoon,' he said, walking around the back of the vehicle.

Shafiq bolted.

Shit, he's fast, thought Connie – stupid but fast.

The driver hesitated, looking from Shafiq to Connie and back again. Decision made, he jumped into the car and it sped off. Then it stopped. The passenger door slammed and the car roared away after Shafiq. She panicked and ran.

Gallagher watched her run through a gate into Crescent Gardens as a policeman jogged along the pavement in her direction. That's not going to end well, he thought.

Connie scanned the gardens as she ran in. Apart from an old tramp asleep on a bench under the wet trees, the place was deserted. She needed to hide. She couldn't think straight. There were evergreen shrubs and trees around the

93

edge shielding the inside of the gardens from the street. The copper wouldn't see her until he reached the gate.

She kept running and headed clockwise through the cover of the shaded borders to the side of a small cream-coloured structure surrounded by dense undergrowth.

The policeman was at the gate looking left and right, but he hadn't seen her. She was now at the top-left-hand side of the gardens. Over the railings would be the entrance to Regent's Park Underground Station. She'd hide, wait, climb over and head underground.

She crouched low, trying to control her breathing. She watched the police officer make his methodical way anti-clockwise around the edge of the gardens. She couldn't run; she'd be spotted the moment she broke cover.

Then he was standing with his back to her, only a few feet away. She held her breath.

'It can't be very comfortable for you in there,' the officer said, still facing the other way. 'You're not going to make me come in after you, are you?'

It might have been a bluff. No need to panic. There wasn't much they could do to her – stupid Shafiq – but it'd mean hours of awkward questions in a police interview room. What was worse, she'd be back on the radar when there was a big day of direct action approaching.

The policeman turned, found the gap and stood over her. He pushed her off balance on to the ground. Then he extended his baton with a menacing click.

'I'll take that camera, miss.'

Connie pulled the camera away.

The policeman gave her a sharp crack on the thigh with the baton. 'Now, now, play nice.'

'Bastard,' said Connie, tears welling up in her eyes.

'Your Paki boyfriend run off and left you, has he? Once I've run you through the system, maybe I'll pay you a visit on my night off – you'd like that, wouldn't you?'

'Go fuck yourself.'

He hit her again in the same place and replaced the baton in his belt. 'Time enough for a quick body search,' he said, kneeling in the dirt and snatching the camera. He put it down and leered at her, then groped at her breasts before grabbing her between the legs as he covered her mouth with his free hand.

Through her tears, Connie saw a man standing behind the police officer. The man placed a finger to his mouth. She tried to concentrate on the police identification number on the right-hand epaulette, but the wide-eyed look had been seen.

The officer quickly stood and began to turn. 'Nothing to see here, just…'

Before he could finish the sentence, Gallagher had hit him in the throat. Not hard enough to do any lasting damage, but it'd shut him up and act as a nice reminder when the bastard tried to eat for the next week or so. The policeman clutched his neck. Gallagher punched him hard in the stomach and then in the ribs, below and to the side of the stab-proof vest. The man was winded but still standing. Gallagher brought his knee up squarely into the policeman's balls, before pushing him into a bush.

A call came across the radio that was clipped to the officer's chest, informing him that the runner was still running, giving a last known location. Had he found the girl? A van was on its way. He should make his way up to Wick Place, off Marylebone Road.

'Handy,' said Gallagher, helping Connie up. He bent down, picked up the camera and put it into his messenger bag.

'Hey, what do you think you're doing?' she asked.

The policeman groaned as he tried to get up. Gallagher kicked him hard and then knocked him unconscious with a blow to the temple. He scanned the area again for onlookers and grabbed a plastic carrier bag, blown by the wind across the gardens, that was hanging on a branch next to Connie. Placing his hand inside the bag, he ripped off the policeman's radio, tied a knot in the bag's handles and tossed it over the railings into the road. A truck drove straight over it. Connie stared at him, her mouth open.

'Trust me,' he said. 'This way.'

* * *

Gallagher guided Connie south, turning right into Devonshire Street where he flagged down a black cab.

'Where to?' asked the driver.

'Oxford Street, the Plaza Shopping Centre.'

'Spending all your money is she?'

'You know how it is, but she's worth it.'

'Love's young dream, eh?' The driver turned up the classical music playing on the radio. He was a romantic.

Gallagher turned to Connie. 'Empty your coat pockets and take it off.'

'What?'

'You might have to dump it, but for the moment just roll it up.'

'Anything else?'

'Take off your hat and let down your hair – give it to me.'

Connie bit her lip and did as she was asked. Gallagher tossed the hat out of the window. The cabbie was busy swearing at a bus driver and didn't notice.

'Who are you?'

'Who are you?' replied Gallagher.

'I liked that hat.'

'It suited you, but don't buy another one – not for a while, anyway.'

Oxford Street was heaving with afternoon shoppers. The traffic was slow, snarled up by dozens of buses.

'Anywhere here'll do, mate,' said Gallagher when they were approaching the shopping centre.

'Keep the change,' he said, handing a note to the cabbie. It wasn't a huge tip, definitely not over the top or flashy, so if asked to recall him the driver might have positive memories but nothing that would stand out.

Gallagher led Connie across the road into Berwick Street and stopped near the doorway of an office building, allowing a group of American tourists to amble past with their flapping maps.

'Why did you do that?' asked Connie.

'Do what?'

'That: the policeman.'

'It seemed a bit off, the way he was handling the situation.'

Connie smiled. 'A bit off? Right. Do you make a habit of intervening in situations that are a bit off?'

'Not really. Drink?' he asked. 'I know I could do with one. We should get off the streets, then go our separate ways.'

Connie still couldn't think straight: everything had happened so fast. The sound of sirens on Oxford Street made her tense.

'OK.'

'I know a place that's a bit out of the way,' he said. 'It should suit us very well.'

Connie looked up at his face. She should walk the other way. She should leave this man standing on the pavement and get as far away from him as possible in the shortest amount of time. She didn't think he'd try to stop her, but she needed time to think. Curiosity was also getting the better of her.

'This is mad,' she said.

'Isn't it?' This is beyond mad, thought Gallagher, as the same thought continued to move across Connie's mind.

* * *

Harry wasn't too concerned that he hadn't heard from Gallagher; if he was underground or too close to the target he wouldn't be in contact. Still, it wasn't ideal and it'd be difficult to react as back-up, stuck with the car in central London on a busy afternoon. Of the two of them, though, Gallagher was the expert. Unlike Harry, a fair bit of Gallagher's time in the army had been centred on surveillance and other specialist work.

Harry had jumped at the chance to work with his old boss again. He didn't dare think what his life would be like without these sporadic jobs, with the adrenaline rushes and heightened sense of awareness. Being a soldier was like real life but with the volume turned up. It had more colour, more, well, life to it. It had been much more than a job. For Harry it had been a boyhood dream, a real calling and it hadn't disappointed – until he'd lost his leg, that is. He could have stayed on: the prosthetic was good but because of other damage he couldn't run fast enough to pass fitness tests. He'd been told there was a desk for him if he wanted it, maybe even a cushy number at a training establishment. God knows he'd thought long and hard. Some amputees were already making it back to operational tours. But he just couldn't get back to fitness and he'd felt a fraud.

He'd made his decision. It wouldn't have been the same. The colour had faded from his life as a soldier, a life that was all he'd known since he'd left school.

A traffic warden was walking towards him noting number plates, so he eased out into the traffic and pulled into another side street. He took his mobile phone from the passenger seat, keeping Bannerman's new toy in his lap, and selected a number in the address book. The number rang and went to voicemail.

'You've reached the Ministry of Defence. We're all a bit too busy to come to the phone right now but, if you're

100

looking for a fight, please leave a message and we'll get back to you,' said a Scottish voice.

'Ross, you knob, it's Harry. Give me a call when you've finished shagging your little sister's mates.'

* * *

They made their way through Wardour Street, across Shaftesbury Avenue and into Lisle Street, moving east from Charing Cross Road. On reaching Floral Street, they turned into an alleyway and walked through to the Lamb and Flag pub.

It was a tall seventeenth-century building sitting in a small courtyard between Garrick Street and the old Covent Garden market. This backstreet area had once been home to whores and bare-knuckle fighters, but at that moment it was populated by bemused Japanese and afternoon drinkers. Three men stood outside smoking and laughing loudly. No one gave the couple a second glance.

Gallagher bought a bottle of red and they made their way through the little bar to a table at the back.

'So what's the score?' Connie asked. 'Who are you? What do you want?'

'Well, at the moment, I'd like to get my breath back and avoid arrest for assaulting a police officer and aiding and abetting a...?'

101

Connie looked away. 'We weren't doing anything wrong.'

'We?'

'It doesn't matter, we weren't doing anything illegal.'

'So how did you come to be hiding from the police in a bush?'

Connie laughed in spite of herself. 'Never happened to you?'

'Can't say it has, no.'

'Oh well, after your performance this afternoon that might change.'

Gallagher was quietly confident. They hadn't passed into the arcs of any CCTV cameras before they got into the cab. The driver wouldn't remember too much about a couple out shopping and they'd been dropped off on one of the busiest streets on the planet – at a shopping centre that they hadn't gone into.

'Why aren't I as suspicious as I should be?' she asked.

'You tell me.'

'I'm Connie.'

'James,' Gallagher lied.

She put out her hand. 'Hello James, and thank you, but this really is too bizarre. I should be going.'

'OK,' said Gallagher.

'What were you doing there, anyway?' said Connie, keeping her seat.

'Where?'

'The park.'

'It's a nice park – I was just out for a stroll. I like to wander around town, it helps me think, but it gets a bit too busy, don't you find?'

'So you live near that end of town?'

'Not far.'

'To think about what?'

'Sorry?'

'You said it helps you to think, the wandering.'

'Oh, right. You know: this and that.'

'You didn't mess about, did you?'

'When?'

Connie rolled her eyes and lowered her voice. 'When you pole-axed the copper, knocked him out and chucked his radio under a lorry – that's when.'

'Oh that.'

She couldn't help smiling. 'You're now in my top ten most-annoying-people-I've-ever-met.'

Gallagher raised his glass and smirked.

'I didn't see you in there when I ran in,' she said.

'I saw him follow you; I was curious.'

'OK, let's try some deduction: you're nosey; you can handle yourself; you like to rescue damsels in distress; you seem confident that the Met's Territorial Support Group aren't going to steam through the door of this pub and kick seven shades out of us; and, unless you've got a very understanding colleague, you're not an undercover copper.'

'Ex-army: I learned a few things over the years. Would you have preferred I looked the other way?'

'So you really just stopped to help because you thought he was out of order?'

'He was a bit more than out of order. I was just going to suggest that he stopped whacking you with his baton, but then…'

Connie shuddered. 'The bastard.'

'Quite,' said Gallagher, topping up her glass.

'And now?'

'And now what?'

'You said you're ex-army, what is it that you do now?'

'This and that.'

'An enigma,' she said.

Gallagher smiled as he remembered his conversation with Harry.

Connie smiled too. 'My brother was a Para,' she said. 'He's a contractor now.'

'A military contractor? A mercenary?' asked Gallagher, sipping his wine.

'I don't think they like being called that these days. He does security work in exotic places, that's all.'

'Close Protection?'

'I'm not really sure. I try not to think about it too much and he doesn't really talk about it.'

I bet he doesn't, thought Gallagher.

She asked him about the pub. He asked her what she did for a job. She told him about university, about being a mature student, about getting carried away and opting to do a PhD. They finished the bottle and he resisted the urge to buy another.

'We'll need to leave separately.'

'I suppose so,' she said, looking down at her empty glass.

He really wanted to buy that second bottle. 'You leave first. Where was it that you said you lived?'

'I didn't.'

'That's right, you didn't. Well, wherever it is, take a circuitous route – don't go straight home. Get hold of a bag and hide your coat.'

'You seem to know a lot about this kind of thing.'

'So you said.'

'You didn't give a particularly full answer.'

'Maybe I watch too many films. Maybe you could ask me again over dinner,' he replied, wondering how bad an idea this actually was.

'Maybe I could,' said Connie.

'Maybe I could have your number.'

'Maybe you can't.'

'May I have your number?'

'No.'

Gallagher shrugged and began to stand.

'But you can buy me dinner,' she said.

'Tomorrow night?'

'Yes, why not? You choose.'

'Meet me outside the National Gallery, by the main steps in Trafalgar Square and we'll walk to the restaurant. Half seven?'

'Yes.'

'And if you've changed your mind you never see me again, right?'

He'd read her thoughts.

'I'll be there.'

'So will I.'

'Good. James, thanks again. It's been bizarre to meet you.'

'And you. I'll stay here, best you walk out alone.'

'OK,' she said. 'Aren't you forgetting something?'

Gallagher put out a hand; he wasn't sure whether she was asking him to do the cheek-kissing thing.

She laughed. 'My camera?'

* * *

Gallagher rang Harry and arranged to be picked up on Eversholt Street, in order that they could collect Gallagher's van. On the way, he told Harry what had happened.

'Oh well, no point in crying over spilt milk, what's done is done. What now?'

'I don't know,' said Gallagher. 'I need a night off and time to think.'

Gallagher got out of the car at the end of the street his van was parked in and walked past Vince, who turned and watched him from the end of the road. Vince had been walking around the side streets every hour or so noting anything that might be police-related. He'd needed to get away from Ray and his hung-over farts for one thing – apart from that he was bored.

The van had been there all afternoon. It had a parking permit. The driver didn't look like a copper but then he wouldn't, would he? Both he and the bloke in the Mondeo had short tidy hair, though – and why had he dropped him off on the corner a few hundred yards from the van? Could have been to save him turning around; maybe he was in a hurry. Vince went back to Ray in the VW Transporter and told him what he'd seen. Ray reckoned that, as they hadn't seen the girl all day, it'd be something to throw to the boss.

An hour later they saw Connie walk past their position as she returned to Kingsland Basin.

* * *

Bannerman was a happy man. Flic had called to thank him for the information he'd supplied. Her thanks had been warm, effusive even. They must meet soon, so she could thank him properly, but she couldn't chat. She'd be in touch.

He called Gallagher's number.

'Owen, Sandy, anything new?'

'No, nothing new. She's a student: she's probably studying.' Gallagher sat down in his uncle's old leather armchair. He was breaking his own rules. He didn't know why but his instincts were driving his actions. Not to mention that he wasn't likely to tell Sandy that he'd prevented an officer of the law going about his duty, by knocking him unconscious in a bush. That could be awkward.

'Oh well,' said Bannerman, 'it's time to pull the plug anyway.'

'That's it?'

'Yes, that's all, stand down. We just need to know where certain people are in case there's any monkey business in the next few weeks – we can't have these lefties spoiling things for our friends in the City, can we?'

'No, indeed not,' Gallagher said, unsure of how much he should believe.

'Look,' said Bannerman, 'we're going to be busier than usual for the foreseeable. There's a big international scientific conference coming up in town and I'm likely to need you. Planning any holidays?'

'I'll be around,' said Gallagher. He ended the call and sent a message to the covert camera, turning off the alerts. Being paid to watch someone was one thing, but he wasn't a voyeur by nature. Anyway, with any luck, he'd be sitting across a table from her tomorrow night.

* * *

Kenny Collins sat on the prison bed. They'd put him in a single cell when he'd arrived back from court – an empty soulless room, only four paces across – so that he could get his head around his new future. The tears were streaming down his face and he rocked back and forth, sobbing and sniffing.

Not such a hard man now, are you? The thought whirled around his mind, taunting him over and over. He lay back and stared at the ceiling. He'd be staring at that ceiling for a long time, or one just like it. The cell would be unlocked in the morning. He'd be unlocked and then banged up again throughout the day and most of the evening day after day, month after month.

Leanne would find someone else; she'd forget about him; she'd move on. She wouldn't come to visit. He didn't blame her. He might be able to shave off a few months for good behaviour, but it'd be too late. In the meantime, he wouldn't even be able to get pissed to block it out. There were drugs on the inside, of course, but that wasn't his style and he wasn't going down that route. He was at rock bottom and he couldn't face falling any further.

Kenny replayed in his mind every wrong turn he'd ever made. He watched as the opportunities came and went and saw the faces of all those he'd ever let down. And there was Mick. He thought of his life in the army: the good times, the great times and how he'd pissed it all away. He'd pissed it all away because he couldn't handle one Afghan afternoon. Because he'd let down a mate. Mate? He hadn't deserved to be called 'mate' when he let his friend die under that scorching sky, bleeding to death in a stinking ditch because Kenny Collins was playing the hard man.

Kenny had survived when all those good blokes hadn't. He'd come back in one piece, his life ahead of him. What had he done with it? He'd pissed it away, wasted all his chances and let them down all over again. You're an arsehole Kenny Collins, he thought.

The guilt swept through him like a forest fire, burning away any right to anything. He stood and undid the button of his trousers. He hadn't needed to be processed through the health centre as that had been done earlier in the week. The short-staffed screws had given him a cursory search on his return, but he'd only been to court and back, under guard, so they didn't put him through the full ordeal. The security blokes on the prisoner-transfer van hadn't asked him to return the plastic sick bag – they'd forgotten he'd asked for it when they'd piled him back in the cage after court. Some Hell's Angel had been head-butting the door and had kicked off when they led him into the sterile area back at the prison, so they'd had more than enough to deal with.

It was now close to midnight. The prison officers were stretched. The door hatch wouldn't be opening any time soon.

Kenny reached into his underpants and pulled out the carefully folded bag, which he laid on the bed. He took off his socks and tied them to the metal end of the bed, lay back and pulled them towards him, stretching them as far as they'd go. He held the position for a couple of minutes and his tears stopped.

He sat up, untied the socks and leaned back against the wall. He thought about waking up on the helicopter, waking up and fighting to show them he was alive. You shouldn't have come back, he thought: you didn't deserve to come back. He looked at the heavy cell door and heard the shouts, the threats, the pacing screws, the jangling of keys. He looked at the barred window, then stood and switched out the light. In the darkness, he placed the plastic bag over his head and smoothed down the open end around his neck, feeling it contract and expand with his breathing. He tied the two stretched socks together and made a slipknot, groping in the dark to tie the makeshift noose to the bed frame.

He lay on the floor and slipped the loop over his head, feeling it travel across his face, across the plastic bag, until it reached his neck. He lowered his shoulders. It was instantly more difficult to breathe as the bag moved to and from his lips. He tightened the knot and shuffled forward on his buttocks, using his heels to pull himself away from the end of the bed. The bag began to move faster as the oxygen was expended and he fought for breath. Kenny placed his hands into his back pockets and let his weight pull his shoulders to the floor.

He felt the panic surging; he felt the instinct to survive. Fuck it, he thought, you're a wanker – you deserve this.

SIX

Mark Keane heard the slow rumbling as he lay curled up in his sleeping bag. The floor was hard. The air was cold and a pungent smell filled his nostrils. He stayed absolutely still as the noise grew louder. He couldn't feel the comforting weight of his personal weapon in the bag with him. Where was it? Sergeant Burgess would kick his arse from here to there and every point in between if it wasn't within arm's length.

Where *was* here, never mind there? The adrenaline was pumping through his stiff body and confusion was gripping his brain. He'd have to move fast to get out of the scratcher and on his feet. The noise was loud and wrong. It was too close to wait to work out what it was. Then he felt the seeping wetness: so wet, so much blood. He was out of the bag, eyes adjusting to the early morning darkness.

His fist clenched as his hand found no weapon. A split second later he'd launched himself at the source of the threat. Keane's fist slammed into the driver of a Westminster Council road-sweeping machine. The man's face, grinning through the open window of the cab, contorted as his cheekbone shattered under the force of Keane's blow and he slumped out of reach, crying out in pain. The machine's water was still spraying the doorway at the side of the Lyceum Theatre where Keane had been sleeping.

Keane's hand was throbbing and the realisation of where he was and what he'd done rose up into his throat, filling his mouth with a vile acidic mess. He bent over, gagging, then looked left and right as he grasped his knees, his eyes watering. The street to his left was empty except for him and the man now sobbing in his cab. Wellington Street, to his right, was a main thoroughfare leading off the Strand. Early as it was, there were people, no doubt some police and definitely a shitload of CCTV cameras.

Keane stuffed the wet sleeping bag into his rucksack, spat again and jogged up Exeter Street, sticking to the right to avoid the camera on the wall on the left. Further on, Exeter Street would lead back around to the Strand – as would a left turn now – too busy. Instead, Keane moved right up the incline of Burleigh Street. He kept right to avoid the shallow angle of a bra shop's CCTV camera on the left.

At the junction with Tavistock Street he looked left and right again. Left would take him across Southampton Street, down Maiden Lane.

Stop. Think.

He'd end up at Charing Cross Police Station if he wasn't careful.

Not funny. So go right.

Remember to breathe.

Into Tavistock Street. Shop camera, shallow angle, cross to the darker area of the scaffolded walkway behind the London Transport Museum. Good cover.

Junction. Wellington Street again.

Shit.

Lyceum Theatre down to the right again.

Shit.

Keep calm.

Slow the breathing, don't look flustered.

Siren.

Shit.

Moving away. Breathe.

Keep going.

Into the next section of Tavistock Street. No cameras.

Junction. Stop.

Camera, corner of the Novello Theatre – two more to the right. Left, then, into Catherine Street. Cross the road, columns, better cover there.

Junction with Russell Street.

Door cameras opposite side of the road, nightclub entrance, no threat. Go right. Walk slow behind the theatre columns. No cameras.

No cameras?

Forget it. Keep moving.

Slow the pace a bit.

Cross into Crown Court: get off the main drag.

Church of Scotland. Camera five metres beyond on the left. Walk slow, head down, other side.

Quiet here, very quiet.

Martlett Court. No cameras.

Go left. Opera House at the end in Bow Street.

Stop.

Stay here a minute, not back on the roads.

Doorway. Sit.

Wait.

Breathe.

Crowds building soon. Wait here. Then drop into Covent Garden, just another bod off the train mooching around the tourist traps or just another homeless loser in a cast of thousands.

A good plan, relax.

Starting to rain.

Raining hard.

Bollocks.

He knew that it was going to be a long day.

* * *

Connie's head was thumping. She was dehydrated and her feet were aching. It was her third cup of coffee and she still hadn't managed to piece together all the bits of the night before. She'd met James – what was his surname? Had she asked? Had he told her? She remembered the meal. The food had been lovely. He was charming, if a little awkward to begin with. She'd had too much wine.

By dessert they'd been chatting like old friends, but she couldn't remember all the topics of conversation: just the usual stuff. There had been a moment towards the end of the meal when she'd asked about his family. His mother had died when he was young. She'd told him about how her parents had been killed in an accident when she was eleven. He'd suggested that they go on somewhere. She'd agreed that the night shouldn't end with such a conversational downer.

They'd gone on to a club. Drinking, dancing, lots more drinking.

He'd insisted on bringing her home. God, she'd let a man she barely knew bring her back; she'd shown him where she lived. Idiot.

But he'd been a perfect gentleman. She hadn't invited him in for coffee – had that been rude? No, sensible. He hadn't seemed to mind. She'd kissed his cheek and stepped on to the boat.

He'd walked backwards, whispering goodbye so as not to wake the neighbours. He'd tripped. She'd giggled as quietly as she could. He'd gone.

Flashes of the club: a slow dance, his eyes, the way he'd held her – her phone number. Shit, she'd given him her phone number. Only two people on the planet had the number – three now. Idiot.

It wasn't that she didn't like him; in fact, she was surprised at how quickly and how much she was liking him. But she should have been more guarded. He seemed genuine, but this wasn't the time to be taking chances.

Did she want to see him again? Did she know much more about him since they'd talked in the Lamb and Flag? Ex-army, estranged from his father, consultant of some kind – did he tell her? His favourite uncle; boarding school; his calm exterior and the sense of isolation that he gave off; the distance in his eyes even when he was looking straight at you; his smile, those eyes, that smile. Steady, Connie, slow yourself down.

* * *

Gallagher looked in the mirror: rough. He stared at himself accusingly. 'What are you doing?' Then he grinned. It had been a great night out. Connie.

Connie Edwards. His reflection gave him a quizzical look as he put the toothpaste on the brush. But she was a target. He'd followed her, photographed her and disregarded her civil liberties.

She was gorgeous.

She was on an MI5 watch list. The police liked to beat her up. And funny, she was really funny. She didn't dance well, but neither did he. She was a troublemaker – must be if she was on Bannerman's radar.

She was great company and she could certainly hold her drink. He remembered a slow dance, her eyes as she looked up at him – questioning, watchful, mischievous eyes. In any other situation he'd be wondering how long he should leave it before he could call her without seeming too keen.

To be fair, she was now a former target. True, he'd taken the opportunity to get close. The policeman's behaviour had forced him to intervene. He should have walked away, but he'd never been able to stomach injustice or casual violence like that. The copper he'd left in the bushes would probably disagree, but that was different. Fuck him.

Did he want to see her again? Bloody right he did. Should he see her again? Bloody right he shouldn't. Was that going to stop him? It should. As would the fact that he'd told her his name was James. It was far too complicated to contemplate.

The name thing could be explained away – not necessarily a big issue. He'd been in shock, he'd say; he was thinking on his feet, not sure what to do, he'd say. As for the rest of it, he was freelance: he didn't work for anyone; he didn't have to follow anybody else's rules anymore; he didn't need to let anyone else fuck it up. He looked back in the mirror. He was breaking his own rules, the rules that kept him together, that kept him safe and sane.

Bannerman had ended the job, but Gallagher had still gone to meet her. He'd still taken her to dinner, a club and home. It would be easy to cross the line again if she was involved in anything heavy. He walked to the shower, turned back, rested his hands on the sink and looked in the mirror.

'Idiot,' he said out loud.

He'd been in the shower for less than a minute when his phone rang. Was it her? Steady. Must have been hammered to give out his number – he'd got hers, though. The phone was on a chest of drawers by the sink, which he dripped his way over to.

'Morning Harry.'

'All right? Didn't wake you, did I?'

'What's up?'

'Nothing's up: just checking you're still on for tonight in Southwark – meeting Mark Keane.'

'Yeah. I hadn't forgotten,' said Gallagher. He had forgotten.

'Right. I'll meet you there at six. Did you get anything more from Bannerman?'

'No, that's it, job done. But more in the pipe.'

'Not surprised,' said Harry. 'They've been picking up suspected terrorists in car stops and raids. Have you caught the news lately?' Harry guessed not.

Gallagher hadn't.

'Six or seven arrested in London last night. Then there's the blokes nicked yesterday after guns were found in a car stopped for having no insurance. You would, wouldn't you?'

'Would what?' asked Gallagher.

'Drive guns around in a car with no insurance. Genius. Car gets stopped on the M1, next thing half a dozen front doors get kicked in around Birmingham.' Harry started to laugh. 'One minute you're asleep dreaming of wide-eyed celestial virgins, next minute you're being dragged through your front door by the Rozzers wearing nothing but your underpants and a pair of plasticuffs.'

'Why would the police be wearing your underpants and plasticuffs?'

Harry paused. 'Dipstick.'

'I'll see you tonight,' said Gallagher, heading back to the shower.

* * *

Ray and Vince were sitting in the van just off the Kingsland Road. The boss had torn a strip off them for leaving the job and they'd been staking the place out ever since. It was a pain in the arse. Parker had been a bit happier when Dave had taken back the images of the boyfriend who'd brought her home pissed – especially when Vince had remembered the van driver was the same bloke. Not a copper, then.

It was now early evening and Dave was sitting in the back. He had a crew-cut sitting above a round, often worried-looking, face. He was about the same age as the men in the front seats but hadn't been working for George Parker as long.

'So what else did he say?' asked Vince.

'Not much, just something as I was on my way out about throwing another bone to the bitch on the phone. Don't reckon he thought I heard that so keep it dark, right?'

Vince turned in his seat and gave an 'of course' look.

'Anyway, next thing I know, Loz Weir has me in and tells me you're to pick up the bird as soon as he calls. Gave me the bag and the keys to a motor and told me to get down here sharpish – like I told you. So now you just have to wait.'

Dave blew smoke out of the rear window on the driver's side.

'So, colleagues, to recap: the syringe and the sedative are in the bag. The dose is marked on the label. Loz will give you the green light. After that, you do it ASAP without making a dog's dinner of it.' He took another drag on the cigarette. 'Stick to the dosage: she might not survive a big shot and we don't want her choking on her own vomit while she's bagged.'

'How are we going to get her off the boat?' asked Vince.

'Carry her?'

'I mean how are we going to get her to the van? We can't carry her down the canal to Kingsland Road and the flats' entrance gate'll be locked.'

'Yeah,' said Ray. 'And even if it wasn't, it's a busy road – even at night – we'd never get away with it. Have you thought about that?'

'There's an inflatable coming,' said Dave, before taking on a storytelling voice. 'Silent running, sliding through the water under cover of darkness.' He leaned forward between the seats. 'Fuck knows who's doing that bit. Anyway, it'll be on the other side of her boat after you've gone in. Knock her out and bag her – there's a body bag in the holdall – just don't suffocate her.'

'An inflatable?' asked Vince.

'That's right. Lift her over the side into the inflatable. And do it quietly, she's small enough but she'll still make a splash if you drop her in.'

'Bloody hell,' said Ray. 'Who'd she piss off?'

'Someone Georgie Boy owes big, I reckon.'

'Then what?'

'Well, Ray, then you fuck off back to the road as quietly as you can, you get in the van and go to the house. And remember to take your masks off, in case someone thinks there's an IRA reunion in town.'

'I meant what happens to her after we put her in the boat.'

'There'll be a black van waiting alongside the canal down the road, out of view – it's all arranged, job done. She'll be delivered to us at the house later. We're not to talk to the delivery blokes. The boss was crystal about that.'

'Nice one,' said Ray, nodding approvingly. 'You used that stuff before?' he asked, looking in the rear-view mirror.

'Nope, but apparently it'll work instantaneously if you give it as an intravenous or intramuscular injection.'

'You what?' asked Vince.

'It doesn't matter where you stick it, dumb ass,' said Ray. 'I'll take care of it; I did an emergency first-aid course when I was a hospital porter.'

Vince looked relieved.

Dave opened the van door. 'I've got to get back or George will have my balls. I'm driving him over to Luton tonight. Just wait for Loz to call and follow the instructions on the label.'

'We'll just sit here, then,' said Vince, folding his newspaper and throwing it on to the dashboard.

'Looks like it,' Dave chuckled. 'Be lucky.'

* * *

Gallagher had arranged to meet Harry at the same pub in Southwark as the time before. Within a quarter of an hour, the two men looked up when they heard a lad in his early twenties at their end of the bar. Taking his change the new arrival walked to their table, waiting to be invited to sit.

Harry spoke first.

'So how are you keeping, Mark?'

Mark Keane took a swig and tilted the bottle out at the world. 'You know how it is: ducking and diving, fucking and skiving.'

Gallagher smiled, but noted that Keane was looking tired and thin. 'You're working, then?'

Keane took another swig and eyed the bar as he reached for his rolling tobacco, looking at his bottle and then at Gallagher. 'Nah, ain't working – apart from the odd day on a site lugging bricks about.'

'Where are you staying?' Harry asked.

'I'm mostly sofa surfing. Didn't work out too well back at home, me mum means well but all that nagging and worrying, well, it gets on your tits. And I missed being down here in the Smoke.'

'Of course, you're from round here,' Gallagher said.

'Dragged up in these very streets, boss.'

Harry pointed at Keane's already half empty bottle and began to stand.

Keane gave a grateful smirk and went back to rolling his cigarette.

Gallagher felt awkward. Small talk had never been his thing but he had less and less to say these days, even to people he knew well. Keane didn't offer him a way in.

'Mark, I'm glad that you bumped into Harry. It helps to be with people who, well, you know what I mean.'

Keane watched Harry collecting his change from the barmaid. 'So what happened, boss, you got back and told them to stick it?'

'That's the long and the short of it,' Gallagher answered. 'There are a few formalities involved when resigning the Queen's Commission, but not as many as might be imagined.'

Keane shook his head. 'I can understand why they didn't give a toss I was leaving, but you? Fuck me.'

Harry carried the drinks to the table and took up the conversation where he'd left it. 'Yeah, it's a bit rough at my gaff. The missus is glad to have me back, but she's not that keen on having me around all day every day, if you see what I mean, Keane.'

'Still funny, sarge,' Keane said, pulling a face. 'How's the stump?' he asked, feigning a kick at Harry's lower left leg.

'The stump itches like a bastard on damp days and I still get phantom pains in the bit that isn't there.'

'You move OK on it though, yeah?'

'Yeah, pretty good, if I do say myself. I've got a small selection of what are known in the amputee business as "prosthetic attachments." I've got my everyday one, my sporty one and this one is my dancing attachment,' said Harry, tapping the false bit under his trouser leg.

'Really?' asked Keane, knowing he was being set up.

'That's right: I'm a regular Ginger Roberts these days.'

'Isn't it Ginger Rogers?'

Gallagher smiled. 'I'm hoping he means Fred Astaire.'

'Fuck off, the pair of you,' said Harry. 'I'm a disabled and you're discriminating. Anyway, how's the shoulder?'

Keane shrugged. 'It is what it is.'

'And your legs?'

'They ain't pretty, but I've still got them and they still work.'

Gallagher turned to him. 'Harry says you had a hard time of it after we were flown back.'

'I was being "difficult" – gobbing off – so the CO sent me back ahead of the battalion, with a group of mongs on the sick. I spent a month digging the Brigadier's garden, taking shit off his wife. When the lads came back I was shoved on to the Guard Room staff – I mean, regimental policeman, me? For fuck's sake.'

Harry laughed and snorted beer down his nose. 'I still can't imagine it.'

'Anyway, I had three months of being dicked about by that arsehole Provo Sergeant, Simmons, and I'd had enough. In the end, I had to pay a few hundred quid for an admin discharge.'

'What happened to your hand, Mark?' Harry asked, looking at Keane's bruised knuckles.

'I caught it in a pile of bricks. They were falling off a scaffold plank at the time.'

Harry shook his head. 'Silly sod.'

Keane stood, indicating with his cigarette that he was going outside. 'I bumped into Frankie Fuller in my old local last night, just down the road, matter of fact. I was meeting a mate about some work. Anyway, Frankie Fuller – you know, Mick Fuller's dad, proper geezer – said he'd like to meet us for a pint sometime. I told him we'd be here.'

As the young man eased his way through the chatting crowd Gallagher looked at Harry, who shrugged.

Gallagher took another pull on his beer. 'This business you mentioned on the phone, it's not looking good?'

'No, he'll do time. He made a right mess of the bouncer and they've done him for assaulting the two coppers. Kenny always was a stupid fucker after a few beers.'

Gallagher felt a pang.

Harry twisted his glass. 'I went to see his mum and she's in a right two and eight.'

Staring out into the packed bar area Gallagher coughed and then took a long drink. 'We should visit.'

Harry was only half listening. The couple in the booth behind had made their tiff audible above the noise of the after-work crowd.

'So, how is Mrs Burgess?' Gallagher asked, watching Mark Keane making his way back through the crush.

The couple behind had fallen silent in sullen anger, simmering before the next bout, as Keane arrived back at the table.

Harry took a long pull on his pint. 'Don't ask.'

While the pub didn't quite fall silent, the noticeable lowering of the volume heralded the arrival of a man in his early fifties. He walked through the spaces made for him and a short glass arrived on the bar as he reached it. He was treated to an expansive smile by the barmaid. The landlord had come down from the flat above for the evening shift and raised a hand in greeting to the newcomer.

'Evening, Eddie,' said the man.

Keane shifted in his seat, as if unsure whether to stand and greet the stranger. He half stood and then seemed to think better of it, before turning to Harry. 'Frankie Fuller.'

Gallagher, looking concerned, sought something from Harry but Harry kept his eyes firmly on the new arrival.

Frankie Fuller, dressed in a tailored suit and wearing a gold watch that measured out the hours since its owner had made good, raised his glass by way of greeting.

Keane smiled like a nervous schoolboy, standing as Frankie asked if he might join them.

Gallagher introduced himself and extended his hand. His hand wasn't taken.

'I know who you are, son, and it's Frankie – everybody calls me Frankie.'

Keane managed a 'Mr Fuller' before dithering and sitting.

Frankie nodded, acknowledging the local boy's deference and raised his glass once again. 'Harry Burgess, I presume. I've seen you in photos Mick sent. He had a lot of time for you. He said you're a right hard bastard, but fair. He respected that, did Mick.'

Harry shook hands. 'I'm sorry we didn't get to meet at the funeral. I would have been there, if they'd have let me.'

'I heard you were in a bad way.'

'It could have been worse,' said Harry, immediately regretting the words he'd chosen.

Frankie showed no sign of noticing.

Keane was on his feet again, attempting to organise a pocket full of loose change into something that might be useful. The big man looked at his empty glass and named his brand.

'There's a tab open, son. Put your money away and get your arse up to the bar.'

* * *

They'd had a few drinks. War stories had been told amid remembrances of Mick Fuller. Frankie was clearly enjoying the banter, somehow holding on to the memory of his son with a newfound vividness as he sat and listened. He told his own stories of Mick's scrapes growing up, of holidays, of his wife's pride in her son when he became a soldier.

Mark had bought pork scratchings at the bar, which he'd crushed before opening the packet to douse the contents with Tabasco Sauce. He indicated that the others could help themselves.

'You really are a disgusting individual,' said Harry, shaking his head.

Mark looked out at the pub crowd and chewed on the concoction. 'Mick always led from the front. Always on the Barma team, if you let him.'

'Barma?' asked Frankie.

'Barma was the code word for clearing routes of IEDs. Either with detectors or on your belt buckle with a bayonet,' Harry explained. 'He preferred "Toyota Barma," though.'

Frankie shrugged to indicate that he was lost again.

Gallagher took a sip of his pint. 'Making sure the Afghan civilian vehicles could drive down the road in front of us – Toyota Barma.'

'Then there was Barma "*Insha'Allah*." That was the A and A – the Afghan Army – method,' said Mark. 'The crazy fuckers would just stroll along kicking at anything that looked a bit dodgy.'

'Those were the days,' said Harry, rubbing his leg.

There followed a lull in the conversation: the kind that can come after sustained laughter, when everyone present recalls the darkness that surrounds them – invisible to others – their own personal set of shadows threatening to pull them back into a heartbreakingly cold embrace.

Frankie offered to go for the next round of drinks – same again.

As he reached the end of the bar nearest their table, two stocky men in their late twenties walked into the pub and stood waiting to be served. The landlord stopped the barmaid as she made a move towards them.

'Gentlemen,' Eddie said.

'Two pints of Stella.'

'Sorry lads, I'm afraid not.'

'You what?'

'Sorry lads, no Travellers, nothing personal.'

'Nothing personal? That's discrimination, that is.'

Frankie stood behind them. 'Eddie, pass me that pen and pad.'

'What's your problem, old man?' asked the tallest.

Frankie smiled. 'If either of you can spell "discrimination" you can stay for a drink.' He placed the pad on the bar and offered the pen. 'In fact, if you can spell it between you I'll buy your beer.'

The shorter one looked at his companion and then at Frankie. 'Fuck you.'

'I'm flattered, but no thanks.'

The taller man took a step forward.

'Can I help you, son?' asked Frankie, tossing the pen back to Eddie.

Gallagher, Harry and Mark began to stand. Frankie gave a wave of his left hand down by his side. They retook their seats.

'Fuck you,' said the taller one.

'So he said.' Frankie adjusted his cuffs. 'Off you go, lads – no hard feelings.'

'Fuck you,' said the shorter one again, as the taller one began to throw a punch at Frankie's face.

Frankie stepped forward and pushed the man's arm away and down with his left hand while simultaneously using his right to punch his attacker's ribs. He followed up with a right jab to the sternum. His opponent collapsed to the floor.

'You bastard,' said the smaller one, who turned and grabbed for an empty bottle to swing backhand at Frankie.

Eddie pulled the man's arm over the bar, grabbed his hair and smashed his face into the solid old wood.

A woman let out a cry as the sound of broken cartilage reverberated across the now silent pub.

Frankie stood back as the taller one got up and helped his brother. 'Off you go, lads – no hard feelings,' Frankie repeated.

The taller man pulled the shorter one to the door, pushed him outside and then turned. 'Fuck you!' he spat. 'Fuck all of you – we'll be back.'

As the door slammed shut, Frankie smiled at Eddie. 'I don't think so.'

Eddie smiled back.

'Like old times. I've come over all nostalgic.'

Frankie adjusted his cuffs and straightened his tie. 'Same again, Eddie.'

'I'll send them over.'

Gallagher watched Frankie walk back to the table as if nothing had just happened. It had been an impressive demonstration of non-institutionalised controlled aggression. Now he saw the dangerous elements of the man that were swirling behind the penetrating and slightly sad eyes of the still-grieving father.

Mark began to say something but then didn't. He couldn't trust himself not to misjudge the situation and he certainly didn't want a slap off Frankie. The stories his dad had told him about Frankie Fuller – you wouldn't believe. You especially wouldn't believe them if you saw this dapper businessman quietly sipping a short at the end of a bar, reading his paper, minding his own. But it was him all right: hard as nails. No one in the pub that night would have been in any doubt. Mark still couldn't quite believe what he'd just witnessed.

'You know the landlord well then, Frankie?'

'I know everyone round here, Harry, but to answer your question, I bloody should do: I own the place.'

'The pub's yours?' asked Gallagher.

'Bought it in '86. I'm what you might call a sleeping partner. Eddie's kept it for me since 1990. The bloke before got his fingers broken in the till – nasty things those old cash registers. Anyway, he reckoned it best to move on and Eddie's been in charge since.'

The evening wore on. Mark told some jokes and everyone followed suit. It'd been a good night but Gallagher thought it better that he left them to it. He was becoming distracted by daydreams about Connie Edwards.

'Thank you for your company, gentlemen,' he said. 'But I think it's time I headed back over the river.'

135

'You can't go yet, boss, it's still early,' Mark replied.

'Yeah, he's right, boss – not often that he is, so you'll have to stay.'

Frankie noted how the other two had both addressed Gallagher as 'Boss' throughout the evening.

'No, I'm off.' Gallagher stood and shook hands with Harry.

'Stay in touch, Mark,' he said, patting him on the shoulder.

Frankie stood. There was a pause in which the two men sized each other up. Frankie held out his hand and Gallagher took it willingly.

'Go careful, son,' said Frankie.

As Gallagher left the pub, Frankie turned to Harry.

'So what's his story? I can't make him out. He's not what I expected for an officer and a gentleman.' He pronounced the last phrase in a la-di-da sing-song fashion.

'He's a good bloke, Frankie, one of the best,' replied Harry. 'He joined up as a private, a Sapper in the Engineers, a ranker like us. He was selected for officer training, chose the infantry and was commissioned into our regiment. He was always at the front, head up and charging. Switched on, tough, loyal, he always put his blokes first.'

'Yeah, not like some fucking Ruperts,' said Mark.

'Ruperts? Officers?' asked Frankie, remembering how he'd tried to keep up with Mick's barrack-room lingo and army jargon.

'Yeah,' said Mark. 'Fucking Ruperts: fucking officers.'

The lad was one over the eight and Harry was slowing down too. It was time to call it a night, after all.

Frankie waved and called out to the bar. 'Three brandies please, Eddie.'

'Frankie,' said Mark, full of boozy courage and familiarity. 'Do you know why officers are like lighthouses in the desert?'

'Go on,' said Frankie. He couldn't help liking the silly young sod.

'Because,' Mark hiccupped, 'they're very bright' – he hiccupped again – 'but they're fuck all use to anyone.'

'The old ones are the best,' said Harry, clipping Mark around the back of the head.

Frankie was still chuckling as the drinks arrived. 'A toast,' he said, looking to Harry.

'Absent friends?'

They chinked glasses.

'Absent friends.'

Frankie downed his drink.

'Right lads, that's me. Now listen: if you need anything – and I mean anything – you call your Uncle Frankie.' He handed them each a card with his number on. 'Now cock off home.'

* * *

Yasir grabbed Syed by the scruff of the neck. 'I told you not to carry anything dirty through this area.'

'Sorry,' Syed answered. 'We'll be finished soon.'

Imran directed his torch at the wall that the men were bricking up. They'd crawled through on arrival and were now sealing themselves into the oldest section of the building's attic space. Progress had been slow, as noise had to be kept to a minimum even when the building was closed. Yasir had used his compass to find which way east lay. He'd marked it with a chalk arrow and had taped off a square area denoting their prayer zone. All washing and sanitation was to be done at the farthest point from this square. Urine was bottled, excrement bagged.

The space was cramped, hot, dusty and dark. It would be a long few days and Imran needed to monitor the men's psychological and physical health. There were too many bodies, too much heat, boredom and excitement – mixed in a small space full of weapons and explosives – not to carefully watch the short fuses that could be lit in men's minds.

Imran moved the bag containing the metal case to a hole in the wall behind his bed space and placed his jacket over it.

138

He hadn't discussed the case with any of the others. Not even Yasir. The Chechen brothers had secured the material; the bomb-maker in Germany had built the device around the canister.

The radiation would be slowly killing them in such a space, but they'd be dead before any signs of sickness showed. They'd be dead and with God and London would witness piles of corpses not seen since the Great Plague of the seventeenth century had killed one in five of the population.

They had water and food enough. They had the Holy Book and God was in their hearts. All they had to do was wait.

* * *

Connie had spent the evening reading, in between bouts of thinking about James. He hadn't called. She hadn't called – probably for the best. It had been a great night and she'd liked him. She'd more than liked him. That was becoming more apparent the longer he didn't call. She'd kicked herself, initially, for leaving herself so vulnerable, so quickly. She'd questioned her sanity for exchanging numbers with him, when only Tom and Benita had hers, true. But that had passed with her hangover.

Perhaps he was too good to be true. The ache in her thigh from the police baton throbbed. Perhaps she had isolated herself too much; perhaps she should let someone in. She was tired but wanted to finish the chapter she was reading. She lit the gas to boil the kettle.

Tom: still nothing. Maybe she should ring the company office if his mobile was still switched off tomorrow. Sod's Law he'd call half an hour after she did – then he'd be mad at her for causing a fuss. She didn't want to bombard him with unanswered text messages.

She drank the tea while wading through the pages, continually having to re-read sections, as thoughts of Tom and James jostled for pole position in her mind. She flicked the pages forward to see if the end of the chapter was coming. It wasn't. It could wait until the morning.

Walking to the front of the boat she checked that the cabin doors were locked and secured a window that was unlocked in the galley. In the bedroom she switched on the radio. The display showed 00:17. That was just over half an hour to the Shipping Forecast, which would help her to doze off.

Vince watched the last light go out on Connie's boat from his hiding place further up the towpath and made his way back to the van.

Two and a half hours later Connie was still wide-awake. Her mind was racing in the darkness. Should she call Tom's company headquarters on the King's Road? Should she call James to thank him for dinner? Should she send him a text onnie woke in darkness. She vomited. Turning her head to ne side, her nose touched a hard surface as she tried to mpty her mouth. She spat. Her hands touched wood either ide. Raising her head a little, she gasped as it touched something hard. She pushed left and right. Amid a terrifying wave of claustrophobic panic, she vomited again. Struggling to breathe, she turned her head again, pushed down with her shoulders and kicked out to the front. The surface beneath the soles of her feet was solid.

Beginning to hyperventilate, she kicked and shoved at the walls surrounding her. She knew they weren't walls. She knew what was containing her. A primal recognition began pumping adrenaline through her body, fear surging through her mind, driving her limbs in every direction, flailing in the stench of her sickness, sobbing in the face of death.

She pulled her knees towards the spasm in her stomach. The hideous reality took hold of her mind. Pushing her knees up, she lifted her palms, shoving with all her strength. No movement. She tried to scream and was sick again.

'All right, all right, fun's over, you sick fucker,' said a muffled voice.

The lid of the wooden crate gave way to her efforts as the sound of boots hitting a stone floor reached her ears. Hands lifted the wooden lid and a black balaclava with a mouth and eyes looked in. Another face, exactly the same but its mouth laughing, leaned in from the other side.

message? Would it be simple or flirtatious? Would he reply? God, what if he didn't reply? How long did Tom have left on his contract in Africa? She tried to count back the weeks from the date he had given her. Maybe he'd met a girl – a South African, a tourist, a female contractor. Maybe he was in the throes of a whirlwind romance and didn't want to jinx it by telling Connie. She smiled in the dark: he wouldn't be able to keep it to himself.

Was that the boat moving? Just the wind shifting it on its mooring. She hoped Tom had found someone, maybe then he'd settle down in the UK instead of being abroad all of the time. Maybe he'd got married one mad weekend and was wondering how to tell her. No, he wouldn't do that.

She sat up. Cracking wood? Boats made odd noises in the quiet of the night, but that was a very strange sound. It had been way to the front of the boat. Why was she beginning to breathe faster? Calm down Connie, you're not a silly little girl. She swung her feet off the bed, pulled on her jeans, t-shirt and a pair of trainers – she might have to look outside.

She picked up a torch that she kept in a drawer by the bed and walked to the bedroom door. Instinctively, she pulled it open sharply and shone the torch forward into the passage that led past the bathroom to the living area beyond. Nothing there. Relax, for goodness' sake.

As she walked down the narrow corridor into the galley she directed the torch beam towards the cabin doors. The wood around the lock was splintered. She dropped the torch as a black cotton bag came over her head and a hand clasped over her face. Her shout was stifled by a rope gag pulled sharply into her mouth on the other side of the bag and she felt a sharp stab in her right buttock. She fought with her elbows, struggling with the bigger body behind hers. Hands – another set of hands – were in front of her holding her arms. A fist slammed into her stomach. The gag stayed firmly in her mouth as the air rushed through her trying to escape. Parts of her body were going numb and she felt the world slipping away, until she sank into nothingness.

SEVEN

Gallagher awoke standing by the window. He'd ma open it in his sleep and the cold air had brought hin He looked back across the bedroom to see the various he'd knocked over as he fought his way out of bed chink of light in the curtains. As usual the alarm cloc gone first and farthest, which is why he had a solid contraption rather than a digital model. There had been many electronic casualties and they weren't cheap.

He rested his head on the glass and looked down to tl street below – down on to normality. Just a bad dream, but bad dream that had happened; a bad dream that flickered behind his eyes as he walked in daylight; a bad dream that consumed him as he slept; a bad dream that released him into this half-life, having fed deeply on his fear and guilt, spitting him out, sweating and frightened, to clamber into any light that he could find. The same dream, over and over, but nothing changed. He could never do anything differently: just watch as it all unravelled towards its inevitable, soul-crushing end.

* * *

'What's going on?' asked a voice several feet away.

'This sick bastard was sitting on the lid reading his book. He heard her wake up and stayed put. Now she's covered in puke.'

'Well he can clean it up,' said Dave, also clad in a balaclava.

'You fucking clean it up,' said Ray the laughing mask.

Connie spat and tried to sit up as she fought for air, the bright light hurting her eyes. She opened her mouth to scream and was sick again. There was movement from the left and the bag came over her head. She struggled for breath as the damp cotton mingled with vomit and was sucked against her mouth. A hand gripped her shoulder hard, followed by a stabbing pain in her arm. She tried to lash out and was struck in the side of the head. Nausea swept over her. Then darkness.

Dave walked over to the two men either side of the crate.

'Nice job, lads.'

'It was this nutter,' said Vince.

'You were told to take her out of the crate and tie her up on the bed. The crate was for moving her across the bloody yard: it wasn't meant to be her new fucking house. Tie her hands and ankles and don't pump any more of that shit into her, for fuck's sake.'

'Whatever,' said Ray.

145

Dave wanted to punch him but thought better of it. 'Vince, get that bag off her before she suffocates – you twat.'

* * *

Tom had been staying with a former colleague, Jonno, in Colchester. Jonno's wife had left him two weeks earlier, so Tom hadn't needed to explain too much. The conversation was pretty circular due to Jonno lurching from hung-over to pissed every day, replaying recent events over and over.

Details of the five funerals had been relayed to Tom through a network of friends he and Jonno shared on the security circuit. Some of the lads they knew had attended, but he hadn't. He felt bad about that but it was too risky to be out in the open at services so closely linked with Iraq.

He'd binned his mobile phone in South Africa and had bought a new unregistered pay-as-you-go when he arrived in Plymouth. Connie would be worried, but he still didn't want to call her number just in case. In case of what? Was he being paranoid? Probably, but five men were dead – five of his friends. A degree of paranoia wasn't to be entirely unexpected.

Stewie Boss in Iraq had been cagey about the team's last contact on the day Tom had finished his contract. Whoever the blokes were who had ended up dead in the brief firefight, someone higher up the food chain wanted the whole thing kept dark. The official line was that Gary, Martin, Chalky, Joe and Gus had been targeted by a local militia group to send a warning to the military contractor community. But why just them? There had been a couple of incidents across the city involving other companies, but why five guys from the same team? It didn't add up and Stewie wouldn't or couldn't help Tom make sense of it. Tom hadn't supposed to have been on that escort job but they were short-handed and he'd volunteered. His replacement had been delayed in Dubai, so Tom's last day hadn't involved lying by the pool as he'd planned.

He had to check that Connie was OK, which was why he was now stepping off the train at London's Liverpool Street Station. He'd have to be careful but he'd see her and tell her he was going on another job – that he'd be out of contact again for a while. Then he'd lie low and see what happened.

He had friends still working in UK Special Forces and a couple of them were using their contacts to glean anything from the intelligence grapevine that they could. If someone was targeting contractors, someone would know – somewhere, something would connect, somewhere with someone. It was a slow process, as there was a risk of drawing the wrong kind of attention to Tom, his contacts and his contacts' contacts. If there was something he needed to know he'd find out in time, but at that moment he had nothing to go on.

He'd taken a late train in order to arrive at Connie's boat after dark. He took the Tube down to Old Street and checked into the Premier Inn around the corner. It was clean and big enough for no one to notice him coming and going. It was close enough to walk to Kingsland Basin, but far enough away to ensure that he wasn't followed. Who was he expecting to follow him? He didn't know. It was doing his head in.

He should have felt safe back in the UK. It was unlikely that anyone connected to a ragtag local militia in Iraq would come after him personally, no matter how pissed off they might be – and, if it had been a series of warning attacks, why would they know who he was? Still, his instincts were telling him to go careful and Gus had clearly thought it necessary to warn him even after Tom was safely out of Iraq. Gus had contacts in all sorts of shadowy places but it hadn't saved him. He'd still ended up at the side of the road stripped, battered and bloated in the morning sun, with the side of his skull blown out.

The boat was in darkness. He didn't want to startle his sister, so he crept to the front and saw that the security bar was across the cabin doors: she must be out. But then he saw the small pieces of splintered wood on the deck and noticed that the security bar was tilted, its padlock closed but not locked and secured through the clasp. He removed the seven-inch folding knife that he'd bought in Colchester from its ankle sheath and climbed on to the boat.

* * *

They needed to extract the camera from the canal basin. Harry would have to do the business in case anyone, especially Connie, came out and recognised Gallagher. They planned to lift it at about three in the morning, but Gallagher didn't fancy explaining why he was hanging around, half way up a tree, by her boat in the early hours.

It was now 02:06 and Gallagher was in the back of the van in Lee Street. Harry was parked around the corner as back-up while Gallagher fired up his laptop to get a view of the boat and basin before Harry's first walk-past.

Connie's boat was in darkness on the screen, which was a good start. They needed to watch a while yet, though. Gallagher opened another screen window to check any images captured in the last few hours, in order to see if she was at home. He smiled and decided to watch what it had picked up when he'd walked Connie home. She hadn't called and he still didn't know whether he should. It was getting more rather than less likely. Idiot.

The laptop screen offered him the choice of a series of recorded clips – captured images recorded when the camera had been triggered by movement – displayed as a row of 'thumbnails.' He selected a file but realised it had been later than he thought it had been. He tried again, watched a few ducks landing on the boat's roof and then there she was. He could see her laughing, finger to lips as he walked backwards out of shot. She laughed again, bending forward, hands on thighs, trying to be quiet. Then there was a wave, a blown kiss, a fumbling of keys, a look, another wave and she went inside.

Connie-bloody-Edwards. He had to get her out of his mind. He'd take Eve dancing. He'd call up Sophie in Putney or that girl from Clapham. What was her name? Poppy? No, that was the crazy one at the Coach and Horses in Greek Street. Whatever: he had her number somewhere. He'd call her to suggest drinks, anything to get Connie Edwards out of his head. It was too complicated, too risky. It was a bloody shame.

Gallagher selected another image and saw Connie at her window late morning the day after their night out. She was wearing some sort of light dressing gown, her hair tied back. She filled a pint glass with water and drank it where she stood. Hangover: unsurprising.

There was always Charlie from Stoke Newington. No, she was mental, too mental for more than a one nighter.

Connie moved across the screen with her bike and was then captured by the camera returning with some shopping.

Zara, from that night down in Fulham? Good-looking girl, but she knew it – dull. The redhead, Isobel? He'd met her in the Walrus and Carpenter near the Monument, the night he was supposed to meet Bannerman for drinks but had thought better of it at the last minute. She was funny, bright, didn't take herself too seriously, liked a beer, great taste in music, lived for the moment and always bought a round. Isobel moved to the top of the list.

Connie was back on screen waving to someone out of shot from the front of her boat, a neighbour probably. Some words were exchanged and then she went back inside after stretching out her arms and shoulders.

Who else could he call? There was the woman in Kennington: Jess. Still too much missing from the memories of that encounter and he hadn't got her number. Why was that?

Gallagher watched the screen as Connie moved about the boat throughout the evening, triggering the camera sensors. A book in her hand at the sink: a study night. More images of a similar sort, then the lights on the boat were turned off and the two screen windows on his laptop looked exactly the same.

That was enough. He was beginning to feel guilty about watching her. His hand hovered over the laptop's control pad, about to select a later file to see if she was home. But then he noticed another file with a timecode from the early hours of the morning before. Curious, he clicked on the image but he couldn't make out what had caused the camera trigger.

He slowed the playback.

The dark figure of a man walked into shot and climbed on to the boat. Another man followed him aboard just over a minute later.

Gallagher felt his heart rate increasing and watched as the two figures huddled around the cabin doors. It took them the best part of five minutes to open or break the lock; they clearly weren't professionals. There was nothing more to see for some minutes after they'd entered, until a torch beam flashed across the boat's interior from the stern – then darkness again. The next activation was triggered by one of the men coming out on to the front deck and moving to the starboard side, just out of shot. Why was he going to the waterside of the prow?

Harry's voice activated Gallagher's PTT: 'Anything doing?'

* * *

At that moment, the man codenamed Mimar was sitting in his office in Kensington, a single desk lamp throwing shadows against the thick curtains that covered the blast-proof glass of the tall windows. The BBC World Service was

152

on in the background, the volume low on a small world-band radio he kept on this desk.

He had been making his way to the bottom of a stack of reports but was now reflecting on what had happened to bring him to this point, thinking about what had brought him to this stage of the most important operation of his career: an operation that wouldn't win him any medals or the love of his countrymen but would save countless lives, perhaps even his country itself. He picked up the cigarette case lying on his desk – presented to him by the Institute's former chief – and took out one of the five cigarettes that he allowed himself per day.

The man codenamed Mimar had been there when the Americans had broken the prisoner. One of his teams had been involved in the extraction from Europe so the intelligence was shared, even though the Americans had kept ownership of the man. Now he'd be in the Back of Beyond, held in an American detention centre somewhere, if he was still alive. One thing was certain: he would never be released.

The information that Mimar returned with had solidified into a plan. The man had first been flown to Uzbekistan. Mimar had watched as the interrogation teams had broken him, over many weeks. He had listened to the venom that the man had spat at his captors, then the lies, the hatred, more lies, more venom. Then there were the small slippages in logic, cracks in the lies, cross-referenced phrases, tired affirmations and irrational denials.

The 'Black Arts' employed by the interrogators were a clever mix of the physical and the psychological. Eventually, under physical torture, prolonged beatings, burns, the use of electricity, tools or surgical instruments, the man, any man, would say anything to make the pain stop. The man, any man, would end up telling you what you wanted to hear. Of course, when the prisoner had first arrived he had been subjected to the usual intense sensory deprivation, mock executions, immersion in water to the point of drowning; he'd been starved, had his circulation clamped off by wire restraints and he'd been drugged to further weaken his resistance. The prisoner knew, of course, that some captives sent to Uzbekistan had been boiled alive. He knew that Uzbek interrogators were Soviet-trained and didn't take no for an answer. He hadn't wanted to meet the local boys.

The use of enhanced interrogation techniques that followed increased the disorientation of the prisoner via stress positions, sleep deprivation, relatively low-level violence and degradation. But then he was offered good food and people spoke more quietly, more kindly. He was offered clean clothing and cigarettes. Here an understanding of kinesis came into play: watching the physical manifestations of attempts at deception, in order to build a baseline from which to spot anomalies that could be exploited with sets of

154

planned, repeated questions. Then more violence, more deprivation, until the wheel turned again. The pressure had been relentless and he had listened as the man was finally broken, the prisoner's mind whirling in fragments, mumbling incoherently at first, until the detail began to pour out of him – long after he had begun to forget who he truly was.

Mimar reached over to the radio and turned up the volume to listen to the news. Amid reports from correspondents covering attacks in Afghanistan and Iraq, was yet another piece speculating on whether the Western powers would support Israeli calls for a large-scale attack on Iran. Some politicians and pressure groups in America were making supportive noises but the Administration was still holding a firm non-committal line. Other sources spoke of the Iranian leadership as having 'malevolent intentions.' A British source had stated that international support for Israel was 'slipping away' due to a 'lack of progress towards peace' and recent unilateral action.

Mimar sipped his drink and smiled.

He now had everything he needed to trigger the groups, the individuals. He now had what he needed to allow them to start the hostile planning cycles. The targets had been provided. The sleepers would now carry out initial surveillance, pre-attack surveillance, planning, rehearsals and execution. And he had his two assets ready to cap it off job by job.

Now it was beginning.

* * *

Gallagher had watched the screen as the body bag had been taken from the boat's cabin and lowered over the side, out of shot. Had they dropped it into the water? He spoke to Harry via his PTT phone: 'H, there's been a change of plan. I need you down under the bridge with a night sight, sweep the basin for me.'

Harry heard the quiet urgency in Gallagher's voice and sought no further explanation.

Fifteen minutes later Gallagher entered Kingsland Basin, ignoring Harry who was hidden in the shadows, and made his way towards Connie's boat. There was no sign of anyone aboard so he quietly clambered over the gunwale. The security bar had been laid to one side. He took the torch from his pocket and held it ready as he eased apart the cabin doors.

Crouching in the doorway he allowed his eyes to adjust to the darker area of the boat's interior and began to discern the layout in front of him. The blinds were down over the windows on both sides of the boat. He switched on the torch with its red filter – fitted so the light wouldn't travel far or be too visible to anyone close enough to see the interior illuminated.

He walked slowly into the cabin.

He froze. The hairs on the back of his neck were up. He hadn't heard or seen anything but his survival gene was sounding the alarm.

He eased slightly to his right, directing the torch beam down a narrow passage leading from the galley area. He saw the eyes of the man low to the ground in what was almost a sprinter's 'ready' position. Then, as his assailant powered forward, Gallagher saw the knife.

He stepped back and to the left as he threw the torch. It tumbled through the decreasing space between the two men and struck the knife-man squarely on the nose. The man made no sound, nor did he give any other indication of the pain that such a blow must have caused. He did, however, stop his forward motion, planting his feet in a low fighting stance.

Gallagher took a fighting stance of his own, his feet hip-width apart, left foot forward. His weight was on the balls of his feet, his hands relaxed at chin height a comfortable distance from his face, elbows in, shoulders square. The blade moved forward and across, slashing the air between them.

Gallagher stepped forward as it passed across his front, tucking his chin down, keeping his head low and sweeping his attacker's arm out to the side as he punched the man in the face. He continued the defence by pushing the knife arm back and down, holding the wrist with his left hand and the man's shoulder with his right, before delivering his knee into the assailant's testicles.

He pulled and twisted his attacker's wrist as the man bent double and the knife clattered across the floor towards the front of the boat.

The man fought back, ramming his head into Gallagher's stomach. As they fell heavily against the sink, a voice outside called at the window.

'Connie?'

Gallagher propelled the heel of his palm into the hinge of the man's jaw below the ear and his opponent dropped to the floor, cracking his head on the sink unit as he fell.

'Connie, it's Tony, what's going on?'

Gallagher stepped back and picked up the knife. The man on the floor spat blood and called out.

'Tony, it's Tom. Connie's away – everything's fine. Go back to your boat.'

'Tom? It's Tony, are you OK?'

Tom kept his eyes fixed firmly on Gallagher and the knife, inwardly cursing Tony for putting himself in harm's way – the man was renowned for being an early to bed and early to rise kind of guy, for God's sake.

'Tony, it's fine. I came back from a club after a skinful, couldn't find the lights. I'll see you in the morning.' He watched Gallagher place the knife on the small table in the red glow of the torch lying on the floor.

'OK, Tom, you take care. See you in the morning.'

'Tom? Connie's brother Tom?' asked Gallagher.

'That's right. Now, who the fuck are you?'

* * *

Net's watch showed 03:13. He could hear Ozi shooting anything that moved in the living room. He threw on a pair of tracksuit bottoms and walked into the hallway on his way to the bathroom.

'Don't you get tired of those games? Don't you ever sleep?'

'I'll sleep when I'm dead. We've had years of people telling us when to go to bed, when to eat, when to shower. I can do what I like,' Ozi called back, eyes fixed to the screen, hands clamped to the controller.

'No one's stopping you,' said Net.

He left the bathroom and sat in an armchair opposite Ozi, who was busy blowing up a car with a rocket launcher.

'You need to sleep; we don't know when the first call will come.'

159

'Relax, Netanel, we're not in the army now and we're not in a military prison. We're in London. Can you believe we're in London?'

'I can believe it, but if we fuck this up we'll be back in our cells – knowing our luck they'll throw away the key.'

'Our luck? We're in London, Net, and we're getting a pardon. We do this and we're free men. I might come back. I love this city.'

Net shook his head. 'Ozi, you're a mad man. Get some sleep, you freak.'

Ozi laughed as Net walked back to his room.

'Good night, Mother!'

* * *

Gallagher called Harry on the PTT and asked him to bring his car into Dunston Street next to the canal steps.

'Are you going to tell me what you're doing on my sister's boat in the middle of the night?' Tom asked.

Gallagher looked around the cabin, seeking possible camera and microphone positions.

'I don't think we should say too much here, do you?'

'I'm asking the questions, shithead. Who the fuck are you and where's my sister, you bastard?'

'Actually, you're sitting on the floor bleeding and I've got the knife you tried to stick me with in the dark.'

'Want to go again?' Tom asked, snorting blood from his nose into his hand.

Gallagher crouched so that he wasn't talking down to the man on the floor. 'Tom, this isn't going to help Connie. We need to get out of here. I'm going to give you back the knife and then we're going to leave quietly to find somewhere to talk about this.'

'Are you Old Bill?'

'No, nothing like that.'

'Well who the fuck are you?'

'I'm a friend and I have a friend waiting on the road. We need to go now.'

Tom saw an image of Gus dead by the roadside, an image his imagination made worse every time it presented the scene he hadn't witnessed.

Gallagher was holding out the knife, the handle towards Tom, who eased himself up and took it. He pointed the blade at Gallagher.

'Nobody fucks with my sister. I get suspicious: I kill you.'

Gallagher raised his palms. 'Like I said, I'm here to help.'

They closed the doors to the cabin and replaced the security bar. Tom locked the padlock and then followed Gallagher down the towpath.

When they reached the Kingsland Road Gallagher turned to Tom. 'Where are you staying? Is it safe?'

'A hotel. I'm not taking you anywhere. I'm not doing anything until I get some answers.'

'No, not a hotel: too many cameras, not enough people coming and going at this time in the morning.' Gallagher broke another of his rules. 'We'll have to go to my place. No one will be watching it.'

'Are you going to tell me what's going on?' asked Tom.

'Let's get off the street, get a drink and we'll talk – there's a car waiting for us over there.'

'I'm not getting into any car; do you think I'm some kind of mug?'

Gallagher wracked his brains. 'You joined the Paras when Connie had just turned fourteen. You were flush with your new wages after training. When you went on leave you borrowed a car and the two of you drove to Wales. You camped near a beach for two nights. You paid for her to ride a horse for the first time. You bought her a new rucksack for school. The car kept breaking down and Connie remembers learning a few new words that came out from underneath the bonnet. She remembers every minute of it.'

Tom looked up and down the street. He grinned. 'I nicked that car – took it back, so technically I did borrow it.' He touched the split skin on his nose where the flying torch had hit. 'OK, let's go. Where's your motor?'

Gallagher led the way. 'I'll introduce you to Harry.'

* * *

Gallagher and Tom had gone ahead to Gallagher's flat while Harry found a place to park. Gallagher made coffee and led Tom into the living room.

'I need to have a quick chat with Harry before we try to work out what's going on.'

'You can start by telling me where my sister is.'

'That I don't know.' The doorbell rang. 'Just give me five minutes to talk to Harry.'

'I want answers quick, or I'm gone.'

'I understand.'

Gallagher let Harry in and Tom heard them as they began to talk in the kitchen in low voices. They joined him within a couple of minutes and sat opposite each other on either side of the room.

'We think Connie's in trouble, Tom. Do you know what she was into?'

'What do you mean "into"?'

'Was she involved in any criminal activity?'

Tom stood up and slammed down his cup, spilling the contents on the table. 'I knew it, you're the Old Bill.'

'We're not coppers,' said Harry.

'Who the fuck are you, then? What's all this got to do with you?'

Gallagher leaned forward and rubbed his temples. The next few minutes would need careful handling. 'Give me a minute,' he said, gesturing for Harry to follow him.

'Fuck this.'

'Please, Tom, bear with me for a minute.'

'You're fucking me about – how do you know my sister?'

Gallagher turned to Harry. 'Sorry, mate, I know it's an arse-ache but could you go and get it?'

'No problem. Like I said, Ross's back. I'll get him to meet me up there.'

'I owe you one.'

Tom picked up his cup and threw it against the wall. Gallagher ignored the mess and walked Harry to the door. When he came back into the room Tom was sitting with his head in his hands.

'Don't worry about the cup,' said Gallagher.

'Fuck the cup. Start talking or it'll be you I'm throwing against the wall.'

'Follow me,' said Gallagher, leading the way to Uncle Edwin's sitting room.

EIGHT

Gallagher pulled open a drawer in the desk and took a file over to the leather chair. He sat facing Tom, who was sitting on the sofa, and placed the file on the coffee table between them. The mantel clock sounded out its doleful ticks and then chimed the quarter hour.

'I'm going to show you some things, Tom, and you're going to have questions – but I'm not going to be able to answer them all. I have a few of my own, too.'

Tom leaned forward. 'If he's gone to get the cavalry, if this is a set-up, you're a dead man.'

'If this was a set-up, you'd have known before now. I wouldn't have brought you to my flat and I wouldn't be about to show you this.'

Tom sat back. 'So my gut tells me. OK, what is it?' he asked, pointing at the file.

Gallagher picked up the bundle of documents and held it out. Tom moved to take it and Gallagher pulled it back. 'I'm not the police and I want to help Connie, remember that.'

He sat back in his chair and watched as Tom first flicked and scanned his way through the documents. Tom looked up and then began at the beginning, this time reading everything carefully. Once he'd finished reading he took the close-up photograph of Connie and stared at it for a couple of minutes.

Gallagher moved to an old globe drinks cabinet and lifted the northern hemisphere. He poured two large brandies and placed one in front of Tom.

'Where did you get this file?'

'I was given it as part of a job.'

'What kind of job?'

'I was asked to find Connie, to provide an address.'

'What are you, a private detective or something?'

'Ex-army, I do some freelance work.'

Tom looked up from the photograph. 'For who?'

'The Security Service.'

'Box?' Tom snorted. 'Why would MI5 be interested in Connie?'

'I was hoping you could tell me.'

Tom gestured at Gallagher with his glass. 'You're the spook, mate. You're telling me that you don't know why you were asked to watch her?'

'That's exactly what I'm telling you. I'm not a spook. I take the odd job from an old colleague once in a while, that's all.'

Tom took a sip of brandy. 'Hang on, how did you know that stuff about me and Connie going to Wales?'

'She told me.'

Tom rested the glass on his knee and leaned back. 'I'm listening.'

Gallagher had crossed too many lines to hold anything back now and he was in no doubt that Connie's life was in danger. He couldn't ask Bannerman outright. For all he knew, Bannerman might have sent the goons to lift her – though he doubted it. So he laid out the whole story for Tom: the find, the fix, the policeman in the gardens, the Lamb and Flag.

'And you went to meet her?'

'I liked her. It wasn't the brightest of moves, I agree.'

'You were using her, you twat.'

'It wasn't like that.'

'You saw an opportunity to get close and you took it – that's what you fuckers do.'

'Things weren't exactly going to plan when I found myself decking a Met copper in broad daylight; anyway, I'd been stood down: she wasn't my target when I met her again.' Gallagher heard his words leaving his mouth and wasn't sure he'd believe him either.

'So Box have lifted her?'

'I don't know. Is there any reason why she'd be seen as a threat or an asset by Five? It's a bit off-piste to pull someone in like that for no reason.'

He didn't mention that the goons on the boat were unlikely to be Five, given their poor standard of Methods of Entry skills. That would come when he showed Tom the camera images. He wasn't looking forward to that.

'So you know they've got her?'

'I know as much as you. No, actually, I think I know less than you do.'

'What's that mean?'

'What was she into? How deep?'

Tom finished his brandy and held out the glass. Gallagher refilled it and his own.

'Thanks. She's part of Occupy. She's always been a fighter. She's got an in-built injustice button, can't help herself.'

'Go on.'

'She was at St Paul's at the start, but she's more likely to wave a placard than blow the bloody place up.'

'What was she involved in more recently?'

'I dunno. There was going to be a day of mass action she kept talking about – she was really excited about that. What did she say? Oh yeah, that it would be the greatest act of civil disobedience of our time.'

'Violent struggle?' asked Gallagher.

'Nah, like I said, demos, occupations, disrupting stuff – passive resistance, being a pain in the arse, getting the message out.'

Gallagher rubbed his temples. 'How about you?'

Tom tensed. 'What about me?'

'She said she was worried that she hadn't heard from you. She'd had a few glasses of wine; she didn't go into any detail.'

'Where's this leading?'

Gallagher stood and paced the room. 'I'm trying to work out what's going on.'

'Yeah, well so am I. I'm going to try calling her phone.'

'I don't think that's wise. Go with me on this. Is there any reason that someone would use Connie to get to you?'

'No,' said Tom, looking back at the papers on the table. 'The spooks gave you no clues?'

'Just something about keeping known troublemakers on the radar.' Gallagher's PTT phone beeped. 'Harry? Yeah, fine, when can we expect you?'

Tom gave him a quizzical look.

'Thanks, H,' said Gallagher as he sat down again, ending the call. He looked across at Tom. 'I've got something else that you need to see. Harry's bringing it here. He'll be with us within the hour. In the meantime, help yourself to the bathroom – your face looks a mess.'

Tom felt the tiredness surge through him.

Gallagher thought about calling Connie's number, but dismissed the idea again. It was an instinct – he didn't want to break cover.

'There are clean towels in the chest of drawers by the door. Help yourself to the brandy, too.'

Tom downed the contents of his glass. 'This doesn't make any sense,' he said, but a terrible idea was taking shape in his mind.

* * *

The doorbell rang and Gallagher went to let Harry in. Harry said hello to Tom and then headed to use the bathroom. Gallagher walked to the kitchen and offered to make coffee. Tom was restless and picked up the TV remote control, watching as the BBC News Channel came on screen.

Two men in suits were shaking hands. The voiceover explained: 'The Israeli prime minister reiterated to the visiting US defence secretary that "time was running out for the international community to halt Iran's nuclear programme by peaceful means".'

'Arseholes,' said Tom to no one in particular. He switched off the television as Gallagher came back into the room. Harry joined them.

'Did you move the van?'

'Yeah, Ross took me up,' said Harry.

Gallagher turned to Tom. 'What are you going to do about accommodation?'

'Back to the hotel, I suppose. I need to grab my stuff and move.'

'Too risky. Give Harry your key; he'll pick up your stuff. You can use the spare room here tonight. And I need to show you something else.'

Tom nodded.

'Sorry, H, can you nip down to Old Street and pick up Tom's things?'

'Not even time for a brew, it's like being back in the bloody army.'

'I owe you one,' said Gallagher.

'I'll add it to the tally. Ross's waiting outside in his car. He's got a couple of hours and then he'll need to go. He's moving on to the night shift tonight – we definitely owe him one.'

Tom gave Harry his room key-card and the hotel details. Once Gallagher had seen Harry to the door, he came back into the room, rubbing his neck. 'Tom, I'll finish making the coffee and then I'll show you this. Do you want something to eat?'

'I'm fine but I will go and wash my face. I'll take my brew NATO.'

Gallagher had set up the laptop while Tom was in the bathroom. He handed him his coffee when he came back. He also placed two more large brandies on the coffee table. Tom raised his eyebrows.

'Trust me: you might be grateful of that in a few minutes.'

Gallagher played back the images, watching Tom's reaction. Tom watched until the screen showed Gallagher climbing aboard; he knew what had happened after that. He closed the lid of the laptop, took a sip of brandy and then threw the contents of the glass into Gallagher's face.

'Fair enough,' said Gallagher, licking his fingers.

'Right,' said Tom, 'how do we find these bastards?'

* * *

Mark Keane felt the early morning chill in his bones. He was lying under some trees in Victoria Embankment Gardens, beyond Somerset House, on the boundary of the City of London district. The gardens were surrounded by railings. The gates were locked at various times during the evening depending on the time of year, but, to the side, by the news kiosk, opposite the entrance to Temple Tube, the wall sloped alongside some steps off Temple Place opposite Arundel Street. The railings were lower there and the wall was much lower, low enough to step up on, drop a bag and climb in after it. It was 06:25; the gates would be unlocked again by half seven and he needed to be gone by then.

He'd chosen a spot near a small structure next to the statue of a child and had laid out his basha – poncho, pegs and bungees – behind a bush. He'd set up his shelter far enough inside the perimeter so as not to be seen from the busy road of the Embankment, sheltered enough from the wind coming up off the river and away from both sets of gates. On the other side, across the little paths and central lawn, in the shrubs, a man and woman were still sleeping, huddled close, sharing body heat. He'd seen them when he'd arrived in the early hours.

He liked to walk the streets for as long as possible in the dark – it was safer – and would kip down when most of the pissheads and druggies were heading home. The sleeping couple hadn't heard him arrive and build his shelter.

He'd heard that, back in the day, dozens would sleep rough in these gardens. On the predatory streets of London at night, they had sought safety in numbers; they'd watched out for each other. Perhaps sometimes they still did. Not last night, though. For the last few hours it had just been him and the sleeping couple. He'd had more comfortable nights, but he hadn't felt so safe since the incident in the Lyceum Theatre doorway, where he'd thought he'd be OK for a few hours under the relative warmth of a cloudy night.

But he couldn't go back: he'd fallen too far. Someone might offer a sofa, a floor, but the price would be questions – too many and not many that he wanted to answer. He was getting the odd job here and there on the sites, so he wasn't starving, but it was strictly cash-in-hand. Times were hard and there were too many hands needing the cash.

Years ago, more people would have slept in the shelter of Shell Mex House down the road, the former headquarters of the petroleum giant. They slept on the river-facing side of the building, rather than the Strand entrance, along the covered walkway, on the beautifully finished stone. He'd read on a wall plaque there that it was where the Royal Air Force had been founded and had its first headquarters in the building, a former hotel, in 1918. Apparently, it was worth hundreds of millions.

The homeless would sleep lined up under the long columned portico, like Londoners sheltering from the Blitz on underground station platforms. He'd heard the story of Old Annie, a lady in her sixties – a former schoolteacher – sleeping at the end of the row. He'd heard how people woke to see her sleeping bag on fire after two men, out and about after a pub crawl, had poured lighter fuel over her for a laugh. Nice.

He'd heard how the homeless there were not moved on by the police at night, because the coppers knew where to go to find information about runaway children. Not any more: now ornate gates and railings kept everyone out.

He'd heard about people sleeping in basement areas, down steps alongside buildings around Covent Garden. How newcomers were guided by experienced Old Hands to places of relative safety, shown where the soup kitchens were and when: passing on the knowledge, giving them the skills to survive on the streets, keeping them away from the drinkers – the homeless underclass. He'd been surprised to learn of such a hierarchy, how the class system trickled down into the gutter with the piss, the vomit and the broken dreams. But that was before all these places had been gated off to keep out the riff raff; to force them out of the trendy areas where money flowed but where charity meant a sponsored, suitably exotic, something or other to be talked about via Twitter or Facebook.

He packed his gear into the rucksack. Then he did his stretching routine, easing his tired muscles into life, teasing the stiffness from his shoulder, feeling the holes with his fingers, trying to will some warmth into the cold dead tissue. Then he found somewhere to urinate, careful that no one should see. That had been what was known as a 'prevalent offence' in the forces: get caught pissing in public and you were for it. You'd be marched up to the Head Shed to see the big boss. Left, right, left, right – treading the boards in front of his desk – halt – interview without coffee – bringing the army into disrepute – a disgusting anti-social act – take him away, Sergeant Major. He grinned as his relief steamed up from the dark soil.

But the biggest crime? You'd got caught. You'd been spotted and you'd been caught. That was the issue, not necessarily what you'd done; that'd be forgotten, but you'd got caught. Muppet: that's all you'd hear off the NCOs for weeks, muppet. Funny, though, you had to laugh.

Mark picked up his bag and walked towards the Temple-station end of the gardens to climb out the way he'd climbed in. He stopped to look through the trees. The London Eye stood across the water and behind it, beyond the bend of the river, Big Ben kept time for the city. The red buses were beginning to line up in the foreground on Waterloo Bridge. You had to love London. She might be a hard bitch with a cruel streak, but you had to love her.

* * *

Archie Keane awoke in his bunk at the Royal Hospital Chelsea. Well, Archie old son, you've survived to fight another day, he thought. Like every other morning in the three years since he'd donned the famous scarlet coat of the Chelsea Pensioners, he'd been up at least an hour before 07:00. That was the rule: everyone out of bed by seven. That way, the staff could tell which of the old soldiers had made it through the night at a glance. It gave them time to call down to the chef to cancel an egg. Archie chuckled at his own joke. He'd try it out on young Mark later when he visited.

He hadn't seen the lad for a while, but they kept in touch. He recalled the visit to the hospital in Birmingham after Mark had been injured: the puckered wound where the bullet

176

had entered the young man's shoulder, the bigger, nastier exit wound to the rear. That had been Mark's first tour of Afghanistan. He was back there within eighteen months. He was a good lad, a good grandson.

Mark had changed, though, that much was obvious to Archie. Not surprising really, but there was something darker about the boy when he came back the second time. He'd been injured again – shrapnel wounds in the legs. They'd patched him up out there and he'd soldiered on, but within a year Mark had returned to Civvie Street. Archie had been surprised about that, but it was Mark's life and he'd done his bit. He was working in the building trade now, apparently doing well. He was a good lad, a fine grandson.

He'd been proud when the young lad had joined his old mob. He'd imparted all his old sweat's wisdom – recalled through the decades since his own army service – before the nervous recruit had left for the depot. Archie had bristled with greater pride at his grandson's passing-out parade and had sunk a few pints with the new breed of drill sergeants populating his former regiment. He'd held court in the bar until late afternoon. 'Pull up a sandbag,' he'd said and the stories had poured out of him as fast as the training staff could pour beer in.

It had been a great day and, looking back, it had been the start of his journey to becoming a Pensioner: that day, that afternoon, when the usually quiet widower remembered the joys of the Sergeants' Mess, the quick-fire banter, the camaraderie, the feeling of belonging.

* * *

Connie was lying on her side staring at the wall. Her hands were tied in front of her, the sharp plastic digging into her skin; her ankles were similarly bound but the ties were looser. She could hear the man in the corner turning the pages of his newspaper. Other than that, there was little noise. She didn't think that she was in London. The dawn chorus had been loud and long, beautiful and sad. She refused to cry.

Her body ached and she still felt sick. She remembered getting out of her bed on the boat, the bag, the struggle, the blows, the sharpness of the needle. She remembered waking up in the box, the fear, the vomit that she could still smell on her clothes, the vomit that was still stuck to her hair. She remembered the shouting, the questions, the gut-wrenching terror.

The man in the corner had brought her a bacon sandwich, which was still untouched on its plate on a chair next to the bed. The smell had made her wretch, but she had nothing left to throw up.

'Any good at crosswords?' asked Dave.

'Fuck off.'

'They're cross words – I'll give you that,' he said with a laugh. 'I've been trying to finish this for two days. Want to help?'

Connie turned over and glared at him.

'I could always tape up your mouth again,' said Dave.

'Why am I here?' she asked quietly.

'Ah, one of the great philosophical questions: why are any of us here? Anyway, you've been asked the question. You know why you're here, what we need to know. Tell us and it'll all be over.'

Connie turned back to the wall as the door to the room opened.

'Help me get her up,' said Ray.

'Where's she going?'

'Into the cellar, for a chat.'

Connie's heart began to beat faster and her mouth became drier – she hadn't thought it possible.

'Sit up,' said Dave.

She didn't move.

'Sit up, or my colleague will help you.'

She turned, swung her feet over the edge of the bed and pushed herself up on an elbow.

'You took the gag off,' said Ray.

'I did,' agreed Dave, folding his newspaper.

'Tape her up again; she'll have plenty of time to do some talking downstairs.'

179

Dave walked over to Connie and placed a length of grey tape over her mouth. She didn't resist. She didn't want the other man near her; he was the really dangerous one – that was obvious.

Ray knelt in front of her and cut through the plastic around her ankles, staring at her through the balaclava holes.

'Don't fuck me about,' he said.

She looked straight ahead.

'Stand up!'

She stood and Ray gestured towards the door.

'Ladies first. That means you, mate,' he said to Dave. 'Then you, sweetheart.'

Connie stepped forward. Her legs buckled. Ray grabbed her roughly under the arm and dragged her forward. 'Give me a hand, for fuck's sake.'

Dave took her other arm, firmly but not as roughly. They dragged her out of the room and into a stone-flagged passageway. To her front she saw a dilapidated country-style kitchen. Halfway along the passage Ray opened a wooden door on the right, behind which were a set of rickety stairs leading to a brightly-lit cellar. Connie mustered all of her remaining strength and placed a foot on the doorframe, trying to stop them taking her further. Ray punched her in the side of her knee and then pulled back her head by the hair.

'Walk down or fly down: your choice.'

* * *

Connie had been placed on a chair by the back wall of the cellar. There was a rope dangling from the central beam across the ceiling in front of her. The cellar was damp and empty, its cold space made colder and emptier by the bright unshaded light-bulb that lit up all but the far corners. The two masked men who had dragged her down the steps were standing a few feet away, whispering to each other. The dangerous one turned and walked towards her.

'Here's the deal: you tell us what we want to know and we all stay friends. Any anti-social behaviour when I take off the gag and I'll give you a slap, right?'

Connie stared past him.

'Look, love, I really don't mind how you want to play this but you will tell me what I need to know,' said Ray, ripping the tape from Connie's skin.

She winced but made no sound.

'Right then, here we go again.' Ray folded his arms. 'Where's your brother?'

Connie said nothing.

Ray turned to Dave. 'How many brothers has she got?'

'Fuck knows – why does that matter?'

Ray shrugged and turned back to Connie. 'Your brother, Tom, where is he?'

181

She stared past him.

He slapped her hard across the face.

Connie glared back, burning with defiance.

'Got your attention, have I?'

'Go easy,' said Dave.

'Fuck off if you don't like it, soft lad.'

Dave took a step forward and then stopped. Ray didn't bother to turn around.

'Simple enough question: Where. Is. Your. Brother?'

She stared past him. He slapped her again.

Ray walked away and leant against the wall. The stone was damp but he'd got the pose he was looking for, so he stayed where he was.

'My problem, apart from you being a stubborn bitch, is that I'm not known for my patience. I get bored easy, you see, and when I get bored I get frustrated and when I get frustrated I get a bit hyper-active, a bit twitchy.'

Connie kept looking straight ahead.

'Then I have to find ways to entertain myself before I get too wired.' He walked back to stand in front of her. Leaning forward, he put his mouth near her ear.

'You. Are. Boring. Me!' he shouted.

Dave shuffled on the spot and then walked upstairs.

Connie said nothing.

Ray called up to Vince. 'Silly Bollocks, come down here and give me a hand.' He moved to Connie's front. 'OK, why

182

don't we make you a bit more comfortable? It can't be very nice sitting there in that puke-stained t-shirt.'

Connie braced herself as Ray grabbed the bottom of her shirt with two hands and pulled it up, tugging it over her head and down until the armholes stopped at her cuffed wrists as she struggled. She tried to kick out but, even though her ankles were free, she was too weak to muster any real force.

'Nice tits,' said Ray.

She hadn't put on any underwear when she'd pulled on her clothes to investigate the noise on the boat. She tried to push him away again.

He pushed back and she toppled off the chair on to the cold hard floor. He turned her on her back, as she tried to bring her knees up into a foetal position, and scrabbled at the button of her jeans, punching her in the shoulder as she tried to resist. She cried out and he laughed. He overpowered her and she felt him rub his groin against her leg as he pushed her face against the cold floor. She could feel his hard excitement through the fabric of his jeans.

'Oi! Come and give me a hand,' he shouted as he pulled down her trousers, slapping her hard as she tried to resist. 'No knickers, either. Nice.' He stood up, breathing heavily, as Connie curled herself into a ball.

Vince came down the steps into the cellar. 'Enjoying yourself?'

183

'Shut it,' said Ray. 'Help me get her up.'

Vince lifted Connie from the floor and carried her to the centre of the room. Ray took the free end of the rope that was tied to the beam, tied it around her wrists, pulled the slack in and walked backwards. Connie's feet were now a foot off the ground and she cried out as her shoulders took the weight, the rope burning into her skin.

Ray pulled harder, walking sideways, lifting her an inch or so more, then tied the rope end to a bracket on the wall. Connie felt the rope cutting into her flesh where her rolled t-shirt wasn't bunched underneath it. She was fighting to keep control of her full bladder.

Ray walked around her. 'She's proper tidy, ain't she?' he said to Vince. 'Great arse, great tits. I don't know about you, but I reckon she looks better with a few bruises.'

He slapped her hard across the buttocks, making her body swing, the rope burning as she heard her shoulder crack. She gritted her teeth.

'Doesn't talk much either. I usually like that in a bird,' he said moving to her front, 'but in this case, she's really starting to piss me off.'

He came close enough for her to smell his breath.

'Where's your brother? We haven't got all fucking day.'

Connie spat. Ray stepped back and wiped the fluid from around his eyes. Vince tensed as the other man slammed his fist into Connie's stomach. The two men turned as Dave walked down the stairs.

'Well done for bringing the phone, lads, did either of you geniuses check her messages and address book?'

They hadn't.

'The last message from her brother on this was ages ago.'

'Give me that,' said Ray.

'So maybe hanging her up isn't going to help us get the info. Let her down.'

Vince eased the rope through the bracket and Connie collapsed in a heap, trying to curl up in an attempt to hide her naked vulnerability.

Ray scrolled through the address book. 'Haven't got many friends, have you? Who's Benita? Girlfriend? Are you a lezza? How about James, who's he?'

Connie stared ahead.

'Lift her up again,' said Ray to Vince, shooting Dave a look.

Connie cried out as the rope dug into her fresh wounds and her weight cracked her injured shoulder again. She couldn't control her bladder through the force of the pain; urine poured down her thighs on to the floor. She closed her eyes in humiliated agony.

'Kinky,' said Ray.

Dave took a step forward. 'Let her down.'

'Who made you the boss?' Ray spat, turning.

'I just phoned the boss. We're to try to flush out the brother with the phone. We need to get it done and get out of here. He says we're taking too long to get an answer to a simple question.'

Ray thought for a moment, gave the phone back to Dave and walked over to Vince. He pushed him out of the way, undid the rope and let Connie fall to the ground hard.

He walked back and leaned over her. 'Plenty more time for us to get acquainted, don't worry.'

'Her brother's phone is switched off. How about this James bloke?' asked Dave.

'The boyfriend?' Vince suggested. 'The bloke with the van, the bloke we saw her with the other night.'

'Oh yeah,' said Ray, kicking Connie in the back. 'Tell us about the van man.'

* * *

Harry returned with Tom's bag. Ross was standing behind him.

'Everything OK?' asked Gallagher.

'Yeah, in and out, no dramas, but Ross here spotted a surveillance team while he was waiting outside.'

'Five?'

'Don't think so, boss, looked like normal coppers trying to look inconspicuous,' answered Ross. 'We watched them for a bit: two blokes in an immaculate car, wedding rings, chunky watches, short hair, didn't look comfortable in their ironed civvies. There was another car, three-up, carbon copies, down the road. They may as well have put a blue light on top.'

'Could be watching anyone,' said Gallagher.

'True, but it's a bit of a coincidence,' Harry replied.

They both looked at Tom, who was looking better as far as his injuries were concerned but still looked stunned from watching the camera footage.

'What?'

'Is there anything you need to tell us, Tom?' asked Gallagher. 'Any trouble with the police?'

'I got a speeding ticket two years ago.'

Ross moved towards the door. 'I've got to be off, boss: I'm on nights for the rest of the week. I'll need to try and get my head down. Just popped in to say hello.'

'Thanks, Ross, I owe you.'

'No bother. I'll let myself out.'

Gallagher turned to Harry. 'I'm going to give Bannerman a call; he said he'd have work for us, so it won't seem odd. I'll see if he coughs up anything useful.'

'OK,' said Harry. 'But watch him: he's a slippery bastard.'

Gallagher went into the kitchen and called Bannerman, who was sitting in a busy coffee shop trying to read his newspaper between calls from his office. He hadn't been overly chatty.

'How was the gimp?' Harry asked when Gallagher returned.

'Sounded a bit jaded, not his usual annoying self. He wants to meet later today, says he's got a little job for us – all of Five's watchers are busy with something else.'

'Is this the bastard who's lifted my sister?' Tom asked, pacing the room.

'We can't rule it out, but my bet would be no. The blokes on camera were goons. Anyone working for Five would have had that lock open in well under a minute,' said Gallagher.

Tom gripped the back of the chair that he was standing behind. 'We need to do something.'

'Like what?' asked Harry.

Tom remained silent.

'Look, this morning we'll piece together everything we know,' said Gallagher. 'There must be something staring us in the face. If it's a criminal kidnapping they'd contact the family – but there's just the two of you, is that right Tom?'

'Yep, just us.'

'So they'd call you. On the other hand, we have to consider that it could be a sexually-motivated abduction but two blokes climbing on to a canal barge and then carting her off doesn't really add up. Do you think it's money that they want?'

Tom bowed his head and stared at his white knuckles as he gripped the chair.

'Is your phone charged, Tom?' Gallagher asked.

'She hasn't got my number.'

Gallagher thought about how to pose the question. Harry looked like he was about to speak but didn't.

'Connie hasn't got your number?' asked Gallagher, but his phone rang before Tom could answer.

'Connie?'

Tom and Harry watched as Gallagher stood and listened to the voice at the other end of the line.

Gallagher shook his head and held up a hand.

'I understand.'

Harry took out a notebook and pen from his jacket pocket.

'Yes, of course, I understand,' said Gallagher. 'No, I'm listening.'

Tom looked at Harry.

Harry watched Gallagher.

Tom paced.

'I understand. No, of course, I'll be waiting.' Gallagher placed the phone on the coffee table and then walked to the drinks globe before looking over at Tom.

'What?'

'It's you: it's you they want.'

Gallagher refilled his glass and walked back to his chair. Harry was leaning against the door, arms folded.

'Are you sure you don't want one?' Gallagher asked him.

'Better not, I'll be driving.'

Tom was sitting with his head in his hands.

'So let's recap,' said Gallagher. 'Persons unknown have abducted Connie in order to get to Tom. The caller spouted the usual about not contacting the police and said he'd call again at six this evening. In the meantime, I'm supposed to find out where Tom is. He has something they want. The caller used Connie's phone, so we're pretty confident that he's directly involved.'

'What now?' asked Tom.

'If it isn't Five, which seems increasingly unlikely, I could ask Bannerman to locate the phone.'

'Are you still going to meet him?' Harry asked.

'Might as well show willing; he's more likely to do me a favour. Connie's phone isn't registered and we didn't have the number originally, so it shouldn't arouse suspicion.'

'Good thinking,' said Harry.

'Thing is, Tom,' Gallagher said, standing and walking to the window, 'knowing what they want presents us with a new set of problems.'

'Yeah, I've just been thinking about that.'

Gallagher said nothing and stared out of the window.

'The way I see it,' Tom continued, 'is we have to arrange a meet. They want me, I go to them and they set Connie free.'

'Or they top you both and bury you in the same hole,' said Harry.

'Got a better idea?'

'He's right, Tom,' said Gallagher. 'We're working blind. We need to work out why they want you in the first place. The caller had a London accent. Let's draw up a list of people who might want to do you harm. Anyone you've pissed off lately?'

Tom fiddled with his glass and took a couple of sips. 'I can't see how it's connected, but something happened at the end of my last job in Iraq.'

Harry sat down in the chair that Gallagher had vacated. Gallagher turned to sit on the windowsill.

Tom told them about Gus and the other four lads, how he'd had a warning from Gus and about the journey back from South Africa to the UK.

'And none of your contacts came up with anything?' asked Gallagher.

'Not yet. It doesn't make any sense.'

'But you were careful about not contacting Connie and you didn't just jump on a plane to come home,' said Harry.

'Gus sent me a warning. He was old-school: nothing put the wind up Gus, but he was worried enough to send me a message. The other thing that bothers me is how he died.

He'd been beaten before he was shot, so he didn't die in a stand-up fight.'

'And?'

'The three of us in this room wouldn't have been able to deck Gus together if he saw us coming. It must have been more subtle, it must have been a crafty hit. He'd have fought them to the death otherwise. I just can't imagine the local militia being up to it.'

'So more questions but no answers,' said Gallagher.

Tom stood and paced the room again. 'I've been going over it since I heard about the lads and I can't see how any of it adds up.'

'Tell us about the contact,' said Harry.

'We were escorting a principal up to an oil refinery, got caught up with a couple of ragheads in the traffic, weapons seen and we took them out – end of.'

Gallagher stretched his back and downed the rest of his drink. 'We're missing something. Walk us through the tour, any leave taken, any run-ins while at home or abroad.'

Tom sketched out the last couple of years of his life.

'OK,' said Gallagher. 'The only thing that's standing out is that last contact, if we dismiss the incident with that chap's wife.' He poured himself another drink and put the bottle next to Tom's glass on the table.

'Grab yourself a coffee, Harry. Tom, I'm going to meet Bannerman but then I want you to talk us through your last day, move by move, round by round.'

* * *

Mark Keane had made his way along the Strand, past Charing Cross, to St Martin-in-the-Fields. The church had a daycentre where he'd showered. Sometimes he went to the centre's café, the food being decent and relatively cheap. There were medical services available, drug and alcohol counsellors, internet access, computer courses and the like. You could get your laundry done, too. A couple of caseworkers and a bloke from SSAFA – the Soldiers, Sailors, Airmen and Families Association – had approached him when he first started going there. They meant well, but he didn't want to start telling his life story and he certainly didn't want to attend art therapy or to be 'befriended.' Christ, anything but that.

It was a choice. At first it had been an escape. He'd gone to a couple of hostels after a bout of sofa-surfing with friends but the hostels were like open prisons – with more drugs and definitely more violence. The shouting and the stench could be unbearable. Some were OK but he didn't want anyone's pity, so he'd gone on to the streets. The streets weren't great – for some it was hell on earth – but ex-squaddies were renowned for being able to sleep on a washing line in a storm. Some nights he really enjoyed the walking, watching the city go about its business and pleasure. In the summer he was happy to be out, but the summers weren't what they used to be and the winters were cruel. If the weather was really bad he'd go to a mate's. If he was ill, he'd scrape together the coach fare and visit his mum up in Birmingham. But the life was beginning to make his bones feel old. The lies and the isolation were ageing him too. He just couldn't imagine living a normal life and it was difficult to sleep when the memory of driving a bayonet through another man's throat had a habit of floating up in the darkness.

At the daycentre, he'd changed into the clean clothes that he kept carefully folded in a plastic bag at the bottom of his rucksack and pulled on the clean training shoes he also kept safely wrapped. Having dumped his rucksack in one of the centre's lockers, he made his way to Chelsea.

Archie had arranged to meet his grandson at the gate on West Road. The lad was looking tired and he wasn't as smartly turned out as he used to be. He's been out on the razzle, thought Archie. Oh well, he works hard so why shouldn't a young man play hard? Archie had.

'All right, Granddad?'

'Great to see you, lad. Keeping well?'

'I'm good, Granddad. You been out chasing the dolly birds again?'

Archie feigned a serious look. 'Don't talk unconscious, you little bleeder.'

'Want to go for a cuppa? A spot of lunch? My treat.'

'Oh no you don't, I'm buying. I don't see you often enough to let you pay.'

Mark didn't show his relief.

They walked to a café a few minutes' walk away that they'd used before and ordered two cups of tea while they looked at the boards on the back wall.

'So, what's the grub like at your digs?' asked Mark, wondering why he'd never thought to ask before.

'We had one of them pizza things last night – you know: the ones with the monsterella cheese on.'

'Monsterella, eh? Nice.'

'It was all right, but I've never trusted the Eye-Ties.'

'The Eye-Ties?' Mark asked, knowing what was coming.

'The Italians: slippery bastards, always pinching women's arses.'

'Right,' said Mark, with an embarrassed look towards the café owner. They ordered a toasted sandwich each and more tea. While they waited for the toasties to arrive, Archie asked after his daughter-in-law. She hadn't been in touch. He didn't blame her. They talked about the football, the weather, Archie's knee and the Polish girl behind the counter

195

at the shop down the road, who apparently made a fuss of the old man every time he went in to buy his Mint Imperials. Archie told a few stories about his fellow pensioners, about their army service, what their children and grandchildren were up to. He was full of it and Mark was glad.

When they'd finished eating, they walked back to the Royal Hospital and through the grounds, laughing at this and that, until they reached a long sandstone portico where they found a bench to sit on.

'So, boy, what are your digs like? Got yourself a nice flat now?'

'It's all right, yeah,' Mark lied. 'You'll have to visit.' He held his breath.

'Nah, wouldn't want to cramp your style. I'm fine where I am. Got a girlfriend? Or is it girlfriends?'

Mark didn't want to lie again so soon.

'I know, I know, none of my business. You sow your wild oats. Don't get tied down too early. Enjoy your life.'

Mark laughed, masking the irony. 'Living the dream, Granddad, living the dream.'

Archie yawned. 'Time for you to make tracks, I suppose. You must have better things to be doing on your day off.'

'OK, Granddad,' Mark said, knowing that he had nowhere better to be that afternoon. 'It's been great to see you. We'll have to go for a pint next time.'

Archie's eyes lit up. 'I'd like that, son. I'd like that a lot.'

NINE

The blonde-haired man with the blue rucksack held open the door to allow the six old ladies to exit the motorway service station's main building. He smiled at their thanks and continued to hold the door as two children under the age of ten charged through the gap going the other way.

As he entered the retail area of the M1's London Gateway services the smell of burgers and coffee filled his nostrils. He watched travellers walk zombie-like into the shops. Others were walking the aisles as if in a trance, eager to buy, to consume – it didn't matter what. Released from their cars and their coaches for a few brief minutes, they filled their baskets and joined the queues in droves.

The blonde-haired man made his way to the Gents. He walked beyond the queue of men lined up behind the roaring hand dryers, past the sinks and mirrors, past the rows of urinals and into a cubicle.

Opening his rucksack, he pulled out a foot-long cylinder and rested it on the flat stainless-steel surface that joined the toilet bowl to the back wall. As he worked, he listened to the harassed father in the adjacent cubicle cajoling his young daughter into using the facilities – while she bombarded Daddy with a relentless flow of questions and requests.

A mobile phone connected to the top of the cylinder showed four bars. The cylinder housed enough explosive charge to demolish part of the room and send a thousand tightly packed nails to seek their prey. His three colleagues would be in the same kind of cubicle, with the same kind of cylinder, in other locations. Their controller, Mimar, had sent them a message detailing the value of such an operation: how it would put fear into the hearts of people travelling the road network; how it would strike a blow against the country's economic infrastructure; how it would make godless men think about going to hell with their trousers down.

He activated the flush sensor with a wave of his hand and put his rucksack back on. The man in the adjacent cubicle was pleading with his daughter to co-operate, his voice betraying how thin his patience had worn.

The blonde-haired bomber took a small tool from his pocket and checked that no one was waiting for a vacant cubicle. In a practiced move, he stepped through the gap, closed the door and used the tool to lock it. All the attention in the room was on a group of men on their way to a rugby match, who had poured into the space speaking too loudly, shoving each other and generally not acting their age. The smell of alcohol, the belching, the fart-induced hilarity, the crude language, the sheer godless idiocy, made the man with the number of the detonator-phone want to dial it

198

immediately. But there was a plan: he had to wait for the arranged time.

He left the building as spots of rain began to land on the empty picnic tables to his right. As he arrived at the car he looked at his watch. He attached his phone to the holder mounted on the windscreen just above the dashboard, before pulling out of the parking space and heading to the exit.

There were no vehicles in his rear-view mirror as he came to a halt at the stop sign. The blonde-haired bomber touched his phone's screen and selected the detonator-phone's number. The call connected and disconnected. He pulled away to join the motorway as the bomb's shrapnel flew outwards, hunting for flesh and bone.

* * *

Bannerman was waiting when Gallagher arrived at Le Lion Rouge, a bottle and two glasses on the table in front of him. He'd spent most of the morning at New Scotland Yard and was glad of the temporary distraction.

'Thanks for coming, Owen.'

'No problem, what have you got for me?' asked Gallagher.

Bannerman poured him a glass of wine. 'The Alsace Pinot Noir is to your liking, sir?'

Gallagher nodded. 'Before we start, may I ask a favour?'

'Ask away.'

'I've got a young cousin, second cousin actually, who's gone off the rails a bit during her Gap Year. Her family are worried because she's on some rebellious road trip with a rather unsavoury group.'

'What's the favour?'

'I've got her mobile number. Any chance of getting a location?'

'Shouldn't be too taxing.'

'Thanks.' Gallagher passed a piece of paper with Connie's number on it across the table.

'No problem,' said Bannerman. 'Now this job, it's actually an extension of the last one.'

'OK,' said Gallagher, feeling anything but OK.

'I'd like you to watch the girl again.' Bannerman took out an envelope from the coat pocket behind him on his chair. 'I'd be grateful to know if this chap turns up.'

Eve was hovering, waiting for Gallagher to acknowledge her. He gave her a 'not now' look and she slinked away. He pulled a photograph out of the envelope. It was Tom.

'Who's this?' he asked.

'The brother, he's a private military contractor. The Friends along the river have an interest and it's believed he's just arrived in the UK. His name is Tom Edwards.'

'Been a naughty boy?'

'Need to know, Owen, sorry. Let's just say that he's drawn attention to himself.'

Gallagher drank some wine. 'And that's it? Watch the girl and see if he turns up?'

'That's it: he's bound to visit her charming little canal basin if he's home, or she'll go to wherever he's holed up. Either way, let me know the minute you spot him.'

'I'll get right on it,' said Gallagher, his mind racing.

'Good man. How are the PTTs working out, by the way?'

'They're good, do you want them back?'

'Keep them,' Bannerman said. His phone rang.

Gallagher watched as the other man's features shifted to show an immediate level of worried concentration.

Bannerman returned the phone to his pocket. 'I've paid for the wine – enjoy.'

'What's wrong, Sandy?'

Bannerman smoothed his hair. 'Well, believe it or not, someone has just blown up the gentlemen's lavatories in four motorway service stations – simultaneous attacks. The world has definitely gone mad.'

* * *

Bannerman buttoned his coat on the pavement outside Le Lion Rouge with a sense of foreboding. Today was going to be a nightmare; he could feel it in his bones. On the plus side, Flic Anderson was back in touch – she'd even given

201

him a mobile number, which he rang as he walked to the Charing Cross Road to find a taxi.

She answered on the seventh ring.

'Flic, it's Sandy. Just wanted you to know that I've put someone on the hunt for your man.'

'An Alpha team?' Flic asked, with some concern in her voice. 'This is important, Sandy. It could be something big, but I don't want egg on my face if the whispers I'm hearing turn out to be of the Chinese variety.'

'No, no, still off the books, as agreed. He's a former colleague. He's the one who found the girl. Owen Gallagher.'

'Thank you, Sandy. I owe you one. I'm still not sure how connected this guy is, but it could be Brownie-points all round.'

'Splendid,' said Bannerman. 'Can't chat, I'm afraid. The balloon's gone up. Why don't we have dinner next week? We can catch up.'

'Sorry, poppet, I'm snowed under – rain check?'

'Of course,' Bannerman replied, hiding his disappointment. 'I'm a bit snowed under myself.'

'Oh and just in case your man crosses the radar further down the line,' said Flic, 'do you have a photo that you could send to this number? I wouldn't want him to be dragged into any crossfire.'

* * *

Once Bannerman had gone, Gallagher tried to gather his thoughts. This was getting worse by the minute. This is what happened when rules were broken. This is what happened when you got involved. He took a sip of wine and then pushed the glass and bottle away before standing up to leave.

Eve looked confused.

'Must dash. I'll be in soon,' said Gallagher.

'But the wine?'

'You drink it.'

He could feel her watching him as he went through the door. Fair enough, it was the first time he'd ever left a drink in Le Lion Rouge and he'd been a bit sharp with her, but he couldn't be doing with all that pouting and flirting today.

He walked into St Martin's Lane and left up Monmouth Street as he put his mind back on the problem in hand. On the plus side, Tom would be safely under wraps at the flat for the time being and there was a chance that Bannerman would unwittingly locate Connie for them. The problem was that Gallagher was up to his neck in it. More importantly, he'd dragged Harry into it. Who and what was Tom Edwards? And why was everyone so keen to meet him?

* * *

Gallagher arrived back at Seven Dials Court to find Harry washing up.

'Mr Edwards is sleeping,' said Harry.

'I was dozing,' said Tom, standing in the hallway behind them. 'I won't sleep until we find Connie. What did the spook have to say?'

'Well,' said Gallagher, 'I think we can rule out the surveillance team at the hotel being anything to do with you.'

'Why's that?' asked Harry, drying the coffee jug.

'Because,' Gallagher said looking at Tom, 'Bannerman has just tasked me to find you, on behalf of Six.'

Tom walked into the kitchen. 'MI6? Jesus Christ, what the fuck's going on?'

'Bloody hell,' said Harry.

'Quite,' said Gallagher. 'We need to think fast. It's time for you to tell us the detail of the contact, Tom. There must be something that connects all this. Either way, you're extremely popular with some serious people. I think it's time that you levelled with us.'

Tom walked to the sink and filled a glass with water. 'I've got no more clues than you have. This is a nightmare.'

'OK, run us through it.'

Gallagher poured some whisky. Harry decided he'd have a drink, just the one, to help him think.

Tom settled into the armchair. 'It was my last day in Dad's Bag. My replacement was delayed so I had to join an escort job up to an oilfield. As usual we headed out up Route Irish dressed as locals, headscarves on, out on to one of the most dangerous roads in the world. We were primed for another arse-clenching ride to the badlands north of the city.'

Gallagher smiled at Tom's use of a mocking melodramatic tone and eased back on the sofa as he listened to the story recounted. The escort team had left the relative safety of the International Green Zone in three vehicles. Gus commanded the lead vehicle driven by Gary. Joe was in the back as rear gunner and medic. Tom was in the passenger seat of the second vehicle with Chalky driving and Martin in the back with the principal. They had a back-marker car following them with a crew of four South Africans.

'We all had our arcs of fire in case of attack and things were going well until the traffic slowed for an incident up ahead. The Iraqi army were dealing with something the best part of a mile up the road and Iraqi police had put a checkpoint on the slip road to stop any insurgents from diverting away. A few of the locals were trying to do U-turns across the central reservation, which was causing chaos but left some space in front of us. Gus ordered us forward to try to create space between us and the traffic behind. His vehicle held the traffic back as we manoeuvred around into a better position.'

Harry nodded approvingly.

'But,' Tom continued, 'we had to be careful as there was a bridge ahead that could have opened us up to attack from above. It'd happened before and a bunch of PMCs had been shot to bits by insurgents. Anyway, we decided against turning back because there were cars all over the place. Next thing, the Yappies, the South Africans in the rear vehicle, are on the radio telling us there's a sedan forcing its way up the inside. Gus told Gary to block it off to stop it getting through to us but it rammed his vehicle and kept coming.'

Gallagher took a swig as Tom did the same.

'Joe had spotted weapons in the car on its way past him, so Chalky tried to get us out of what looked like becoming a killing zone between the sedan and the bridge, but the road was blocked by U-turning Flip-flops. The sedan stopped behind us as me and Martin debussed. The two guys in the car saw us and started firing as they tried to get out. We'd taken cover and hit them both through the windscreen. The driver died instantly but the passenger made it out on to the road.'

'Lucky boy,' said Harry.

'Not really,' said Tom. 'I ran forward to stop him causing any more trouble and he pulled himself up on the car door. He wasn't interested in me. He had a chest wound and his face was cut by the shit that had shattered off the windscreen. He was fiddling with this grenade in the car. It

206

was strange: he had a pistol and a grenade but he didn't look at me or Martin, or at Gus and Joe who were running up the road screaming at him. He kept looking in the car. At first I thought he was trying to work out how to help the driver, but half of that bloke's head was missing.'

Tom leaned forward and sipped some more whisky. 'Gus was shouting for me to slot the bloke and I did: double-tap in the head before he could pull the pin. It was over in seconds.'

'So what was he up to, do you think?' asked Harry.

Tom sat back again. 'I dunno. When I got to the car, there was a long behind the front seats – a 7.62 PKM – but he hadn't tried to use it. It was chaos and we needed to get the principal out. Chalky and Gary had moved the vehicles and Gus and Joe were covering the area shouting for me and Martin to get going. I spotted something in the footwell next to the grenade and grabbed it. I don't know why. I suppose I was still surprised at how the bloke had reacted after he'd been shot: he'd been holding his pistol and the grenade and he'd got a belt-fed fuck-off machine gun in reach, but he didn't fire again. Anyway, the checkpoint on the slip road had gone to shit in the mayhem and the traffic was powering away in any direction it could – the Iraqi police had long gone – so we got the fuck out of there.'

Tom stared ahead and drank from his glass, lost in his thoughts.

'What did you pick up?' asked Gallagher.

* * *

Bannerman entered the Joint Terrorism Analysis Centre, JTAC, at Thames House. The duty officer, Will Sorsby, was young and excited and came bounding across the room to greet him. Bannerman stepped to the side and took a breath, as though ready to grapple with a muddy puppy.

The young man caught himself smiling too much for the circumstances and was wearing his most professional face by the time he began to speak. 'Four bombs: one at London Gateway, M1 and the others around the M25 at South Mimms, Thurrock and Clacket Lane.'

'Casualties?'

'Still counting, but it's a mess. We think the bombers at all M25 sites died at the scene – possibly malfunctioning devices. Regardless, the motorways are backed-up for miles in every direction after the police closed sections to get fire and ambulance through. I doubt you'll be able to get a cup of tea on the M25 for a while, either.'

Bannerman ignored the attempt at humour. 'Nothing from the cameras yet, I suppose?'

'Not yet: the CCTV at the service stations will be some time coming and the police control centres are a bit stretched; they're trying to give us their footage now.'

'And no one has claimed credit? We've got two thousand known terrorist suspects in the country, working within two hundred separate networks and no one is putting their hand up?'

'Not a dicky-bird.'

'OK,' said Bannerman, looking across the ops room with all its technological hustle and bustle. 'I've got a meeting to go to at the University of London. I'll call you in a couple of hours for an update.'

* * *

Tom rummaged in his bag and pulled out a brown leather wallet with a zip running around its outside.

'This is it. I'd shoved it in my pocket and forgot about it. When I got back to the compound that evening I had to finish packing and then catch my plane. It wasn't until I'd got to South Africa and did some washing that I found it in my map pocket.'

He handed it to Gallagher who pulled the zip round in order to lay the wallet flat. On the left were three cardholders, two were empty. The other contained what looked like a hotel key-card but it was more substantial than thin plastic. It was silver in colour with no other embellishment: no branding, no logos, just plain silver. It almost had the feel of a large casino chip with a magnetic strip on the reverse.

On the right of the wallet's inside were elasticated loops holding a USB stick firmly in place. Below the memory stick, on small metal clasps, hung three keys. Two were the kind used for filing cabinets or security boxes, while the other was heavier and made of better quality metal. Also in the wallet was a set of rosewood prayer beads with a brown silk tassel.

Harry moved to take a closer look. 'What's on the memory stick?'

Tom turned to answer him. 'There's nothing on it – just random photos of some Holy sites and mosaics.'

'Why did you keep it?' asked Gallagher.

'I was straight out on a job the next day and when I got back I found out about the blokes on my team. I suppose I just gathered it up with my stuff. It wasn't until I was getting ready to leave Africa that I looked at it. If there'd been anything interesting on it I would have told the boss back in Iraq.'

'Do you mind if I have a look?'

Tom passed the memory stick to Gallagher.

Gallagher inserted the device into his laptop port and opened all the files. 'Harry, would you mind checking to see if the memory used matches the file sizes? You're good with figures. Have a play with it and see if you can spot anything hidden. I can't say it looks too interesting on first view. There can't be many more than three dozen photographs on it.'

Harry took the laptop to the desk and began making notes on the content. Gallagher and Tom remained where they were in silent contemplation.

Tom was the first to speak. 'What's next?'

'I'll be getting a call at six from the chap with Connie's phone. Bannerman won't expect a report for a day or two so we're OK on that front. In the meantime, he might come back with a location for her mobile. So first we have to come up with a strategy for the phone call tonight.'

Tom rubbed his temples. 'It'll have to be a meet. Can you get guns?'

Gallagher paced. 'Let's say we track them with the phone and go in guns blazing, we'd be on the wrong side of the law and we'd be putting Connie in danger. I could level with Bannerman, as he clearly doesn't know she's been lifted. He could bring in the police negotiators but it's still not adding up, we don't know who's behind all this.'

'It'll have to be a meet,' said Tom.

Gallagher walked to the drinks globe. 'I'm not saying I wouldn't do it – God knows I feel a weight of responsibility – but I couldn't drag Harry into a situation like that.'

'Piss off, boss,' said Harry, glancing behind him.

'Don't you think you've had enough of that, you pisshead?' Tom asked, as Gallagher poured more whisky.

'No, it helps me to think. Anything Harry?'

'Nothing. The file sizes match the memory and I can't see anything dodgy – not that I'm an expert.'

'So what are you going to say when this bastard calls again?' asked Tom.

'I'm going to tell him that I've got a lead but I need to follow it up – it might buy some time. If they want you that badly they won't do anything to Connie if they think they're close to getting you.'

Tom flashed him an angry look. 'You know that for sure, yeah?'

'Calm down, mate,' said Harry. 'We know fuck all for sure at the moment. He's trying to help.'

'Yeah, well,' said Tom, 'I'd like to see how fucking calm you'd be if it was your sister.'

Harry's phone rang and he left the room. Gallagher walked to the window and stared down into the street.

Tom simmered, his mind whirling.

'That was Mark Keane,' Harry said as he returned. 'Said he was calling from a mate's phone, still hasn't sorted out a new mobile. He wanted to know if we fancy a beer again soon. I told him to call back in a few days. He sounded disappointed.'

'He'll live,' said Gallagher, with some irritation.

'Yeah, I was just saying,' said Harry.

'Sorry, H. Do you think Ross could help?'

'I dunno. He's only recently made it into the TSG. He's not that long out of his probationary period.'

'The bloke who was with you this morning? He's a copper? He's TSG?' asked Tom. 'After all you fuckers said.'

'Relax,' said Gallagher. 'He's one of us. He was out with us in Afghanistan: he wouldn't turn us over.'

'Sure about that as well, are you? Bollocks to this.'

'Where are you going to go, Tom?' asked Harry. 'It's Owen that they'll be calling about Connie. It's him who has the contact at Five. What are you going to do, run around London asking if anyone's seen your sister lately?'

Tom took three steps towards Harry, his fist clenched and ready to swing.

'Easy, Tom,' said Gallagher. 'We've got enough battles to fight outside.'

Tom took a deep breath. 'Well let's start fucking fighting them.'

TEN

Connie flinched as the door was kicked hard. It remained closed and she held her breath. She saw an eye at the keyhole. She sensed it was the dangerous one.

'Feeling lonely?' said a voice through the door. He laughed. She heard him stand.

'What now?' he shouted. 'Can't you two manage to clean up for five fucking minutes? For fuck's sake.'

A door slammed.

She'd been taken from the cellar and placed in a damp pantry. She could hear the men banging around as they shifted whatever they were shifting. Above and to the sides were shelves, which were empty except for a few cans of tinned food, half a loaf of bread and a bottle of tomato ketchup. There wasn't quite enough space for her to stretch out her legs. Her back and shoulders ached and the cuts from the rope were making her wrists itch and burn.

The kinder one had helped her on with her clothes and had brought her to this cupboard before retying her ankles. He'd left her with a rough blanket. He hadn't spoken. Later, he brought her a plate of tinned tuna and some Philadelphia cream cheese, which still lay on the floor to her left. The airbrick in the corner was allowing in some clean air. Her

214

nostrils were full of the smell of mould and decay, but now they were burning wood outside and the smoke found its way into the house.

The initial shock of capture had given way to a desperate sense of helplessness and crushing isolation. One minute she was sure she'd be killed, the next she imagined Tom or James coming to rescue her. She berated herself: Tom wouldn't know she was missing and how could James help? If they'd contacted him, he might go to the police. The dangerous one had told her what would happen to her if he suspected that.

She tried to find a more comfortable position. She'd lost the feeling in her buttocks and wished that the rest of her aching body would go numb too.

* * *

Hafs and Eshan had known each other since primary school. They'd been born and brought up in South London and had known nothing else in all their nineteen years of life. They'd played football for their school and still played in the local Sunday league. Most evenings were spent at either of their parents' houses playing Xbox games. It had been a year since they'd returned to worshipping at the local mosque, which had pleased their parents, who were hard-working people and worried that the sometimes hot-headed boys were mixing with radical elements of the faith. They had passed through that phase unscathed and were settling down into working life in preparation for – their fathers prayed and mothers hoped – prestigious matches in marriage. A selection of local girls from good families had been paraded and there were a couple of candidates in Pakistan but both families were happy to allow the boys some freedom of choice, for the time being at least.

They had entered the City, having walked across Southwark Bridge. Hafs was sitting outside Starbucks in Paternoster Square looking up at the great dome of St Paul's, the symbol of London's rebirth after the Great Fire; the first dome in the city, a symbol of classicism and perfect order – or so said the guidebook that lay on the table in front of him next to two cups of green tea.

He watched Eshan walk across the square.

'How was it?' he asked as his friend joined him at the table.

'Ridiculous, innit?' Eshan answered, putting his own guidebook on the table. 'You walk straight in.'

'No checks?'

'You walk straight in, man. The ticket desks are well inside.'

Hafs looked at the other customers sitting outside: a businessman talking loudly on his phone and a woman wearing patent-leather high heels at another table, tapping at her laptop. An elderly couple were the closest to them and were prattling away in what Hafs guessed to be Dutch. He looked back at the woman's legs.

'Is it really going to happen? Are we really going to do it, bruv?'

'We were chosen, so we've got to.'

'I feel a bit sick, bruv,' said Hafs.

'Me too, but we're up for it – right?'

'We've been dreaming about it for years, yeah?'

'So we wait. He'll call with the details of where the stuff is and we'll do it when we're told to do it. *Insha'Allah.*'

'*Insha'Allah,*' said Hafs, the blood pulsing into his face as the woman caught him staring at her hemline.

* * *

Harry had been home to check in with Lynne. His wife had been busy with her Open University course work and Harry Junior had been playing quietly with his toy cars on the floor. She hadn't given him any grief for being out so long or for having to go out again so soon. He'd made the boy his tea. Then he'd had a shower, changed his clothes, kissed Lynne goodbye and made his way back to Gallagher's flat for a quarter to six. Now he sat with Tom and Gallagher waiting for the call.

217

The old mantel clock chimed six times and then fell silent. No one spoke.

Gallagher's phone rang.

Tom stood and began pacing the room. Harry flipped open his notebook, pen at the ready.

'Yes, it's James,' said Gallagher.

Tom looked at Harry, puzzled. Harry shook his head and raised his index finger.

'Yes, I know. Look, I've got a lead as to where he might be. Yes, I know what you said. I've been working on it all day. I'm confident, yes.'

Gallagher listened to the caller. 'I think it's best if we all stay calm, we can work this out.'

Gallagher walked to the window as he listened again. 'I understand, but there's only so much I can do in a few hours. Yes, I understand.'

He moved back to the centre of the room and placed his phone on the coffee table.

'What did the bastard say?' asked Tom.

'The usual threats, but I've got until midnight to come up with something.'

'Or?'

'They'll dial my number with one of her fingers before putting it in the post. The guy obviously watches too much TV. I doubt he knows where I live, for a start.'

218

Tom sat down again, visibly shaking with rage. 'Bastards, I'll kill them.'

'We've bought ourselves some time,' said Gallagher. 'Let's hope Bannerman delivers on the phone location.'

Tom stood and moved to within three feet of Gallagher.

Harry stepped forward.

'I thought your name was Owen,' said Tom.

'It is. I told Connie it was James – stupid of me, I know.'

Tom swung a punch at Gallagher's head, which he ducked as Harry shoved Tom off balance on to the sofa.

'Sit there and be a good lad,' said Harry.

Gallagher walked to the globe. 'Drink?'

'Is that your answer to everything?' asked Tom, with audible scorn.

'Mostly,' said Gallagher. 'Want one?'

'Bollocks to it, why not? Nothing else we're doing seems to be of any bloody use.'

'Harry?'

'Not for me, boss. This probably isn't the best time, but I picked up the Evening Standard earlier. I think you should take a look at this.'

Harry opened the newspaper. There was a still from a CCTV camera taken after a council worker had been attacked near the Strand.

'The picture's fuzzy and the angle's crap, but I'm pretty sure it's Mark Keane and the description from the victim is pretty close.'

'Mark? Why would Mark attack a council worker?'

'That I don't know but the attacker was a dosser sleeping in a Lyceum Theatre doorway, it says here.'

'Shit,' said Gallagher.

'Which is how I'm feeling about giving him the brush-off when he called.'

'There's not much we can do about it now. Let's hope he calls you back.'

Tom kicked the coffee table. 'Are we forgetting that a bunch of bastards have kidnapped my sister and are threatening to chop bits off her?'

* * *

Tom was dozing on the sofa and pretended to have been awake as Gallagher entered the room and switched on the light. The mantel clock chimed a quarter to midnight.

'Tom, get your things together we're leaving.'

'Why's that? What about the phone call?'

'It's my mobile number they've got, I can still answer it. Ross's on nights, he had to help an inspector set up a briefing room for a raid by TSG and SO15 in the morning.'

'What's that got to do with us?'

'It's my front door they'll be kicking in.'

'You couldn't make this shit up,' said Tom. 'It's a shagging nightmare and I'm gonna wake up any second.'

'Harry will be back in five minutes, we need to be ready to go,' said Gallagher grabbing his laptop and placing it in his messenger bag. He took this to the kitchen table where Harry had left the holdall he'd retrieved from the surveillance van when he'd returned it to the lock-up.

Gallagher heard Tom at the sink in the bathroom throwing water at his face. In Uncle Edwin's room he spotted the zipped wallet and took it to the bag in the kitchen.

His phone beeped as he went to get two bottles from the drinks globe. Bannerman had the cell-site tracking data and had texted the co-ordinates and a cheery message. That was something at least. It also pointed to Bannerman not knowing about a pending arrest – although you could never tell with the likes of Sandy Bannerman.

He went back to the kitchen and placed the bottles in the holdall, followed by four bottles of red wine from the rack. He wasn't going to leave any of the good stuff for the police to smash during a search.

In his bedroom, Gallagher opened a secure cabinet in the wardrobe. He removed a small covert camera unit, the other two PTT phones, a SIG Sauer P228 pistol, a suppressor unit, a holster with a magazine pouch, a box of 9mm ammunition and two magazines. He turned and saw Tom in the doorway.

'Got another one of those?' said Tom, pointing at the pistol.

'No. Come and give me a hand.' Gallagher held out the camera. 'Hang on, take this too,' he said, reaching into the cabinet and pulling out a block of bank notes wrapped in cellophane. 'Put both of these in the holdall on the kitchen table, would you?'

'Fuck me,' said Tom. 'There's a few quid there.'

'I don't think it's a good idea for either of us to rock up to a hole in the wall and withdraw cash for the foreseeable, do you?'

'Fair point. What happens next?'

'In the next few hours a bunch of coppers are going to come through that door. At least we'll be able to watch the fun.'

'Eh?'

'There's a covert camera covering the door.'

Tom leaned out into the hallway and scanned the walls and ceiling.

'I can't see it.'

Gallagher raised his eyebrows.

'Yeah, yeah,' said Tom. 'The clue's in the name.'

'Do me a favour, go and get Connie's file from the desk. We can't have that lying around when they arrive.'

'Where are we going?'

'Bermondsey. There's a warehouse down by the river that belongs to a friend. Harry's sorted it.'

'Why would someone like you have a friend with a warehouse in Bermondsey?'

'Someone like me?'

'You're an ex-Rupert, aren't you? Pretty obvious, everyone keeps calling you "Boss".'

'His name's Frankie. His son was one of my corporals. I sent his boy home from Afghanistan in a box.'

'What happened?' asked Tom.

There were three quiet knocks at the door.

'Go and let Harry in. We've only got a few minutes before we leave and they call again.'

* * *

Bannerman switched on his bedside lamp and answered the ringing phone.

'Sorry to wake you, Sandy. It's Gerry Stowford, duty officer, JTAC. We've had notification of a raid due for first light. We cross-referenced the target name and address and it flagged up one of your contacts.'

'Who?' asked Bannerman, reaching for the glass of water next to his bed.

'It's an Owen Gallagher, Seven Dials Court?'

'Gallagher? Who's the local commander?'

223

'The chap holding the reins is an Inspector Slater. He's assembling a team at Charing Cross. TSG have been tasked to co-ordinate support for SO15. Details are a bit sketchy so the divisional commander is reluctant to send in the guns before they've got more info – but the intel calls for it.'

'Why are they sending in an armed-response unit?'

'Apparently, there's a red flag from SO15. The ball was set in motion by a tip-off from an informer with an old handler code. They weren't too sure about what was going on but the intel mentions arms dealing and knowledge of impending attacks. I'm trying to find out more now.'

'So why has Gallagher been flagged by the counter-terrorism unit? Sorry Gerry, I'm just thinking aloud. This makes no sense to me.'

'The supervising ranking officer is a Superintendent Austin, but he's still at home. That's all I've got at the moment. The borough's Counter Terrorism Liaison Officer is on his way to Charing Cross now to provide the link with SO15 – Andy Jenkins.'

'Right, thanks Gerry. Would you let Slater know I'll be arriving within the hour? I want to be there when they go in and I want everything that he's got the minute I walk into that police station. I'll want to speak to Jenkins as soon as possible – understood?'

Bannerman ended the call and got out of bed. The rain was pelting against the glass and the wind was rattling the sash window like it was auditioning for a Hammer Horror. He'd been dreaming of Flic Anderson and now he was going to have to travel across London in a storm to watch the goons of the Territorial Support Group kick in Gallagher's front door for a Heckler-toting firearms squad.

'Owen Gallagher, what have you been doing?'

* * *

They had loaded Harry's car and were driving along the outskirts of Covent Garden when Gallagher's phone rang.

'Yes, I think I know where he is. I'm driving there to confirm it now.' He paused and listened. 'OK, but it might take a couple of hours to be certain.'

He paused again.

'I understand; I'm doing what you've asked.'

There was yet another pause.

'I thought you just wanted an address.'

There was a longer pause.

'OK, I understand.'

Gallagher placed his phone back in his pocket.

'There's been a change of plan: they want me to find you and then deliver you. They'll be calling back with instructions at six this morning.'

Tom looked out of the car window at the passing lights blurred by the rain and said nothing.

'I'm going to use Waterloo Bridge,' said Harry. 'OK?'

Gallagher hesitated before answering. 'H, turn around and head up to King's Cross and give me your PTT.'

Harry handed him the phone.

Gallagher held it up between the front seats so Tom could see it. 'Tom, there are two more of these in that holdall next to you. Pass them to me, would you?'

'Bannerman?' asked Harry.

'I don't know,' said Gallagher. 'But there's a chance of being pinged by one of his friends at GCHQ if he's setting us up and he may not have any choice but to join the hunt. I'll wipe them down, so be careful of prints.'

As they arrived in the King's Cross area Gallagher asked Harry to pull up in Pancras Road.

'I need to stay in the car away from the police and cameras. Take two of these each and get rid of them. We need to be out of here as soon as possible, but be creative.'

'I'll have a look up and around Euston Road,' said Harry. 'Tom, you take the station area and see what you can do – but wear this baseball cap and try to stay out of the camera arcs.'

Gallagher sat low in the passenger seat and locked the car's doors as Tom and Harry walked away. Harry put on his gloves as he headed towards King's Cross Mission Church and found a street drinker huddled in a doorway asleep. He leaned forward and held his breath. The man's face was weathered, his skin like cracked leather. His right eye was surrounded by a black bruise and there was a fresh wound just above the cheek bone. He'd pissed himself in his sleep.

Harry's thoughts turned to Mark Keane for a moment and then he slipped one of the PTTs into the sleeping man's coat pocket.

Tom walked to the front entrance of King's Cross Station. Two men were arguing in a language he couldn't identify and three Police Community Support Officers were trying to restore calm. Tom moved nearer the road and was about to turn when a young woman brushed past him.

'Sorry, sweetheart,' she said, throwing a coquettish smile over her shoulder as she walked on.

She couldn't have been much older than twenty and might have been pretty, but the drugs had begun to ravage her looks even at that young age. He smiled and waved his acceptance of her apology as she walked quickly in the direction of York Way. She'd taken the PTT from his back pocket as she'd bumped into him.

He turned and picked up a McDonald's bag blowing down the pavement towards him. Putting his hand in the bag, he reached into his jacket pocket and used it to wrap the other PTT. Inside the station he looked at an information board and then at his watch, turning as a station cleaner pushed her trolley past him. He smiled and dropped the McDonald's bag into the bin on the front of the trolley.

'Thanks,' he said.

Harry returned to the car first.

'Both gone?' asked Gallagher.

'Yep, one in a street drinker's pocket and the other at a bus-stop down the road. It'll be on a night bus to God-Knows-Where as soon as someone spots it.'

'Nice one,' said Gallagher. 'Here's Tom.'

Tom climbed into the back.

'All done.'

'Good,' said Gallagher. 'Harry, take us around the houses a bit and then head south of the river. Keep heading south and then come back in an arc, east and then north again to Bermondsey.'

* * *

Harry turned right into Tooley Street and then out on to Jamaica Road. He turned left after a mile or so and they wove their way through a number of streets towards the river before stopping at the gated entrance of a disused warehouse. The rain had stopped but the tarmac glistened in the car's lights.

'This is it. Frankie said it'd be unlocked. He'll be waiting inside,' said Harry switching off the headlights.

Gallagher got out and walked to the gates. The padlock was fastened but not locked. He pushed the gates open for Harry to drive through and then closed them without locking the padlock. He didn't want to cut off a possible retreat. Harry edged the car forward as Gallagher walked slowly behind, his hand resting on the pistol holstered at the right side of his lower back.

A torch flashed from a Judas gate set in the large green wooden doors of the warehouse. Harry flashed back with a pen torch. The doors opened for him to drive in.

Gallagher walked to the side of the building and looked out at the surrounding area. When he was satisfied, he entered through the Judas gate and closed it behind him. A coarse blackout curtain hung from ceiling to floor. He found the divide and walked into the dimly-lit space behind. Harry and Tom were out of the car and talking with Frankie.

Footsteps on a set of wooden stairs above and to his right sent Gallagher into a low crouch, hand on the pistol grip.

'Easy, son,' said Frankie. 'No need for any of that. We don't want any accidents now, do we?'

Gallagher inwardly flinched and avoided eye-contact with Frankie, looking instead at the legs of the man who walked into view down the stairs. The man stopped halfway, crouching under a beam.

'This is Teddy Southall,' said Frankie. 'He's my right hand. I'd trust him with my life and I have done.'

229

'Lads,' said Teddy. 'Frankie, all the gear's fine. The camping stove works and the water from the taps is all right if it's boiled.'

'Cheers, Teddy,' said Frankie. 'Let's show these two where they'll be sleeping.'

They followed Teddy up the stairs and he led them into a room running the length of the building.

'There's a bog in the corner over there,' he said. 'I brought you some shit-roll.'

Frankie laughed. 'He's all heart is our Teddy.'

'There are six camp beds in that crate over there, so work out which are the best. The box on the left is full of blankets. They'll be a bit musty but you'll cope, I'm sure. The box on the right is full of camping bollocks: cups, plates, lamps and that. The stove is new and the spare gas canisters are over in the cupboard on the wall. The cupboard next to it is full of tinned food and there's some bread and coffee. There's no electricity or heating – sorry about that.'

'You've had guests before,' Harry joked.

'We have,' said Frankie. 'But the less you know about that, the better. Let's just say that there have been times that the Old Bill has been swarming over London looking for blokes who were reclining on those very camp beds waiting for the fuss to die down.'

'Did it?' asked Gallagher.

'Oh yeah,' said Teddy. 'They're all enjoying a well-earned retirement in the sun. Well, most of them – but no one's ever been lifted from here.'

'So that's why you keep the place?' asked Tom.

'Just how it worked out,' said Frankie. 'I got it as part of a deal years ago and it comes in handy now and then. The big property developers are creeping this way. A lot of the old wharves east of London Bridge and City Hall have been turned into swanky housing developments or bars and shops – like they have over the water in Shadwell and Wapping – but they're still arguing about where to put the new Super Sewer. Once that's sorted, I'll sell up. Now,' he said, adjusting his cuffs, 'who's going to tell me what this is all about?'

* * *

'Tom,' said Gallagher opening the laptop case on the workbench, 'I want you to stay here while we go to find Connie.'

'I don't think so. You're the one that the police are looking for, not me.'

'At the moment, it seems like they're the only ones not looking for you. I'll take my chances,' Gallagher said, laying out the laptop's spare batteries.

'Good, so will I,' said Tom.

Gallagher reached inside the inner flap of the case for the Broadband dongle – with it came the zipped leather wallet, which he placed to one side.

'OK, there's no point in wasting time arguing. H, I'll need you to go and clear the lock-up of any useful kit. It's in my uncle's name, so it won't have been pinged. The van is compromised as it's registered to me, but the motorbike has a set of false plates in the cupboard on the wall, so it might still be of use in the near future.'

'OK, no problem. Everything?' said Harry.

'Please, the OP gear, the lot. The house is in a rural location, so bring the jackets, the cam cream and scrim.'

Gallagher tapped at the laptop's keyboard. 'While you're gone, we'll check out Google Maps of the area identified by Bannerman's cell-site tracking of Connie's phone. He reckons the interpolation of the base stations and GPS is accurate to about fifty metres. We could do with an Ordnance Survey map, would you mind picking one up?'

Harry took out his notebook. 'No problem. I'll nip to the big bookshop on my way back in the morning.'

Gallagher checked the laptop. 'It's OS Explorer map sheet 182 and get 194 as well – the location might be on the adjacent sheet.' He held out ten £20 notes. 'And if you could get London North 173 and South 161, they might come in handy over the next few days. There's money there for your fuel, too.'

'No worries,' said Harry, noting the numbers. 'When do you want me back here?'

'We'll try to get our heads down for a couple of hours, after we've watched my front door get kicked in, so go home and get some rest. Shall we say late morning, unless we need you before?'

'OK,' said Harry. 'Frankie, what's it like for coming and going round here?'

'You should be fine. Teddy has left you two keys to the padlock on the workbench.   There's not much in the way of residential or business down this end, but there's plenty of construction traffic up the road for you not to be too noticeable to any passing Plod.'

'I'll dig out a hi-vis vest and a hard hat,' said Harry.

'Can we fix it? Yes, we can,' said Teddy, chuckling on his way to the stairs. 'I'll go and check the coast is clear, Frankie. You want Chris to bring the car to the end of the road?'

'Five minutes.'

Teddy disappeared down the stairs and Harry stood to follow him.

'Give us twenty minutes before you leave, Harry,' said Frankie.

Harry sat back down in his chair and Gallagher patted his shoulder as he walked past him.

'I appreciate this, H.'

233

'What else would I be doing on a wet night south of the river?'

'Is there anything else you need, lads?' asked Frankie.

'Guns,' answered Tom.

'No,' said Gallagher.

'We need more guns.'

'Tom, I don't intend shooting up a corner of the Home Counties. No more guns.'

'And if we get there and find them mob-handed and tooled up?' asked Tom, kicking over a chair and stalking to the other side of the room.

'He's got a point,' said Harry. 'Whoever we're dealing with, they're not messing about. If Bannerman and the police are involved we're in the shit and the rulebook's out the window – unless you turn yourself in to Bannerman and hand it all over.'

Tom walked back down the room and stood at the opposite wall. 'Whatever this is about, you know as well as I do that Connie's not going to walk away from this unless we take the fight to them. We can't go to your spook friend: he's the common-fucking-denominator in all this. We can't go to the police. We're fucked.'

Gallagher looked at the floor, then raised his head again. 'It looks like I'm not destined for a quiet life. Frankie, any chance?'

Frankie shrugged. 'Short notice, beggars can't be choosers.'

'OK, thanks, just a couple of pistols, we don't need to be armed to the teeth and I don't intend getting into a firefight.'

'Teddy'll bring you the gear in the morning. I'll try for clean but they might have history. Ditch them if you need to, you don't want to be in the frame for an unsolved case from ten years ago.'

'Let me know how much I owe you,' said Gallagher.

'Bring them back unfired and forget about it. If not, we'll talk about it later – if you make it back, that is. They won't be traceable to me.'

'Appreciated, thanks,' said Gallagher.

'I'll leave you to it,' said Frankie.

Gallagher shook Frankie's hand. 'I owe you,' he said.

'We'll see about that, but now isn't the time. Getting the girl back is all you need to worry about today. A couple of my lads will be watching the place, but you won't see them.'

They heard Frankie go out through the Judas gate.

'As soon as the coast's clear I'll be off,' said Harry, yawning. 'Is there anything else you need me to do?'

'No thanks mate. You've been a star, as usual,' said Gallagher. 'Tom, we need to begin to have a look at the area we think Connie's being held in. Then we'll get our heads down. We can relax for a while with Frankie's boys keeping watch.'

* * *

Gallagher's phone beeped on the floor next to him. He rolled over on the camp bed to retrieve it. Tom was sitting in a chair opposite, illuminated by the pale light of a camping lantern. 'They've arrived at the flat. That's the SMS alert for the camera being triggered,' said Gallagher as he activated the camera app on his laptop.

Tom carried his chair over.

They watched the screen as two armed police officers cleared the hallway beyond the battered front door. They'd sent in 'the hounds' first – dogs trained to ignore gunshots – and Gallagher watched as they returned to the handlers outside. Another pair of armed officers followed as the first two cleared the bedroom and the bathroom, before moving beyond the camera's field of view. Within minutes two men in suits followed three TSG officers wearing overalls and riot pads through the door. Sandy Bannerman followed up behind. It was obvious that a vigorous search was underway and two more officers came through the door to assist. Various bits and pieces were thrown into the hallway as they went to work with enthusiasm.

'It's going to take you a while to clear that lot up,' said Tom.

'It's just stuff, I really don't care. We've got more important things to deal with.'

They continued to watch as various police personnel walked in and out of the flat.

'I bet your neighbours are none too pleased,' said Tom.

Gallagher laughed. 'It'll give them something to talk about. Those lads shout so loud the neighbours will think it's them being raided.'

An hour later, Bannerman walked into shot as the last of the uniformed officers left the flat. He allowed the two men in suits to pass him, turned, and looked straight at the hidden camera's position, giving a wry smile before moving to the door.

'He knows you're watching,' said Tom, stretching out his arms.

'He's guessing I am.'

'How did he spot the camera?'

'I doubt he did – the search team didn't – but it's where he'd have put it.'

A uniformed officer turned off the light in the hallway and the screen dimmed as the door was closed. 'Some poor probationary copper's going to be standing out there all morning while they get that secured,' said Gallagher, lying back on the camp bed.

'Fuck 'em,' said Tom.

ELEVEN

Gallagher had been asleep for half an hour when his phone rang. He propped himself up on an elbow and looked across the room to where Tom was sitting in the canvas chair.

'I wondered how long it would be,' he said before answering it.

Tom gave him a puzzled look but remained silent in the half-light.

Gallagher held the handset to his ear.

'Sandy, how are you? Did you enjoy the party at my place?'

'Owen, would you mind telling me what's going on?'

'I was rather hoping that you might be able to tell me.'

'I'm afraid not, old boy, but you're on SO15's naughty list – that I can tell you.'

'Someone's playing silly buggers, Sandy,' Gallagher said, swinging his legs off the bed. 'I need to find out who. Are you tracking my phone?'

There was a pause.

'I don't think it's necessary just yet. They've asked, of course, but I foresee some technical glitches. How long do you need?'

'As long as you can give me, but a couple of days at least. I've got to be able to move if I'm going to get to the bottom of this.'

'No promises, but I'll keep you dark for as long as I can.'

'Thanks, Sandy.'

'Any luck with that niece of yours?'

'Cousin, second cousin,' said Gallagher. 'Not yet, but I appreciate your help. Thanks again.' He ended the call.

'Bannerman,' he said to Tom. 'I think he may still be on side.'

'You trust him?'

'No, but this phone is our only link to the kidnappers. I can't ditch it until we find her.'

'And if he turns you over?'

'I'll be sitting on a plastic chair in a room with no windows, listening to the same repeated questions until they get bored and send me to a detention centre.'

'It's a big risk.'

'We'll worry about it after we've got Connie back. Until then, I've got no choice.'

Tom nodded, opened his mouth to speak and then closed it. Gallagher waited for him to find the words.

He picked up Gallagher's cup. 'Brew?'

Gallagher nodded as his phone rang again. It was 05:58.

'I'm listening,' he said.

'Yes, I know where he is, but I can't go knocking him up at this time of the morning, he might do a runner.'

Gallagher listened.

'I understand but you do want me to bring him, don't you? You'll need to give me some time to approach him in the right way.'

Gallagher listened again, picking up a pen and pad lying next to the camp bed. 'No, but I'll find it.'

Tom paced behind him.

'I understand. Of course, yes.'

Tom sat back in his chair, listening intently.

'One followed by three, yes, I understand.'

Gallagher put the phone down on the pad. 'They want me to deliver you to Paddington Old Cemetery at midnight. It's up Kilburn way, off Willesden Lane. They want the wallet. No coppers, no funny business, etc. The bloke's in danger of becoming a parody.'

'He's in danger of being fucking dead,' said Tom. 'Why are they giving you so long?'

'I said I needed time, but he didn't seem to want to argue. They're obviously setting up an ambush and they don't want any witnesses.'

'What's with the "one followed by three"?'

'Torch signal, it doesn't matter. We'll hit the target house after dusk. I can't imagine they'd actually bring her for exchange, even if they intend to release her. By the time the

240

meeting is supposed to happen we'll have her and they can whistle.'

* * *

Harry arrived twenty minutes after Teddy Southall had left Gallagher and Tom with the pistols that Frankie had promised them. Upstairs, he took the maps Gallagher had asked for from a carrier bag, followed by a carton of milk, all of which he placed on the workbench next to the guns.

'Brownings. Well maintained by the look of it.'

'I'll put the kettle on,' said Gallagher. 'You two strip those down and load the magazines.'

He walked to the holdall and took out a full bottle of brandy before moving to the shelf with the camping kettle and the coffee. He lit the small gas stove and poured some of the brandy into a cup.

'Gunfire?' said Tom with disdain, nodding at Gallagher's cup.

'Breakfast of champions. There's a cleaning kit and gloves in the holdall. I'll get them for you.'

Tom shook his head.

Harry took off his jacket and caught a pair of surgical gloves thrown by Gallagher. Tom caught a second pair and then the cleaning kit. Harry laid his jacket on the bench and placed two pistol magazines on to it, before picking up the

241

Browning on the right. He pulled back the slide and engaged the safety in the slide notch, checking the chamber for a round. Having cleared the weapon, he pushed the slide stop pin and pulled out the slide-release bar. Then he carefully held the slide, released the safety catch from the holding notch and pulled the slide forward and off the pistol's frame. He removed the recoil spring and guide rod by compressing the spring and pulling it out. He then slid out the barrel. Tom followed suit and both men checked and cleaned the component parts before reassembling the Brownings.

'What's with him and the booze?' Tom whispered to Harry.

'It's his way of coping. Problem?'

'Is it likely to be?'

'Hasn't been, for as long as I've known him. It helps him to think and sometimes it helps him not to think. It's never affected his work. I think he's got hollow legs.'

'So it doesn't worry you that he might fuck up in a situation?'

'He's self-medicating. Sometimes I worry he might fuck himself up further down the line, but he doesn't let people down – never has, never will. Just leave it, yeah?'

Gallagher placed two coffees on the bench. 'All good?'

'Fine,' said Tom. 'Did you see Gaddafi's Browning? It was gold-plated with a picture of his mug on the grip. The rebels were waving it about after they stuck that pole up his arse.'

Gallagher poured another shot of brandy into his cup. 'He was a classy guy, old Muammar. There are two boxes of ammo in the bag there.'

Harry inserted an empty magazine in order to fire off the action. He and Tom then wiped the individual pieces of ammunition before loading each magazine with thirteen rounds. Tom inserted a freshly loaded mag, cocked his pistol and reached for another loose round to make it fourteen.

'We won't be travelling with one up the spout,' said Gallagher.

'OK.' Tom removed the magazine and pulled back the slide to eject the round. 'You planning on shooting pissed?'

'I'm not planning on shooting at all,' said Gallagher. 'Remember: the aim is to scare the shit out of them. We don't want a body count.'

Tom slipped the pistol into the back of his trousers, picked up his coffee and walked to a chair on the other side of the room. Harry looked at Gallagher, who shrugged before unfolding one of the map sheets on the now cleared workbench. He turned his laptop to face Harry.

'From the co-ordinates Bannerman gave us we're pretty sure that this is the house where Connie is being held. The properties in the area are spaced a good way apart and the cell-site tracking puts her here, within fifty metres.'

243

Harry sipped his brew. 'Want to walk me through the plan?'

* * *

Harry met Frankie at the Judas gate. Upstairs, Gallagher tensed. He knew that Frankie would bring Teddy Southall but there were four pairs of feet climbing the stairs. He gestured for Tom to take a position on the farthest side of the room, diagonal to the opening. Gallagher moved to his right to watch the heads emerge in front of him, listening for the sound of more bodies. He heard none.

Harry came first and seemed at ease, followed by Frankie and Teddy. A few seconds later Mark Keane emerged. Gallagher took his hand from the holster and waved for Tom to relax.

'I've picked up a stray,' said Frankie. 'Battersea Dogs' Home is full, so I had to bring him here.'

Gallagher walked across the room. 'Mark, how are you?'

Mark looked embarrassed. 'All right, boss, you?'

'He's been telling us porkies – haven't you, boy?' said Frankie.

Harry slapped Mark on the back. 'Come on, Mr Keane, help me make a brew.'

'What's up?' Gallagher asked Frankie.

'The silly sod's been sleeping rough. Got himself into a spot of bother and gave me a call. I'm going to try to find him some work. In the meantime, he can kip down here with you.'

'Just like old times,' said Harry, spooning coffee into the mugs. Mark gave him a sheepish grin.

'What you tell him about your business is your business,' Frankie said to Gallagher.

'Was that you in the paper, Mark?' Gallagher asked.

'Yes, boss.'

'OK, you can tell us about it in your own time. I need to talk to Frankie downstairs. Harry's going to tell you a story. You're not the only one in a bit of bother.'

'Don't forget your coffee,' said Harry. He held up the bottle of brandy that had been sitting next to the kettle.

Gallagher shook his head.

Teddy was lounging in one of the canvas chairs. Mark took a coffee to him and then one to Tom, who was sitting on the workbench. Mark placed the mug on the bench next to Tom's Browning.

'What's with the gats?' he asked.

Tom sipped his coffee and said nothing.

'Come over here, Mark,' said Harry, 'and I'll bring you up to speed.'

* * *

245

'I'll come with you,' said Mark, after Frankie and Teddy had gone.

'Not this time.'

'Come on, boss.'

'No and that's final. We'll be back before you know it. Then we'll talk.'

Harry laughed. 'You're too keen, Keane. I've always said so.'

'Still funny,' Mark said without smiling.

Harry raised a finger. 'Don't you dare start sulking, you stroppy fucker. Do as you're told, there's a good lad.'

Gallagher called them together to look at the map of the area that he'd drawn, which was lying on the OS map sheet.

'OK, one more time. This is far from ideal. We haven't been able to check out an OP site on the ground and this afternoon will be our first close-target recce, so we'll have to improvise when we get into position.'

He tapped the laptop keyboard and brought up the aerial Google Maps view of the area.

'The Drop Off Point is in this layby here. You can see the alternative drop-off marked here, in case the layby is being used. Tom and I will walk down the road to this stile once Harry is clear. From here we follow the public footpath along the edge of this field. We cross this bridge across the small stream and then move along this field boundary – as the path goes straight across and we want to avoid moving across such a big open space – then re-join it here. Once we hit these woods we move south away from the path again, pick up this stream and head east through the trees. The ground rises here and we follow the hill across these two streams to the OP. It'll give us a view of the target house and everything around it.'

Gallagher paused for questions while they took in the detail.

'You'll see that the path we leave continues through this wood to the south east and comes out at this gate on the road. That's our ERV if it all goes tits up. Harry, your turn.'

Harry pointed at the map. 'Once I've cleared the DOP, I'll drive the long-way round to my lying-up position here, just down the road from the Pick Up Point. I'll head straight to the PUP when you call. If you don't call within an hour after dusk, I move straight to the ERV.'

'Good,' said Gallagher. 'Have you got a cover story?'

'I'll think of something on the way. Oh and I spotted the cat's eyes attached to the wooden baton at the lock-up. I'll leave the car in the LUP and walk down to place the baton here in front of the PUP gate, so I can spot it in the dark. I'll be back at the car before you reach the OP position.'

'He thinks of everything,' said Tom.

Gallagher stretched and leaned over the maps again. 'The most dangerous part of this is going to be the rescue and

247

extraction, but we need to remember the risk of compromise during the insertion. We can't move in during dark hours, as we can't take the chance of them moving her early without our knowledge. We'll be playing walkers. Tom, dress accordingly, you've got boots and stuff to look the part?'

Tom nodded. 'I'll be all map pockets.'

'Tom and I have discussed our initial thoughts for hitting the house. It'll be dark a couple of hours after we arrive at the OP. We'll wait for twenty minutes after that and then we go in. Any questions?'

'Piece of piss,' said Tom.

'No questions,' said Harry. 'Mark, come and give me a hand with the car.'

Gallagher took out his pistol for cleaning. 'Just remember, we don't know who we're dealing with and we need to get a clue to which part of the house Connie's being held in.'

Harry turned and walked back to the workbench. 'Like I said, the chances are you'll be outnumbered. I don't like it.'

'And like I said, we've got no bloody choice: things are moving too quickly.'

Tom walked away. 'If you two have finished, do you mind if we get the fuck on with it?'

'Right,' said Gallagher. 'I want to be on the road on the hour. Harry, once you've checked the car over, spend some more time with the maps if you need to. I'll pack two daysacks: one with the binos and night sights etc., the other with the camo gear, shit bags and water. Tom, you'll have the latter, if we need to bug out you can dump it.'

Half an hour later, Gallagher picked up his daysack and handed the other to Tom. 'Help yourself to food Mark, but we'll bring something back. We'll need to feed Connie.'

'Let's get on with it,' said Tom. He picked up his pistol and walked to the stairs. When he reached the second step he turned to Mark. 'There's a broom down there; the place could do with sweeping out while we're gone.'

'Just don't go opening any bloody windows,' said Harry.

Mark gave Gallagher a pained look and Gallagher rested a hand on his shoulder. 'Just take it easy.'

Tom left the warehouse and checked the area. He opened the heavy doors and parted the blackout curtains to allow Harry to drive out with Gallagher in the front seat, before calling up the stairs.

'Come and shut these, will you?'

He heard Mark moving on the stairs and jogged forward past the car to the gates, climbing into the back seat once they were through and the padlock was fastened.

Harry turned into Jamaica Road and headed down to the A13, along the A12 and then picked up the M11 to take them to the M25. Thirteen miles later they left at Junction 24 for Potters' Bar. Having cleared the town, they picked up the

Great North Road before branching right towards the drop-off point.

'It's coming up on the left,' said Gallagher, checking his mobile was set to silent. 'Ready, Tom?'

'Ready,' he said, pulling out his own phone to switch it off.

Once they'd pulled over in the layby, Gallagher and Tom took the two rucksacks from the boot and gave Harry the thumbs up to drive away. Gallagher had insisted on that signal, rather than a slap on the bodywork. He'd seen too many misunderstandings occur because of kit banging against drop-off cars. He carried out a radio check with Harry, followed by Tom who then took out his earpiece and placed it in a pocket. There was little point in reducing their combined hearing ability by half, especially when approaching a target through woodland.

To anyone watching, they looked like a couple of walkers but no one passed them on the road before they reached the stile. They followed the track that led to a larger field, moving left to follow a ditch along a low hedgerow. They reached the woods and stopped, careful to open their mouths to improve their ability to hear the smallest of sounds.

Gallagher took out the camouflage jackets from Tom's pack. Both men then smeared their faces, ears, necks, wrists and hands with cam cream, before moving off through the trees.

Ten minutes later Gallagher signalled another stop. They had reached a burbling stream, which they planned to follow to the base of the hill. He checked the map indicating with a hand signal that Tom should be scanning the area. Gallagher pulled out his pistol, which he loaded and put back in its holster, the noise of the stream reducing the sound of the cocking action. Tom did the same and placed his pistol in the right-hand map pocket of his trousers, so he could crouch more easily without fear of it dropping from his waistband.

Gallagher pointed ahead as they kept close to the ground moving towards the OP position, stopping short in a hollow. They crouched, silent and still, waiting ten minutes before moving again, listening and watching, familiarising themselves with their surroundings. Satisfied that they weren't being followed or observed, Gallagher began to unpack the equipment and then crawled to the treeline a few feet away. The target house was clearly visible, their position allowing a view of the side windows and door, the rear windows, most of the front yard and the driveway. Gallagher wrapped scrim netting around the binoculars, careful to ensure the lenses were covered to reduce reflections.

Tom followed up behind and laid out a green waterproof sheet for them to lie on, before taking the high-power zoom monocular that Gallagher held out for him.

* * *

They had watched in silence for half an hour.

'No movement,' Tom whispered. 'Anything?'

'Nothing,' replied Gallagher. 'They must be keeping away from the windows.'

Tom adjusted his weight on his elbows. 'No sentry.'

'It'd look suspicious. Scan the lanes, see if you can spot any parked cars. I'll keep watching the windows.'

Tom swept the monocular across the countryside, first checking along the road nearest to the house. He saw nothing of interest and widened his search to the other visible roads and lanes. The only other high ground beyond the house was at least half a mile away and offered little cover for anyone that might have been watching the house from that vantage point.

'Nothing,' he whispered. 'Up here is the best position with cover.'

Gallagher lowered his binoculars and turned his head.

'That's what I was thinking,' said Tom.

Gallagher went back to watching the windows and Tom slid down the slope. He crouched next to the bags in the hollow and scanned the area behind them with the monocular, before moving east, checking the area to the rear of the OP position that they hadn't walked through on arrival.

He made his way slowly back to the hollow, stopping at intervals, waiting and listening, checking for signs of anyone else's presence.

'Rabbits and squirrels. There's no one near. Anything?'

Gallagher shook his head.

'Not too long until the sun sets.'

Gallagher nodded, keeping his gaze firmly fixed on the house. 'The back door lock is a Yale. Keep watching the doors and windows. I need to get my MOE kit ready.'

Gallagher kitten-crawled backwards down the slope to the bags. He took out a leather-wrapped toolkit and removed a small pouch. From this he took a tension tool, a half-diamond pick and hook, ball, rake and stagle picks. He put these in the left chest pocket of his jacket. Quietly unzipping one of the side pouches of his rucksack, he pulled out a small but high-powered black hunting catapult.

As dusk approached and no lights came on in the house, Gallagher's sense of unease grew. Either the kidnappers were keeping themselves to the central parts of the house, perhaps even a cellar, or the place was empty. Another thought flashed across his mind with an image of Connie's dead body lying in a room – her captors long gone.

Twenty minutes after darkness fell they were in the hollow, the rucksacks repacked. Tom inserted his earpiece and carried out a radio check. Gallagher clicked an affirmative with his pressel switch. Harry's voice sounded in their ears, loud and clear. Gallagher led as they made their way east before dropping down the hill, their descent covered by the smaller wood that lay behind and slightly to the right of the house. Once they'd entered the new wood lower down, Gallagher took out his pistol and made his way to the treeline nearest the back door. It would be a short run from the trees. He took the night-vision goggles from the top of his daysack and scanned the area. There were security lights fixed to the building's walls over the back door and at each corner of the house.

Gallagher selected two round stones and placed one into the catapult's sling. The stone narrowly missed the central security light and ricocheted off the stonework. Waiting for a couple of minutes, he was confident that no one inside the house had heard the noise. The second pebble found its mark and the bulb made a dull pop as it broke. He pushed the goggles on to the top of this head. Gallagher checked that the safety was off on his pistol and ran forward from the treeline, moving fast and low, trying to judge the sensor fields for each of the lights at either end of the back of the house. He reached the back door with neither of the lights activated so he depressed the pressel switch in his pocket five times, signalling for Tom to move into position at the side door. Tom would wait at that door before gaining entry on Gallagher's command. By then the noise wouldn't matter.

Gallagher tried the doorknob and felt its locked resistance. He listened and took the tools from his breast pocket. Inserting the tension bar, he checked the way that the lock turned. He applied some pressure to the bar and inserted a tool to rake the upper section and locate the pins. Raking the lock allowed him to push each pin, starting at the rear and moving forward. Once all the pins had moved, he turned the tension bar and the lock opened. He stayed in the crouch position and listened. No sound. He took a deep breath and eased the door ajar with his shoulder, poking the barrel of the SIG 228 through the gap.

He stayed low and entered the damp-smelling kitchen that looked like it hadn't been used in years. He could smell a faint trace of food in the air – food that had been prepared and eaten recently, although there was no sign of anything like used plates or wrappers. He pushed the door behind him so it remained slightly ajar and listened. The house was silent. He pulled the night-vision goggles down and moved forward into a small passage that had a door to the left, a door to the right and a door at the other end. The farthest door was open, so he crept forward past the other two, his pistol held to his front in a two-handed grip.

Tom had stayed in the trees, ready to move to the side door. Now, having received Gallagher's signal, he crouched to the left of it and peered in through the lower panes of glass that began half way up. He waited for the best part of ten minutes in the silence, straining his ears to pick up any indication of what might be going on inside. Gallagher's voice whispered in his earpiece.

'I'm coming to the side door.'

Tom pressed his radio switch twice as he felt a sinking sensation in his stomach. He saw Gallagher move through the narrow passage as he came to open the door, which he did by turning a key that was in place in the mortise lock.

Inside, Tom held his pistol up to cover the area behind Gallagher.

'Relax. There's no one here,' said Gallagher, removing his night-vision kit.

'Shit,' said Tom. 'Any sign that she was here?'

'There's a single bed in what would have been the parlour. I found a cut plasticuff under that and then cleared the other rooms. Apart from the cuff, it looks like they've been pretty thorough in cleaning up but we need to do a proper check.'

* * *

Having searched around the exterior of the house, they'd gone back to methodically clear through the building by torch light and had found no other clues. A fire pit recently dug in the garden had consumed anything of interest and what remained in the ashes amounted to nothing more than blackened ends of planks and a charred rope knot. The last room that they checked again was the kitchen.

'Tom,' said Gallagher. 'That's a pantry in the corner. I didn't check the shelves carefully.'

Tom walked across the kitchen and opened the pantry door as Gallagher checked the cupboards on the wall and under the sink.

'Blanket. Blood on it,' said Tom.

Gallagher joined him at the pantry door and shone his torch inside. There was a blanket on the floor, shoved into a corner, and a tin of baked beans at the back of the third shelf.

'This tin is in date and the label is clean.'

Tom bent down to examine the blanket more closely. 'The blood is dry. There's not much of it but it hasn't faded and the blanket doesn't feel or smell too damp. I don't think it's been lying here for long.'

Gallagher crouched next to him and shone the torch on the blanket. 'Lay it out, let's get a better look.'

Tom began to push the far corners of the blanket away from him. He stopped, lay down and removed the torch from his mouth, using its beam to illuminate an area of plaster underneath the lowest shelf. He looked over his shoulder at Gallagher, who leaned forward to get a closer look. Part of the plaster had given way over time and small fragments of brick and stone had been dislodged in front of an airbrick.

On the surviving plaster, a piece of the masonry had been used to scratch the words 'Connie Edwards' next to a date.

'That's today,' said Tom.

* * *

Tom and Gallagher had thrown the bags and jackets in the car boot and had cleaned off the cam cream with wet wipes as they drove back to London. No one had spoken for half an hour. Harry broke the silence as they crossed over to the south side of the Thames.

'What now?'

'I'm still thinking,' Gallagher answered.

'We'll be going to the meet in the cemetery, no question,' said Tom.

Gallagher stared straight ahead. 'There are plenty of questions.'

'Like what, for fuck's sake?'

'Like the ones I'm still thinking about.'

Tom resisted the urge to comment for a moment.

Harry switched on the car radio.

Gallagher switched it off.

'Need a drink, Rupert?' asked Tom, leaning forward from the back seat. 'Will a little drinky make everything better?'

Harry saw Gallagher tense and gripped the steering wheel in readiness.

Gallagher took a deep breath and relaxed. 'That's the best idea you've had all day.' He opened the glove compartment and pulled out a leather-covered hip flask with a hinged screw-top lid. He took a sip and offered it to Harry who waved it away.

'As the Buddhists say: don't just do something, sit there,' said Gallagher, proffering the flask to Tom without turning around.

Tom took it and laughed, easing the tension. 'You're such a twat,' he said.

Harry parked down the road from the warehouse, allowing Gallagher and Tom to check the area. Tom waved him forward and closed the gates as Gallagher opened the big warehouse doors. Harry reversed the car in beyond the blackout curtains.

Tom was the last to climb the stairs having stayed to watch outside before entering through the Judas gate.

'Fuck me, someone's been busy,' he said as he reached the top.

The room had been thoroughly swept and Mark had organised three separate sleeping areas rigged with blanket-curtain partitions hung from the beams. Each area had a bed, a canvas chair and a makeshift bedside table made from some small wooden crates that had been stacked downstairs. In the part of the room containing the cupboards and kettle, he'd arranged the remaining chairs around a table he'd created from four more crates topped with a broken door.

'Who's been a busy boy, then?' asked Tom.

'OK, lay off him,' said Gallagher.

'I was just saying. You've done a good job, mate. Any fool can be uncomfortable.'

Mark shuffled on the spot. 'Brew?'

'Good lad,' said Harry. 'I'm bloody parched.'

Gallagher switched on his laptop and opened out the OS map sheet for London North on the workbench. 'Everybody relax for twenty minutes. Then we'll reconvene around Mark's new table.'

He walked over to the brandy bottle near the kettle, picked it up and put it down again. 'Plenty of sugar in mine, please Mark.'

Tom was sitting staring at the ceiling, arms crossed, ignoring the coffee that Mark had placed next to him on the floor.

Mark had moved to his camp bed, staying well out of the centre of the room with its building tension. Gallagher poured over the map by the light of one of the camping lanterns and tapped away at his keyboard.

Tom stood, walked past Gallagher, picked up the wallet he'd brought from Iraq and flung it across the room. The memory stick, keys and beads skidded across the floor planks. He walked over to where they had landed, picked up

260

the memory stick, walked another three steps and threw it hard at the opposite wall.

'What the fuck is all this about? It's driving me mad.'

Gallagher looked over to where the thumb-drive had landed. The casing had cracked down the middle and brick dust lay on the floor around it. He looked at Harry, who was sipping his coffee. Harry raised his eyebrows and shrugged.

'I don't know, mate. Let's go through it again,' said Gallagher.

Tom began to pace. 'I've told you everything. For fuck's sake, we need to do something, sitting here is doing my head in.'

Gallagher walked across the room. He picked up the memory stick and held the plastic device between his thumb and forefinger. 'This is all we've got. This has got to have something to do with it – it must be the key.'

Tom grabbed it from him and threw it against the wall again, dislodging more brick dust. 'It's got some Flip-flop's holiday photos on it, how the fuck is it the key to anything?'

Gallagher walked over to the seating area and sat down, placing his head in his hands.

Tom kicked over a chair and went to lean against the wall.

Harry moved to the chair opposite Gallagher, where he closed his eyes, trying to make sense of everything. When he opened them he looked across at the thumb-drive on the floor. He stood and stretched, then walked over and picked up the now badly fractured casing. As he returned to his seat he pulled at the plastic, which came apart in his hands. 'Well, key or no key, it's properly banjaxed now.'

Mark yawned, walking out into the centre of the room, watching as Harry turned the pieces over in his hands. From where he was standing Mark could see the electronics board attached to the USB connector that had been on the outside of the device.

Harry turned the pieces over again. There was a layer of insulation on which was another circuit board attached to another port – a port that hadn't been visible on the outside.

'Erm, I think you might find this interesting,' Harry said, looking at Gallagher.

'What is it?'

'It's amazing,' said Mark, walking over to Harry.

Tom stopped pacing. 'What's shagging amazing?'

Mark held out his hand for Harry to give him the parts of the device. 'It's a thumb-drive hidden inside a thumb-drive.'

'I'll drive my thumbs into your bloody eye sockets in a minute. What the fuck are you talking about?'

'Tom, calm down,' said Gallagher. 'Mark, carry on.'

'Well, that's it really: someone's hidden a device inside the casing of another device.'

Tom sighed and walked to the brandy bottle next to the kettle. He picked up the cleanest mug he could find and poured a generous measure.

'You know about this stuff?' asked Harry.

'I've done a few courses, read some books. It's really interesting. At the drop-in centres it's either computers or art therapy half the time. I've spent a lot of days in libraries keeping warm and dry.'

'OK, so now we know your specialist subject, Einstein, how does that help us?' asked Tom.

'Let's have a look,' said Mark, pointing at Gallagher's laptop. 'All right, boss?'

Gallagher opened his palm and gestured towards the workbench. 'Be my guest.'

'I don't just want to boot this up without thinking about it first, though,' said Mark.

'OK,' said Gallagher. 'But we're going to have to leave for the meeting.'

'I'll come,' said Mark.

'You're more use here. Anyway, we haven't got enough of these,' Harry said, holding up his pistol. 'You don't want to be standing in the middle of a bone-yard at midnight waiting for the mob to arrive with your dick in your hand, do you?'

'I could keep watch.'

'Or you could break the habit of a lifetime and do what you're asked at the first time of asking,' said Harry, feigning a slap across the back of Mark's head.

Gallagher took a night sight from his rucksack and passed it to Harry.

'You're staying, Mark. Work on the memory stick. It could be what we're looking for.'

* * *

By 23:13 Gallagher, Harry and Tom had left the car in Lonsdale Road. Gallagher entered Paddington Old Cemetery over a gate by the junction with Donaldson Road, while Tom and Harry had headed in the other way entering between the primary school and the fitness centre on Salusbury Road.

Gallagher moved along the south side and took up position behind a large plinth on which stood a statue of an angel guiding a child. A stiff breeze was blowing a light rain across ageing headstones and memorials. Apart from an old fox patrolling its territory, he saw no movement for twenty minutes.

At 23:45 Gallagher spotted two men cautiously make their way east to west from the direction Willesden Road. They moved slowly into the cover of a large monument and then the shorter of the two gingerly walked forward into the central area of the cemetery designated for the meet.

Gallagher scanned the cemetery through the thermal-imaging camera and counted six heat sources, in addition to the man in the middle, all of adult-male size hiding among the stones within ten metres of the meeting point. He whispered the various positions across his radio and Harry acknowledged each one with two clicks, before identifying another three men hiding north-east of his and Tom's position.

The man in the middle turned and looked back in the direction he had come as he took his phone from his pocket. It looked like he'd received a text message. Gallagher saw him move his head from side to side, replace the phone in his pocket and jog back to his hiding position. Within seconds, all the heat sources withdrew and Gallagher watched as they headed for different sections of the road running along the eastern edge of the graveyard.

Harry reported a similar withdrawal from the north-east.

'What's happening?' asked Tom in Gallagher's earpiece.

'Don't know. Hold your position.'

They waited another fifteen minutes and saw no other movement.

Harry transmitted. 'Something spooked them. We should leave.'

'Agreed,' whispered Gallagher. As he stood he felt his phone vibrate in his pocket. It was Connie's number.

'We fucking warned you,' said a voice. 'We warned you about calling the Rozzers. Now the girl is really going to get it, you stupid bastard.'

Gallagher leaned against the marble plinth. 'What are you talking about? We were in the cemetery waiting. We didn't call the police.'

'Fuck off. Don't take me for a twat. There were at least two fucking surveillance vehicles on the Willesden Road and they're just the ones our man spotted. You've fucked it mate.'

* * *

'Bannerman?' Harry asked.

'Must have been. He's either put a tracker on my phone, Connie's or both.'

'We're screwed then. They could be following us back to the warehouse now.'

They pulled into a supermarket car park and Harry switched off the engine. 'Even if they haven't got the car, they've got your phone signal.'

'I've been thinking about that, why wait for us up there when they could have hit us in a building away from prying eyes? I don't think they've got the warehouse.'

He turned in his seat. 'Tom, I want you to send a text to Connie's phone. Say that it's the new contact number and we think my phone is compromised. They might not buy it, but at least I can ditch this bloody thing. They'd have been too suspicious before, so at least there's one positive.'

'Positive? Are you fucking mental?'

'For Christ's sake, just do it man,' shouted Harry.

'OK, OK, I'll do it now.'

Gallagher reached inside his coat for his hip flask. 'Harry, drive down through Maida Vale. We'll head just beyond Warwick Avenue Tube and I'll chuck it in the canal.'

'Right, boss,' said Harry.

'Then we'll head back to the warehouse. Mark may have a lead.'

TWELVE

Mark stretched out his shoulder and then pointed to the laptop. 'It's a password protected memory stick.'

'So we're still fucked,' said Tom.

'No, because I cracked the password – piece of piss. I just downloaded a USB Sniffer.'

'A what?' asked Harry.

'This memory stick has FIPs certified encryption. You see them advertised as military-grade kit, but most of them are far from it. Some of them encrypt the password to the chip, this isn't one of them.'

'Go on,' said Gallagher.

'With the sniffer, you can check what's being sent to the drive. The software asks the drive if the password is correct but then unlocks the drive using a fixed string, so I used a dictionary attack program to find out what it was.'

'It's been a long night, Einstein,' said Tom.

'So you've unlocked it?' asked Harry.

'Yep, the dictionary attack didn't work on its own but I tried a couple of other things and cracked it. Not surprising as most brute force decoders can unscramble a data-encryption-standard transmission, like the banks use, in about five minutes.'

Tom looked at Gallagher. 'Have a word, will you?'

'Just cut to the chase, Mark.'

'That's when it got really interesting, because then nothing happened. I did the old reboot and guess what? It's an operating system.'

Harry looked at Tom and then back at Mark. 'I'm not sure I'm going to be able to stop him if you don't get on with it.'

'Well, that's about it so far. I didn't want to open it up too much until you were here, but I've had a look at one of the other programs on it. It's an S-Tool but nothing off the shelf. This is custom-made hard-core programming.'

'That's it,' said Tom. 'I'm going to lamp you!'

Harry stepped between them.

'It's a tool for hiding and finding data; it's steganographic,' Mark said quickly.

Harry stepped aside. 'OK, Tom, get in the queue. Mark, it's been a long day and my patience is wearing thin.'

* * *

In a Croydon bedsit, Faaz sat opposite the hard rectangular case. He'd been sitting staring at it for the last hour. He knew what it was. He'd opened it when he'd arrived at the flat the evening before.

Faaz had told his parents in Tipton that he was going to stay with friends from university for a couple of weeks. And

269

he prayed that he'd be back with them after it had been done. He was starting a new job in a month's time. His life was just beginning. He didn't want to go to prison. He certainly didn't want to die. *Insha'Allah.*

He'd been waiting for the call. He'd kept his head down. He'd stopped attending a particular mosque, as instructed. He was ready, but he didn't want to die.

Faaz leaned forward and clicked open the case. Inside was a Beretta Sniper: a conventional Mauser-type bolt action rifle – 7.62 – with a five-round magazine capacity and telescopic sight. The rifle was lying in its component parts, ready for assembly. He closed the lid of the case and rested back in his chair.

Now he had to wait again. The mobile phone had been lying on the case when he'd arrived. The bedsit was well stocked with food, spare clothing and cash. He'd been told to bring nothing: no phone, no identification, no bank cards, nothing. He didn't even have a return train ticket. Next to the phone was a set of numbered keys for a building he'd never seen. Instructions would follow.

Now he had to wait to be given an address for the firing point, along with the targeting details. The code system was simple enough and a pad and pencil lay next to the laptop computer that he'd found on his arrival.

He would try to sleep. He just had to wait.

* * *

'Like the typists in a court?' asked Harry.

'That's stenography. Steganography is hiding stuff in other stuff. It means the art of hidden writing. If you encrypt something there's obviously something hidden, which is why steganography can be more effective.'

'OK, I get it. How does this help us?'

'You can do it with computer files. You just stick the steganographic coding inside a transport layer.'

'Of course you do. I really am going to punch you in a minute,' said Tom.

'Like a document file or an image. You adjust a pixel here and there, changing the colour or something to indicate something else – or you can actually insert a message. Post it to a bulletin board, a blog, or newsgroup and Bob's your uncle.'

'Who'd use something like that?' asked Harry.

'Criminals, terrorists, spooks, government agencies, they're all at it. Cryptography can be really hard to crack, right? But it's obvious something has been encoded. With stego the transmission might never be detected. The Americans use something called inference tracking to build up a picture of terrorist activity by following encrypted traffic. The codes might not be cracked but the activity can be monitored for clues. If you use encryption it stands out to

271

the NSA like a sore thumb. Using stego, having covered your tracks, you can be confident that no one is looking at your traffic for anything hidden in the stuff you're using. Al Qaeda has been ahead of the game for years. The Yanks had hundreds of al Qaeda emails to sift through a couple of months before 9/11 but found nothing because the terrorists stuck to open codes.'

Harry pulled up a chair. 'And this is a new thing?'

'Nope. The earliest examples come from ancient Greece. Like shaving slaves' heads, tattooing a message and letting the hair grow back. That's not a great example but think invisible ink or microdots. The internet just makes it possible to hide shitloads of stuff in with billions of pieces of data. Take Facebook as an example: it's got something like a billion active users who are all uploading photos and all sorts of other bollocks. That's only one example; it's a big bastard of a haystack. I love this stuff.'

'And you've found something hidden?' asked Gallagher.

'The operating system directs the browser to a site full of photos. That's all I've got so far.'

'Why is that so fascinating?' Harry asked, retying his bootlace.

'Look,' said Mark as he began to roll a cigarette. 'If you've got, say, a JPEG image like these, they use a discreet cosine transform to change the pixel blocks. The bits that aren't that important can have a message inside without any visible changes to the image.'

'So you search that lot? How many do you reckon there are?'

'Three thousand, give or take.'

'Three thousand? Brilliant,' said Tom, walking away.

'OK,' said Harry. 'If you're right and I was the bloke who was meant to pick up the messages, how would I know which photos to pick?'

'I dunno,' said Mark, fumbling for his lighter. 'I was just explaining how it might work. Mind if I go for a quick smoke?'

'I might start smoking again if I have to listen to any more of this,' said Harry.

Mark stood at the top of the stairs and turned. 'I'll be back in a minute. There's something else I need to tell you about that S-Tool program, the one you use to decode the transport files.'

Harry rolled his eyes. 'Yeah, hurry back, I can't wait.'

Gallagher stood up and looked at Mark. 'Photos.'

'Yeah, photos. Three thousand photos in some mad mosaic,' said Tom from his camp bed.

Gallagher ignored him. 'No, the photos: the photos on the original memory stick. Mark you're a genius.'

'Who'd have thought it?' said Harry.

'Fucking get on with it!' shouted Tom.

It was morning. The room was cold. The noise outside had been building for three hours as she drifted in and out of consciousness. The morning before, they'd lifted her hooded and gagged into the boot of a car and she'd heard two new voices. The boot was small and she'd still felt sick after the injections and the lack of food. She'd thought she'd suffocate in the enclosed space, with her legs folded, further restricting her ability to breathe. She'd had a surging desire to try to escape as she smelt the fresh air and wood smoke on the way out of the house, but she was securely bound and knew they wouldn't hesitate to beat her if she tried.

Now she was somewhere new. It was difficult to tell how long the journey had taken. She'd passed out a couple of times but woke to hear heavy traffic and the sound of what could only be moving through London. The smells, too, or rather that smell – only London smelt like that. But why had they bothered to bring her wherever they had brought her?

Connie tensed as she heard the door open. There were whispered voices as footsteps sounded on the room's bare boards. Her body was racked with pain in the cold air, her nostrils full of the bitter smell of dried vomit and the damp cotton of the bag covering her head. She was sitting on a hard wooden chair that seemed to sigh at her slightest

274

movement. Her wrists were bound in plasticuffs behind the seat back, her ankles were zip-tied to the front chair legs and a length of tape covered her mouth. The hardest thing was the lack of conversation. She liked her own company but not having anyone to speak to, even for a minute, was driving her mad.

The room had fallen quiet after the door had shut, but she sensed that there were at least three other people now in the room. She could hear the rumbling of traffic, voices, horns, the airbrakes of buses, all somewhere below her and to her left.

The floorboards creaked and she counted the footsteps as someone walked towards her. She reached the count of twelve. The room was quiet again but for the sound of low breathing near to her. Then the heavy blow struck the outside of her left knee. The shock and pain caused her to cry out. The balance was tipped and she heard herself sobbing.

'Morning, darling – sleep well?' asked Ray the laughing mask, as he took the bag off her head and ripped the tape from her mouth.

Connie blinked in the harsh fluorescent light. The windows, stretching along the left-hand side of the room, were covered with steel shutters fixed beyond what remained of the glass in the frames. Faded velour curtains hung from sagging poles either side of each one, matching the worn red fabric of the seating around the edges of the large room.

Behind her, though she couldn't see it, was a small bar, its grill locked shut, the hand pumps tarnished with age and lack of use.

She screwed up her eyes, looking past the masked man who had hit her. The tears rolled down her face and she tried to sniff up the mucus that was dribbling from her nose before it reached her lips. Behind the man, near the door in the far corner, were two other men wearing balaclavas, both with their arms crossed.

'Your boyfriend doesn't care if you live or die,' said Ray. 'Did you know that?'

Connie took a breath to control the sobs. 'He's not my boyfriend – I told you.'

Ray placed the baseball bat on the floor. 'That's OK: I'll be your boyfriend. But we've still got the problem vis-à-vis we haven't found your twat of a brother.'

Connie lowered her chin but the slap connected with her left cheek regardless. Ray clicked his fingers and gestured to one of the men behind him. 'Next time I ask you something and you fuck me about,' he said, pointing at the bat, 'I'm going to whack a kneecap. You can choose which one if you like.'

Vince took a mobile phone from his pocket and handed it to Ray, avoiding eye contact with Connie. Ray stared at him for a moment and then held the phone in front of her face. 'Look at me.'

276

He slapped her again.

'Recognise this? It's your phone, but there's a new number in it: your brother's. The van man fucked up, which is why you got a slap for breakfast and not a bacon sandwich.'

Connie stared up at him, blinking away her tears.

Ray leaned in close. 'My colleague here is going to dial the number and tell your brother we'll be calling again in two hours with details of a meeting. He'll have time to sort himself out and lose your boyfriend. Then you're going to tell him to come alone. Any sign of the van man or the police and they'll never find your body. Understand?'

Connie nodded.

Vince rang the number and said his piece before holding the phone to Connie's ear.

'Tom? Tom? It's so good to hear your voice.'

Ray jabbed a warning finger at her, walked around Vince to her other side and picked up the baseball bat.

'Tom, they want you to come alone; they don't want you to bring James or anyone else.'

She braced herself for what she knew would follow.

'Tom, don't come, please don't come.'

Ray shoved Vince away and brought the end of the bat round hard to the side of Connie's left knee. She screamed and Ray grabbed Vince's arm, pulling the handset near her as she continued to cry out. Then he grabbed the phone.

'Now, now,' he said. 'There's no need for that sort of language, Mr Edwards. Be ready, bring what we need and come alone – or I'll make sure your sister wishes she was dead.'

* * *

Tom was visibly shaken by the call and had taken to pacing the room – mainly to hide the tears in his eyes, thought Gallagher. As Tom moved up and down the bare boards he relayed some of the details of the conversation and let out his rage at Connie's screams.

Gallagher took control. 'We're going to have to get organised. We need to be ready to move as soon as we get the details. The meeting could be anywhere and any plan of attack will be on the hoof. Now my phone's been ditched, we should have the bastards to ourselves.'

'What do you want me to do, boss?' asked Mark.

'I need you to keep working on that. This won't be over when we've got Connie, we need to know who's behind this and why.'

Mark turned back to the laptop as Gallagher began checking and packing equipment. Harry had gone to the toilet at the other end of the room. Tom walked to the workbench where Mark was seated.

'Fancy a brew?'

Mark looked surprised. 'Er, yeah, thanks.'

Tom returned with the coffee, moving one of the map sheets to clear a space. As Mark checked his notebook and then peered intently at the screen, taking a sip from the mug, Tom made a show of looking at the map. He was trying to find the wallet. It wasn't there and he realised that Gallagher must have taken it.

An hour and a half later, Tom felt his phone vibrate in his pocket. Gallagher and Harry had gone to the lock-up to fetch the motorbike. Mark remained busy at the keyboard. Tom moved quickly to the room with the toilet and closed the door, running the cold tap so that the water splashed loudly in the sink.

The voice on the phone gave him a location and a time, reiterating that he was to bring the wallet and to come alone. He agreed the terms and ended the call. Back in the main room, he walked to where Mark was sitting.

'How you getting on?'

'Fine,' said Mark, engrossed in the contents of the laptop screen.

'Nice one,' said Tom, scanning the map for a route to the meeting point.

'You feeling OK?' asked Mark, not looking up.

'Actually, I need the bog again: something's going straight through me.'

279

'You haven't been drinking the water out of the taps, have you?'

'That'll be it, yeah, I forgot.'

Tom shut the door to the toilet and ran the tap again. Opening the window, he looked left. The nearest part of the old cast-iron fire escape was five or six feet away. He climbed outside the window and faced inwards. The iron drainpipe was rusting and he didn't trust his weight to the bracket directly to his right. He took a deep breath and jumped sideways, throwing his right arm through the gap between two of the open metal steps of the fire escape. The iron clanged and he hung for a moment before hooking the other arm over. Reaching forward, he pulled himself up into the gap and reached out to grip the edge of the next step down, allowing him to pull himself through and on to the staircase. He went down four steps on his belly, before bringing his legs up and around into a seated position. He listened for a few seconds, descended to the bottom of the fire escape and headed away from the side of the warehouse.

There was a hole in the fencing, which he crawled through before running across the vacant plot adjacent to Frankie's land. He continued running to the cover of a concrete storeroom, waited and listened and then sauntered over to the gate located next to a service road. He checked the area for cars and people and then climbed the gate where the

280

barbed wire above had become detached, rolling over the top to reach down, holding the central mesh and throwing his legs up and over. He landed feet together, knees bent. He checked left, right, behind and moved off towards the main road.

The weight of the pistol in the small of his back was comforting, but he felt the anxiety building beneath the adrenaline. If the memory stick that Mark was working with was the key, then he had nothing to bargain with, nothing to exchange – but he doubted that an exchange was on the cards. He'd have to think on his feet and get Connie to safety any way he could. In all probability, she wouldn't be brought to the meeting. So that's the plan, he thought: meet kidnappers, get kidnapped.

Plan A wasn't great, he had to admit, but he was on his own and it was the only plan he had. Now he needed to find a car to steal.

* * *

Gallagher downed the wine in his cup. He was running out of supplies.

'I still can't believe the stupid bastard went off on his own.'

'What now? Did Frankie's boys see where he went?' asked Harry.

'No, they had no reason to follow him. They're watching the place for people arriving, not leaving. Tom's not answering his phone, so, for now, we listen to what Mark has to say and see if we can work it from the other side. I'm pretty sure that we still have what they want.'

'Whoever they are,' said Harry, moving the bike helmet off a chair. 'And if we have, it's not looking too good for Connie and Tom from where I'm standing.'

Gallagher poured himself another drink and walked with Harry to where Mark was waiting to brief them.

'You were right about the original photos,' said Mark. 'I've found three of the images and they all have hidden data.'

'What have you got?' asked Harry.

'Like I said, it's using what's known as an amnesic system independent of the laptop's normal operating system. It works on a hidden network by bouncing your traffic around a global network of relays. It stops anyone tracking you or finding your physical location via your IP address.'

'And?'

'That way you can do what you like without being tracked.'

'Like the Dark Web? I've read about that,' Gallagher said. 'Isn't it full of paedophiles and crooks?'

'And gunrunners, assassins, drug dealers, spooks, nutters. Yeah, you've got the Dark Web, the Deep Web, the Hidden

Net – whatever you want to call it. But that's not the point of it. Look, every time you use the internet, every picture, every document, every email you've ever sent or received, it's all still out there somewhere stored on a server, recorded forever.'

Harry laughed. 'Don't tell Lynne that.'

Mark ignored him. 'This way those in the know avoid the advertisers, the police and prying governments. Did you know that in Russia any encrypted file found on your computer can land you in the nick? Doesn't matter if it's just your shopping list.'

'You have been spending a lot of time in the bloody library, haven't you?' said Harry.

Mark smiled and continued with his explanation. 'Your supermarket tracks your shopping preferences, advertisers see your search terms and bombard you with targeted adverts. Some people don't like that. Journalists, bloggers, activists, whistle-blowers, all sorts of people get off grid. People in countries with strict government surveillance go deep and off radar. They encrypt their data; they route their traffic through proxy servers using Tor: the onion router. They say what they want and stay safe behind a shield of anonymity. That's what this is: it's a shield created by the operating system. But these photos are out in the open. They aren't hidden deep on some dodgy Dark Web platform. Look, it's like someone's photo blog.'

'Fascinating,' said Harry. 'But how do you decode the hidden stuff?'

'Along with the operating system, the hidden memory stick has the S-Tool. You can download them off the internet, but this one isn't off the shelf. Someone was serious about hiding stuff in plain sight. Without this program you'd have no chance of getting at the hidden data.'

'So what is it you've got exactly?' Gallagher asked.

'Not much. I'm still playing with the S-Tool. I'll keep working at it.'

Harry laughed. 'And you ended up in the infantry how?'

'I wanted to join the Royal Signals. I scored high enough, but the recruiting sergeant said they were full up. Not to worry, he said, the infantry has got loads of spaces. I couldn't face another few months kicking around waiting, so I signed on.'

'I think he might have been telling you porkies. You should have said it's the "Scaley Backs" or nothing.'

'I know,' said Mark. 'I'd like to meet that fat bastard on a dark night. I'd have been a good Bleep.'

'But then we wouldn't be sitting here all cosy,' said Harry, lifting the collar of his coat against the cold.

Mark grinned. 'Made my granddad's day.'

'Oh yeah,' said Harry. 'He was one of ours, wasn't he? He's a Chelsea Pensioner now, didn't you say?'

284

'He is, yeah. He wants me to take him out for a beer, but I'm brassic.'

'Once this is all sorted,' said Gallagher, 'we'll all take him for a beer.'

Mark grinned again. 'That'd be bloody brilliant, boss – he'd love that.'

'So would I,' said Harry. 'But I reckon we've got a way to go yet.'

Gallagher gave a weary nod. 'In the meantime, I'm going to call Bannerman. Harry, would you drive me to a phone box a few miles away once we've finished prepping the kit?'

'Sure, what have you got in mind?'

'We're pissing in the wind here – no offence, Mark. We haven't done anything illegal and we need help with this.'

'You trust Bannerman, after he blew the cemetery meet?' Harry asked.

'We still don't know what happened there. It's either Bannerman or a walk into the nearest cop shop. At least this way might save us some time. If he tries to do me over, I'll know for sure.'

* * *

Tom had found a Vauxhall Corsa to steal, half a mile from the warehouse. Driving east, he'd crossed the river at the QEII Bridge. He'd driven along the Purfleet By-pass, skirted

285

Romford and picked up the A104, ensuring that he'd avoided the motorways and big town centres en route to Epping Forest.

He'd followed the Epping New Road, turned left on to Fairmead Road, left along a track and through a gate. The track took him between a group of pollarded oaks interspersed with Hornbeam, Holly, Rowan and Maple trees, leading him up the high ground overlooking Chingford Plain to a large clearing.

He was now sheltering in the trees as the rain swept in from the south west. He'd been searching through the area for half an hour. Adrenaline pumped through him.

He heard the VW Transporter pull up at the entrance to the clearing, followed by a blue Land Rover Discovery.

Tom stepped out from the trees and into view, his Browning held in his right hand at his side, clearly visible to the two men who stood at the front of the VW and the one standing behind the open driver's door of the Land Rover. Both vehicles had privacy glass and it was impossible to tell from his angle whether there were more men hiding inside. The man to the left of the van had a phone to his ear and a Colt Python revolver cradled across the bend of his elbow pointing at Tom. All of them were wearing balaclavas.

The Land Rover bloke, carrying a CZ100 9mm pistol, walked forward, the gun in his right hand at his side, mirroring Tom's posture.

'There's only one way this can go,' said Dave.

'And how's that?' asked Tom.

'Toss the gun, show the wallet and walk forward with your hands on your head.'

'Or?'

'One way out of here or die where you stand, shortly before this gentleman to my right gets to know your sister a bit better and then digs her a shallow grave.'

Tom raised the Browning, pointing it at Dave and then at Ray. Dave took another step forward, the pistol still at his side.

'Look, this can all be over and done with today. See it as a simple business transaction. We get what we want, you get your sister.'

'Simples,' said Ray, in what he thought sounded like a Russian accent.

Dave kept looking at Tom, who lowered his gun.

'Ignore him: he's an arsehole. Me and you can work this out. My boss isn't interested in you or Connie – it's just business.'

At the sound of Connie's name, Tom tensed and brought the Browning up into a two-handed grip.

'I'll fucking slot you,' shouted Ray, raising what Tom recognised as a Baikal IZH-79.

'Shut it,' said Dave, still looking at Tom. 'He will, though. Don't be stupid. Drop the gun, you're coming with us, you know that.'

Once Tom had dropped the gun and knelt on the ground he was gripped by two of the men.

'Search him,' said Dave.

'Shite,' said Ray. 'He hasn't got it on him. Silly Bollocks, check the car.'

Tom was loaded into the back of the van, his ankles bound and the zip-tie secured with rope to the tie at his wrists.

'Nothing,' reported Vince.

Dave shrugged. 'Fuck it, let's go, we've been here too long.'

The van drove slowly over the gravel path at the end of the track and then turned right on to the smoother surface of Fairmead Road, heading back the way Tom had come. Keep calm, he thought. The hood and gag were conspiring to send him into a claustrophobic meltdown. Stay calm. He tried to concentrate on the turns made by the van, to keep a sense of how long the journey was taking but, sense-deprived as he was, it was hopeless. What was the point? He didn't know the area anyway.

* * *

The van stopped. The van travelled forward in first, then stopped again. He'd heard a shutter door rolled down somewhere to the rear. The back door of the van opened and he was yanked out and dropped on to a cold surface – smooth, concrete. The rope attaching his ankles to his wrists behind his back was untied and the cramp screamed through his muscles as his legs straightened. His hands and ankles were still secured but the pain in his knees and back eased a little.

Tom was lifted and dragged forward. His head was dipped by a hand and he thought he passed through a low opening before being pulled down a short flight of steps. Pulled forwards again, he was thrown against a wall. Hands on his shoulders forced him into a squatting position as he tried to make sense of his surroundings. The hood and gag were making it hard to breathe. The adrenaline and limited oxygen were fragmenting his thought processes. He struggled to control his breathing, trying to bring himself under control.

He heard the rasp of a handcuff opening, which was then fixed to his right wrist. The plasticuff was cut, his hands moved to the front of his body and his other wrist cuffed. He pulled and heard the chink of metal on metal. His fingers found a pipe attached to the wall, to which he was now attached. Three pairs of feet shuffled around him. Something heavy and metallic was dragged across the concrete floor to his left. A door opened and closed to his right. The gag was tight across his mouth through the bag but not as tight as the ankle tie, which was cutting off the blood to his feet. From the left came a sound like a toolbox lid opening. His arms were forward in line with his face. He sank back on his haunches as his exposed flank took the full force of something heavy. He grunted and tried to form an image of the implement that had struck him. He tried to breathe slower. It was a bloody big spanner and he was pretty sure it had cracked a rib.

'Relax,' said a voice. 'I'll be back in five minutes.'

* * *

'What do you reckon to this, boss?' asked Mark.

'It looks like a word-search puzzle,' said Harry.

'Have you found anything else like this?' Gallagher asked.

Mark flicked through some pages of the notepad. 'Yeah, look, these other blocks and some number strings – horizontal and vertical.'

Gallagher looked through the pages. 'I'm not sure about these short sequences, but these blocks and strings could be the basis of a one-time pad.'

'Right,' said Harry. 'It looks like BATCO.'

'Exactly,' said Gallagher. 'And it's unbreakable without the right setting.'

Mark stood up and began to roll a cigarette. He looked in his tobacco packet at the few bits remaining and put it away. 'So why would anyone go to all this trouble to get back a hidden memory stick that takes you to hidden messages that no one can read?'

'Someone can, obviously,' said Harry.

Gallagher picked up his pistol and placed it in its holster. 'We're wasting our time. I need to see what Bannerman has to say. This is really starting to piss me off.'

'Well, we're no closer to finding Connie. We've lost Tom and that bloody thing is just giving us more puzzles to stare at,' said Harry. 'What's the plan?'

THIRTEEN

Bannerman had finally managed to get through to Flic. He wasn't happy. Her tone had been abrupt, to say the least. He'd been given the brush-off. She'd more or less told him to mind his own business. He was in danger of getting in over his head, things had moved out of his league. She was grateful, of course, for his earlier assistance but that was to be the furthest extent of his involvement. It would be noted and praise would be flowing his way once the situation had been dealt with. She'd softened at the end of the call. They'd have dinner at some point in the undefined future.

He wasn't sure which hurt most, his personal or professional pride. Fuck it: it was both and he didn't like it.

He climbed the steps to the door of his club, the dark sky tinting the tall Georgian windows. He nodded to the doorman and walked into a large reception area. He waved away an offer to take his coat and crossed the lobby with its oil paintings of members past, great and good. His reflection greeted him in the huge gilt-edged mirror at the foot of the ornate staircase. He looked tired, but better than he felt.

At the top of the stairs, he walked through the door to the members' bar and ordered a gin and tonic. Drink in hand, he found a chair in one of the rooms off the main bar area. A grandfather clock ticked its stately tick and a fire in the grate flickered in the late afternoon gloom. Peace at last. Voices carried through from the bar, but he had the small room to himself. He eased back into the old leather of the chair and sipped his drink, closing his eyes to listen to the clock and the crackle of the fire.

Through the growing fug of his easeful state Bannerman heard his name. He ignored it and stretched out his legs, holding on to the moment of calm for as long as he could.

'Sandy?'

He opened an eye.

'Working you too hard, are they?'

'Perry, how are you?' asked Bannerman, not caring how, who or what Perry Fairbrass was or wasn't doing.

'Good, yes, splendid, thanks. Haven't seen you here in an age, what brings you in off the streets at this hour?'

'In need of sanctuary.'

'Far from the madding crowd?'

Bannerman sat up and took another sip. 'Quite.'

'Mind if I join you?'

Bannerman gestured to the seat opposite, an exact copy of the high wing-backed leather chair that he occupied, flanking the other side of the fire. 'And you?'

Fairbrass sat and adjusted his trouser creases. Perry didn't get his suits from Savile Row, his shirts weren't hand-stitched. He looked like an absent-minded academic who had

293

found himself surprised that he was wearing a suit at all, but he was sharp in other ways.

'Meeting one of the colonial cousins,' Fairbrass said, easing back in the chair.

'An agency man?'

Fairbrass nodded. 'He'll be here in a few minutes. I wanted to enjoy a drink in peace before he arrived.'

'How are things south of the river?' asked Bannerman, still struggling to feign interest.

'Oh, you know, fighting the good fight.'

Silence descended between them as they both stared into the fire. The quiet was broken by the arrival of a tall man in a well-cut dark suit and polished brogues. The man nodded to Bannerman.

'Perry, good to see you.'

The man's quiet voice belied his solid stature, close-cropped grey hair and craggy features.

'You guys watching Ranger TV?' he asked, pointing at the fire.

'Just the same old repeats, I'm afraid,' said Fairbrass. 'John, please join us. This is Sandy Bannerman, one of our friends across the river. Sandy, this is John Kinsella, one of our friends across the ocean.'

Bannerman mustered a weak smile in acknowledgement of the even weaker wordplay, stood and shook Kinsella's hand.

'If you don't mind, Sandy,' said the American, 'I need to steal Perry away. I can't stay long, there's an embassy function this evening and I'll need an hour to fix my bow tie.'

'Please, take my seat,' replied Bannerman. 'It's time I was getting on. I hope that we can become better acquainted at our next meeting.' As he stood, his phone began to ring.

'You'll be up before the committee,' said Fairbrass, wagging a finger. 'You know the rules.' He looked at Kinsella. 'The old guard aren't too keen on the march of progress and a ringing phone is more frowned upon than cuffing a waiter.'

Kinsella smiled and made space for Bannerman to pass.

Bannerman waved apologetically and answered the call as he entered the bar, ignoring the critical glare of the assembled members sitting in their cloistered dotage. The information was relayed swiftly by the JTAC duty officer. A car bomb had exploded in Manette Street, between Charing Cross Road and Greek Street. Three workmen in Orange Yard had been killed in the blast that had ignited propane cylinders being used to lay asphalt. Four other people were reported seriously injured and many more had been hurt by flying debris when the surrounding buildings took the force of the blast in the narrow street. Foyle's bookshop, on the corner, was still burning.

A suspicious car had been found an hour earlier in White City. The bomb disposal unit were working on a device thought to be similar in size to the one in Manette Street. Traffic was building in the grid-locked area and the police were reporting chaos at local underground stations. Two other reports of abandoned vehicles were being dealt with in St John's Wood and Waterloo East but it was unclear if these were related to the bombs.

He took the last three steps of the staircase in one bound. Two former cabinet ministers, talking by the front door, looked disapprovingly as he barged past them into the street.

'I'll be there in a few minutes,' said Bannerman, waving down a black cab.

* * *

Traffic Warden Mandy England – known as 'Come on' to the officers at the station – approached the black Mercedes parked on double yellow lines on the corner outside the Waterstones bookshop in Richmond. A bus driver sounded his horn and raised his hands in disbelief before manoeuvring his vehicle around the obstruction. The car was a soft-top and had seen better days. She checked the tax disc. It was in date. A scrawled note on the dashboard read: 'Gone for petrol.'

Pillock, thought Mandy, why not push it around the corner away from the bloody junction? It was always a busy road, but the traffic was only going to get worse in the next hour. She looked to her left and saw two men smoking at the top of the steps to a cellar bar while they watched her go about her work. Laughing at the size of her arse in her uniform trousers, no doubt. She didn't care. She was used to it. Anyway, she liked her bum and so did her husband Kev.

Continuing to make her way around the car, she took a note of the registration and photographed its position in relation to the curb, the junction and the pedestrian crossing. The driver's window was half open. It was threatening to rain and it'd serve the owner right if he had to drive home on a wet seat. She looked in through the window. The key was in the ignition – a lone key, no fob, no house keys. The car was empty: no sweet wrappers, drinks cans, coffee cups, maps or bits of paper.

The two men had returned downstairs to the bar. Mandy waited for a young woman with a double buggy to weave her way through a group of shoppers chatting on the pavement and then took up position where the men had been smoking just inside the railings out of the wind. She looked back across the road at the car and reached for the radio clipped to her stab-proof vest.

The light was so bright and the glass so sharp that it didn't dawn on her that she could have been so injured, so badly, so quickly.

The shimmering glass seemed to fall silently, glinting like snow as the dullness of evening began to wrap itself around the town. The smoke in the road changed colour, swirling and pulsing around the flames dancing in the hot wind. Figures seemed to pass through the billowing clouds in slow motion. The shop fronts looked different from where she was lying. She felt different.

Mandy recognised one of the faces leaning over her and then the other. It was the two smoking men. They were touching her. Why were they touching her? Then there was a voice, a man's voice telling her that she'd be OK. Then more noise, dull but recognisable: alarms, women screaming, children crying, shouts, sirens in the distance. She looked at the man cradling her head in his hands. She tried to smile but saw the sadness in his eyes and the fear in the face of his friend. The pain in her ears was unbearable, a piercing whine of knitting-needle intensity, modulated by the dull shouts of those assisting the wounded and the urgent sounds of the sirens growing nearer. She could smell an earthy smell. No, she could taste a metallic smell. She'd never tasted a smell like that before. What was burning?

She watched a tear roll down the face of the man holding her head. She thought of Kev. The pavement was cold. She was cold but the noise began to lessen and it was a relief, as quiet descended with the darkness of dusk, to be able to sleep.

The first paramedic team to arrive surveyed the damage and began to put their procedures into action. Steve Moore carried his rescue bag up the street. Burned and bleeding survivors were walking by him towards the sirens, moving towards a sound that told them help was coming, away from the smoke and flames, the blood-stained glass – moving as far away as they could stumble from the familiar corner of a familiar street where death and chaos now reigned.

An elderly woman was sitting in a shop doorway. She looked like she'd been turned to stone. She was covered in dust and still wearing her glasses but the glass had shattered inwards. It was sticking out of her eyes. He couldn't tell, as he approached her, if she was alive or dead. She was dead.

He moved closer to the immediate vicinity of the blast. He knew about the risk of secondary devices but he had a job to do. A young man was lying several feet away. Steve jogged over to the casualty, unhooking his medi-pack from his shoulder, but then saw that the boy had lost an arm and a leg. He had no face. The lower jaw had gone and the face and scalp had been ripped off. What remained was lying in a thick pool of blood and dust.

He glanced back at his colleague, Tris, who had stopped to tend to a woman who was struggling to lift herself from the floor. The young mother was rocking the remains of a pushchair back and forth next to a wrecked litter bin. The front of the buggy had been blown away with its occupant. The woman hadn't seemed to have noticed that her left arm was missing.

As he got closer to the burning car, Steve tried to take in the scene. It was a grotesque mosaic of glass, blood and body parts. He could identify arms and legs, shoes, a handbag, lumps of intestine. There was a child's lunchbox and an exercise book lying open in the gutter, but he couldn't see anyone that he could treat. Then he saw two men leaning over a casualty at the top of some steps to a cellar bar, next to some mangled railings, and made his way over. He looked down at the woman lying between them.

He threw up.

* * *

Bannerman walked along the blue carpet of the basement corridor at Thames House and took out his ID to swipe through the card reader next to the unmarked door of JTAC. His phone rang.

'Owen, where are you?'

'We need to meet,' said Gallagher.

300

'Agreed but now isn't a good time, I'm afraid. You've seen the news?'

'No, why?'

'Switch on the news and call me back in two hours. I have to go.' He placed the phone back in his jacket.

Inside the ops room he was greeted by the duty officer, Gemma Godrevy.

'Gee Gee, what have we got?' he asked, as he looked behind her at the monitors covering the back wall.

'Since we spoke there's been an explosion in Crouch End. We think the bomber was killed in that one. Also, a device exploded in Richmond outside the Waterstones – another car bomb.'

'Another bookshop? Casualties?'

'Thirty-seven confirmed dead but it's difficult to tell before they've matched up all the body parts. Ninety injured at the last count. Massive damage to property and chaos on the roads for miles around.'

'Any warning?'

'None, like the others.'

'The Manette Street bomb, anything from the Congestion Charge cameras – any facial-recognition matches?'

'Nothing. The bomber is probably a clean skin but the cameras might have pinged him. Once we get more on the car make and model, we can start looking at camera footage of the area to see if we can spot it arriving. The bookshop won't be able to give us anything from their CCTV for a while.'

'So we've got eight square miles of Congestion Charge cameras able to track known criminals via facial-recognition software, several hundred ANPR cameras linked to police databases and someone has managed not only to have driven a car bomb into central London but has walked away?'

'That's about the size of it, for the moment at least. It's chaos. All our resources are stretched to the limit, both here and out on the ground. We'll pick him up but it'll take time.'

'You'd bloody hope we'd pick him up. The average Londoner is caught on CCTV hundreds of bloody times a day. Jesus. Any intel?'

'Nothing. GCHQ, NSA, MI6 and the CIA are analysing data from the Echelon feed, but report no recent chatter that would indicate any hit of this kind and nothing remotely juicy in the last few days.'

'What's the analysis of the modus?'

'Take your pick of any number of attack templates, from the IRA to al Qaeda via all stops in between. For all we know, it could have been the bloody Basque separatists.'

* * *

Gallagher carried a camping chair across the room to where the laptop was showing rolling news coverage of the bombings.

'Who do you reckon's behind it?' Mark asked.

'It could be any number of groups but, whoever it is, they know what they're doing.'

'They say that there are already more casualties than 7/7.'

Gallagher stretched. 'I can't see it being Ireland-related but it's a step up if it's home-grown Islamists. It's like George Orwell said: "a complex weapon makes the strong stronger, while a simple weapon – so long as there is no answer to it – gives claws to the weak." The car bomb is a very simple weapon.'

'It's a bloody mess, whichever way you look at it,' said Mark. 'I'm going for a piss and a smoke.'

Gallagher nodded and continued to watch the screen. A car smouldered to the rear of the camera shot. He thought of his mother as the picture filled with ambulances and scurrying members of the emergency services. Walking to the other side of the room, he picked up the last bottle with something in it – about a quarter full – and poured a large measure of whisky.

Mark returned and retook his seat in front of the computer. 'Want to watch anymore or do you want me to carry on searching these images?'

'Carry on. I'm going to get some air.'

* * *

Mimar sat back in his office chair and watched the BBC News channel on his laptop. The men he had chosen held ideological beliefs that were non-negotiable. They were, in their own minds, already martyred. All they needed was someone to co-ordinate an attack, someone to tell them which targets to hit, where to go, what to do. Mimar, in the guise of the fixer controlling a network of jihadists, just provided what they needed. They were there, they were ready and they would have acted sooner rather than later. This way, the world would have to sit up and listen. This way, the world would see how the hand of Iran could probe the sacred environs of a capital thousands of miles from Tehran. People would have the threat brought home to them as they travelled around their city, reminded that they were always in striking distance. In striking distance day after day, just like his family, friends and colleagues.

None of the operatives that Mimar had recruited had any communication with the other cells. One aspect of the Technological Age was the ability to conscript young people into terrorism via the privacy and anonymity of their bedroom and computer.

Some had found and stored the cars. Some had trafficked the explosives but hadn't known what they were couriering.

304

Two had hidden the explosives in the cars and had driven them to the pick-up points. Others had taken the cars to target, told that the police cameras would be deactivated and that they had a window of fifteen minutes to deliver the bombs to the chosen sites before walking away. They were fools, every one of them. One man had been chosen to drive into central London. He was the keenest, the angriest. He was the one with Iranian heritage.

The bombs had been placed in carefully thought-out locations. The Manette Street bomb was the most daring. Near to Oxford Street, Theatre Land, Soho, it was a device to cause maximum disruption. The plan hadn't been for mass casualties but to create the chaos that rippled out across the capital at the moment of the explosion.

The Richmond car bomb had similar thinking behind it. The idea was to hit a wealthy area to the west, with its high-end shops and American school. A place where decision makers and money lived, a place full of diplomats, politicians and business people – all living near the vast expanse of Richmond Park with its roving deer, within ten miles of central London but far enough away to escape at the end of the day. A place to escape for weekends of bucolic and cultured pleasures by the green banks of the winding Thames, just as the great and the good had done since the eighteenth century.

The British Government had refused a US request to use its airbases in the UK and in Cyprus to launch strikes on Iran if the time came. Legal advice had been cited. The British didn't have the stomach for another war. The British would have to think again now that gore-spattered Gucci accessories were lying next to body bags in the centre of a well-heeled town. They would think again every time a siren wailed or blue lights flashed; every time they saw a car parked suspiciously in the street; every time they saw a Pakistani or an Arab.

Mimar turned off his laptop, inserted a memory stick and rebooted the system to run on the USB device's operating system. Now he was all but invisible as he stalked the internet. He opened the email account and typed a message: a name, an address, a date and a time. He saved the message under 'Drafts' – it wouldn't be sent.

The memory sticks held details of bomb-equipment hides, safe houses, CCTV systems, target lists and instructions, timings, contacts – everything that would point to another source when they were eventually found.

Over the years, he had run dozens of agents. Agents were just weapons, a means to an end, that's all. If he had to send an agent to the hanging tree, he wouldn't give it a second thought. The agent was always a cipher, never a person. With these operatives it was even easier because killing the likes of them had always been his job.

Netanel would check the account three times a day. He would read and delete the message. Then he and Ozi would go to work. It was simple: always make them look the other way – enemies or allies, it was all the same.

* * *

The woman codenamed Hariq stared up at the ceiling, holding the phone to her ear.

'What do you mean there's no wallet?'

On the other end of the line, George Parker took a breath and repeated what he'd said.

She swung her legs off the bed and began to pace the room. 'George, I'm unhappy. Actually, George, I'd go so far as to say that this is upsetting me a great deal.'

'What do you want me to say?' Parker asked.

'That you have what I asked you to find.'

'If he hasn't got it, he hasn't fucking got it. What can I say?' There was a long pause. 'You still there?'

'I'm still here, George. I'm just trying to imagine why you'd think it was a good idea to lose your temper and swear at me. You seem to be forgetting that, figuratively speaking for the moment at least, I've got your balls in my hands and I'm partial to a new set of earrings every now and then. Understood?'

Parker dug his nails into the palm of his hand and coughed. 'What do you want me to do?'

'The boyfriend must have it. The way I see it, our mercenary friend is past his use-by date.'

'I'll take care of it.'

'I'll leave the details to you. Make sure he doesn't turn up on the bloody news or you'll be the next big story. Don't contact me when it's done, just get it done.'

* * *

Cyrus opened the door and beckoned Ozi and Net to enter. '*As-salamu alaykum,*' he said.

'*Wa alaykum salam wa rahmatullah,*' they answered in unison.

'I am Rasul. This is Abbas.'

'I know who you are. I was told to expect you. Tea, brothers? Or juice?'

'No, thank you,' said Net, glancing through to the living area where a television was tuned to the Sky News Channel. Cyrus led them into the room. Footage from the car bombing locations was being shown on a loop. The volume was down low.

'Want me to turn it up?' Cyrus asked.

'No brother, we are well aware of your triumph,' said Ozi.

'It was God's triumph only,' said Cyrus. 'Mimar has sent you to brief me.'

'He has,' said Net, holding up a grey and black rucksack. 'We have everything needed for your next mission to be equally successful.'

'*Insha'Allah.*'

'*Insha'Allah.*'

Ozi walked to the window and looked out at the myriad lights illuminating the area around a small park. The pub on the opposite corner spilled out a soft glow on to the wet pavement, along with several drinkers who had clearly stayed longer than just-the-one-after-work.

'A pleasant view,' he said.

Cyrus joined him. 'It is a picture of decadence and immorality. The world of the *kuffar* has nothing that I find pleasant.'

Net took the stun gun from his inside jacket pocket and pushed it against Cyrus's neck in one smooth movement. The gun didn't rely on pain to do its job. The energy transferred into Cyrus's muscles depleted his blood sugar immediately, converting it to lactic acid. Starved of food, his muscles couldn't function and he collapsed to the ground. Net kept the charge against the prone subject's neck until he was sure that Cyrus had lost consciousness.

He pointed and Ozi grabbed a large cushion from the sofa running along the wall. Net put on a pair of surgical gloves, opened the rucksack and pulled out a hand grenade.

'Put the cushion on the floor. I don't want him to feel this when he wakes up.'

Ozi did as he was asked. 'What's the idea?'

'Help me to turn him over and you'll see.'

They rolled Cyrus over and placed him in the recovery position, his chest on the cushion.

'He'll wake up and push or roll himself off the cushion.'

'Boom!' said Ozi, a little too loudly.

'Fool,' said Net, unable to suppress a smile. 'His body will take most of the blast. The floor is concrete so the building won't suffer too much damage. The police will find all they need to link him to the car bomb.'

He tipped up the rucksack, out of which spilled some documents and CDs containing training manuals on forging identity documents, weapons training, planning assassinations, surveillance and counter-surveillance, how to build and detonate car bombs and some video footage of torture in Chechnya. Net's personal favourite was the manual entitled The Nuclear Bomb of Jihad and the Way to Enrich Uranium. A dangerously impressive document that wasn't available on Amazon.

'I'll put these around the place where they won't be damaged. Put these on.' He threw a pair of surgical gloves to

310

Ozi. 'Find his wallet. Make sure it's away from the blast. In the kitchen would be good, by the kettle.'

As Ozi returned from the kitchen, Net was carefully placing the grenade under the centre of the cushion. It was a standard time-delay fragmentation anti-personnel grenade. He pulled the pin and wedged the striker lever against the carpet, before easing himself back on his heels and placing the pin next to Cyrus's right hand.

'Playing with a grenade in your living room wasn't the best idea, was it my friend?'

'Is it secure?' asked Ozi.

Net pushed himself up and slowly stepped back. 'It is but I don't think we should hang around, do you?'

* * *

Salman and Syed were sleeping. They were always sleeping. Yasir had just finished wiping the prayer area. Zeeshan was reading by the light of his torch.

Imran wrapped the Holy Book in its protective cloth and placed it carefully inside a cavity in the wall behind him. 'Is the time weighing on you, brother?' he asked Yasir.

'No, brother. I'm ready and waiting, that's it.' He took out his smartphone. 'Time to switch this on and check the news?'

311

Imran stood and eased the tension in his hamstrings and calves with a series of stretches.

'The car bombs have caused chaos and panic. They're speculating about links to the motorway attacks,' said Yasir, showing Imran the screen.

'Let them speculate, it doesn't matter to us.'

'Do you want to read the report? There's video, too.'

'No, switch it off and save the battery. That and the spares need to last until the end of the operation. Did you check that the Bluetooth is off?'

'I always check.'

'And so will the police when they're carrying out their searches. Stupid mistakes lead to failure.'

Yasir sighed. 'I know. You've told me a hundred times. Relax.'

'We're on the final journey to God and you think it's time to relax?'

Yasir lay on his blanket and placed his hands behind his head. 'Relax, don't relax, it's up to you. I just think we'll be better prepared if we don't get too stressed.'

Imran sat opposite, legs crossed, his hands resting on his knees. 'It's better to seek peace, you're right.'

'It'll be fine,' said Yasir. 'The plan is perfect, you worry too much.'

* * *

312

'I'll do it,' said Ray. 'No bother. Then we can grab some breakfast.'

'The boss said Dave was to do it, we've got to meet Loz and relieve Gel and Matt.'

'Shut it, Vince, you're really getting on my tits. It won't take a minute. Those two arseholes can wait.' Ray kicked Tom hard. 'Wakey, wakey, dickhead.'

'All right, ladies, calm down,' said Dave, cocking his pistol. 'You've had your marching orders. You'd better get off. I'll finish up here.'

Tom's leg cramped but he didn't move. His ankles and wrists remained bound and he was still fixed to the wall. Gagged and hooded as he was, it was pretty obvious what was about to happen.

'Sure?' asked Ray. 'I won't tell if you don't.'

'Go on, fuck off, unless you want Loz Weir to tear you a new arsehole.'

Vince swallowed hard. 'Yeah, come on, I don't need the grief if we're late.'

'Fair enough,' said Ray. 'I've been missing little Connie while we've been away.'

Tom stayed absolutely still.

Ray crouched next to him. 'See ya then, mate. Oh no I won't, will I? Never mind, I'll give your best to your sister.

313

Yeah, I'll tell her you said hello while I'm giving her one later.'

'Right, go on, piss off,' said Dave. 'I'm wanted back at the club once this is done.'

He waited for them to drive away in the van before picking up an orange plastic chair, placing it a few feet in front of where Tom was kneeling.

He sat. 'You did well not to react there. He was dying for an excuse.'

Tom remained motionless.

'OK,' said Dave, 'this is what's going to happen: I'm going to take off the hood and the gag and you're going to stay staying still. Nod your head if you understand.'

Tom nodded.

Dave stood and placed his CZ100 on the chair. Standing to Tom's left, he removed the hood and gag.

Tom blinked and spat, then glared at his captor.

'Next,' said Dave, taking a pair of pliers from his pocket, 'I'm going to untie your ankles. OK?'

Tom nodded.

Dave crouched and snipped through the plastic tie. 'Thing is mate, I've been told to shoot you.'

Tom kicked out, pushing Dave off balance, twisting and clamping his legs around Dave's neck and pinning him to the floor.

'You were saying?'

Dave fought back as he struggled for breath. He angled around and aimed a kick at Tom's head but connected with his chest.

'You'll have to do better than that,' said Tom, increasing the pressure with his calves. 'Where's the key to these cuffs? What? I can't hear you.'

Dave's face was approaching scarlet. Tom released some of the pressure.

'Pocket,' gasped Dave.

'Give it to me.'

'Can't breathe,' Dave gasped again.

'You can speak: you can breathe,' said Tom, but released some more pressure. 'Give me the bloody key or I'll kill you and get it myself.'

Dave removed his hands from Tom's leg and moved the right one towards his pocket. He punched Tom hard in the balls and as the legs parted he pushed himself back and out of Tom's range. He coughed and crawled back to the chair, where he picked up the gun.

'As I was saying' – he coughed again – 'I've been instructed to shoot you but I'm not going to.' He chuckled quietly. 'How are your knackers?'

'How's your windpipe?' Tom replied, trying to control his breathing.

'We're getting out of here, but I need to know you're on side.'

'Who the fuck are you? I keep meeting people who are somebody else and it's starting to piss me off.'

'It doesn't matter who I am. We need to get out of here.'

'And that's the second time someone's said that to me this week. Where's my sister?'

'Last time I saw her she was sitting in the upstairs function room of a derelict pub owned by George Parker.'

'Who the fuck is George Parker?'

'You don't know?'

'Of course I don't fucking know – I'm asking, aren't I?'

'He seems to know you, that's all.'

'Never heard of the twat, but I'm planning on paying the fucker a visit. Where's Connie now?'

'I don't know. Two blokes came to move her when we were ready to pick you up. The other two have to meet a bloke called Loz Weir, Parker's fixer, to find out.'

'So take me to Parker.'

'I don't think so.'

'Have you got my gun?'

'Yeah, it's in the Land Rover outside but you're not having it back. Look, I'm not taking you anywhere near George Parker. What's going to happen if I turn up with the bloke I'm meant to be disposing of as we speak? You can walk away now.'

'You look: tell me where he is and I'll give you a realistic slap – you can say I overpowered you. He'll have more to worry about than your annual fucking appraisal by the time I'm done with him.'

'This isn't some half-arsed TV cop show, you know,' said Dave. 'George Parker is a seriously dangerous individual, or did you miss the clues?'

'So what are you going to tell him?'

'I'm telling him fuck all. I'm out and so are you, if you've got any sense.'

Tom thought for a few seconds. 'Come on then, take these shagging cuffs off.'

One moment Dave was undoing the cuffs, the next he was lying on his back staring up at Tom and the wrong end of the pistol.

'Right, who the fuck are you?'

'Easy, mate, I'm one of the good guys – although I'm not so sure about you.'

'Police? You're an undercover cop?'

'No. Listen, will you? We need to get out of here before Loz Weir arrives with a van-load of meat-heads carrying guns and machetes.'

Tom kept the pistol pointing at Dave's face. 'Who do you work for?'

'You don't need to know, but waving that thing in my face really isn't a good idea.'

Tom kicked Dave in the balls. 'You listen: you're my only link to my sister. Tell me how I can find her or I'll kill you. I don't care who you are.'

'I don't know where she is, I told you,' said Dave, clutching his aching groin.

'Car keys.'

'What?'

'Give me your car keys. You're taking me to Parker.'

'Am I fuck.'

Tom kicked Dave, grabbed the back of his collar and put the gun to the side of his head. 'Car keys.'

FOURTEEN

The meeting with Bannerman was set for ten o'clock at Holy Trinity Church, Bryan Road, Rotherhithe. Mark had taken position near the health centre at the end of Downton Road. He called Bannerman at 09:58 and told him the location had changed to the bridge across the lake in Russia Dock Woodland. He gave Bannerman the directions and waited for him to walk past the hiding position by the surgery. Gallagher had said that this would put Bannerman on the back foot and it'd be easier to spot any surveillance teams moving to catch up.

Harry had dropped Gallagher off near Stave Hill Ecological Park at 08:30. While Gallagher familiarised himself with the area and checked for ambush positions and alternative escape routes, Harry began to drive around the sweeping arc of Salter Road to look for anything suspicious. The ERV was set for the corner of Quebec Way and Canada Street. Gallagher would bug out and follow a track through the park area, skirting the wood and nipping through Russia Walk to Archangel Street. He'd come out in the middle of some residential streets, with a church and two primary schools, surrounded by industrial estates and business centres. There were plenty of routes back out once Harry had picked him up.

Bannerman replaced his phone in his pocket and checked his watch. He'd expected nothing less and smiled as he crossed the busy B205 Downton Road. The road curved right. He passed a health centre before turning left, following a short track into the park area. He made his way to the centre of the bridge and looked out at the water shimmering in the cold morning sunshine.

Gallagher stepped on to the bridge from the other side.

'Sandy, thanks for coming.'

'Owen, what's going on?'

'I still don't know.'

'How much trouble are you in – beyond what I already know?'

'Well that's the first thing: what do you know? Because I don't know if I can trust you.'

'So why are you here?'

'Like I said, someone's playing silly buggers.'

'What do you want?'

'I want to know if I can trust you.'

Bannerman smoothed his hair. 'You won't be aware of the amount of chest-poking I've had to endure on your behalf. I'm not sure I want to endure any more. What else are you mixed up in?'

'What do you mean, what else?'

'Arms dealing?'

Gallagher laughed. 'What do you take me for, Sandy?'

'Owen, I have to admit some ambivalence towards you, your current situation and our friendship.'

'End of conversation, then.'

'You asked me here for a reason, what is it?'

'First, were you tracking my phone? Did you mount surveillance at Paddington Old Cemetery?'

'Nothing to do with me. Why, what's been going on?'

'Never mind. I need your help.'

Bannerman smoothed his hair again. 'Still missing a second cousin?'

'Look, Sandy, I've stumbled across something, but I'm out in the cold and I need to know who I can trust.'

'It sounds like we have some unravelling to do. What have you got?'

Two black Range Rovers with blacked-out windows screeched around the corner of Downton Road, a few metres from where Mark was keeping watch and drove in the direction of the track.

Gallagher opened his mouth to speak and then closed it again. He took the beeping phone from his pocket and listened to Mark's breathless speech. The Range Rovers arrived in view, skidding to a halt. Black-clad armed officers began shouting instructions at a distance.

'Sandy, you bastard,' Gallagher said, pulling his hand away from his pistol as the police-issue MP5s got closer.

Bannerman span round following Gallagher's gaze.

'I didn't know,' he shouted at Gallagher's disappearing back.

Gallagher sprinted towards the cover of the woods. 'Bug out, Mark,' he said into the phone as he ran. 'Harry will call you to pick you up once we're clear. Tell him to go to the ERV now.'

Gallagher continued to run to the gap that would lead him down Russia Walk.

He emerged in Archangel Street just as Harry arrived.

Harry checked his mirrors as he pulled away. 'Clear. They won't have the car.'

'Not necessarily,' said Gallagher. 'Head for Kennington Park and drop me off.' He reached into the glove compartment and pulled out a baseball cap. 'I'm going to lie low for a few hours. Call Mark once you've dropped me off and pick him up after you've called Frankie to warn him that the warehouse is likely to be compromised; he'll need to get his lads clear. We can't risk going back there now: there could be covert cars and choppers on us.'

'OK,' said Harry. 'I'll get on it. I'll report this car stolen and dump it. I don't want the coppers at my gaff upsetting Lynne.'

'Sorry, Harry.'

'Piss off, Owen. You didn't start this.'

'I'm going to bloody well finish it, though. The last girl I took on a date has been kidnapped and God knows what's happened to her only relative. I'm wanted by the Security Service, my flat has been turned over and armed police have tried to take me twice. To cap it all, I haven't been to a pub in days and I've been drinking good Scotch out of a mug.'

Harry laughed. 'We've been in worse scrapes, Owen. We'll get through this one.'

Gallagher undid his seat belt and took off his coat before reaching through to the back seat to grab a jacket. 'Well someone's yanked my chain and now it's time to start yanking back. I'll call you to regroup once I've done some thinking. It's not too late to walk away, H.'

Harry tapped the indicator and said nothing.

* * *

Harry picked up Mark half way between Surrey Quays and New Cross. They were now driving to Frankie's warehouse.

'Sorry,' said Mark. 'I thought it'd be safer to leave it hidden there.'

'Don't worry about it, but we'll have to go careful. I'll drop you a few streets away. You do a recce and I'll come to back you up. Any sign of activity, walk away. Once you've got it, we'll dump this car and head into town to somewhere busy while we wait for Owen to call.'

He picked up the Browning that was wrapped in a duster in the driver's door compartment. 'You'd better take this. If the police are there chuck it down a drain, but we don't know who's involved.'

Harry pulled over and watched as Mark walked away. For all the supportive words he'd offered Gallagher, Harry had a bad feeling – the kind of bad feeling he'd only had three times in his life.

His phone rang.

'Lynne, what's up?'

'The police are here. They're looking for you.'

'Tell them I'm on a job. Tell them I was about to report the car stolen, I've been busy.'

'They're searching the house.'

'Have they shown you a warrant?'

Harry Junior began to wail in the background.

'What?' asked Lynne Burgess.

'A warrant – a search warrant – have they shown you a search warrant?'

'Hang on, Harry, one of them wants to speak to you.'

Harry swore under his breath and checked his watch.

'Mr Burgess? Mr Harry Burgess?'

'Speaking.'

324

'Are you on your way home, Mr Burgess?'

'No, I'm working and – I was just telling my wife – I need to report my car stolen.'

'OK, Mr Burgess, perhaps we could deal with the stolen car when you come to the station. We're based at Paddington Green. When can we expect you?'

'Why are you searching my house?'

'We'll be happy to explain that when you arrive at the station. When can we expect to see you, Mr Burgess?'

'Like I said, I'm working. Look, give my wife your number; I'll call you in a few hours.'

'Mr Burgess, this is an urgent and important matter. I think it best that you co-operate so we can clear it up.'

'I'm working. I'll call you,' said Harry, hanging up.

He started the car and moved it to the corner he'd agreed with Mark. His phone rang.

'All clear so far,' said Mark.

'Moving now,' said Harry, easing the car into the next street.

'I'll go forward,' said Mark. 'Keep the engine running.'

Mark slipped in through the Judas gate and froze as he heard voices. A Browning came through the blackout curtain attached to Tom Edwards.

'Don't shoot, I'm having a shit day as it is,' said Mark.

Tom gave him a wide grin. 'I didn't think I'd ever say this but it's good to see you.'

Mark looked over at Dave, who was standing by the Land Rover. 'Who's that?'

'Dave the Kidnapper, aka Constable Intheshit. Where's everybody else?'

'Long story. We've got to get out of here. The boss thinks this gaff's blown. I've just come back for the memory stick. Harry's got the rest of the gear in his car. He's down the road.'

Tom tensed. 'Is that him pulling up outside?'

'Doubt it,' said Mark, pulling out the Browning Harry had given him.

'Watch him,' said Tom, as he moved through the curtain. The Judas gate opened.

'Don't move!' Tom shouted.

'Calm down, mate,' said Chris. 'Frankie sent us to clear the place before any Old Bill arrive. We were watching when you arrived, waiting to see if you'd been followed. Harry sends his best and says hurry-the-fuck-up.'

'Right,' said Tom, turning back through the curtain. 'Mark, get the thing and let's go.'

'We haven't long,' said Chris, following. 'We can flannel the cops if needs be, but it sounds like you need to be on your toes sharpish.' He looked over at Dave. 'I've got a message from Frankie. What about him?'

Tom turned to Dave. 'You, get in the back of the Rover.'

Dave hesitated. Tom raised his pistol. Dave climbed into the car and closed the door. Tom nodded to Chris.

'Frankie says to meet him at this address at half four this afternoon.'

Tom took the piece of paper offered. Mark rejoined them from upstairs.

'Got it,' said Mark. 'The boss just called. I told him about your friend in the car, he said to let him go.'

'What?' said Tom. 'That twat is my only link to the bastard who kidnapped my sister, George Parker.'

'Gallagher said let him go; otherwise it's kidnap, false imprisonment, whatever. We don't need any more hassle.'

'He knows about this place,' Tom answered.

Chris laughed. 'I don't think that's really an issue anymore. Anyway, everyone knows who George Parker is – where have you been living, Africa?'

'Let's go,' said Mark. 'Harry's got to ditch his car. The boss wants me to find a new place to hide the memory stick.'

'We'll take Dave's, then.'

'He'll report it,' said Mark.

'Don't worry about him' said Chris. 'We'll get someone to look after him for a couple of hours, but you'll need to ditch it. Don't take it to the meet with Frankie, for fuck's sake.'

* * *

327

Gallagher had walked through Kennington Park to the Oval where he'd taken a tube train to Stockwell. From there he took the Victoria Line to Oxford Circus.

He'd now finally arrived at the back of Le Lion Rouge. He heard the bolt pulled and the latch turned. Eve looked through a small gap in the open door.

'Gallagher, why are you coming to the back door? Have you come to take me dancing?' She smiled. 'Come in.'

'Eve, I need a place to sit and think for a couple of hours.'

'That's what you do in the bar, no?'

'Not today, there are certain people I'd rather avoid today.'

'You will bring me only heartache, I know,' she said, taking his hand. 'You can use my room. I'm about to start my shift.'

'Thank you,' he said, squeezing her hand.

'You're welcome. A glass of the Alsace Pinot Noir?'

'A bottle? Put it on my tab.'

'Moreau was worried that we hadn't seen you. He kept looking at your bill and shaking his head. I think he was afraid you were dead.'

'I've only been away for a few days.'

'Like I say, he was very worried.' She stood on her tiptoes and kissed him on the cheek. 'You know where it is. I'll bring you the wine.'

* * *

'So you're telling me that Special Branch – SO10, 12, 15, whatever they're calling themselves this week – put a team of Greys on me and no one knew anything about it?' Bannerman asked.

'I knew about it,' said Nicholas Drummond. 'Are you telling me that you really didn't spot them?'

Bannerman ignored the sleight. 'Jesus, Nicholas, since when did we have Plod watching our own?'

'SO15 were somewhat frustrated that you weren't giving up your man, that you cited technical glitches at the Burrow.'

'So why didn't they liaise with GCHQ themselves?'

'They did, eventually. JTAC provided this man Gallagher's details through the SO15 chap in their ops room, but Gallagher's phone was untraceable by that point.'

Gallagher's phone would have been sitting in several feet of water by that point, thought Bannerman.

'And you sanctioned a Branch tail?'

Drummond eased back in his chair. 'The word "sanctioned" would imply a choice on my part, old boy. SO15 went bleating to the Home Office, who were uncomfortable to say the least. After some deliberation a green light was shown and S-squad was tasked.'

'How far up Shit Creek am I?'

329

'You've managed to go quite a distance. The question is: do you still have a paddle?'

'Let's start with where SO15 got their intel about Gallagher.'

Drummond leaned forward in his chair and steepled his fingers beneath his chin. 'I don't think you've quite grasped the gravity of the situation. A blame-thrower has been ignited at the Home Office. Why were you protecting a man on a Counter Terrorist Command arrest list? You do know the penalties for Misconduct in a Public Office? Who the hell is Gallagher anyway?'

Bannerman smoothed his hair. 'Owen Gallagher is a freelance watcher, who I've known since I met him at Sandhurst.'

Drummond opened a drawer in his desk and pulled out a bottle and two glasses. 'I might as well hear the lot.'

He poured. 'No need for a horoscope. Start with the military service and stick to the headlines.'

Bannerman took the glass he was offered. 'Owen James Gallagher: enlisted as a private soldier and was picked up for officer training during his first posting at a working unit. They packed him off to Sandhurst, where I met him. He opted for a commission in the infantry. Did his stint as a platoon commander, including a tour in Iraq and then put in for special ops. He spent a couple of years with the Special Reconnaissance Regiment – usual places. He was part of a team supporting the SBS and SAS seeking high-value Taliban leadership targets for a while and then went back to Northern Ireland to watch Republican dissidents.'

'Bugging, burglary and covert surveillance.'

'Quite,' said Bannerman. 'He "returned to unit" when his home regiment were given notice for deployment to Afghanistan. Two tours of Afghanistan. During the second tour he was injured: one bullet to the shoulder, shattering his collarbone; moments later, he took another in the calf and one in the thigh while crawling to pull an injured corporal into cover. He was awarded the Military Cross for his actions that day.'

Drummond raised an eyebrow and sipped his drink.

'His CO described Gallagher as "a man drawn to chaos and easily bored, but an inspirational leader." He had a reputation for being fearless – a real soldier's soldier. He was also known for having little interest in small talk, or doing anything, including drinking, in moderation.'

'So he had a good career ahead of him, what happened?'

'He resigned his commission the day he was discharged from hospital. Never speaks about it.'

Drummond took another sip of his drink. 'What was his last job for you?'

Bannerman shifted in his seat and waved away the offer of a top up.

'If you leave this room knowing something about this that I don't, Sandy, I shall personally hole your boat, throw you to the waiting piranhas and wave to what's left of your eviscerated carcass as it floats downstream.'

'It was off the books.'

Drummond topped up his own glass and tilted the bottle towards Bannerman. 'Sure?'

'Thank you, no. I was contacted by an old friend, one of "the Friends," who asked me to locate a young lefty activist. Initial investigations pointed to involvement with Occupy and as I've been running operations in connection with them it was of interest.'

'Who at Six?' asked Drummond.

'Flic, Felicity, Anderson. I knew her at Oxford. The target wasn't on any of the usual radar so, as it was off book, I tasked Gallagher to carry out a find and a fix.'

'Who was the target?'

'The first was a City of London PhD student, Connie Edwards. The second was her brother, Tom Edwards – ex-Para and jobbing military contractor.'

'So now we have a left-wing activist, a mercenary and a gunrunner in the mix?'

'Gallagher isn't a bloody arms dealer, for Christ's sake.'

'Are you saying that this is a set up?'

'To be honest, I'm at a loss.'

Drummond stood and began to walk the carpet behind his desk. He paused at the window. 'Thoughts?'

'Gallagher is as straight as they come and I can't imagine why anyone would be setting him up. He keeps himself to himself and I've never known him demonstrate anything but the utmost integrity.'

'But he ran today.'

'What would you have done in his position?'

Drummond continued to look out of the window. 'I wouldn't have been in his position.' He turned. 'But I take your point. Go on.'

'Gallagher has gone to ground for a reason. You've seen the transcript of our brief conversation at the bridge. He's on to something.'

'Or into something. Let's recap: one, we've got a missing Occupy activist.'

'Correct: her neighbours report that she's away.'

'Two, the brother is also on Six's radar and has been neither seen nor heard from.'

'Correct: last known travelling from Johannesburg to the UK via Germany and Spain.'

'A circuitous and, some might say, torturous route. And into the fray comes an ex-army officer with an alleged penchant for illegal arms deals.'

'The operative word being "alleged." Let's remember that SO15's intel is sketchy to say the least.'

333

'Let's not forget, Sandy, that he may have known about the raid, hence he wasn't at home and, therefore, someone may have tipped him off.'

'Not necessarily.'

'Well, we know where the finger is pointing regarding that. The Home Secretary has made space on the mantelpiece for your severed head. But we'll gloss over that small matter for the time being. The main pointers are that Gallagher hasn't been back to his flat; he's ditched his mobile phone; we know he's armed and he claims to have information of some kind – as per the intel – which he didn't relay to an officer of the Security Service who had obstructed a counter-terrorist investigation.'

Bannerman kept quiet.

Drummond continued. 'During this clandestine meeting – having possibly, let's remember, already been tipped off about an imminent raid on his flat – Gallagher flees the scene being pursued by the armed back-up. Several police officers brandishing automatic weapons in a primary school playground was one particular point of the report that specifically impressed the Home Secretary. That really was the icing on the cake.'

'But it doesn't add up.'

'Is there anything that I've just said that isn't based on known facts?'

'No, but that doesn't mean that it adds up to the truth.'

Drummond sighed. 'I'll try another: can you understand why certain members of certain government agencies would like to see you sitting in a cell down the corridor from the one in which they'll be housing your friend Gallagher?'

'Do you trust me, Nicholas?'

'Yes, Sandy, I do. So I want a list of known associates. I want, nay insist upon, your full co-operation in finding Gallagher and anyone else caught up in this sticky web of unknown provenance. The Home Secretary has thrown this across the river as a result of your involvement and the Iraq connection. I've been called to a meeting at Vauxhall Cross in two hours' time and I need something to take with me.'

'Will you be releasing Gallagher's photograph?'

'We don't want to muddy the waters at this point. The Home Office is clear on how they want to steer the news coverage. The TSG constable – Ross McGregor – has been cautioned pending investigation. There's no tangible evidence against him, just the link to Gallagher that was in your files, so it's on the QT and he hasn't been suspended.'

Bannerman pushed his empty glass across the desk.

'We keep a watching brief,' Drummond continued. 'The Home Secretary doesn't want anything to detract from the calls for public vigilance regarding terrorist attacks. Another?' he asked, lifting the bottle.

'A double,' replied Bannerman.

Mark had left Harry and Tom to dispose of the two cars, while he took the motorbike that Gallagher had collected from the lock-up. They'd have to carry the bags of kit to the meeting with Frankie. Gallagher had given Mark clear instructions regarding the memory stick and Mark knew exactly where he was going to hide it. He pulled into the curb, turned off the engine and put the Triumph Speed Triple on its stand.

Archie Keane was already sitting in the café nursing a cup of tea. Mark removed the crash helmet and waved at him through the window. Archie looked surprised and beckoned him in.

'Two more teas, please mate,' said Mark, as he passed the counter. 'All right, Granddad?'

'I'm all right, son. Is that yours?'

'A friend's. Gleaming, isn't it?'

'It's a corking-looking bike. I wanted one once: it was a second-hand BSA Gold Star I had my eye on. I can see it now – lovely sleek beast, it was.'

'Why didn't you?'

'My old dad said that if I came home with one of those death machines, as he called them, he'd wrap the bleeder around my neck.'

Mark laughed.

336

'Not sure how he'd have managed that,' said Archie. 'But I decided against it. Then I met your granny and that was the end of that.'

The tea was placed between them on the table.

'Thanks, mate,' Mark said to the café owner. 'Granddad, I've got a favour to ask.'

'Ask away: I don't keep credits and debits, you know that, lad.'

'I need you to keep something for me.'

Mark pulled out a small envelope.

Archie slurped at his tea. 'Should I ask what it is?'

'Two computer memory sticks. There are some contact details inside. If I don't come back for it in a week, I need you to get it to the person whose name and number is on the piece of paper.'

'Are you going somewhere?'

'I'll either be back for it or I'll call you. If I, Harry Burgess or Owen Gallagher don't collect it, open the envelope and call the number.'

'Burgess? Your old sergeant?'

'Yep, or my old boss Captain Gallagher.'

'Right, got it. I know better than to ask too many questions. I take it that you aren't in trouble if those two are involved – and that's enough for me.' He leaned forward conspiratorially. 'What's it all about then?'

'I thought you knew not to ask questions,' said Mark, smiling and lifting his mug of tea. 'To be honest, Granddad, I'm not too sure myself – but it's important. Will you do it?'

'Of course, son, of course.'

'Thanks, Granddad, I owe you one.'

'You owe me nothing – have you eaten?'

'I've got to go, but thanks.'

'You know,' said Archie, leaning back, 'I saw a picture of some homeless prat in the paper the other day. He'd attacked a council worker down by the Strand. Gave me a start, it did: he looked a bit like you. The picture was all fuzzy and at an angle, though, and it obviously wasn't. I tell you, I thanked God that you've turned out all right.'

* * *

The woman codenamed Hariq inserted the memory stick into her computer and switched on the power. The separate operating system booted up and presented her with a welcome screen. Now she could communicate anonymously, her traffic routed through dozens of servers across the global network, protecting her IP address, protecting her identity.

She selected a photograph that had been left with no hidden data. Using the code matrix she inserted the message into the image that would temporarily retask one of Mimar's

338

operators, before leaving a draft message on the agreed email account to alert him to the new information.

She opened the trip-wire program and saw how many files had been opened with the S-Tool. At first she'd thought Mimar was accessing the hidden data in some sporadic manner for reasons she couldn't fathom. She'd checked: he hadn't. Tom Edwards had obviously found the hidden stick; he'd been groping around the files – she couldn't be sure what he'd found. It was time to up the ante and make her move.

She secured the ankle holster to her leg as George Parker made excuses on the phone.

'George, my tolerance levels are very low so listen to me carefully. I'll be seeing you in your office at some time between ten and midnight. Be there, with answers; otherwise, your grubby little world will unravel so fast you'll wish you were someone else.'

She moved her shoulder bag from the floor on to the desk and continued. 'In the meantime, you will call your men and tell them I'm coming to see the girl. They will keep her hooded and they will do as I say. Are we clear? Good. Now what's the bloody address?'

Parker told her.

'See: that wasn't so hard, was it? Oh and George, do remember that discretion is the better part of valour –

339

particularly when dealing with me. Tell them to expect me soon.'

She placed the phone on to her desk and picked up the Makarov. She liked the gun – standard Russian military issue from 1951 to 1991 designed by Nikolai Federovich Makarov, popular for its simplicity and stopping power. The semi-automatic was compact, holding eight rounds in its magazine and was accurate enough over 50 metres. She'd liked the man who had owned the gun. Having to kill him hadn't changed that. It was a shame she'd have to ditch it.

Pulling back the slide, she checked the chambered round, eased the working parts forward, added an extra round to the magazine and checked the weapon's slide-mounted safety lever. She placed the pistol into the ankle holster and covered it with her trouser leg.

She stood and pulled her waistband outwards, slipping a spare magazine into an elasticated loop sewn into the lining on the left. She opened a drawer, took out the Makarov's suppressor unit and placed the silencer into her bag. Her jacket was lying across the armchair on the other side of the room and, having put it on, she walked to the full-length mirror on the back of the door and checked each angle to ensure the weapon and magazine weren't visible.

She took a step forward, checked her make-up and tucked some hair behind her ear. She was looking forward to this.

* * *

James Rutherford stood at the window in his office at MI6's Vauxhall Cross headquarters and stared out over the river. The meeting with Drummond hadn't been too disconcerting. The situation could be salvaged, even if things had unravelled rather more than he'd realised. Bannerman had given up what he knew and had been dragged over the coals at Thames House. That Bannerman knew next to nothing was good, but his man Gallagher posed a problem. For the moment, Gallagher wasn't Rutherford's problem; his problem was bigger, the picture that he was looking at was much bigger.

He had to make a decision and he needed to make it fast. Things were getting messy: there were flies in the ointment and for the ointment to be effective, to be kept clear and clean, the flies would have to be removed.

Rutherford also had to decide what and when to tell his own masters. It didn't help that an officer of the Security Service would, at the very least, need reigning in. Bannerman had to be put off the scent; he had to be convinced to stand back – to leave well alone.

There was a knock on the door and Alexis Clark's brown-haired head came into view.

'Sir, your next appointment is here. I'm sorry.'

'Thank you, Alexis. Come back in ten minutes and tell me again, would you?'

The door closed and Rutherford watched a wooden-hulled Thames sailing barge glide by on the river below. An incredibly versatile craft, the Thames barge could move quickly into the heart of the city. Dropping its masts to slip effortlessly under bridges, the barge was a majestic courier that was just as at home in the river's narrow tributaries as amid its main arterial flow. The flat-hulled boats would float in as little as three feet of water, getting in close, going where others couldn't go, sitting out the changing tides without rolling over.

Rutherford saw himself reflected in the window glass as the clouds moved across the sky. He saw his reflection transposed on the barge slipping by and recognised two fine examples of British practical style: understated and eminently useful, with an elegant gracefulness; solid, dependable, versatile; steady workhorses serving the country; part of the landscape and extremely pleasant to look at.

He made his decision.

* * *

'What's wrong with it?' Atif asked.

'That's what I'm trying to find out,' Saeed replied without looking up from under the bonnet. 'It's been sitting idle for long enough: it's probably forgotten it's an engine.'

Atif looked around him. They had come together to finish preparations for the attack. Saeed was attempting to get the stolen ambulance started. It had been stolen months before. Its plates had been cloned and its radio and locating equipment stripped out and dumped in a canal.

He walked along the side of the vehicle to the rear. The ambulance would be driven forward to the target and would create an effective focal point prior to a main attack.

Hammad and Waleed were working at the back of the ambulance. The inside was now armour-plated. They were fitting defensive metal shields either side of the medical bay – where the stretchers would have been – behind which they'd take cover when the shooting started. He was particularly pleased with the hatch that had been created in the floor.

Bilawal was preparing the other vehicle – a black London Taxi Company TX4 Elegance Automatic: the diversion car.

Atif looked around him and smoothed his beard. The men that had been brought together had bonded well in a short

343

time. They were good workers, true believers striving in one true purpose. If the other crew were as single-minded and disciplined the mission would be an inspiration to fighters all over the world. Not that he knew who or where the other crew were, or how their part of the mission would work. He just knew what he and these men had to do and when – and that they were the diversion.

The ambulance's engine turned over and exhaust fumes filled the space in which he was standing. Saeed's oily features appeared from under the bonnet, showing a toothy grin. Atif gave him the thumbs up and felt a shiver of excitement thrill through his body.

FIFTEEN

Harry had transferred the kit from his car to the Land Rover Discovery that Tom had driven, before dumping his Mondeo in a side street a few miles from Frankie's warehouse. He and Tom had then ditched the Land Rover near Stockwell, before heading to Clapham. They'd managed to pack the kit into a holdall and two large rucksacks, so they looked like a couple of tourists. After sitting in cafes and pubs for a while with the newspapers, they took a train out to Walthamstow.

When they arrived at the rear of the derelict cinema they were met by Teddy Southall, who was wearing a hi-vis jacket and a hard hat.

'Not a fucking word,' he said to Harry.

Harry smiled and whistled the tune 'Bob the Builder' as he walked away.

Four more of Frankie's men were milling about trying to look like a surveying crew.

Gallagher had been collected from the rear of Le Lion Rouge by Chris and was inside waiting for them with Frankie, sitting in what had once been the manager's office.

Tom relayed his tale.

'So who is George Parker?' asked Harry.

'He's a dangerous bastard. He reckons he's gone legit but blokes like him can't help themselves. Well, they can, but that's the trouble,' said Teddy.

Harry chuckled. 'It looks like one of his lads was an undercover – he's dropped himself right in it.'

'He's got it coming, we all know he's a grass; otherwise, he'd have done more time than he has.'

Tom turned to look at Teddy. 'What do you mean?'

'You can't be as naughty as George Parker has been and stay out of the nick for thirty years. He did some bird early on, but nothing since. He's a grass, it stands to reason.'

'Never proven,' said Frankie. 'But Teddy's not wrong.' He stood and walked around the desk. 'Teddy, give Loz Weir a bell – you and him go way back.'

'Loz Weir?' Harry asked.

'George's right-hand man,' Teddy explained. 'We went to school together. Why he got mixed up with that twat Parker, I'll never know.'

'But you're mates?'

'Haven't spoken to him in a while but we've never had a ruck. I've got his number somewhere.'

'He'll listen to you?' asked Gallagher.

'Loz might, but George Parker doesn't listen to any fucker. He hears what he wants to hear, does what he wants to do. One night he was entertaining some of his flash mates. One bloke, some twonk off the telly, was smarming with

346

George's missus – we're going back a bit, mind you. Anyway, this bloke's giving her all the chat – just doing his smooth TV act – and he says something about her dress, how it shows off her legs. Next thing he's lying on the floor, arm in the air and George Parker is breaking three of the fingers on his left hand. "I know you weren't really thinking of laying a finger on her" says George, "which is why you've still got the use of your good hand." Like I said, he's a mad bastard.'

'Did the guy press charges?'

Teddy laughed. 'No he fucking didn't – you been listening? Georgie boy sent him round a couple of bottles of champagne with a high-end tom to show no hard feelings.'

'Nice,' said Harry.

'What do you want to do?' Frankie asked Gallagher.

'I want someone to send me some champagne and an expensive prostitute, tip-off the police and let them sort it out.'

'And we're not going to do that last bit because?' Harry asked.

'Because there's something not right here and it could be our best chance to find Connie if we keep the police out of it.'

'And how are we going to do that?' asked Harry.

'We need to arrange a chat with Mr Parker for starters.'

* * *

George Parker was not a happy man. The woman had shouted down the phone. She'd yanked his chain, she'd detailed his fuck-ups and she'd demanded a meet. She was coming to his club tonight and he'd be there, with solutions, or things would get even messier and he'd rue the day he'd let her down. Bitch.

He sat in his office above the club just off Oxford Street. He'd bawled out a couple of people on the phone; he'd shouted at Loz and he'd scared the shit out of his club manager. He'd made his wife cry when she nipped in on a shopping trip and he'd told his mistress that she was boring him when she'd phoned. He still didn't feel any better.

Parker stubbed out his cigar, which was just adding to the bitter taste in his mouth. What he really wanted to do was dig a hole for the stuck-up cow pulling his strings and take the great and personal pleasure of putting one in the back of her head as she knelt staring into the pit. It wasn't going to happen: she'd got him by the short and curlies. Bitch.

She'd wanted to know the girl's location – the place that Gel and Matt had taken her before being relieved by Ray and Vince – she hadn't wanted to know details before. That was niggling him, what was she up to? Why was she coming to the club? He'd find out before midnight.

She'd arrive like a punter, ready to be shown upstairs, ready to give him grief, standing on his carpet, in his office, in his own fucking club. She'd stroll in to give him a dressing down under his roof on his turf: taking fucking liberties. Bitch.

There was a knock on the door and Loz walked in – no fear of Parker, no sign of anything bothering him in the slightest. If Parker had trusted anyone, it would have been Loz.

'All right, boss?'

'What?'

'Teddy Southall just called.'

'Teddy-fucking-Southall? What the fuck does he want?'

'He says Frankie Fuller wants a meet, tonight.'

'Fucking does he now? Has he gone fucking mad? And while we're at it, where the fuck is Dave?'

* * *

Mark had arrived back on Gallagher's motorbike and had stored it in the cinema's old ticket hall. Harry had been out to call Lynne from a payphone – he couldn't risk using his mobile. The call had been short in case of eavesdroppers. She wasn't happy but the news she'd relayed put her annoyance in the shade. Harry had made another call and then found the nearest off-licence.

Two hours later, he was sitting on a dusty pink-upholstered pull-down seat in the auditorium of the cinema. Gallagher poured another whisky into Harry's cup. Tom was dozing a few rows up from where they were sitting.

Harry nodded his thanks. 'I'm drinking all the booze. To Kenny.'

'To Kenny. We wouldn't have any booze if you hadn't done the resupply. This Balvenie is just what the doctor ordered.'

'I still can't believe it,' said Harry. 'Why would he do it?'

Gallagher swirled his drink in the chipped mug. 'I suppose he couldn't face the time. I'm not sure I'd take to the life either.'

'It wasn't going to be a bloody life sentence. He could have put his head down and fought through it. I thought he had more balls.'

'Who knows what state you have to be in to do something like that.'

Harry took a sip and looked away. 'He was one of the best blokes I ever stood next to in a fight. He had no fear. The times he scared the shit out of me, never mind the Teletubbies.'

'What did he used to say?' asked Gallagher. 'The Dad's Army thing?'

'They don't like it up 'em?'

'Yeah,' Gallagher laughed. 'That.'

350

They heard Mark sniff behind them in the aisle. Harry looked up.

'Any more of that, boss?'

'Sit down, Mark, I'll get you one.'

Harry looked at Mark's swollen red eyes.

'It's all right, son, sit down.'

Mark took the seat next to Harry. 'Kenny was a legend. I looked up to him. If I could have been half as good as he was.'

'He was a good bloke.'

'I can't believe it.'

'I know.'

Gallagher handed over the cup. 'To Kenny,' he said.

Harry chinked cups with Mark and then Gallagher.

'Did he ever tell you why he didn't sleep in his own bed when we were in Afghan?' asked Mark.

'No,' said Harry. 'That's right: he'd only sleep in a cot vacated by somebody on leave, why was that?'

'Dunno,' said Mark. 'He never told anyone why, that I know of.'

'Do you remember the silly fucker on top of that ditch near Compound 9 outside that last patrol base we were at before we went back to Lashkatraz? What was that shithole of a PB called?' Harry said, reaching for the bottle. 'I think I might have had too much of this.'

'I remember him standing there with the Jimpy, screaming at them to come and get him,' said Gallagher. 'We couldn't get the ammo to him quick enough he was putting so many rounds down.'

Harry nodded. 'When they opened up on three sides that day it sounded like the world was unzipping. The nutter just stood there as the rounds hit the bun line in front of him.'

Mark smiled. 'I was underneath him in the ditch. I said to him, why the fuck are you standing up there? He shouted back that he was trying to draw fire so he could shoot the bastards. I couldn't help laughing. Then he said, why the fuck are you hiding down there? I told him: I'm waiting for you to get their attention.'

Gallagher took a sip. 'He certainly managed to do that. I'm not sure we'd have moved the casualties so quickly if he hadn't. He saved some lives that day.'

'That was a good day at work,' said Mark. 'About fifteen-nil to us, wasn't it? Kenny said it was the best drug in the world: proper war fighting, seeing the near misses, turning to your oppo and laughing it off in the middle of a contact.'

'Yeah and now he's killed himself – the soft twat,' said Harry, staring into his cup.

'Have you ever thought what it must be like?' asked Mark.

Harry looked up. 'What?'

'Going from this to whatever's next.'

'Eh?'

'Dying: going from all this – seeing, hearing, feeling – to, I dunno, nothing, to not be anywhere, not feel anything, not know anything.'

'Exactly, you wouldn't know.'

'Must be weird, though.'

'How could it be weird if you don't know anything about it?'

'What if you did?'

'Did what?'

'Know. What if you knew you didn't exist?'

Harry placed his cup on the floor under his seat and stood up. 'Right, that's it, my head is messed with enough, thank you very much. I'm going to get some water.'

Gallagher thought about Kenny standing under the glaring sun, firing like a mad man. He remembered when he'd heard, two months later, that Kenny – injured and slipping in and out of consciousness – had found himself next to a body bag on the medevac helicopter as he was flown to Bastion for treatment. The soldier in the bag, thought to be dead, had come round kicking and screaming, trying to fight his way out. Kenny hadn't been able to laugh that one off. It had haunted him for the rest of the tour and he'd confided to Gallagher that he'd often dreamt that he was the man in the bag and that no one could see him moving. No one could hear his cries for help.

Gallagher remembered the attack they'd repelled on the day that Harry had mentioned. They'd been in danger of being cut off by dozens of enemy fighters, from the seriously well-armed and trained jihadists to the local ten-dollar Taliban. He remembered the sound of the RPGs, the SPG-9s, the RPKs and AGS-17 grenade launchers. He could almost hear the rhythmic chatter of the Dushka anti-aircraft machine guns, the thuds of the 82mm mortars.

Gallagher remembered the roots of the mulberry trees, the fields flooded by the Taliban, the tall maize crops. He remembered the fear of those long hot days and how he had pushed that fear deep down inside himself.

He'd quickly realised that the only way to deal with it was to consider yourself already dead. Nothing to worry about on that score from then on. You could think about it and drive yourself to mad distraction, but then you'd fuck up, other people would get hurt. Far better to accept that you were already dead – walking, talking, eating, shitting, pissing, sleeping, running, sweating, shooting, diving, crawling, dead.

That was the mental toughness that it took — and it did take. It took away bits of you that wouldn't come back, even if you made it back. You came home but you didn't, not all of you.

Some died in the ditches, in the compounds, in the fields, on the dusty roads, on the choppers, in the hospital tents, or in a clean ward back in the UK. But those that came back didn't come back entirely. Part of them would be forever running, sweating, shooting, shouting, diving, crawling through those ditches and fields, forever sheltering from the heat in the shade of a baked-mud wall, forever in that moment, those moments of walking and running and crawling, when each step, each move, might trigger the bomb that took your arms or legs or sent your detached head, still in its helmet, rolling through the endless grey-brown dust.

One moment like that after another for months on end. One moment followed by another when an aimed shot or stray round could slam home and end it all in an instant.

And the smell: the dust and the diesel, the gun oil, the cordite and sulphur, the rotting vegetation, the sweat, the shit, the blood, the stinking wounds and decomposing bodies. How could it leave you? Why would it leave you?

Who would you be without it ripping you back in time to see things you wished you'd never seen in places you wished you'd never been? Who would you be? How could it not be there, behind your eyes and coursing through your brain as you walked down a street, chatted over a drink, smiled or laughed, or watched the sun set in a place you called home? How could it not be there as you fell asleep, as you dreamed and as you woke?

'Boss?' said Mark. 'Boss?'

'Mark.'

'What do you think? Have you ever thought about it?'

'No, that kind of thing will drive you mad.'

Harry came back down the central aisle. 'Frankie's back.'

The doors to the auditorium opened and shut at the top of the stairs.

'Keep your seats, fellas. Harry just told me your news. What a bloody waste. I met him a few times when Mick was on leave. They used to tear up the town, those two. How are his parents doing?'

'Kenny's dad flew in from Jamaica a couple of days ago. They're bearing up,' said Harry. 'I called them as soon as Lynne passed on the message.'

'Shame you can't go to the funeral,' said Frankie.

'We are,' said Gallagher.

Tom was walking down the steps to where they were sitting. 'You're mad. He worked with you, didn't he? I mean since you were in the army.'

'The coppers could be waiting, if they've made a connection,' said Frankie.

'Even if they haven't, Bannerman and his crowd will have,' said Gallagher offering the bottle to Tom, who took it and used it to point at him before taking a sip.

'You're a maniac, Gallagher. What's the plan?'

'First, we'll need some clothes – we can't turn up to Kenny's funeral dressed like this.'

356

* * *

The knock at the back door made Vince jump.

'Calm down, soft arse,' said Ray. 'It'll be the woman. Go and check the street from the front bedroom. I'll check the back.'

'Shouldn't we let her in?'

'Don't make me ask you again, dickhead.'

Vince was dithering at the foot of the stairs as Ray descended. 'All clear.'

'Good. I got her mug shot on my phone camera. Go and let her in.'

Vince unlocked the mortise lock and then turned the Yale latch above. A striking blonde woman entered carrying an umbrella. He shut the door behind her.

'What took you?' asked the woman codenamed Hariq.

'Just being careful.'

'Where's the girl?'

'Upstairs, back room.'

'Where's the other one?'

Vince looked confused. 'We've only got one girl.'

'The other guard,' said the woman, with a pitying look.

'Through here.'

She followed Vince into a musty-smelling room containing a threadbare three-piece suite that had lost all sense of its

357

own identity shortly after it had been placed on the mind-bendingly psychedelic carpet many years before.

Ray offered his hand. 'Ray Carver, at your service.'

She gave him her best smile and pulled back the edge of a dirty net curtain to look out into the street.

Vince shifted his weight from one foot to the other. 'George, Mr Parker, said you were coming but he didn't say why.'

She smiled another sweet smile. 'Nothing to worry about, boys: I'll be out of here in a few minutes. Would you show me the bathroom before I speak to the girl?'

'Yeah, right,' said Ray, positioning himself in front of Vince. 'Allow me.'

'Thanks.' She looked at Vince. 'Be a poppet and take her hood off, but keep her gagged, would you?'

'But George, Mr Parker, said to keep her hooded,' said Vince.

He saw the warning flash in the woman's eyes, nodded and dipped a little.

The prick might as well have curtsied, thought Ray.

She allowed Ray to follow her up the stairs so he could get a good look at her backside. She locked the bathroom door, lowered the toilet seat and lid with her foot and removed the Makarov from its holster. Reaching into her bag, she took out the suppressor. Once the silencer was fitted she flushed the toilet using her elbow, walked back to the door and placed the gun flat against the wall at face level, as if she was leaning her palm against the plaster.

She opened the door.

'Have you seen this window?' she asked Ray, who was loitering on the landing. She could see Vince standing with his back to her, looking at Connie. Both men had put on their balaclavas.

'The window? Why?'

'Come and look,' she said, watching Ray the grinning mask as he came towards her.

She angled her body to the side and allowed him to brush past her.

'Look at the latch.'

Ray moved to the window as the woman eased the door until it was just ajar. 'What's up with it?'

She stood close behind him, making sure her breath touched his neck, her right hand behind her back. 'I thought it had been tampered with. What do you think?'

Ray turned slowly, maintaining the close proximity of the encounter. 'From where I'm standing, everything looks fine – more than fine.'

She touched his lips through the mask with her left index finger. 'No time for that,' she said, moving the flat of her hand down to his chest.

Ray placed his hands on her waist. 'What's five minutes between friends?'

She feigned a giggle and pushed him gently so that the back of his legs made contact with the toilet. 'Five minutes? Well, all work and no play.'

She stepped forward, forcing him to sit.

Ray grinned at her chest as she brought the Makarov around and fired a single shot up under his chin. His head snapped back and the remains of the rear of his skull settled on the cistern with chunks of his brain.

The woman turned quickly, walked forward and peered through the crack in the door. Vince had also turned and she watched as he stepped out on to the landing. As she opened the door a question formed in his mind but died with him before he hit the bare paint-splattered floorboards.

Connie stared, wide-eyed.

Flic removed the Makarov's suppressor, placed it back in her bag and refitted the pistol in its ankle holster. 'Hello, Connie. I'm a friend of Tom's. Shall we go?'

Connie's eyes filled with tears as Flic undid the gag. She coughed and stretched her jaw. 'Thank God,' she said. 'Please, get me out of here.'

'My car is two streets away – can you walk?'

'Watch me.'

'Good girl, come on.'

Flic led Connie to the back door.

'After you,' she said. 'I think you deserve the honour of opening your prison door.'

Connie undid the latch and allowed Flic to walk through, before pulling the door closed behind her. 'What about them?' she asked.

'What about them?' Flic replied. 'They aren't going anywhere.'

It had started to rain again. They passed through a small yard full of rubbish and Flic ensured that Connie opened and closed the back gate. They came out into an alleyway. It was empty except for two mangy-looking cats eyeing each other up on either side of the six-foot wall at the rear of the next-door property. Flic opened the large black umbrella and used it to shield their faces.

She helped Connie along the road, smiling at an elderly lady who had given a look of concern when she saw Connie's haggard features limping along the pavement under the brolly.

They hurried, as quickly as Connie could manage, to where Flic's car was waiting.

Flic eased the car out of its parking space and checked the parked cars for occupants as she approached the junction. She made a left turn and headed for the busy main road two hundred metres away.

'They said they'd got him,' said Connie quietly.

'They did, he escaped.'

'How did you know where I was? How come they let you in?'

'Forget about it for the moment, they had it coming. I've got a lot to tell you but not just now. Relax and get your strength back. You've had quite an ordeal by the look of things.'

Connie eased back in the passenger seat. 'I can't believe it's over.' She rubbed the welts and cuts on her wrists. 'I can't believe it. Thank you.'

'Just relax. Are you hungry?'

'I'm starving but I want to see Tom. Are we going to him now?'

'He's meeting us later. I'll get us a take-out while we're waiting for him to arrive. Fancy an Indian or a Chinese? There's a great pizza place I know, too.'

'Honestly,' said Connie, closing her eyes, 'I don't mind.'

'OK,' said Flic. 'We can decide when we get to my place.'

* * *

Wayne Dalton had been working the door of Luca's for three years. There were more than enough perks that came with the territory – and it offset the boredom of his day job. The queue of young trendy types stretched down the road to his right between the red ropes. In twenty minutes he and

Charlie Vaughan would be relieved by two colleagues, then he'd work the bar area and catch up with the girl who'd given him the eye on the way in. It was one of those nights: he was going to get lucky. He could feel it in his bones.

He watched as the group of lads that Charlie had just refused crossed the road, turned the corner and headed towards Oxford Street. Charlie was a big bastard of a Welshman who spoke softly with a patient, knowing air. The lads had actually thanked him before walking away. Of course, it was the sensible thing to do. Charlie had only recently left the Marines and he gave off an aura of quiet but potentially deadly menace when the need arose. He was a bit twitchy and serious for some of the other bouncers, but Wayne liked him well enough and he was the kind of bloke you wanted next to you if it all kicked off. He looked at his watch and considered which of his chat-up lines he was going to use on the cheeky buxom brunette.

A bottle hit the brickwork above his head. A scrawny-looking Asian lad was standing on the other side of the road waving the come-on.

'Little bastard,' said Wayne.

Charlie held the queue. 'Stand your ground, Wayne. He'll fuck off in a minute.'

Wayne ducked as the next bottle flew past him and hit the club's inner glass doors.

'Oi, you skinny bastard!' he shouted, walking into the road.

The next bottle glanced his shoulder on its way past his head and the thrower ran.

Wayne gave chase. The scrawny fucker was fast, but he stopped at the corner goading Wayne on before disappearing down the side road on the right. Wayne heard Charlie shout something but you couldn't let liberties be taken like that – you just couldn't.

Charlie sighed and waved a group of six girls through. He was going to ditch this job as soon as he could. Some mates of his were earning good money on the security circuit but Charlie needed some time before he carried a weapon or endured the heat again. Two couples were next in line and Charlie waved them on as he looked at a white male in his mid-twenties further down the queue. The man didn't seem to be with anyone and was doing his best not to make eye contact from beneath the peak of an oversized baseball cap. There wasn't a chance in hell that he'd be coming through the doors to the club. Not tonight, not any night.

Charlie heard two gunshots from the direction that Wayne had given chase and instinctively ducked into the cover of the club's entrance. When he emerged a few seconds later the lone male was standing in front of him, a Steyr machine-pistol in his hand, sticking out from beneath his coat.

'*Allahu Akbar*,' the man said quietly.

The first round hit Charlie in the chest. The second passed up through his chin spraying blood and brain matter into the faces of two girls standing in the entrance. As Charlie fell, the gunman pushed the screaming girls back into the club.

'*Allahu Akbar*!' he shouted against the thumping bass of the music, a wall of sound that sent him into a killing rage.

Upstairs, Loz Weir was watching the security monitors as the first grenade exploded among the packed-in clubbers. As he ran from the control room he heard another two explosions. He heard the fourth as he kicked open George Parker's office door.

'Out the back, boss, we're being hit.'

Parker was already stubbing out his cigar and had one arm in his coat. The monitor on his desk was scrolling through cameras: three showed thick smoke and strobe lights, while all the others seemed to be broken. He opened the middle drawer of his desk and lifted out a heavy security box, from which he removed two CZ100 pistols.

He threw one to Loz.

Loz went through the fire exit at the top of the back stairs first and looked down into the stairwell. 'Clear.'

'Someone's going to fucking pay for this.'

'We need to get out of here first, George,' Loz said, pressing a speed dial on his phone.

'Bish, you still round at the bookies? Good. Bring the car to the junction with Great Titchfield Street. Do it now: the club's being hit.'

As they reached the bottom of the stairs at the rear of the club, Loz charged through a barred exit and into the rear lobby next to the doors to the smoking area outside. One of the security staff was out in the yard trying to unlock the back gates, surrounded by punters shouting and screaming.

Loz caught his breath. The small crowd surged out into the road behind. The bouncer with the keys came back into the club as the door leading off the main dance floor opened.

There was a wildness in the eyes of the man who emerged flanked by billowing smoke. The music had stopped. The explosions had stopped. The crying and screaming were only just beginning.

'This way!' shouted the bouncer to the clubber.

Loz saw the gun come up and track from the bouncer to Parker. He pushed the older man back into the stairwell and fired, hitting the gunman in the chest as he felt a round strike him in the shoulder.

Parker picked himself up, walked over to the gunman and double-tapped him in the head. 'Cunt.'

'Come on, boss, there might be more. You: Tommo, isn't it?'

The bouncer nodded, still staring at the widening pool of blood and the exploded head on the floor in front of him.

'We weren't here tonight. Got it? The Old Bill will be here any minute. I need to get Mr Parker away. Get upstairs and switch everything off in the boss's office. Lock the upstairs off and tell Sean in the control room to erase all the camera footage for the cameras in this back area and the stairs. Two days' worth should do it. Get him to scribble a fault report card, sharpish.'

The bouncer nodded. He was fixated by the remaining eye that was dangling on the cheek of the dead man.

'Oi, Silly Bollocks! Do as you've been told,' said Parker. 'Loz, let's go, there's no time for fannying-a-fucking-bout.'

Faaz was parked in shadow diagonally across the street about thirty metres from where Loz and Parker appeared. He leaned forward in the back seat and operated the front passenger window, lowering it half way.

He sat back again, rested the free-floating barrel, with its harmonic balancer, on the front seat and cocked the bolt-action Beretta Sniper. Through the telescopic sight he could see the design on Parker's blue tie. He began to control his breathing and prepared for a headshot.

Loz looked left and then right in the direction of Great Titchfield Street. He looked left again, saw the glint on the sight's glass and pushed Parker back through the club's rear gates. It felt like someone had punched him in the throat and his gaze followed the moving stars in the night sky as they passed over his head.

He gurgled something to Parker, who was pulling him into cover.

'Got him, Loz, got him,' said Parker, swinging low around the gate post and putting three rounds into various parts of the parked car before taking cover again.

'Cheeky bastard. I'll fucking string him up, Loz, see if I don't.'

Two more shots were fired, ricocheting off the ornate iron gates behind and above Parker's head.

Parker fired three shots as the gunman moved around the outside of the car. Two quick shots hit the brickwork as he pulled his head back out of the shooter's line of sight.

'I'll hang him up by his bollocks,' said Parker, reaching for Loz's pistol. He heard an engine rev and saw the car begin to pull away at speed. He stood, a CZ100 in each hand and fired the remaining rounds contained in the two magazines.

'Wanker!' he shouted, as he heard the second click of an empty chamber.

He put the pistols into his coat pockets and walked back to Loz. 'Someone's going to fucking pay for this, my friend – that I fucking promise you.'

Parker crouched and brushed Loz's staring eyes closed as Bish screeched to a halt in the Range Rover.

'Boss, what the fuck's going on?'

Parker stood and looked first at the smoke pouring out of the club and then down at Loz. The sound of sirens was getting nearer. He jumped into the passenger seat and Bish hit the accelerator.

'Some fucker's just mugged themselves. Some fucker out there, tonight, has just signed up for a course of advanced torture and a long stay in a shallow-fucking-grave.'

* * *

Lynne Burgess had handed Harry's suit in a bag to Mark, who was on Gallagher's motorbike, at a meeting at the local park, along with her little brother's suit for him – and an earful to be delivered to her husband.

Gallagher and Tom were wearing suits that had belonged to Mick Fuller. The sleeves were slightly too short for Gallagher and the jacket wouldn't button. He thought he looked like a waiter in a back-street restaurant.

As the service around the open grave was nearing its end, Gallagher watched three vehicles with tinted windows roll along the cemetery's central track north of where the mourners stood with heads bowed. Bannerman's immaculate trench coat moved into view from Gallagher's left as its owner made his way through the gravestones. Bannerman nodded and took his place in the rear rank of the black-clad crowd.

'Friends of yours?' Gallagher whispered.

'Out of my hands,' said Bannerman, feeling the end of Gallagher's gun in the small of his back. 'At a funeral?' he whispered. 'Badly done, Owen, badly done.'

The mourners began to drift away, shaking the vicar's hand as they went.

'I'll do you if you don't do exactly as I tell you. What's the plan?'

'You'll be picked up as you try to leave, all the exits are covered.'

'I thought they might be.'

'Don't tell me: I'm going to help you escape with a gun in my back. I didn't have you pegged as the melodramatic type.'

Gallagher gripped the pistol hard in his coat pocket and jammed it purposely into Bannerman's left kidney. 'Let's go and say goodbye to Kenny's mum; it'll give you a chance to pay your respects. She's offered us a lift in the family car: Kenny's dad and uncles are walking to the pub where the wake is being held so they can have a smoke on the way. I don't think your gun-toting Plod friends will want to stop a family car at the funeral of a local war hero who has just died in prison – do you?'

'Not unless they want a week of riots, no.'

'You'll be joining us for a drink, then?'

'Rude not to, Owen, rude not to.'

Gallagher jabbed him again and followed Harry and Mark, who were flanking Valerie Collins on the way to the car.

'And how wise do you think it would be for the police – undercover or otherwise – to be within half a mile of that pub now that we all know they're here?' asked Gallagher.

'I see worrying potential for a serious breakdown in community relations.'

'As do I,' said Gallagher as they reached the car. 'Shall we?'

The funeral cars began their slow procession to the main entrance. Bannerman's phone vibrated loudly in his pocket.

'I'm sorry, Mrs Collins,' he said.

His apology was acknowledged with a nod. Valerie Collins went back to gazing out of the window as they drove past the rows of headstones.

'Will work be trying to get hold of you, Sandy?' Gallagher asked quietly.

'I should think they have a few questions, yes,' said Bannerman, looking across at the grieving mother. 'But I'm sure that they understand the importance of paying one's respects.'

Valerie smiled sweetly and dabbed her eyes with a handkerchief.

371

'Let's hope so,' said Gallagher.

Harry winked opposite Gallagher and Bannerman caught it.

'I'm sure that all the necessary arrangements for a good send-off have been made, Owen.'

Gallagher twisted his neck to the left and right, easing the tension until there was a dull crack. 'Indeed, Sandy, indeed. Just relax. Days like these are emotional – you don't want to become overwrought.'

'Don't worry, Owen, the first round is on me.'

* * *

Harry was standing by the large bay window at the front of the pub. He'd positioned himself so that he could glance past Kenny's Uncle Rodney as they talked – in order to keep an eye on the car park. Rodney was telling him stories about growing up in Jamaica.

Mark was smoking outside the back entrance with Kenny's dad and had a good view of the rear approach to the beer garden that lay off another road.

Gallagher was searching Bannerman in the Gents.

'Lay the contents of your pockets on the sink.'

Bannerman placed his wallet and phone on a dry part of the sink surround.

Gallagher stuffed the phone into the pocket of the black Crombie that Frankie had given him. 'You can keep your wallet; you'll need it at the bar.'

Harry turned as Gallagher and Bannerman came back into the room. Gallagher beckoned him to join them.

'Anything?'

'Two unmarked cars have done four drive pasts,' Harry reported.

'OK, keep Sandy company. I'm going out to see Mark.'

'It'll be nice to catch up, won't it Harry?' said Bannerman.

'If you say so.'

'Come on, Harry, I'm not the bad guy in this.'

'So who is?'

'Try not to make this too public, chaps,' said Gallagher walking away.

He passed Kenny's dad who was on his way to the Gents. 'Mr Collins, I'm so sorry for your loss.'

'Call me Kenneth. You're Captain Gallagher, right? I'll buy you a drink. I'll be back in a minute.'

Gallagher made his way outside. 'Anything, Mark?'

'Three drive-bys – one unmarked car, no uniform.'

'See if you can spot the nearest static surveillance, but don't venture out too far. I don't want them snatching anyone.'

Mark nodded and took a drag on his cigarette. 'Kenny was born in this road. I'll ask his dad to point out the house from the car park.'

Gallagher's phone rang. 'Tom?'

'I'm ready, front or back?' asked Tom.

'Back: there's a small fence with a gate to the beer garden, you can reverse right up to it through the rear car park. Give us twenty minutes.'

Gallagher ended the call and walked back to Mark. 'I'm not happy about what I'm about to do, but there's no choice.'

'I know, boss. I don't think Kenny would mind.'

Kenneth Collins came out of the back door with three glasses of whisky in the triangle made by his hands. 'A toast,' he said.

Mark and Gallagher took a glass each.

'To Kenny.'

'To Kenny.'

Gallagher downed his drink in one. 'Excuse me a moment, Mr Collins – Kenneth.' He walked back into the pub and found Harry and Bannerman in the same place he'd left them, still in an awkward attempt at civil conversation. 'Right, we're leaving in about fifteen minutes through the back. I'm going to say my goodbyes to Mrs Collins and then I'm going to talk to Kenny's Uncle Rodney.'

'Understood,' said Harry.

'Very clever,' said Sandy, raising his G&T. 'Ruthless but clever.'

'I don't feel good about it, but you've backed me into a corner. This is on you.'

'Quite so, Owen, and so is the last drink before we leave. It'll be on the bar as you come back this way.'

Having said his goodbye to Mrs Collins, Gallagher approached Uncle Rodney. Bannerman watched the man's features change from mildly jovial to a look of deadly seriousness. Rodney grabbed the arm of his brother, Richard, who was standing a few feet away talking to a woman wearing an enormous black hat. Rodney whispered in his brother's ear and then took out a mobile phone as his brother did the same. Uncle Rodney made his way to the bay window and made his call. Richard moved through to the back of the pub and spoke animatedly but quietly into his phone as he went.

'Oh dear,' said Bannerman to Harry. 'Someone's about to get a nasty surprise.'

'So will you if you try anything, you posh twat.'

Bannerman finished his drink and picked up the one he'd just ordered. 'Harry, I'm hurt. I thought we were friends.'

'Well, you know what Thought thought,' said Harry.

Bannerman looked puzzled but was saved from the need to pursue the semantic conundrum by Gallagher.

'Stay away from the windows and exits,' said Gallagher, reaching for the drink that Bannerman had placed waiting. 'I'll tip you the wink when it's time to move, H. If Sandy decides to go off script, lay him out.'

'With pleasure,' said Harry with a wide grin.

Tom had waited until the last minute before stealing the catering van. It was a white Citroën Berlingo, fitted with white rear-window security blanks and emblazoned with the sandwich company's logo along both flanks. He pulled down the peak of the red baseball cap, which he'd found on the dashboard, as he sat at a set of traffic lights. To his front, on the left, he could see three black Range Rovers parked in a line next to four police vans.

Once through the lights he drove half a mile and pulled over outside a parade of shops, where he sent a text message to Gallagher detailing what he'd seen. Gallagher acknowledged with a message of his own. Tom checked his watch and pulled out into the traffic. He looked left into the road at the front of the pub and saw a small crowd converging on a parked car. Several men, some in black suits, were gesticulating at the occupants. Tom moved forward in the traffic. A similar scene was unfolding at the other end of the road he turned into. Pulling into the rear car park of the pub, he saw Mark stub out a cigarette and turn to the back door. Manoeuvring the van, Tom reversed to the beer garden gate, jumped out of the cab and opened the back doors.

Mark returned, nodded and took up position at the side of the van with a view of the road. Bannerman came out of the pub first, followed by Harry and then Gallagher.

Harry pushed Bannerman. 'Your coach awaits, Cinders.'

'Most kind.'

'Shut the fuck up and climb on top of those crates of sandwiches, we've all got to squeeze in tight.'

Bannerman did as he was bidden. 'Do I send you my dry cleaning bill, Harry?'

'Shut it or they'll be charging extra for the blood stains.'

Bannerman smiled. 'One should always seek out new experiences.'

Harry followed him into the back. Mark came next. Gallagher was the last to climb aboard and Tom shut the doors. The sound of sirens grew loud.

Tom pulled out of the car park. To the left three police cars had blocked the road and several officers were attempting to extricate their undercover colleagues from the midst of the crowd. A dozen local youths, wearing a variety of headgear and scarves, were moving in from an alley opposite the rear of the pub carrying half-bricks and other makeshift missiles.

Tom indicated right and looked left just as Kenny's Uncle Rodney was shoved by a policeman. The group of youths began taunting the uniformed officers and a brick landed on the bonnet of the nearest patrol car. Two police vans had joined the fray and helmets and shields were being deployed in haste.

'Arseholes,' said Tom. As he turned left on to the main route out of the area two more patrol cars passed him at speed, lights flashing and sirens wailing.

'Never met you, Kenny,' he said aloud, 'but I reckon you'd have enjoyed this. No one round here's going to forget your last party in a hurry.'

* * *

George Parker was shown into Frankie's makeshift office at the disused cinema.

'You two wait out there,' he said to the men he'd brought with him.

'George,' said Frankie.

'Don't fucking George me – what the fuck's going on?'

'Connie Edwards,' said Gallagher from behind the door.

'Who the fuck's this?' Parker asked, still looking at Frankie.

'This is a friend of mine. The man in the corner waiting to shove a gun in your mouth is Connie's brother. Where's the girl?'

'Fuck knows. The two lads who were looking after her are dead. She's disappeared.'

378

Tom pulled his Browning from the back of his waistband. 'You'd better start making yourself a bit more useful or you'll be useless and dead.'

Parker undid his suit jacket. 'Teddy Southall calls Loz. Not long after, two of my men are shot dead by some posh bint, then some twat starts chucking grenades around my club while waving a machine-gun like he's Rambo-fucking-Schwarzenegger.'

He paused and gave Tom and the Browning a sidelong glance. 'The evening progresses and Loz takes a bullet meant for me. In other news: we shoot the bastard in the club only to find some other bastard's outside firing a fucking rifle at us down the street. While we're standing here chewing the cocking cud, Loz Weir is dead and what remains of my club is full of bodies and dozens of fucking coppers in forensic-fucking-paper-suits. Now, like I said, what the fuck's going on?'

Gallagher brought his right foot down on the back of Parker's knees and placed the end of his pistol behind Parker's ear.

He patted him down for weapons. 'Where's Connie?'

Parker straightened his tie and managed to look dignified in his kneeling position.

'For the hard-of-fucking-hearing among us: I. Do. Not. Know. Look, the house was cleared by some of my lads. I knew the woman was going to the house to see the girl so I

379

told Ray Carver to get a photo. Inside my jacket pocket: his phone.'

Tom placed his gun on Frankie's desk, walked over to Parker and pulled out the phone. 'This her?' he asked, holding it in front of the kneeling man's face.

'That's her.'

'Who is she?'

'She's the bitch who's been pulling my strings. I've never met her. She called herself Amelia.'

'And kidnapping Connie was her idea?' asked Gallagher, jamming the barrel of the gun into Parker's neck again.

'Well it wasn't fucking mine. I don't go around kidnapping young girls.'

Tom punched him hard in the stomach. 'But you did, didn't you? It was you who kidnapped my sister.'

He punched Parker again.

'I'll let you have those, son,' Parker said looking up at Tom. 'I can see you're upset. But if you touch me again in this life, it'll be a slow and painful death – that I promise you.'

'That'll do, Tom,' said Frankie. 'Do you recognise the woman?'

'No,' said Gallagher. 'Sandy?'

Tom passed the phone to Frankie who looked at the screen and passed it to Bannerman. Bannerman smoothed his hair and Gallagher watched as the blood drained from his face.

'Oh Christ, it's Flic Anderson.'

'Who's Flic Anderson?'

'She's who asked me to find Connie – you were essentially working for her.'

Tom grabbed his pistol from the desk and pointed it first at Bannerman and then at Gallagher.

'Easy, son,' said Frankie.

Tom turned and kicked out at a three-drawer metal filing cabinet until his rage began to subside. Then he stood resting his forehead against the wall, the weapon down at his side, his knuckles white.

'How do we find her?' asked Harry, moving his pistol from on top of his knee back to between his thigh and the chair.

'I'll find her,' said Parker. 'You can have what's left.'

'I doubt she's working alone,' said Bannerman, staring at the image and then looking at Parker. 'What did she want?'

Parker nodded towards Tom. 'She wanted him and whatever was in a brown leather wallet.'

'And then she'd have let the girl go?'

'I wouldn't have bet on it.'

'What else have you done for her?'

'Just this and a coded tip-off to the Old Bill.'

'About what?' asked Bannerman.

'Some bloke named Gallagher.'

Bannerman and Gallagher exchanged glances.

'How did that work?' Gallagher asked.

'There was a code – a handler's code – she said it would get to the right people. I just had to use the word and say that this bloke had been selling guns and had information about terrorist attacks.'

'And what else have you been doing for them, Mr Parker?' asked Bannerman.

'Who the fuck is this, Frankie, the Prime Minister's bum boy?'

'Answer the question, George.'

'It's complicated. I was involved in a deal a few years back. Let's just say that from Moscow to Mile End, via Istanbul, it all went a bit pear-shaped. It was put to me by certain types – types like our friend Prince-fucking-Charming sitting in the corner there – that things could be smoothed out. For a few favours. They just never stopped asking. This Amelia bird wasn't someone I'd dealt with before. She was the worst, though. That stuck-up cow wasn't asking: she came telling. Bitch.'

Bannerman rubbed his eyes and then crossed his arms. 'So you work for MI6?'

'It's mainly about fucking over foreigners: traffickers, dealers, nonces, ragheads; delivering packages; arranging the odd punishment beating. We lifted a few people off the street in London and arranged some hits over the Channel. I didn't lose any sleep over it.'

'Paid well, too, I'll bet,' said Frankie.

'Oi, watch yourself. I was no grass – not in the real sense, not to do with any of our own. Jonny Foreigner, though, he can go fuck himself, can't he?'

'A wonderful sentiment, beautifully expressed, Mr Parker,' said Bannerman. 'But why is Flic Anderson so keen to cross the line on this?'

'All we found were codes hidden in Web images. It could be anything,' Gallagher answered.

'I have a friend on secondment in London. He's usually based at GCHQ. The man's a genius,' said Bannerman. 'You need to let me go so I can get to the bottom of this.'

Tom raised his pistol. 'How do we know you're not involved? You're the only connection to this that I can see.'

'Thanks for the vote of confidence, Tom. Owen?'

'He has a point, Sandy. You're going nowhere for the moment. And be clear: if you try to fuck us over you'd better hope that Tom gets to you first.'

* * *

The house was in Cricklewood, in easy walking distance of the railway station. The house was a safe house, an MI6 safe house, which had been cleared for redecoration and updating. The work wasn't scheduled to begin for another three weeks and was part of a larger refurbishment

383

programme. The covert cameras and microphones had been stripped out. The old red carpets were still down but most of the furniture had been placed in large crates, ready for collection in a fortnight. She only needed to be there for a night. The two men would arrive in the early hours. She'd be back at the house to clean up in time to be gone by mid-morning.

There were four dining chairs left out of the crates. Flic sat opposite the one to which Connie was tied.

Connie jerked awake. There was an acid taste in her mouth behind the gag. Her vision was blurred and she felt sick. The smell of cooked food sent a wave of nausea through her.

'Hope you don't mind,' said Flic, dabbing the corner of her mouth with a paper napkin. 'I opted for pizza. Would you like a slice? It's spicy chicken.'

Connie glared as normal vision began to return.

'Suit yourself,' said Flic, closing the pizza box lid and placing it on the floor. 'I suppose you'll be feeling a bit woozy after the stun gun. It'll pass.'

Connie continued to stare.

'Questions? Yes, you must have questions. But, as neither of us are James Bond, I'm afraid I shan't be disclosing the details.'

Connie tried to push her feet off the floor, but she was secured to the chair legs with tape and her arms were tied behind the chair back. Her only wish was to get to the

384

woman sitting opposite, to head butt the supercilious smirk from that supercilious face.

'Take it easy,' said Flic, laying the silenced Makarov on her crossed thighs. 'You've had a rough few days – best not to exert yourself too much.'

Connie grunted her frustration.

'Suffice to say,' said Flic, pushing a strand of hair behind her ear, 'things haven't gone quite to plan. I'll need you for a little while longer. Sorry.'

SIXTEEN

Flic answered her phone. It was 09:21. 'George?'

'Yeah, look, I suppose you saw the mess at the club when you arrived. We'll have to arrange somewhere else to meet.'

'Yes,' said Flic, gathering her thoughts and taking a more authoritative tone. 'Do you have anything for me?'

'We found what you were looking for.'

'That is good news. And the business at the club? Were you hurt?'

'No, I'm all right but I've got some cleaning up to do. Let's get our business finished so I can track down the bastards who've got it coming.'

'Any leads?'

'Plenty but that's nothing for you to worry about. Do you want the wallet or not? I'm getting tired of these fucking games.'

'I imagine you've had an emotional time, George, but don't forget who you're talking to. You wouldn't want any further complications in your life just now, would you?'

'Yeah, like you said, it's been emotional. Name the time and the place. I'll bring it to you myself.'

'What about Edwards?'

'Resting in peace somewhere inside the Bermondsey Triangle.'

'The where?'

'The Bermondsey Triangle, you know, like the Bermuda Triangle but nearer the Thames – people go missing. What about this meet?'

'OK, George,' she said. 'I've got something that needs putting to bed as well. Give me a couple of hours and I'll call you back with the details.'

She ended the call and rested the phone beneath her lower lip, flat against her chin. It was an interesting development. She pushed her hair under a blue beanie hat and put on a pair of matching gloves, along with a pair of glasses, before walking towards the ringing doorbell. She checked out of the window and saw the Ford Transit van parked with two wheels on the pavement. The letters down the side spelled out 'ALAN THE VAN MAN. NO JOB TOO SMALL' above a mobile phone number.

The man at the door was in his early thirties, stocky, with greasy brown hair.

'Alan,' she said. 'This way.'

'That's a lot of crates,' said the man, with a worried look.

'Just the one to be moved today, as arranged,' Flic replied. 'But it's through here in the dining room. I hope that's OK.'

'No problem,' said Alan.

'It's an heirloom, so you're going to have to be very careful.'

'Careful is my middle name. Any chance of a brew?'

'Sorry, everything's packed away. How about we agree that the sooner we're done, the bigger your tip? Being very careful, of course.'

She watched as he pushed the crate through to the front door on a porter's trolley.

He stopped and lowered the crate so he could undo the door latch. 'Blimey, have you got a dead body in here?'

Flic laughed. 'No, all the bodies are under the floorboards. You know where to deliver it?'

'Yeah, yeah, the self-storage place over at Hammersmith. Have you got the paperwork and the spare key?'

Flic passed him an envelope and held out some bank notes. 'You'll leave the key inside? You can relock the padlock without it.'

'No worries,' he said, stuffing the money into the pocket of his jeans. He placed the envelope under his belt. 'I'll go straight there. It's on the way to my next job.'

* * *

388

Harry and Mark arrived in Chelsea in one of Frankie's cars and parked outside the café. A couple of minutes later Mark was back and opening the passenger door.

'Granddad wants to meet you.'

'OK,' said Harry. 'I'll find a meter; I could do with a brew.'

The café wasn't too busy. The back half was populated by three tables of men, in hi-vis vests and jackets, reading newspapers, slurping tea, surrounded by plates that had previously been home to the café's trademark full English breakfast. Mark was sitting nearer the front, opposite the counter hatch, with a grey-haired man in his sixties, who was wearing the navy-blue 'undress' uniform of the Royal Hospital. His 'shako' peaked cap with the 'RH' badge was on a chair beside him. Harry held out his hand as Archie stood.

'I got you a tea,' said the Chelsea Pensioner.

'Thanks. We can't stay long, though, sorry.'

Another tea and an hour later, Harry gathered together the empty mugs. 'We need to be getting off,' he said. 'It's been great to meet you, Archie.'

'The pleasure was mine,' Archie replied, standing to shake Harry's hand again. He reached into his pocket and pulled out the envelope he'd been keeping for Mark. 'Don't forget what you came for, son.'

389

'Cheers, Granddad. We'll go for that beer soon. Harry and Captain Gallagher said they'll come too.'

'Try and stop us,' said Harry, picking up the mugs and returning them to the counter.

Archie beamed as he picked up his cap. 'I'm looking forward to it. I don't know what you lads are involved in but you take care. Look after the boy, Harry, won't you?'

'Of course,' said Harry. 'He's no trouble really.'

Archie laughed. 'And you, Master Keane, you keep your nose clean.'

'He's as funny as you, sarge,' said Mark, as he hugged Archie goodbye.

* * *

Harry and Mark had returned to the old cinema to be briefed by Gallagher. Gallagher and Mark were being taken to one of Parker's properties in Kilburn to collect equipment. Harry was to babysit Bannerman, who was still looking at the stego material that Mark had downloaded. Parker was waiting for Flic's return call.

Gallagher handed a list to Frankie, who handed it to Chris.

'Clear?' asked Gallagher.

'Yeah. Six of everything: covert neck-loops and microphone systems; wireless receiver modules, with built-in PTT; wireless key-fob PTT pressel switches; shoulder harnesses; sub-miniature wireless ear pieces, with anti-interference squelch gates, and a pack of zinc air batteries. They'll know what I'm talking about?'

'They will. I've already phoned the order through, just check the bits off. I've got an account so there won't be a credit card for any police monitoring to ping.'

An hour later in Kilburn, Gallagher was led through the door of a lock-up workshop under the arches of a railway bridge. Mark followed him in. The other of Parker's goons waited in the car.

Goon One took a torch down off a shelf and told Mark to close the door behind him. They followed the torch beam to the rear of the space between a mess of lathes, workbenches and boxes. The Goon stopped and began pulling out various bits of machinery and dusty industrial detritus, clearing a path to the left-hand corner. Once there, he dragged a heavy piece of sheet metal to one side and illuminated a trap door with the torch.

'I'll go first,' said the Goon. 'Wait a minute. I've got to do something before you can come down.'

Gallagher watched the Goon descend a short set of wooden steps into a small cellar.

The man was sweating as his head re-emerged. 'Follow me.'

Gallagher and the Goon had to stoop but Mark could just about stand with a straight back. Each wall had tarpaulin-covered lumps running alongside.

'Don't touch the left-hand tarp. Don't go anywhere near the bastard.'

Gallagher nodded and watched the Goon pull the tarpaulin from the pile on the right, sending a plume of dust across the room. They all coughed.

There were at least twenty crates and boxes in this section. Gallagher prised the lid off a long crate as the Goon removed the tarp lying up against the back wall.

'FNCs,' said Gallagher, as he pulled out an assault rifle. 'What is this place?'

'Arms dump. IRA. The old fella who owned it was a sympathiser. When he died his son sold it to Mr Parker, lock stock – doubt he'd ever been here and if he had, he couldn't have seen this lot. George, Mr Parker, had heard a whisper, didn't give the bloke a choice. He said some contacts had told him the street was up for regeneration, but it never happened.'

'When was this?'

'Ten years ago, give or take. Loz Weir reckoned the IRA left it in reserve after decommissioning – maybe they forgot about it.'

'I doubt it,' said Gallagher. 'They've got long memories in Ireland.'

392

'Well, if they do come back they're in for a surprise. I had to disconnect the booby traps. There's enough to bring the roof down and the blast from the explosives and ammo should send it back up again. They'll be blown back to Belfast.'

Mark opened a box. 'Frag grenades. There's some good kit down here. Hey, boss, this is like that film, the one in Vietnam.'

'Eh?'

'They go searching for some missing PoWs but they lose all their kit. Anyway, they end up in a cellar sorting through a load of shit old gats.'

'You've lost me.'

'Patrick Swayze's in it and that other geezer, Gene something.'

'Hackman, Gene Hackman?' Gallagher asked. He stopped what he was doing. 'What's your point?'

Mark tossed a grenade from one hand to the other. 'Just reminded me, that's all. There's this big meat-head in it who wears a grenade around his neck. He says if he ever gets bored with life, he'll just pull the pin and see what happens next. Good film, funny. That Patrick Swayze was in it.'

'So you said. Keep chucking that about and we'll all be seeing what comes next. I don't want to be standing next to you when you turn into pink mist. Put it back in the box.'

'Boss, you're no fun anymore.'

Gallagher shook his head and smiled. He pointed to the crate he'd opened containing Belgian-made FNC assault rifles with folding stocks. 'Grab those bags in the corner. Fill the long canvas one with eight of those FNCs and find six mags for each. Actually, bring as many as you can in case any of the springs have gone. Bag the 5.56 ammo in that crate, too.'

'Fuck me boss, are we going to war again?'

'Let's hope not, but I'm sick of being at a disadvantage.'

'Fairy snuff,' said Mark, picking up the bags.

Gallagher finished examining the contents of the two piles and turned to the Goon. 'I'm going to want that box of Browning pistols, a suppressor unit for each, that box of 9mm ammo and that box of magazines.'

'Suppressor unit?'

'Silencer.'

'Oh yeah, right, no problem. George, Mr Parker, said you could have what you like except anything in that pile there. The explosives in those boxes were rigged by the same lot who set up the trip wire.'

Gallagher stopped pointing at the boxes and turned. 'Which lot?'

The Goon tried to backtrack. 'Just don't touch that pile, that's all. I'll move your boxes for you.'

So old George really has been playing with the big boys, thought Gallagher. He could imagine the Secret Intelligence

Service reeling Parker in until they had him over a barrel. Six would have handled him and his operations at home and abroad. Perhaps the police serious crime mob had lost him to the spooks before they could make an arrest – a matter of national security: hands off, lose the file, he's ours now.

The spooks would have instructed Mr Parker, The Puppet Gangster, to make the approach, to accept no refusal, to buy the workshop – cash, over the odds – no questions and quick. They'd probably been watching the place for years having followed the shipment from Libya in the eighties. They wouldn't have just walked away because the owner had popped his clogs. They wouldn't have risked someone arriving to tidy the place up. They'd have removed the listening devices and any cameras, set the place to blow – it wasn't a residential area, after all – then they'd have withdrawn the watchers and allowed events to take their course. Simple, cost-effective and ruthless. Maybe the IRA had gotten wind of something, or maybe they just weren't risking annual audits at the moment. Either way, there'd be an IRA quartermaster somewhere who knew exactly where this stuff was stored.

'Finished?' asked the Goon, after he'd taken the last box upstairs. 'I've got to put it all back as it was.'

'Finished,' said Gallagher. 'We'll be in the car. Careful now.'

* * *

Dilawar and Barraq were sitting at the kitchen table. In front of them lay four blocks of explosives, several bags of nails, two pistols, three mobile phones, various maps of the London area, a pile of clothes and a black holdall.

'When did the message say they'd be here?' asked Dilawar.

'I told you, midday. Dil, stop asking me. They're only five minutes late.'

'And they'll have the detonators?'

Barraq looked at Dil and raised a warning finger. 'Stop. And no more about that pretty cousin of yours, either.'

'Second cousin,' corrected Dil.

'Or her,' said Barraq.

'Are you still happy we were chosen as *Shahid*?'

'We've talked about this, we'd never get away. Are you worried about never having sex with that pretty cousin of yours?'

'Second cousin. No, of course not.'

'So what are you worried about? If we mess up, you'll be in prison watching your arse in the showers – so keep your mind on the job.'

'I was just saying.'

'Well don't. I want to think, to run through the plan in my head.'

'Tea?'

Barraq shook his head and lifted his palms. 'If it makes you happy, make tea, but please shut up.'

The doorbell rang as the kettle boiled. Dil went to open it and beckoned the two men to enter.

'I am Rasul, brother,' said Ozi.

'And I am Abbas,' said Net.

Dil indicated the door to the kitchen and led them through. 'You are welcome, brothers.'

Barraq got up from his chair as they entered.

'This is Barraq,' said Dil. 'Would you like tea?'

Net began to speak quickly in Arabic.

'I'm sorry,' said Dil, 'I don't speak fluently and you're a bit fast for me.'

Net smiled. 'I said thank you, brother, no. We have work to do elsewhere. We must do what we came to do quickly and go.'

Barraq nodded. 'Of course.'

Net took a pair of surgical gloves from a pocket in his coat and pulled a small package from another.

'The detonators?' asked Dil.

'The detonators. I need to prepare them with the explosives. I need peace. Take Rasul into the living room and run through the plan with him.'

'But,' said Dil.

397

Net raised his eyebrows, daring him to speak again.

Dil closed his mouth and looked at Barraq, who moved to the door. 'Of course, brother.'

Barraq followed, grabbing a map from the table. Ozi nodded to Net and followed the two men across the hallway into the other room.

Once he was alone, Net carefully unwrapped the detonators and inserted them into the explosives. He looked through the open door and heard Ozi demanding answers about the mission plan. Net placed the explosives to one side and took out another small block from his pocket. This block was fitted with two small detonators attached to a compact electronic timer. He set the device's countdown to thirty minutes before lifting the base inside the holdall, under which he hid the initialising bomb. Then he placed the other explosives – with the detonators fitted to the mobile phone – on top of the detachable base and packed the bags of nails around the device. He packed the rest of the bag with the clothes that Barraq and Dil had prepared. Everything was in place: explosive, switch, initiator, shrapnel and power source.

This one was going to be easy. The blonde man who had bombed the M1 service station had given them some trouble, but not too much. It had been worth the effort and they'd left a stack of damning evidence.

Net zipped up the holdall and placed the two pistols on top. 'Rasul,' he called.

Ozi brought the two men back into the kitchen. 'They're ready. They leave in an hour.'

'Good,' said Net, looking at Barraq and Dil. 'I know we're on the top floor but take the stairs, not the lift, when you leave. Your martyrs' video is ready?'

They nodded.

'And it'll be found when the police search this flat?'

'It's stored on a memory stick on the coffee table in the living room,' Barraq replied.

Net pointed at the bag. 'Neither of you are to let that bag out of your sight. We can't risk either of you tampering with it. There are spies and traitors everywhere. You will watch each other, understand?'

Dil looked horrified. 'We've known each other since we were children.'

'Do you understand?' shouted Net. 'We have lost two bombs in the last few days because people we have known, men we have trusted, have betrayed us, have betrayed God.'

Barraq stepped in front of Dil. 'We understand, brother. He meant no offence.'

'You have no need to check it: it's ready. You just need to dial the number when you reach the target. But remember to shoot as many unbelievers as you can first – with your thumb on the speed dial, of course.'

'Of course,' said Barraq.

Net smiled. 'You are warriors of God, remember that. *Allah akbar wallilahi'l-hamd.*'

'*Allah akbar wallilahi'l-hamd*,' repeated the other three in unison.

'Now we must leave you,' said Net, spreading his arms to embrace Barraq and then Dil.

Ozi did the same.

Dil escorted the two men to the door and closed it behind them. His legs felt as if they might not hold his weight and he steadied himself taking deep breaths. Having composed himself, he rejoined Barraq at the kitchen table and stared at the bag. 'She is beautiful, though,' he said.

'Who?'

'My cousin.'

'Second cousin,' said Barraq, grinning at his friend.

* * *

Gemma Godrevy met Nicholas Drummond as he entered the JTAC operations room.

'What have you got?'

'An explosion in a block of flats. Fortunately, it was on the top floor and the damage was contained – relatively speaking.'

'Bodies?'

400

'Two in the flat: Asian males, probably early twenties – or so the neighbours say. There isn't much to go on, given what's left of them.'

'Cause?'

'Definitely a bomb. The first indications are that the explosives weren't homemade. Preliminary notes on the scene suggest the same type as we've found elsewhere – similar to the cache seized in the Gulf, origin Iran. So we're back to the Tehran connection. Fragments of gun metal are also being analysed.'

'It doesn't make sense to me. Do they think we're stupid? How's the incident being controlled?'

'The Met have issued a press release about a gas explosion.'

'Identities?'

'Nothing yet. The search team will gather evidence when forensics have finished. It'll be a long job: the place is a mess. But we've found a suicide video and details of targets: nuclear power stations, oil and gas terminals, the Shard.'

'OK, thanks,' said Drummond. 'Keep me posted. I'm on my way to a meeting, but call me if you need to.'

* * *

'Anything?' Gallagher asked.

'Nothing mind-blowing, but I think I've found someone's mistake,' said Bannerman, pointing at the laptop's screen. 'This line here has been left in clear text. It hasn't been transcribed into code groups. There's so much of it hidden and fragmented it doesn't jump out.'

Bannerman passed Gallagher a sheet of paper.

'An address? Any context?'

'No, but it's a lead and we haven't got any others. You do see the wisdom in letting me leave to have this worked on by our analysts and GCHQ, don't you?'

'Sandy, some of us are wanted men and Connie is still missing. Getting her back is my top priority.'

'I understand but the odds are that whatever is on this memory stick led to Connie's kidnap, the kill order on Tom and no doubt the attack on Parker's club. You haven't got a chance of picking up Flic until tomorrow morning's meeting – this could give us the edge.'

'Sorry, Sandy. I can't risk being arrested, we might never find Connie. That said: this address could move things forward. If not, tomorrow we find Connie and you're free to do as you please. As of now, that memory stick is the only bargaining chip we have.'

'What are you going to do?'

'We'll watch the address, check for occupants and gain entry for a search if possible.'

402

'And if someone's home?'

'Interview without coffee. I want some answers and I want them quick.'

* * *

Gallagher had parked his motorbike at the end of the road. He had a good view of the door to the target flat. Tom was watching the back, Harry was at the other end of the street and Mark was about to begin his first walk past. Parker's driver, Bish, was seven cars along from the motorbike.

Gallagher's voice came through each man's earpiece. 'Possible standby, standby: the lights in Charlie One have been switched off. Harry acknowledge.'

Harry gave two clicks.

'Yep, that's Alpha One: IC1 male – hat, dark suit, trench coat, black and grey rucksack – exiting front of Charlie One. Tom keep eyes on the back.'

Tom gave two clicks.

Gallagher continued. 'Mark, hold your position. H, trigger Alpha One away to Mark as he passes you.'

Harry gave two clicks.

'Mark, you need to be ready to follow him on to public transport, it doesn't look like he's using a car.'

Two clicks.

Gallagher started the motorbike. 'Tom, hold your position. Bish, keep eyes on the front door. He might lead us to the woman, so it's worth a punt. If not, we'll house him and come back for a search. Bish and Tom acknowledge.'

'Got it,' replied Bish.

Two clicks.

'That's Alpha One approaching the junction,' said Harry.

'I have,' said Mark. 'He's heading to the station.'

'Harry, back Mark. I'll ride around the other side. If he enters the station, we three follow. All call-signs acknowledge. Tom?'

Two clicks.

'Bish.'

'Got it.'

'Mark.'

Two clicks.

'Harry.'

Two clicks.

* * *

The man they followed on to the train at Balham and off at London Bridge had been born Peter Vickery. His name on conversion became Ramzi Rahman. He walked through the bustling streets with a sense of purpose that he'd never before experienced. Thirsty City workers were beginning to slip away from their offices, scuttling into the pubs and bars for a few drinks before catching their trains out of London. It was his birthday.

His choice of target had been immediately obvious when he'd been offered the means. He smiled as he saw the lights of the pub ahead of him. He knew the pub's layout well. He'd sunk many a pint in there himself when he was working as an office drone – before he found God, before he'd started to consider his immortal soul.

Beneath his long coat, he wore a suit and tie. There was a rucksack over his left shoulder and a brown fedora rested on his head at a slight angle. The pub's lone CCTV camera was above the inside of the side door that he'd be entering through, covering the bar area. He could hide his features by walking beneath and away from it. He didn't want to be seen going in and out of the same door in the space of minutes so he steeled himself to walk the length of the pub.

He took a deep breath and walked into the heaving one-roomed bar, angling sideways through groups of drinkers, politely touching backs, nodding his thanks and avoiding elbows connected to full glasses.

The two barmen were preoccupied with the orders of waiting customers leaning on the curving mahogany. Ramzi slipped through to the stairs next to the door he would use to get back on to the street. The stairs fell away to the right and he descended the steep steps to the toilets, which were situated directly beneath the bar.

As he entered, he saw the familiar cubicles, the urinals and, to the right-hand side, padlocked cupboards. A portly man in a suit was sighing into a urinal, his back turned to the newcomer. Ramzi ducked into one of the cubicles and locked the door. He waited for the sound of the taps and then the hand dryer. Finally, he heard the door swing closed and he was alone.

He dropped the toilet lid and placed his rucksack on it, before carefully pulling out the large package wrapped in birthday paper. The timer was visible from the underside. He set eight minutes on the clock and then covered the gap with a piece of gift-wrapped card that he'd prepared earlier, securing it with the double-sided tape affixed to it. The phone signal wasn't particularly strong down in the depths, so he'd opted for a timer to detonate the bomb.

He laid the birthday present on the cistern and climbed up and over into the next cubicle. He adjusted his clothes and was careful to tilt his hat to the left, which would guard his face from the CCTV camera. He climbed the stairs and exited through the door at the top, walking back out on to the street.

Harry still had eyes on both exits from the doorway of a sandwich shop opposite the pub. The rain had returned and

406

was getting heavy. He gave the standby to the team as Ramzi came out. A bus on its way to Aldgate pulled up in the traffic and obscured Harry's view, so he left the doorway and moved to a better position.

'Got him,' said Gallagher, who was watching in the reflection of a shop window. 'He's gone left, through the alley. I have.'

'He was in there just long enough for a piss,' said Harry. 'Have we got the wrong bloke?'

'That's what we're here to find out. I'll follow him through here. Hang back, Harry, and see if anyone follows.'

Two clicks.

Gallagher walked under the overhead walkway that crossed the alley as the target followed it round to the right.

Ramzi felt the hairs on the back of his neck standing up. He looked behind and saw no one. A woman was approaching him, heels clacking and puffing on a cigarette. Both being Londoners, they avoided eye contact. She passed him and he began to walk quicker.

'He's cleared the alley,' said Gallagher. 'I still have. He could be heading back to the station. Mark, are you ready?'

Mark replied with two clicks from his position on London Bridge, where he was sitting wrapped in his coat wearing a woollen hat with flaps over the ears. A discarded paper coffee cup in front of him was a third full with coins. 'I'll take him if he passes me. I reckon I've made a fiver already,' he whispered.

Gallagher followed the target along Eastcheap, past the Monument to King William Street and left on to London Bridge.

'Definitely looking like London Bridge Station. Get ready, Mark,' he said, slowing to a halt. 'Stop, stop, stop. He's on the bridge just north of your location Mark, looking east towards HMS Belfast.'

Two clicks.

'What's he doing?' Harry asked.

'Nothing and there's no one near him on the bridge rail that he could be talking to.'

'A few punters have gone into the pub but no one else has come out,' said Harry. 'Do you want me to do a walk-through?'

Gallagher thought for a moment. 'Yeah, check the pub for the Anderson woman. If there's no sign, head for London Bridge. We'll see where he's going next.'

'OK,' said Harry. 'There are buses lined up here so I'm finding it hard to keep eyes on without looking odd. I might as well go in now.'

Harry crossed the road, heading for the nearest entrance to the pub. The ground shook beneath him and a bus rocked on its wheels as the etched windows of the bar shattered out on to the pavement. Smoke and dust began to fill the street.

'He's just looking at his watch,' said Gallagher in Harry's earpiece.

Ramzi counted down the seconds and then pulled up the collar of his coat. The sound of sirens erupted in the evening air.

'Bomb at the pub. Standby.' Harry walked to the rear of the bus and looked across at the shattered windows. He hadn't seen anyone leave the building. Through the settling dust and grey smoke he saw a hole where the bar had been. The floor had collapsed taking everything and everyone with it. A burst pipe sprayed water towards the ceiling. Harry helped a pedestrian to stem the bleeding from her wound and then walked away from the scene.

'I'm going to have to move,' he said. 'I feel shitty leaving the wounded but the Old Bill are starting to arrive. Will they shut the stations?'

'No, they won't know what's happening yet,' said Gallagher. 'They won't want the panic to spread. The phone networks will stay up, so there could be secondary devices. The full response will take a while to kick in. It'll be chaos, though, so get moving.'

Two clicks.

* * *

Gallagher and Mark had followed the target on to his train. Harry managed to catch the one after.

Gallagher rode the motorbike back to a position in the road further up from where he'd been earlier. Mark had watched the man re-enter the flat. Bish and Tom had nothing to report.

'What now?' Tom asked from his hiding place.

'We wait for Harry, he shouldn't be long. Then we go in.'

'I can't get in through the back without making a lot of noise. I'll come round the front,' Tom explained.

'Boss,' said Mark, interrupting. 'There's two geezers approaching your location. They're looking at the house numbers.'

'OK, standby.'

'They've stopped. Yep, they're going to the door.'

The door opened and light flooded the steps where the two men were standing. Code phrases were exchanged and Ramzi ushered them in, checking the street before he closed the door.

'You've picked up a tail. We're here to get you out, brother.'

'I was just getting ready to leave,' said Ramzi, leading them into the living room, where his bags were stacked.

'So I see,' replied Net.

Ramzi moved to the window and pulled back the curtain.

'Unwise,' said Net. 'They'll be watching front and back.'

'Who? Who is watching?'

'Police, MI5, probably both – we should go.'

'Go where? Won't they have the place surrounded? Why not stand and fight?'

'You have your weapon?' Net asked.

'There's an AK under my bed with four full clips and I have this,' Ramzi said, pulling a Turkish-made Kirrikale 9mm pistol from the back of his trousers.

'We must go now,' said Ozi. 'They'll be calling reinforcements.'

Ramzi raised his gun. 'Cowards! Why not fight? I'm not leaving. No one is leaving. I'm not going to rot in a prison. We're at war and I'm a soldier.'

Ozi looked at Net but his friend kept looking at Ramzi.

'You are right, brother. We stand and fight. Get the AK and we'll work out our defensive positions. If we can hold them off, the television crews will be here to witness our martyrdom.'

'Now you're talking. We, you and I, are directly responsible for protecting and avenging our brothers and sisters,' said Ramzi, putting the pistol back in his waistband. He walked forward, embraced Net, turned and fell to his knees. '*Allahu Akbar!*' he shouted, before lowering and raising his palms in worship, smiling, eyes closed.

Net's bullet slammed through Ramzi's spinal cord, unzipping his throat and collapsing the lower part of his face.

The gun's suppressed noise made the damage seem surreal in the context of the soft-furnished living room.

Ozi walked to the body. 'I thought it was my turn.'

'Shut up,' said Net. 'And plant the evidence. You take the kitchen and I'll take the bedroom.'

'I'm just saying that we agreed.'

'Move!' shouted Net. 'This isn't one of your games.'

Ozi pulled a face and went into the hallway, turning left into the small kitchen. Net kicked Ramzi's corpse as the front door to the flat flew open. He raised his pistol, thought better of it, turned and ran to the bedroom.

Ozi stuck his head around the kitchen door as Harry came into view.

Gallagher fired two rounds.

Harry threw himself past Ozi's position and took a round in the leg as Ozi fired blind. Ozi now had a gunman either side of the door to contend with.

'Throw the weapon out,' Gallagher called.

Ozi glanced back at the three solid walls of the kitchen – no windows, no escape. He wasn't going back to prison. His next shot was fired high around the corner towards Gallagher, who was crouching low.

Harry fired and grazed Ozi's right arm as the weapon was pulled back into the kitchen.

Tom had joined them in the hallway, leaving Bish to keep watch.

'OK, OK,' Ozi shouted. Netanel would finish them off any second, he'd have the AK.

'Throw your weapon out,' Gallagher called again.

'OK, OK, I'm bleeding.'

'Throw it out or I throw this grenade in,' shouted Harry, bluffing.

Ozi couldn't call for Net and he couldn't stall much longer.

'Do you want me to spell it out for you?'

'OK, OK,' said Ozi. Net would take them when he heard the pistol hit the floor. He knew how his friend's mind worked.

Harry called out again. 'Throw it to the right and wait for my instructions.' The pistol landed on the polished wood floor and slid towards him. 'Show me your hands.'

Gallagher moved to the opposite wall, arms and pistol extended in the Weaver position.

'Now!' shouted Harry. 'Show me your hands now.'

Ozi's lower arms came into view, the right covered in blood.

'Yours, boss. We need to clear through.'

Gallagher eased along the wall and motioned that Mark should cover the man. Tom kept his pistol pointing down the hall at the opening to the living room beyond Harry.

'Walk slowly forward,' Gallagher instructed. 'Down on one knee. Hands on your head. Now the other knee.'

Mark stowed his pistol before grabbing Ozi's wrists and pushing him face down on the floor.

Gallagher threw him a zip-tie.

'Careful,' said Ozi. 'That hurts.'

'Shut the fuck up,' Mark replied, dragging Ozi back into the kitchen by his tied hands.

Tom passed the kitchen door and took up position. He glanced at the tear in Harry's trousers where Ozi's bullet had struck. 'Not bleeding much.'

'That's because it's the prosthetic, but I think I'll let you go first.'

Tom nodded and launched himself into the living room, diving behind a sofa angled side-on to the hall door. Harry dropped to his belly and peered into the room.

Tom nodded again and crawled around the furniture to get a view of the bedroom.

Harry glanced back at Gallagher. 'Room clear, apart from a body on the carpet,' he whispered.

Gallagher moved forward to where Harry was lying and received a nod from Tom, then angled his way along the living room wall to the bedroom door.

'Throw your weapon out,' Tom shouted. He counted to five, crawled to another position and fired one round through the open door. 'Do it now.'

Gallagher waited several seconds and then signalled for Tom to stay where he was.

414

'Bring the other one in, Mark,' said Gallagher. 'We haven't got time to fuck about. Man in the bedroom: throw your weapon out now or I'll throw your friend's body in.'

Mark pushed Ozi down the wall to Gallagher, who in turn shoved him forward, hooking his front leg with a foot as he passed. Ozi fell heavily with his head in front of the doorway.

Gallagher pointed his pistol at Ozi's temple. 'Tell him to throw his weapon out.'

Ozi laughed. 'He's gone.'

Gallagher dragged him back and lifted him to his knees, using him as a shield. He pulled back and nodded to Tom, who crawled forward behind an armchair.

'Clear from here,' Tom whispered.

Gallagher shoved Ozi through the door. There was a bed and a clothes rail but no other furniture. The window was open. 'Looks like you're the only one coming to the party,' he said. 'Who's that relaxing on the floor in the living room?'

Ozi turned to look at Ramzi's corpse lying in a widening pool of blood. 'He's no one. I'm no one. Go fuck your mother.'

'Not that it'd change matters in the slightest, but I'm afraid she's long dead,' Gallagher answered. He cracked Ozi across the head with his pistol. 'Let's go, lads. Silenced rounds or not, the neighbours will have heard a kerfuffle.'

415

SEVENTEEN

The two men in running kit, both carrying large rucksacks, jogged with an easy rhythm down the tree-lined avenue of Kensington Palace Gardens. A police car drove slowly past them on the other side of the road and the runner nearest the kerb offered a friendly wave. With all the barracks and embassies on this side of London, men running with packs were not an uncommon sight this early in the morning.

Danny Cooper, now known as Danyal, pointed to a clump of trees ahead of them. The man jogging next to him had changed the spelling of his name to 'Kamran' on conversion.

'Fifty metres on the left,' said Danyal. 'There shouldn't be another patrol car for fifteen minutes or so.'

'I wonder if HRH Bastard is at home,' said Kamran. 'It'd be good to get Captain Wales dead in his bed, wouldn't it? He survives his tours of Afghanistan, brags about killing Taliban and then gets blown up in a London palace. Beautiful.'

'Right,' said Danyal, as he began to slow the pace. 'Stay alert. We need to unpack with no fuss before moving forward. Once the first rocket is fired they'll be all over us. What's our priority?'

'The priority is four hits on Nottingham Cottage, residence of His Royal Highness Prince Harry. Two rockets in the direction of the main palace building for effect – just in case we can get a lucky shot on Kate and Wills. After that we take as many with us as we can,' Kamran replied, repeating the rehearsed instructions.

'We try to get away but we're not to be taken alive, got it?'

'Yeah, got it, I'm not thick. Let's get on with it before our sweat starts getting cold.'

They moved into the cover of the trees. Danyal took off his rucksack and removed the RPG launcher and three rockets. Next he clipped on a set of military-issue webbing: a belt with a holster containing a Yarygin 'Grach' 6P35 pistol, balanced with two double magazine pouches on the other side. To the front were two larger ammo pouches containing magazines for the Russian AKS-74U with its reduced barrel and folding stock, which was the last thing he removed from the bag.

Kamran was going through the same well-drilled process. When he'd finished loading his first rocket, he unzipped the side pouches of his rucksack and passed three hand grenades to Danyal, keeping three for himself. Both men secured these to the chest straps of their webbing.

'Ready?' asked Danyal.

'Ready.'

They moved to the position that had been plotted to allow the best available trajectory and distance for the rockets to reach the targets – and out of view of the side gate to the right.

'We'll be on camera now – go!' said Danyal.

His first rocket followed Kamran's across the high wall and hit the left side of the cottage's roof. Kamran was aiming right.

The shooting started as they fired the last two rockets at a higher angle hoping to hit Kensington Palace beyond the cottages.

The SO14 protection officers at the nearest gate called for reinforcements while firing three-round bursts at the two attackers, who began retreating to the trees.

Danyal was running back to the relative cover these offered when he heard Kamran cry out.

'They shot me in the arse!' Kamran shouted over the sound of exchanged gunfire. The adrenaline pumped through him and he laughed as he emptied a magazine in the direction of the gate. He limped towards Danyal, who was by now crouching a few metres away giving covering fire.

'In the arse, they shot me in the arse!' Kamran reloaded with his third magazine and fired. He was still laughing. His finger kept its pull on the trigger after the single round from a Heckler and Koch G3 travelled through his right eye and removed the back of his head.

418

Danyal watched his friend turn and fall on to the grass. He crawled forward, firing continually. He reached Kamran's body and pulled off the webbing. Back in cover he unpinned Kamran's three grenades and threw each one as far as he could.

He heard the cars braking hard. He couldn't run in the direction of the nearest gate as reinforcements would be rallying there. To his right there were now two armed response vehicles, the crews shouting for him to drop his weapons.

He fired two long bursts with the AK and threw a grenade, causing the ARV officers to take cover behind their vehicles on the road. Danyal knelt and changed magazines before firing a series of short bursts.

His weapon jammed. Placing it on the tarmac, he pulled out his pistol and fired six aimed shots. Four police bullets knocked him to the ground. Danyal cried out in frustration and pointed the pistol down his body, firing over his outstretched foot. He loaded a fresh magazine, eased out the pin of a grenade and held it to one side – waiting for them to come.

* * *

Nicholas Drummond was attending a briefing in Counter Terrorism Command's operations room, known as 1600, at New Scotland Yard. It was 08:03.

'So what have we got?' he asked the tall senior police officer at his side, as they watched the bank of plasma screens filling with live operational detail. Sky News was playing on another monitor in the corner.

'We're hoping to finish sweeping the area in the next couple of hours. Two terrorists, well-armed, in what looks like a well-planned operation,' replied Commander Ketteridge.

Drummond watched the screen as a television reporter gestured into the distance behind a police cordon. 'Armed with?'

'Russian pistols and AKs, grenades from God-Knows-Where and two RPG-7V3s with sighting devices – or so I'm told. The army specialists at the scene think the rockets were high-explosive anti-tank rounds, given the damage that was inflicted. I don't know where the terrorists got their intel, but it was wrong. None of the royals were in residence but six members of staff died. We've got three of SO14 critical, two dead from the ARVs and six other officers wounded.'

'Who's under the white tents?'

'We're still trying to ID them. What we do know is that they're both white males in their late twenties.' The policeman indicated to a map of the area that was lying on the desk in front of them. 'It seems that they assembled the RPGs here and moved to the firing position here.'

'Is that where they died?' asked Drummond.

'No. Number One died here after engaging the protection officers with an automatic. The other one was killed on the road in a firefight with two area ARVs.'

'Any connection to the other attacks? Anything from the motorway or car bombs?'

'We're checking the faces lifted from CCTV after all the attacks. If they were there we should get a match. Still nothing on your list of Trojans?'

'Nothing, our watcher teams have checked in.'

'So we keep looking.'

'Indeed. Keep me posted,' said Drummond. 'I've got the conference to worry about now. Any sign of trouble and we'll need that building locked down immediately. No one goes in, no one gets out. We'll hold the perimeter and wait for the various extraction teams to remove the delegates after we've dealt with whatever we have to deal with.'

'Are Special Forces in place?' asked the policeman.

'We've got teams standing by at Regent's Park and Duke of York's Barracks. Another lot is due to arrive at Wellington Barracks from Credenhill this afternoon.'

'And we've got members of the Special Reconnaissance Regiment out on ops with our lads, trying to find who's behind all this.'

421

'We can't do much more,' said Drummond, wiping his glasses. 'Bannerman signed off plans with the Americans, the French DST, the German BND and the Israelis at their embassies. I'm going to chase up the rest now.'

'Will they cancel it?'

'Not likely. I get the feeling that most of the talking will revolve around what they think the North Koreans and Iranians are planning to do next.'

'Change of venue, perhaps?'

'Not a chance. It's billed as an academic scientific conference. The organisers don't want any military or state background to it. It's one of the main reasons that they chose London.'

'And you say that Sandy Bannerman will be back to run the show from your end?'

'That's the plan,' said Drummond. 'It's his baby and I'll be returning the screaming bundle of joy to him the moment he walks back through the door.'

'By the way,' said the policeman, 'anything new regarding Occupy?'

'No, all the chatter has stopped. Nothing from our agents, either. I'd bet they've shelved their plans because of the terrorist attacks. We'll carry on monitoring, obviously, but they aren't our biggest priority.'

'Well that's something,' said Ketteridge, checking his phone's screen. 'They're a pain in the arse we don't need.'

* * *

George Parker watched as a bookseller at the South Bank Book Market organised boxes of books on rows of tables underneath Waterloo Bridge, near the National Theatre. The wind was blowing cold rain off the Thames. He saw the woman pass him without acknowledgement and then turn when she reached Festival Pier.

He picked up a book from one of the tables and saw her approach from the corner of his eye.

Flic took up position on the opposite side of the table from Parker. 'I haven't got long, where is it?' she whispered.

'I've got it but there's still the matter of payment.'

She didn't trust Parker. That's why she'd picked a meeting in a public place. Having done so, she couldn't threaten him too loudly – or shoot the old fox, as she was tempted to do. 'You'll get your money, don't worry about that.'

'Thing is, I do worry about that.'

'I'm gone in five minutes. What's the deal?'

Parker began to speak but she didn't hear what he was saying because a figure approaching from the direction of County Hall had her entire focus. As the man got closer her initial thoughts were confirmed. What were the odds that Sandy-bloody-Bannerman would be out for a bloody stroll on the South Bank at this very moment?

She picked up a book and pretended to flick through it. 'George, there's a man walking this way. I don't want him to see us together.'

Parker nodded and went to stand at another table of books, his back turned.

Flic braced herself and conjured up one of her best smiles. 'Sandy, what a pleasant surprise – not holed up in Thames House, then?'

Bannerman smoothed his hair. 'They allow us out on occasion.'

Flic replaced the book she'd been holding. 'It's a shame we can't go for coffee. I'm afraid I must dash, I was just killing time before a meeting.'

'I'm sure you could spare some time for an old friend.'

'Sorry, poppet, must go.' She began to walk backwards. 'Call me, yeah?'

'Ooh, sorry,' she said, turning to the person behind her that she'd bumped into.

The man didn't reply.

'Excuse me,' she said, trying to side step around him.

The man blocked her path. He looked familiar. She saw Parker walking back towards her as the man to her front jammed the barrel of a pistol into her stomach through his coat pocket.

Bannerman was at her side. 'Don't make a scene, Flic. We can do this quietly or we can do this with armed police and sirens. We can go to a windowless room, or we can go for a quiet chat somewhere more neutral.'

Parker was standing at Gallagher's shoulder.

Bannerman tilted his head closer to Flic's ear. 'All your favourite men in one place, you must be thrilled. George, would you mind helping Ms Anderson with her bag?'

Gallagher opened Flic's coat as Bannerman ran his hand across the small of her back. Parker took her bag and checked inside while Gallagher removed the magazine secreted in her waistband, before deftly transferring the ankle-holstered Makarov to his other coat pocket.

'So it's up to you,' Bannerman continued. 'At the very least, I'd bet that the gun connects you to a couple of recent murders. Shall we attempt some civilised dialogue, poppet?'

Gallagher watched the stall owner, who was showing interest in the unfolding scene from a distance.

Flic considered her options. She'd recognised Gallagher and saw an intensity in his eyes that left her in no doubt that he'd kill her where she stood if he had to. Parker was like a dog on a short leash, straining to take chunks out of her. Bannerman was politeness personified but she'd royally stuffed him. If she was going to extricate herself from the wider situation it'd have to be while not in police custody.

'Why not?' she said. 'Do lead the way, Captain Gallagher.'

Gallagher leaned in. 'Any trouble and I'll shoot the bits that Mr Parker hasn't chewed off.'

'You are a charmer. I'll be good, promise.'

'Come on,' said Bannerman. 'We're starting to draw attention. Keep smiling Flic, you really don't want anyone coming to your rescue.'

* * *

The man codenamed Mimar – real name: Mordechai Mofaz – turned over the cigarette case in his hands and read the Hebrew inscription from the 121st Psalm: 'the defender of Israel shall neither slumber nor sleep.'

It had taken two years to set up, to find the right people, to slowly build the layers of fiction, the back-stories. Two years to build the trust, to isolate them from other influences and contacts.

It had taken two years to bring together the right combinations of men in the right places – months of work to ensure that they'd do his bidding, no questions. It had taken over a year to move weapons and explosives. The weapons and explosives that could be sourced back to the enemy.

It had taken months to hide the stolen vehicles and the arms caches and to bring the volunteers to the correct psychological pitch. Two years with no sanctioned support, no official communications, no official budget, oversight, or logistical back-up – just a handful of contacts in the service pulling the strings in the background. Two years of running this alongside his other duties. It wouldn't be spoken of. There would be no presentations, no applause and no engraved cigarette cases. This one was different.

Two years, with the help of the British contact, to agree the targets, the safe houses, the timings and to set up the digital dead-drop boxes and the incriminating evidence to be embedded in the whole endeavour. Nothing could be sent through normal channels. Nothing could be detected by the British or Americans using the all-seeing and all-hearing Echelon – the US communications-monitoring system trawling the world's electronic signals: phone calls, emails, whatever they wanted to see or hear. Within Europe all email and telephone traffic was intercepted by the United States National Security Agency and transferred from the European mainland through a strategic hub in London, via satellite through Menwith Hill on the North Yorkshire moors and on to Fort Meade in Maryland.

The man who'd provided the information under interrogation had, of course, only been part of a wider picture but he'd been well connected within his organisation. Put together with other information already known, the detail he provided was gold standard. The interrogation, the torture, had been long and painful to watch, even for a man of Mofaz's long experience and pragmatism, but the end more than merited the means.

427

The Americans had lapped it up and Mofaz had been given the time that he needed with the man. He had sent the intel back home about Iraq, Afghanistan, Syria, Libya, Pakistan, Egypt, Yemen, Jordan, Saudi Arabia, the Palestinians and all the rest. The Americans had thrown the whole weight of their counter-terrorist apparatus behind this package of intelligence, which assisted in filling in important gaps in the battle plan for their War on Terror. Within eighteen months Obama got Osama and the Americans lay to rest another ghost of 9/11.

The Mossad, along with the Shin Bet internal security service, the Aman – military intelligence – the Sholdag special forces battalion and the Israeli Defence Force's secret Unit 8200 signals intelligence detachment went to work. Tunnels were discovered in Gaza and the West Bank, attacks were thwarted, arms intercepted. High-profile targets were fixed, tracked and neutralised across the Middle East by the Special Operations Division, Metsada. Others were taken care of by the covert marauder squads operating in the occupied territories. Some of the weapons seized had made their way to him: weapons and explosives that came from Iran, weapons and explosives that were now in the UK and USA.

But Mofaz had wanted other details. He'd wanted details of active service units, sleeper cells. Not Trojans trained in terror camps and tracked by the intelligence services, but 'invisibles' – with no criminal or terrorist history – living and working in Western countries. More importantly, he'd wanted to know the manner in which these disparate cells and individuals could be activated and controlled from afar. He'd wanted the network of dead drops and mosque contacts, the codes, the authentication procedures, skill levels, specialities, locations and men who could train other men. And he'd got them.

This had been the prisoner's main role. He was the fixer, the facilitator. He'd been the still centre of a web-like structure stretching up from Africa and across Europe, east and west.

Mofaz had used Yoshi Elkabetz to compartmentalise the operators who were to execute various parts of the plan. Al Qaeda wasn't, as some believed, some kind of linked-in corporation with an HR department and an intranet. Some of its plots were carried out by small groups or individuals working on their own initiative. They'd contact someone who knew someone who was connected to the hard-core and approach them for help. It might be for funding, or training, or they might just ask permission to claim the attacks for al Qaeda. Since the death of Bin Laden, battalions of misguided souls had been queuing up to avenge the death of the great man.

Elkabetz should have been running the operation on the ground, but he'd gotten himself killed on his last trip to Iraq.

Mofaz had been required to get closer to the day-to-day execution of the mission than he'd liked.

He'd allowed some to succeed, but others had to fail. The failures would harden the attitude of the British public just as much as the operations that were successful. The British public could be relied upon. They'd been bombed countless times before. They'd get on with life while calling on the government to get the job done. The British government wasn't having an easy ride in general. They'd have to respond robustly. If they could throw blood and treasure at Iraq, Afghanistan and Libya, and assist in counter-terrorist operations in Africa, they would back the US and Israel if push came to shove. The Americans were also getting in step. The American public were foaming at the mouth, the ghosts of 9/11 still harrying them forward to war.

The plan was working well here, as was the parallel mission unfolding in the States. In war there was no black and white. Israel was in striking distance of Iranian-sponsored terror, day after day, year after year. Iran knew that terrorism was seen by the West as war, but attacks weren't treated as an act of war. Iran had sent Saudis to blow up military bases, Syrians to attack buses and Kashmiris to attack the Indian Parliament. They'd trained jihadists, armed them and financed terrorist atrocities across the world with impunity. But there was the bigger threat of Iran's nuclear ambitions.

Iranian long-range ballistic missiles were now easily capable of hitting Israel and US bases in the region. Israeli jets hitting Iran's nuclear sites unilaterally was one thing, but that wouldn't necessarily stop research and production. Tehran had promised on a number of occasions to 'wipe Israel off the face of the earth' – but that didn't mean a stand-up fight was on the cards. At the very least, Israeli and Jewish targets would be hit hard by the unleashed jihadists around the world. The suicide bombers would rise up in battalions. The clock was ticking and force was the only answer.

The Pentagon had already drawn up a battle plan. Tomahawk missiles would be launched from ships and submarines in the Gulf. Iranian air defences would be attacked. B2 stealth bombers flying out of Diego Garcia in the Indian Ocean and Fairford in Gloucestershire, England, would drop the 4,500-pound bunker-busting bombs and all hell would be let loose. There was no guarantee that the bombs would penetrate the metres of protective concrete, but the alternative could be the end of Israel. The Western powers had to be on board – time was running out.

Diplomacy had failed.

* * *

Rutherford gestured for his subordinate to take a seat.

'Justin, are you in contact with any of the reliable deniables?'

'Sir,' said Hancock, suppressing a grin.

'I need you to arrange a pick up. The man's name is Mordechai Mofaz. He works at the Israeli embassy, as you probably know. I think he might be in danger and I need to speak with him face to face. An embassy meet is too risky. I want him taken to a safe house.'

'Understood, sir – which safe house?'

'I'm working on the details now.'

Justin Hancock stood up to leave. 'Anything else, sir?'

Rutherford picked up his pen and pulled a manila file from a stack on his desk. 'That's all. Don't hang about on this. Tell me when they're going to move in.'

'Sir.'

Hancock left Rutherford's office and winked at Alexis Clark, who straightened in her chair and looked back at her computer screen. Out in the corridor, he selected a number from the contacts list in his mobile phone. After six rings his call was answered.

'George,' said Hancock. 'It's Mike Peabody, how's business?'

* * *

'Where's Connie?' Gallagher asked again.

'Oh, come now, this is dull. I'm hardly likely to tell you.'

'But you will.'

'No dancing? No courtship? I'm afraid I'm not as easy as all that – perhaps Ms Edwards was. And no doubt our friend Mr Parker spilled his guts with little persuasion, but I'm an entirely different animal, Owen. It is Owen, isn't it?'

'We're wasting time. Bag her.'

'Boss?' asked Mark.

Harry pushed him out of the way and picked up the clear plastic bag that was lying on the floor behind the chair that Flic had been secured to. He pulled it down over her head and pulled the end tight behind her neck. Gallagher began silently counting.

'Boss?'

Harry raised a warning finger. 'Shut it, Mark.'

Gallagher finished counting. 'Take it off.'

Flic gasped for air.

'Where's Connie? Do you think we won't kill you?'

Flic coughed. 'Not likely: if you kill me, she's dead too.'

* * *

Rutherford picked up the phone on his desk and dialled a number on the secure line. He was calling a friend in the MI6-Special Forces cadre, E Squadron, known as 'the

Increment' – made up of SAS and SBS operatives – who were tasked to support MI6 work around the world. The capacity for special ops had been increased by the Operational Support Directorate in 1994. Some, particularly the British press, had been sniffing around this most shadowy of shadow units for years, yearning for a story regarding 'black ops' and such like. Rutherford preferred to think of the operations as efficient pre-emptive strikes in the defence of Britain and its allies' national interests – but, of course, that phrase didn't have the same ring to it. His call was answered.

'Scotty, James Rutherford. Yes, I'm well, thank you.'

'How's Jenny?'

'She's in fine fettle. Is the lovely Alice well?'

'Super, thanks. What can I do for you?'

'It's off the books. We have a rogue individual operating out of the Israeli embassy. He's due to be picked up by a team of Russians.'

'You want us to stop him? Can't you use Plod?'

'I want you to kill him, so no. Scotty, it's what he's carrying in his head that's dangerous. If we stop him today, they'll get him out tomorrow.'

'What do the Israelis say?'

'They don't know.'

There was an extended silence.

'Scotty, don't make me say it, please.'

'I owe you,' replied Major Scott. 'What about the Russians?'

Rutherford felt a surge of frustration. 'Fuck the Russians!' He took a breath. 'But it would be better if they didn't take any casualties. I'm not suggesting a firefight on the streets of Kensington. We've had enough of those for one week.'

'Easier said than done. I assume you want this to look like a professional hit?'

'I'll leave the details to you, Scotty. Make it look like a hit and run, if you like – just make sure he's dead. It can't lead back to HMG, clear?'

'Let me guess: you won't be following up this call with a memo.'

'Which call?'

'Who's the target?'

'Mordechai Mofaz. He's on the attaché staff. I'm going to send a courier with a photo. You won't be asked to sign for the envelope, just be ready to receive it directly into your own hands.'

'OK. When does this need to happen?'

'Soonest. Thank you, Scotty. If you're at the club this evening, I'll buy you a drink.'

'You'll buy me a bottle.'

'Done.'

Rutherford ended the call, turned his chair and stared out across the Thames. He'd deal with Flic Anderson separately.

Alexis Clark knocked and put her head around the door. 'Mr Kinsella,' she said.

'Send him in.'

Kinsella watched as Rutherford paced the room. 'When did you hear?'

'An hour ago,' replied Rutherford. 'An old Russian contact.'

'And what did he say exactly?'

'They'd been looking for the stolen nuclear material, as you know, John. They picked up the trail in France but lost it. That was a few weeks ago. New intel from a Chechen they've been talking to points to a UK destination via Calais. It took them a while to break the man. A bit bloody late in the day to tell us, but at least they did.'

'Well, it might stop World War III when it gets traced back to Moscow after devastating London.'

'Let's hope it doesn't get that far,' said Rutherford.

'What are you doing to find it?'

'We already have all our guns on the ground, you've seen the news. There are no leads.'

'We've heard no chatter,' said Kinsella. 'I just got off the phone. There's no Sigint. We've trawled our Intelink and we've got nothing to give you, I'm sorry.'

'And your side of the pond?'

'The NSA and Homeland have nothing. The bomb in Times Square definitely contained explosives from the same Iranian shipment that you guys identified. Even the doves in Washington can see we're likely going to war.'

* * *

Gallagher motioned for Harry to join him on the other side of the room.

'She's hard as nails, this one,' said Harry. 'This isn't really my bag.'

'Very droll,' said Gallagher. 'Mine neither, but time's against us and she knows she's holding the better cards.'

Flic laughed behind them. 'Time for a rethink, boys?'

Harry scowled and took out his pistol. 'How about I shoot your extremities off with this? Would that be funny?'

Flic managed a nonchalant shrug, even though she was tied up.

The door opened and Teddy Southall stepped inside. 'The boss wants a word,' he said to Gallagher, motioning outside the room with a nod of the head.

'OK. H, watch her. Mark, stop dancing about – come and see if Sandy needs any help.'

Gallagher followed Teddy. Mark trailed behind. They walked through to the old manager's office, where Frankie was sitting with his hands steepled under his chin watching

Bannerman at the laptop. Tom was sitting sullenly in the corner. Gallagher had insisted that he be kept well away from Flic. He'd also refused to let Parker assist with the interrogation.

Bannerman turned his head. 'Owen, this might be a bit easier if you allowed me access to the internet.' He looked at Mark. 'When the Boy Wonder isn't hovering. Even better if you'd let me take it to an expert.'

Gallagher patted the broadband dongle in his pocket. 'I don't think so.' He turned to Frankie. 'What's up?'

'Parker's lads have been having an extended chat to the bloke you brought in, as you know. They've cracked him and he gave up this.' He held out a piece of paper.

'An email address and password.'

'A dead-drop, he called it.'

Gallagher looked at Bannerman and passed him the dongle and the paper. 'A digital dead-drop. Sandy, check it out. Mark, hover.'

'What's a bloody digital dead-drop?' asked Frankie.

'Spooks used to leave messages under benches, or in Coke cans, they'd tape coded instructions in telephone boxes and so on. There'd be an agreed signal left when there was something to pick up,' said Gallagher.

'Chalk marks? Like Alec Guinness in Tinker Tailor?'

'Exactly, this is just the same. An agent creates a message and saves it to "drafts." Another agent has the email username and password and reads the message. The message is never sent, so can't be read or traced by anyone else.'

'Clever,' said Frankie. 'What's wrong with one of these? Just change the SIM card and don't register your phone, right?' he asked, picking up his mobile.

'Every call you make can be monitored or traced,' said Bannerman. 'If you're a target – or you're daft enough to use a word like "bomb" – various agencies can have your position to the nearest few metres in not very long at all. It can be triggered by names, localities, phrases and subjects, not necessarily from specific telephone numbers or email addresses on a target list.'

'Is nothing sacred? Where's the trust gone in the world?'

'Never was any, I'm afraid. Think of an email as a postcard that can be read by anyone and you won't go far wrong,' replied Bannerman, as he connected to the internet.

'There's something else,' said Teddy. 'He was spouting all kinds of random shit for a while, probably down to Bish whacking the gunshot wound with a length of pool cue before Tom patched him up again. Anyway, then he starts gibbering away in Hebrew. I reckon it was the morphine speaking.'

'How do you know it was Hebrew?' asked Bannerman, turning around in his seat.

'Because Bish is East End born and bred and he knows it when he hears it,' answered Frankie.

Teddy scratched his head. 'What I want to know is what's a Four-by-Two doing in a flat with a bomber's corpse?'

'What do you think? A Mossad hit team?' Gallagher asked Bannerman, who had only just worked out the meaning of Teddy's cockney rhyming slang.

'Could be,' said Bannerman, tapping the keyboard. 'Here we go: this message saved to drafts has the address you lifted him from.'

'Anything else?'

'In the trash – schoolboy error by the recipient by the look of things – two more addresses. Give me a minute.' He typed the first address into Google. 'First one is the road where they found the car bomber who'd blown himself up with his own grenade.'

Frankie whistled.

'And the second?' asked Gallagher.

'Just a mo. Right, here it is: the second is the street where a gas explosion killed the two unnamed Asian chaps. Look, Owen, this is bigger than we thought. You've got to let me go and chase up these leads. I'll take the chap with the bullet wound. You don't want him dying of that, do you?'

'Or pool-cue-poisoning,' said Teddy. 'He's looking a bit peaky, that's for sure. I got some gear and Tom has managed to patch him up, like I said, but he needs a doctor.'

'We still need to find Connie,' said Gallagher. He looked at Tom, who was clenching his fists in an attempt to control

440

his temper. 'Unless we convince your friend Flic to tell us where she is we've got nothing.'

Bannerman threw down his pen. 'Now look here, Owen, I'm losing patience with that particular stream of logic.'

The door swung open. George Parker adjusted his cuffs and walked through into the room. 'Ladies,' he said. 'I've just had an interesting phone call. They want me to arrange a lift. Some geezer who works at the Israeli embassy, Mordechai Mofaz.'

'Morde Mofaz?' asked Bannerman.

'Friend of yours?'

'Not exactly but I do know him. He's an attaché at the embassy – or, more accurately, Mossad's man in London.'

Gallagher leaned against the wall, stretched out his arms and laid his palms flat against the cold plasterwork. 'Why would Six task Parker to lift a Mossad agent?'

'They just want a chat, no rough stuff allowed. I'm to call for a drop-off point when I've got him.'

'Our friend here is deniable,' said Bannerman. 'He's a cut out, a criminal. That's why they use people like him. No comebacks if things start to look embarrassing.'

'All right, Lord-fucking-Fauntleroy,' said Parker. 'If you've finished gabbing with that silver-fucking-spoon in your gob, they're waiting for me to get the job done.'

'They'll have to wait,' said Gallagher. 'We'll be bringing him here first.'

441

'Well, that's the other thing,' Parker said, buttoning his jacket. 'What am I supposed to do, walk up to the embassy gate and ask if he's coming out to play?'

Gallagher turned to Bannerman. 'No, Sandy can do that.'

'Chris is available,' said Frankie.

Parker sat on the edge of the desk. 'You can take Bish and a couple of the lads, if you like.'

'Thanks, I'll take Bish and Chris for their driving skills,' Gallagher replied. 'We're going to need a couple of disposable cars.'

* * *

Gallagher pulled his chair in front of Flic. 'What do you know about a man called Moshe Mofaz?'

'Why do you ask?'

'Because we're going to kidnap him and bring him here. I think he knows something about the attacks and I think you know him.' He watched her eyes and imagined the rapid calculations leaping across the synapses of her brain.

'This is your chance,' he said. 'You've been waiting to make your play, this could be it. But I'm out of here in five minutes.'

'Untie me and we'll talk.'

'Start talking and I'll think about untying you.'

Flic looked at the ceiling, weighing each option one last time. 'We need to make a deal and I need to speak to Mofaz.'

'No deals until we have Connie safe and well.'

'That's the deal. You give me Mofaz and the wallet, I give you Connie.'

'You want the memory stick – that's what this is all about, right?'

Flic laughed until she was gripped by a coughing fit. 'The memory stick? You think this has been about a bloody memory stick?'

Gallagher turned. Bannerman had entered the room and was standing behind him.

'She wants time with Mofaz.'

'He has something you need, is that it Flic?' Bannerman asked.

'He has information I need, yes.'

'Why don't you tell me what this is about? Perhaps I can help you.'

'I can help me, no one else can. Give me half an hour with Mofaz and this ends today.'

'How much trouble are you in?'

Flic ignored the question and looked at Gallagher. 'One thing: Edwards – the brother – was Parker lying or is he dead?'

443

'He's dead,' Gallagher lied. 'I couldn't save the brother but I'm going to save the sister. Why did you want him dead?'

'He and his team killed a friend of mine – a very close friend. The sister was just a way to find him. I've got no argument with her, I'm not a monster.'

'Owen,' said Bannerman. 'Would you mind leaving us alone for a few minutes?'

Gallagher shook his head. 'Because of you two I'm wanted by the police, as are my friends. Another of my friends is still missing and in danger. I don't think I want to leave two spooks alone to work out yet another way to shaft me, no.'

'Let him stay,' Flic said. 'Just take off these bloody restraints so we can have a grown-up conversation.'

* * *

'The two cars you wanted are outside, everything's sorted,' said Parker. 'There's a grey Audi Q7 3 litre and a blue Skoda Octavia 2 litre.'

'And they aren't stolen?' asked Gallagher. 'We don't want to be pinged by police ANPR cameras.'

'Of course they're fucking stolen,' Parker replied. 'The coppers won't spot them, though. They've got clean plates, cloned off kosher cars – same make and model, out Essex way.'

'Right,' said Gallagher. 'I'll take the Audi with Tom. Mark, you ride shotgun with Bish in the Skoda. Pistols only, Mofaz isn't likely to be armed and Sandy has asked him to come alone. Comms check in ten minutes, we leave in fifteen. If you want to check the maps again, do it now.'

'What about me, boss?' asked Harry.

'We've discussed this, H. You need to rest that leg. Sit this one out.'

Harry nodded but wasn't happy. 'Anything I can be doing?'

'Those FNC rifles we picked up could do with checking in case we end up needing them. There are gloves and a maintenance kit in my black bag.'

'I'll get them stripped, cleaned and the ammo loaded before you get back.'

'Thanks,' said Gallagher. 'Let's get our shit together. Everyone needs to be wearing gloves before we touch those cars.' He looked over at Bannerman, who was leaning against Frankie's desk. 'I'll see you around, Sandy.'

'Good luck,' said Bannerman. 'Try not to cause an international incident, won't you?'

Bannerman had arranged to meet Mofaz near the tennis courts east of the Albert Memorial in Hyde Park. Gallagher was parked in a Knightsbridge side street with Tom. Bish and Mark were to enter the park from the north travelling down West Carriage Drive.

Mofaz had left the embassy on Kensington Palace Gardens in his grey tracksuit. He entered the park via Palace Gate, turned right and jogged along The Flower Walk. Mofaz wanted to arrive at the meeting from another direction, so he headed across the park to the Serpentine Gallery, planning to cross West Carriage Drive and then to go around the Princess of Wales Memorial Fountain. Then he'd go via Rotten Row and approach the tennis courts from the other side. He didn't have anything to be suspicious about. He'd met Bannerman a number of times before and often away from formal surroundings. That didn't mean he wasn't going to be careful.

Mark and Bish had just crossed the Serpentine Bridge and were about to pull into the car park when Mark spotted Mofaz.

'Alpha One travelling east. He's wearing a grey tracksuit.'

'Roger that,' said Gallagher. 'We're entering the park now.'

Gallagher pulled the Audi over to allow a sporty blue BMW through. He didn't want to be sitting in the car too long drawing attention.

446

As Mofaz came to the road he began jogging on the spot, waiting for the BMW to pass so that he could cross. The blue car accelerated and swerved towards him. Mofaz bolted across the road as the vehicle mounted the grass. The BMW span through 90 degrees and Mofaz heard the familiar sound of a silenced weapon being fired.

'Someone just tried to take him out,' said Mark in Gallagher's earpiece.

'Seen,' said Gallagher. 'Bish get in between him and that Beamer.'

Gallagher bounced the Audi diagonally across the park in an attempt to head off Mofaz. He could see Bish and Mark in the Skoda on an intercept course with the BMW.

Mofaz felt the bullet enter his left shoulder. The force of the impact span him around and he lost his footing temporarily before powering off again. He saw the Audi coming from his right. There was a cafeteria by the lido. If he could make it there he had a chance. The car travelling across the grass to his left hit the BMW across its front, glancing away at speed. He was losing blood and momentum. He reached down to his running belt for his phone but the zip jammed as he fumbled, still trying to run as fast as he was able.

Gallagher threw the car into reverse and put on the power while turning the steering wheel through a three-quarter arc.

He completed the fast J-turn and drew level with Mofaz. His window was down. 'Get in!' he shouted.

Tom manoeuvred his body through the open passenger window and fired three times at the BMW.

Gallagher saw the blood widening across the fabric of Mofaz's tracksuit. He saw, too, the confusion fizzing through the man's mind. 'Bannerman sent me. Get in the bloody car!'

Tom fired again as Mofaz opened the rear door and dived in. He watched as Bish tried to put his car between the Audi and the Beamer. The BMW's passenger aimed his pistol at the Skoda. Tom hesitated for a second, recognising the gunman, then fired several more shots from the suppressed Browning.

Gallagher accelerated away and Tom changed magazines.

'Keep your head down,' Gallagher called out to Mofaz. He drove fast and swung the Audi left on to South Carriage Drive before turning right and exiting the park through Prince of Wales Gate. 'Where are you, Mark?'

'We took rounds through the back, but Tom took out two of their tyres. We're heading south.'

'Chris, are you in position?'

'Engine running.'

'We'll be with you in two minutes.'

Gallagher turned off Exhibition Road into Imperial College Road. Chris was waiting in a VW Transporter van in

Wells Way. Gallagher heard police sirens as he pulled into the side road.

'We're coming in from Queen's Gate,' said Mark. 'Thirty seconds. Can't tell if we've been followed but the Beamer didn't come out of the park behind us.'

Gallagher hauled Mofaz from the rear of the Audi while Tom opened the back of the VW. The blue Skoda came carefully around the corner. Mark and Bish jumped out and piled into the back of the van.

Gallagher was the last one in. 'Go!'

Chris eased on to Queens Gate heading out in the direction of Hammersmith Bridge.

As they passed through Putney, Tom secured the dressing across Mofaz's wound. 'You'll live,' he said. 'Morphine?'

Mofaz looked at the men around him and shook his head. 'Where is Bannerman?'

'Couldn't make it in person, after all,' said Gallagher. 'Just sit back. I'll explain when we reach our destination. Who were the men in the BMW?'

'That's the other thing I want to find out,' replied Mofaz, wincing at the pain.

Chris drove them to Battersea. They transferred to a Transit van that had been left in the far corner of a yard owned by a scrap merchant on Parker's payroll. The VW would be crushed into a cube before they reached the derelict cinema.

They drove on past Nine Elms, Vauxhall, Elephant and Castle and on through Bermondsey, crossing under the Thames at Rotherhithe Tunnel, heading for Walthamstow.

Tom looked across at Mofaz, who had his eyes shut, and leaned close to Gallagher. 'I recognised the passenger.'

'In the BMW?'

'Yeah, last I heard he'd passed SAS selection. I'm pretty sure he's still in. I would have heard if he was on the circuit.'

Gallagher nodded. 'Keep that to yourself. Things are complicated as it is. When we get back, stay in the van until I give you the all clear. I don't want Flic to know you're still alive.'

* * *

'Hello, Morde,' said Flic.

Mofaz tried to place the face. He would have remembered if they'd met in person before. He'd never have forgotten those pale cold blue eyes that hinted at the toughness her pretty face masked.

'Yoshi showed me a photograph – just in case I ever needed to find you.'

Mofaz shrugged.

'He was worried that you might renege on our arrangement after you'd stitched me up.'

Mofaz smiled. 'Ms Anderson, of course.' He'd seen a photograph but it hadn't done her justice. 'He was a smart boy – a terrible waste for him to die at the side of an Iraqi road like that.'

Flic's smile evaporated and she felt a stab of emotion that flipped her stomach.

Mofaz continued. 'I knew he'd taken you to his bed. I hadn't realised that he'd taken leave of his senses.'

'Love does that,' she said, wishing she hadn't. 'He did his job, he followed orders. He kept the key, he believed in the plan. He didn't betray his country.'

'But he also wouldn't betray you. That was his job. He always did have good taste, if not the best judgement.'

'You can dispense with the flattery. You know what I want.'

'And what happens to me?' he asked, looking at Gallagher who was leaning against the wall.

'That's up to you. This man isn't going to kill a Mossad agent. He's in enough trouble as it is. Although, from what I hear, he'd have to join the queue.'

'London can be a dangerous place.'

Flic pulled up a chair. 'Your man in Baghdad, Yoshi's friend, messed up. I met him at the zoo. Don't worry, he said, we'll get him. But the mercenary got home and he

451

started asking questions, stones were turned. I'm standing here because of you.'

'You're standing there because your masters knew you'd fit the bill. You're standing there because you signed up for the plan with your eyes wide open. The rest of it was merely part of a bigger insurance policy. Yoshi should never have told you.'

'I've been in this game long enough to know that the old adage "what you don't know can't hurt you" is bullshit. It's gotten messy and I want out.'

'It doesn't matter how messy it is, you know that as well as I do. The plan is working, the Iranians are the enemy. The British public can never know about the operation, nor can the American voters – and it's a sway in public opinion we want. There will be a cover-up because nothing can be proven. Let the Palestinians bleat, let the Iranians roar, there will be a reckoning and it's coming soon. Even the Saudis will have to choose a side at last. Pakistan won't relish the thought of being bombed into the Stone Age with Iran. The plan is perfect.'

'You're right, of course, which is why you won't mind giving me what I need.'

Flic pulled the brown wallet from her pocket, unzipped it and removed the silver key card.

'Where is the deposit box? What's the pass number? I have the other keys,' she said, dangling the small metal objects from the wallet's hook. 'That's all I need.'

Mofaz stared at her. 'It's you that jeopardised the mission – you and Yoshi. He'd still be alive if he hadn't gone to visit you that afternoon. There was to be no more contact. He was weak and it cost him his life.'

'He was in love,' she said quietly.

Mofaz pursed his lips and shook his head.

'We were in love!' Flic shouted, picking up her chair and throwing it at Mofaz. It bounced away from his chest, one leg clipping his face and cutting his lip.

Flic walked around him. 'Your *kidon* team should have taken out the mercenary as he meandered through Europe. If anyone fucked it up it was Mossad.'

Mofaz licked the blood from his lips. 'I'm not worried. Who has the memory sticks now?'

'They're on their way to GCHQ.'

Mofaz laughed. 'Excellent. Even if you were believed, there's enough evidence leading back to Iran to make a far better case in public.'

It was Flic's turn to laugh. 'I shan't be saying a dicky-bird. You give me what I need and I disappear. I don't think an inquiry would lead to my promotion, do you?'

'You have friends in high places that you've yet to meet but, no, I doubt they will step from the shadows and come to your aid this time. Who was your London contact?'

'I don't know who I was working for,' she lied. 'But I'd bet he or she is behind your little adventure on the way here. They know that Five are sniffing around this thing.'

Mofaz thought for a moment and licked some more blood from his lips. 'The game is in play. If I give you what you need it makes no difference – but why should I?'

'Because if you don't, these men will deliver you to where they were supposed to deliver you. I assume the people pulling my strings don't want the Iranians to get hold of either of us. People talk about the 'Mad Mullahs' but you and I both know the Iranians aren't stupid. Their VEVAK teams will be working overtime trying to pick up a lead and I don't doubt that the Chinese are assisting in London.'

Mofaz stretched out his back the best he could. 'And I travel back to Kensington in disguise?'

'Quid pro quo: you have something I want and I have something this man wants. You help me deliver it and he helps you. Right, Owen?'

Gallagher stood in front of the Israeli. 'How many more attacks are planned?'

'I don't know what you're talking about,' replied Mofaz.

'He won't tell you,' said Flic. 'And I don't know. It doesn't matter how many plastic bags you've got, it won't

454

lead to any more information.' She took a step closer to him. 'Concentrate on getting Connie back and leave the rest to Sandy and his friends in Cheltenham. Get Mofaz back to his embassy or you'll have more than the police to worry about.'

'I would like to see Bannerman again before I go home,' said Mofaz, on hearing the name.

'I bet you would. Sorry, poppet, can't help you with that one. Live and let live?'

'There will be another time. There always is.'

'OK,' said Flic, turning to face Gallagher again. 'This is how we're going to do it. I'll need my bag.'

EIGHTEEN

'There's nothing here,' said Mark.

They'd walked in from different directions, following the Grand Union Canal's towpath along the south side of Kensal Green Cemetery. Across the canal lay the Gas Works and, further down, the railway sidings of the North Pole International Depot – the old Eurostar yard named after North Pole Road. Sunrise was still an hour and a half away. The sounds of night traffic floated across the still water from the roads criss-crossing the canal. Somewhere in the distance a dog's insistent barking made Mark remember lonely nights bedded down without warmth.

'She said Connie's here. I think it's this bridge up ahead,' Tom replied.

'Just saying.'

Tom flashed him a look through the gloom and pointed the yet to be used torch at him as a warning.

They'd walked another fifty metres or so and were approaching the bridge when Tom held Mark back by the arm. 'Go careful. I don't trust that posh cow.'

Under the cover of the bridge, the two men drew their pistols and cautiously approached what looked, in the dark, like a hole in the wall. It was an alcove in the blackened

Victorian masonry protected by a rusting ironwork gate that was slightly set back in the bricks.

Tom crouched to the right of the alcove and pointed his gun into the space that lay behind the gate. He switched on the torch in his other hand. The light illuminated a low wooden door, covered in flaking red paint, a few feet away.

Mark took up position on the other side of the gap, keeping watch along the towpath.

Tom shone the torch at the gate lock. It was obvious that it hadn't worked in decades, but just above it was a brand new padlock. He fished around in his pocket and found the two keys that Flic had given to Gallagher. He checked the lock make and selected the appropriate key.

Mark followed him through the gate and took cover in the dark shadow, putting his head torch in place – off but ready. He could see by the light cast from Tom's torch that the space was full of bottles, cans and other rubbish. 'Watch out for needles,' he whispered.

Tom was inserting the other key into an equally new padlock that secured a clasp on the wooden door. He pulled it open and peered around the frame. Torch and pistol scanned the void behind the door and found no threats.

The room had a low ceiling and was less than ten paces deep. The bodies of two men lay directly behind the entrance. Both had been shot in the head.

Connie was lying on two wooden pallets laid end to end. On top of these was an insulating camping mat. His sister was in a sleeping bag. The hood was up but the bag wasn't zipped to the top. Over this lay a heavy coarse blanket. As he moved the torch beam away from her face it illuminated a plastic tube leading to an IV drip bag hanging from a nail in the wall.

He eased back the blanket, exposing the cannula that had been inserted into the back of Connie's hand. He checked his sister's pulse at the carotid artery. It was slow and irregular.

'Connie. Connie, can you hear me?' He shook her gently. 'Connie, wake up, please wake up.' The emotion caught in his throat as he tried to speak louder in an attempt to rouse her. He pinched her earlobe. No response. He pulled back her eyelids and took a deep breath.

Tom stepped over the two dead men and called Mark inside. 'Stay with her. I'm going to phone an ambulance.'

'You know what the boss said. We can't wait for them to arrive – too much explaining to do. And these two bodies wouldn't help, either.'

'We'll go when I say we go. It's still dark, so stop whining.'

'Just saying,' said Mark.

Tom raised the hand carrying the torch. 'Are you looking for a slap? I know the fucking score. You can see my sister over there, can't you?' He kicked one of the corpses and began to tap out the numbers 999.

* * *

Faaz had been waiting and watching. He'd watched his target cycle past this vantage point on several mornings over the last few days. Today would be the day if the man took this route again. Faaz had cleaned the Beretta Sniper for what he hoped was the penultimate time. He'd loaded it, checked the telescopic sight and had rested it on its bipod on the long table opposite the window. Today was meant to be the day. He didn't know why but he'd been told not to do it before this morning. What he did know was that once it was done he'd be gone, back to his home, back to his life. The man on the bicycle had to die or Faaz would pay the price. It was a simple equation. There was no choice.

Faaz checked his watch and then straightened the yoga mat on the table behind the rifle. The sash window was open about six inches and wasn't overlooked by any of the surrounding buildings. It was enough and would be hard to spot from the street. He'd be gone before anyone thought to organise a search.

He lifted the stock to his shoulder and looked down the sight at the road ahead. It wouldn't be long if it was to be today.

Twenty minutes later, Faaz saw the man on the bicycle turn the corner. He pulled the stock of the rifle into his shoulder. He held the crosshairs of the sight over the man's shock of blonde hair and then scanned to the point in the road that he'd chosen. He'd checked the distance and the elevation. There was no wind to speak of.

He took a breath, focused on the bridge of the man's nose and fired.

* * *

Kieran Fellows was sipping coffee in S-squad's main office – the specialist surveillance unit of SO15 Counter Terrorism Command. The pager on the desk in front of him beeped, along with those worn by everyone else in the room at Tintagel House. He'd been there all night watching the rolling news coverage of a series of car bombs that had exploded in Washington and New York, interspersed with coverage of the Kensington Palace attack. As part of the Special Projects Unit, hunting down contract killers, it had been his job to infiltrate George Parker's organisation. Parker had nightclubs because they were public places. Once he owned a club it didn't matter who he was seen with. Parker could go about his business pretty well unmolested by the authorities. They'd needed to get someone inside.

Since he'd left his Dave Greene cover behind, Kieran Fellows had been trying to trace the owner of the warehouse he'd been taken to. He was waiting to hear back from a team at New Scotland Yard once they'd unravelled the puzzle of ownership.

In the meantime, Parker had gone to ground and Kieran hadn't had any luck regarding Tom or Connie Edwards. He'd spent the night looking through the covert photographers' images and the transcripts from the unit's technical support guys. It had been the photographers who'd ballsed-up the surveillance at Paddington Old Cemetery.

It'd have to wait, though. Pagers were beeping and phones were ringing. The shit was obviously hitting the fan somewhere. There hadn't been time for him to be debriefed.

As he reached across for the pager, the door flew open and his section commander, Tim Nugent, entered the room.

'You lot: briefing room eleventh floor – the mayor has just been assassinated.'

'Has the Prime Minister got an alibi?' asked Kieran, eliciting nervous laughter from his shocked colleagues.

'Move your arses!' shouted Nugent. 'The Commissioner wants every gun we've got on the streets within the next half hour, so get a bloody shift on.'

* * *

A short bus ride away, Eshan and Hafs walked up the front steps of St Paul's Cathedral. Perched at the top of Ludgate Hill, sitting at the highest point of the City of London, it was drawing its sightseers as it had since the late seventeenth century. Something like two million people visited the church every year. Hafs remembered that from a school trip. The cathedral had dominated the skyline for three hundred years, regardless of its proximity to modern high-rise competitors.

The day of the school outing had been the day that they'd thought up the plan. Later, when they were offered any equipment they needed, if the plan was ambitious enough, they'd smiled at each other. It was ambitious enough by anyone's standards.

Hafs and Eshan walked through the opening at the side of the Great West Door. There was a queue of tourists waiting to buy tickets. It was just as they'd planned, just as they'd imagined it would be.

The two men dropped the rucksacks from their shoulders as they stepped backwards and closed the doors behind them.

'Excuse me,' called a woman at the ticket desk. 'Would you mind leaving those open? It isn't too cold inside, I promise.' She gave an encouraging smile and those at the front of the queue chuckled.

One of the security staff, who'd been chatting to a female colleague, looked less impressed and walked forward with an air of disgruntled authority.

Hafs and Eshan pulled out their machine pistols and cocked the weapons.

'Nobody move!' shouted Eshan. 'Keep calm and do as we say.' He opened his jacket and undid his shirt so that he could access the spare magazines hanging down under his arms.

The security guard held up his hands and felt a coldness run down his spine. The woman at the ticket desk activated the emergency alarm.

Hafs focused on his breathing, slow and steady, as he put his pack back on. They'd rehearsed this moment many times. He adjusted his stance and then raised and lowered the barrel of his weapon in the agreed way.

'*Allah akbar*!'

The sound of the automatic weapons filled the cathedral. The two friends moved past the bodies piling up on the floor, firing and changing magazines as they walked further into the building, killing visitors and members of staff as they went. When the immediate area was clear of the living they took the steps up to the Whispering Gallery, shooting anyone they came across and pulling the bodies down behind them.

From the gallery they saw three policemen scuttling out to various bits of cover below. Hafs let his gun hang from its sling around his neck and took two grenades from his rucksack. He held them out so Eshan could pull the pins, then tossed them out over the balustrade and stepped back.

'That should give them something to think about,' said Hafs after the two explosions. 'Cover the stairs while I get the kit ready. We only need to hold them off for about twenty minutes. Remember there's another staircase above us.'

'No worries,' Eshan replied. 'Anybody up there is staying up there, but I'll keep an eye out.'

Hafs looked out at the circular gallery and up at Thornhill's paintings of the life of St Paul that adorned the great dome. It was one of the largest cathedral domes in the world, reaching over a hundred metres from the ground. Sixty-five thousand tons of it was begging to be collapsed. The devastated London skyline would be filling TV screens around the world within the hour. The cathedral would be destroyed and Wellington and Nelson would be reburied under tons of debris, the shrines to their imperialist crimes smashed, desecrated.

He smiled. 'They'll be coming down soon enough, bruv. You're right, though; the main threat is from below. Let a grenade roll down the steps occasionally or the coppers will be forming up ready to rush us.'

* * *

464

She walked into Chancery Lane. The City was filled with the sound of sirens echoing around the narrow streets. Flic had insisted that Chris drove her. She'd left him with an envelope and a message for Gallagher. She was going to make Rutherford pay for pushing her out into the cold. He thought he had his scape goats. He thought the plan was fool proof. He'd have to think again. She'd be gone and now Gallagher's fate was back in his own hands.

She was greeted by a man in an expensive suit, to whom she handed the silver key card. He led her to an office on the ground floor.

Once the key had been drawn through the man's card reader and she had given him the passcode that Mofaz had given her, she was shown into the vault. She took the keys from the wallet and waited for the man to withdraw into the anteroom before selecting one and opening the deposit box. She pulled out a metal container from inside the drawer and carried it to a table in an inspection booth. She removed the contents and sighed. Yoshi had kept her as safe as he could. The evidence against her was now in her hands, along with the money he'd arranged to allow her to get away and start again if the need arose.

She felt the tears pricking her eyes and berated herself. Hold it together Anderson, she thought. There'll be time enough for licking wounds. You're not out of the woods yet.

* * *

Due to the speed that events were unfolding, Bannerman's debrief at Thames House had been rapid. Loose ends would have to be tied up later and Drummond had almost shoved him out of the door. The memory sticks had been dispatched to GCHQ for analysis. The suspected Mossad hitman had been taken to hospital in protective custody.

Bannerman was now standing in 1600 at New Scotland Yard, listening to the tall senior policeman who had briefed Drummond.

'We were lucky. Well, relatively – dozens were killed and they'll have to get the decorators in,' said Ketteridge.

'How bad was the damage from the bombs?' asked Bannerman.

'Bomb Disposal think that there wasn't enough explosive placed in the right places to bring the dome down. That's odds-on what they were trying to do. I'm awaiting the full report.'

'Has anyone claimed responsibility?'

'No and we can't ask the perpetrators as they saved a round each for themselves.'

'Anything from your sources?'

'Nothing. These people are ghosts and they've got every swinging dick chasing around town following the merest sniff of a lead. The media are in a frenzy, as you know. The PM is still in COBRA and he's screaming blue murder. Special security measures are in place at all airports and as many public buildings as we can cover. And now there's a no-fly-zone over London. The Commissioner has been purple since the car bombings. That throbbing vein in his temple looked set to burst when he heard about the mayor.'

'I didn't think they got on.'

'He couldn't stand him. That's not the point. It's the sheer audacity of it all. What's the endgame?'

'If I knew that,' said Bannerman, 'I'd have a bigger office.'

Ketteridge placed his hands behind his back and lifted his heels from the ground momentarily. 'We've got nothing to go on so we plan for the worst. Problem is we haven't got the manpower to respond to every lead. We could have bombers marching down the Mall to the palace and we could still be looking the wrong way.'

Bannerman nodded. 'This bloody conference is still going ahead, the Cousins and the Israelis are insisting that we don't back down in the face of terrorism. We're to lock it down and let them get on with it.'

'Surely it isn't worth the risk.'

Bannerman sat on one of the nearby desks. 'The complex has been searched and sealed for days. We'll have it cordoned off for the duration. The word is that this is a prelim to more sanctions and strikes on Iran. The bombs in New York and Washington are throwing up the same questions as we're dealing with. The White House is already talking publicly about an Iranian connection to the US attacks.'

'I heard that on the radio this morning,' said Ketteridge. 'Hence they're so keen for the conference to go ahead, I suppose. Way above my pay grade, thankfully.'

'Mine too,' said Bannerman. 'I'll let you get on.'

* * *

'Mimar's plan is working like a dream,' said Yasir.

'Mimar is a Zionist plant. I need to speak with you now the others are sleeping.'

Yasir moved closer. 'What are you talking about?'

'The whole thing is an Israeli plot.'

Yasir looked nervously at the sleeping men.

'They're fine,' whispered Imran. 'They've been carefully watched. But I couldn't tell anyone. Mimar's plan is working. It's just that it's going to work in a different way. The attacks are real. The brothers carrying out the attacks do so with true hearts. But it was organised by Mossad – it's a False Flag operation: a Black Flag.'

'I don't understand,' said Yasir.

'A Black Flag is when one nation launches an attack on another, or even on its own people, and blames another nation. The attacked nation then responds and attacks the country that's being set up.'

'How do you know this?'

'They think they are so clever, but the Quetta Shura has been aware for months.'

'And they let it proceed?'

'Of course, the attacks are sending waves of fear across Europe and America – what's not to like?'

'I don't get that, either.'

'The plot hinges on Iran being blamed, because the Israelis want support for attacks on Iran's nuclear installations. Our job is to let the world know about the plot and to punish the West for dealing with Israel. We've used the plan, the equipment, the men, but we've used it to deliver a bigger message.'

Yasir glanced behind Imran. 'The case?'

'Yes, the case.' Imran lowered his voice so it was barely audible even to Yasir. 'It's radiological, a dirty bomb. It's a chunk of nuclear material that will cleanse part of London's West End and signal the final jihad. The dust and debris from our conventional explosives should help the main bomb to disburse the material effectively in this area of town.'

Yasir let out a long breath.

469

'You look shocked, brother,' said Imran.

'I'm just trying to take it all in. It's not as if we weren't all going to die anyway. How did the elders find out?'

'We have spies everywhere, but the first signal came from a duress code given by a tortured martyr. A phrase was used when recruiting the men. After that, it was a case of watching and listening.'

'*Allah akbar wallilahi'l-hamd*,' said Yasir under his breath.

'Allah is our objective, jihad is our way. The Western powers will be in turmoil, the UN will be discredited and old alliances will falter.'

'Incredible. The material is from Iran?'

'No. That would help the Israelis. It's Russian, stolen by Chechen brothers.'

'It's almost unbelievable.'

'It is God's will and nothing more. We are truly the chosen, Yasir. *Insha'Allah.*'

* * *

Several miles away, Atif's team were lined up in their paramedic uniforms. Only Adham, the driver, really needed to wear one but Atif liked the idea of confusion – and the force of the image of dead gunmen dressed as medical technicians. Fear was the key and the fear would remain long

470

after they had been martyred. The men were facing him and the other driver, Ian.

Ian, a 27-year-old convert to the faith and an ex-soldier, was to drive the black cab. The veteran of Iraq and Afghanistan was going to drive the diversionary car bomb into his capital city, where he would detonate it while still in the driver's seat. The car was clean, bought from a dealer in Edmonton. It was taxed, insured and was registered to Ian. The tyres were at the correct pressures and the tread was good. The indicators and lights had been checked. The driver was white, had short tidy hair and no criminal record. There was a tabloid newspaper on the dash surrounded by food wrappers and other bits of rubbish. Only the Hackney Carriage licence plate on the rear was fake, cloned from a cab operating in Clapham, but a good enough copy for the short journey that the taxi would be making. Nothing was out of place. Nothing would draw attention from the overstretched emergency services. But beneath the rear seats and in the cab's boot was the bomb.

The car bomb: the poor man's air force – indiscriminate and perfect for a strategy of tension and diversion. The black cab's bomb was a mix of potassium chlorate, sulphur and powdered aluminium, augmented by TNT and RDX explosive. It was a fuel-air thermobaric explosive device capable of creating a devastating blast wave. The ringing circuits of three mobile telephones were attached to bulb heads surrounded by match heads in syringes. Petrol cans full of fuel would ignite on detonation, setting off two gas canisters, heating the nail-shrapnel densely packed in bags – crammed into the remaining spaces around the device – that would travel outwards at incredible speed. The multiple detonators left nothing to chance. Many people would die but the victims were all *halal* – all were permitted.

* * *

Faaz was sitting in the quiet coach of the train listening to the throb of its engine as it prepared to depart from Euston Station. He'd be home in a couple of hours or so. He'd dumped the gun as instructed, careful to clean off his prints and any stray strands of hair or fibre. He'd cleaned the flat in Croydon until he'd reeked of bleach. The men who he'd been told would visit him with further instructions hadn't arrived, so he'd decided to leave. It was too dangerous to stay. Mimar would understand.

Now his life could begin again. He looked out of the window as the train moved along the platform edge. He closed his eyes as it moved into the daylight. An image flashed in his mind of a man with a shock of blonde hair. An image flashed in his mind of a man dying in his rifle sight – the image of a man he'd never met, the man he had murdered.

He opened his eyes as the train picked up speed. He looked out at the graffiti and the rubbish at the trackside.

He prayed that his life could begin again.

NINETEEN

Tom was talking to Mark when Gallagher walked into the old manager's office. 'I'm not sure she's going to make it. I still can't believe I left her there alone.'

'She'll make it. You don't want her visiting you in prison, do you?' said Mark. 'At least this way there's a chance you'll be visiting her soon.'

Harry was making coffee. 'So what was in the envelope, boss? You've been a bit cagey. She's not coming back?'

'Didn't expect her to, did you?' Gallagher handed him two hand-drawn building schematics contained in the envelope that Flic had given Chris.

'University of London building – roof space? What's she playing at?' asked Harry.

'She told Chris to warn me that we're being set up. I've been mulling it over. There's a scientific conference being held on the campus. It could be another attack. Maybe she's seen the light.'

'And maybe she's a manipulative cow and she's still pulling the strings. What do you reckon, a crisis of conscience? Or does she want us implicated and out of the way for good?' Harry asked.

'She gave us Connie. Now we've got to get ourselves out of the hole that's been dug. I'm going to check it out.'

'OK, we'd better get our kit together.'

'H, I'm going alone. I've dragged you into this far enough.'

Harry looked at Mark and Tom, who both nodded. 'Don't be a twat, Owen. We're coming with you, whether you like it or not. One question, though: we're not giving these bits of paper to the police because?'

'Because we won't see daylight anytime soon if we do and we won't get a chance to fix this. If we're being set up, I want to play it out on my terms. And I don't want Connie visiting Tom in prison, she's been through enough.'

'That's settled, then,' said Harry. 'Have I got time to finish this brew?'

'If you're quick. Mark, still nothing on any of the news sites about us?' asked Gallagher.

'Nothing,' Mark replied.

'OK, let's not look a gift horse in the mouth. The police will probably be on the lookout for us, but they've got other worries. Let's get moving.'

* * *

475

Netanel had travelled to Ireland via the Holyhead to Dublin ferry. He was sitting in a café in the Temple Bar area of the city drinking his second black coffee. He had a copy of The Irish Times open in front of him, but he hadn't read a column inch. The rain was beginning to fall heavier and his view from the window was becoming obscured by condensation.

This was the third day that he'd watched the bookshop across the road. The third day that he'd flirted with the waitress who thought that the olive-skinned man with the beautiful eyes came every day to ask her out, but remained tongue-tied and pensive over his coffee and newspaper.

The bookshop owner was a *sayan*, a word derived from the verb 'to help.' The *sayanim* were trusted and often well-connected members of the Jewish Diaspora and, as the name suggested, were there to help facilitate operations carried out by Mossad abroad. The man held the passport that Netanel needed. Once he had it, Net had been instructed to fly from Dublin to Frankfurt and then on to Tel Aviv. The bookshop owner would arrange the tickets when contact had been made.

Net had been given no information about Ozi. He hadn't been told if he'd made it out of Ramzi Rahman's flat alive. He missed the idiot. He knew that they'd never meet again, whatever happened next. Net's part in the mission was over. He was compromised. He was a liability and had to be

476

extracted. He would be met at Ben Gurion Airport and taken for debriefing. Except that he wouldn't be arriving in Israel – not if he valued his liberty.

He and Ozi had only served two years of their sentence for killing an Israeli Defence Force officer in a drunken brawl. They'd probably just throw him back in his cell. If he made it that far. He wasn't deluded about his own importance. He knew he was entirely expendable. What he knew of the London operation was dangerous to him and to Israel. That's why he'd watched the bookshop and the owner for the last three days.

Net finished his coffee, folded his newspaper and waved goodbye to the waitress, who mustered a smile to mask her disappointment. Outside, he raised the paper above his head and jogged between the cars as the rain drops exploded off the tarmac. He checked through the window, even though he was sure that the last of the customers he'd counted in were counted out.

The bookseller, a man in his late fifties, looked up from an auction catalogue.

'*Shalom.*'

'*Shalom,*' said the man, closing the catalogue.

'I'm looking for a book on Israeli history,' said Net.

'Ah, Israel first and last.'

'And always,' replied Net, also in Hebrew.

'I was expecting you some days ago,' said the bookseller in English, his voice laced with the lyrical inflection, soft vowels and hard consonants of his adopted city.

Net looked around at the bookshelves and display stands.

'Where are you staying?'

'The Ard Na Sidhe, around the corner from Fitzwilliam Street.'

'I know it. I'll send the courier with your tickets. You're not to come back here, understood?'

'The passport?'

The man reached under the counter and opened a locked box. He took out a book-shaped package wrapped in brown paper. 'I think you'll enjoy this. You can keep it.'

'Nationality?'

'Romanian. You speak your grandparents' language? You are a linguist, am I right?'

Net ignored the question. 'When will I have my tickets? I stop over in Frankfurt?'

'You do. Don't worry, I'll arrange everything. I need the French passport back.'

Net reached into his jacket pocket for the passport and handed it over.

The bookshop owner locked it in the box, which he replaced under the counter. 'It'll take a day or so. Rest, see the sights. I hear you have an admirer at the café.'

* * *

Gallagher and Harry were dropped off by Chris near Euston Square and walked separately towards the University of London, coming around via Oxford Street. There was a visible increase in police numbers on the streets, including pairs of armed officers patrolling the shopping areas or guarding sites such as the British Museum.

Bish had left Tom and Mark at Great Ormond Street Hospital. They walked in from the bottom end of Russell Square Gardens. There were police vans parked in side streets and beside the formal green squares, tangible symbols of the anxious readiness of a metropolis waiting to be attacked again.

Gallagher and the team had converged on a small gallery at the edge of the university estate when Ian's taxi exploded outside the Warburg Institute on the other side of the School of Oriental and African Studies.

The fireball roared outwards filled with the bomb's primary fragments, propelled at high velocity over a huge distance. The shattering effect – the brisance – of the blast wave, created by the expanding gas, sent secondary fragments of glass, roof slate, timber and metal flying across a massive area as the ground shock split the tarmac, blowing open a crater where the car had been. Those that died first were killed by the direct weapon effects of the primary fragments, torn apart by shrapnel. Others were killed by the secondary fragments and crush injuries from debris. Those who were lucky lay on the floor with thermal burns, lung blast damage and eardrum rupture.

Police officers began running to their vehicles or away on foot towards the smoke that began to billow through the streets and float above the rooftops.

Gallagher watched as the policeman guarding a side door of the target building spoke into his radio and walked around the corner.

'Christ,' said Mark, 'that sounded like that 500-pounder the Yanks dropped next door to us in Helmand.'

'They haven't got the manpower,' said Gallagher. 'This is our way in.'

He led them through the door and along the service corridors linking the kitchens to the rest of the building. Young waiting staff, dressed in black and white, scurried past them chattering about the bomb as trolleys were left discarded.

Tom spotted a floor plan on the wall and they headed up the east staircase to the top of the building.

* * *

Imran supervised the kit checks. Each man was to carry a rucksack, the explosive booby trap devices shared between them. Each man carried an AKS-74U, ammunition and a two-way radio. All wore *shemagh* scarves, either red or green. Lufti had checked the video camera and laptop. He'd given Mahir the tripod to carry.

Imran adjusted the pistol on his belt and gave it a reassuring pat. He watched as Yasir attached the shape charge to the far wall, before carefully laying the det cord across the length of the space that they'd inhabited for so many days and nights. Each man knew his position and each man had made his peace with God. Now they would wait for the diversion to begin.

* * *

When they reached the service hatch that Imran's team had used, Gallagher checked the two schematics that Flic had drawn. Harry stripped away the police search team's tape that sealed the entrance to highlight any tampering.

'This one shows a solid wall ahead, the other one shows a partial wall.'

'Meaning?' Harry asked after they'd climbed up.

'Well, that's a solid wall. I'm wondering which version the police had when they searched up here.'

'It's not that solid,' said Mark, as he crawled forward to the wall. 'The mortar is fresh in this bit. The rest is the original brick.'

481

'So what now?' asked Harry, straightening his leg.

Mark ran his hand down the wall and lay on the floor, kicking out with both feet. 'There's a bit of give. I reckon we could break through with something hard and heavy.'

'You're having a laugh,' said Harry. 'What are we doing here, Owen?'

Gallagher shone his torch around the low room.

Mark kicked out again. 'I'm not joking. I've done enough time on building sites to know that this is a recent build and whoever did it didn't know what they were doing.'

'You're really thinking of breaking through?' Harry asked Gallagher.

'I'm thinking about it.'

'What the fuck is going on?' asked Tom from his position at the hatchway.

Gallagher continued to examine the space with his torch. 'Flic obviously knows that there's something behind that wall. A bomb has just gone off outside and the place is crawling with coppers. Sometimes we don't get to choose the field of battle. I say we go forward.'

'OK, just a minute,' said Harry. 'One question: we're not heading back out the way we came in because?'

'Because we're likely to be shot by the police or the SAS. If this is the hostage situation I think it is we'll just get eyes on and guide in the cavalry.'

Harry smiled. 'Yeah, I had a feeling you'd say that.'

482

Gallagher directed his torch beam to the left and illuminated the far corner where an assortment of old cast iron pipes had been piled. 'What about this lot, Mark?'

Mark joined him and began sorting through the discarded junk. Behind the pipes he found a short-handled lump hammer that had rusted. The head was loose on the wooden shaft. 'It'll depend on how much of a shit job they've done, but I'm game if you are.'

Adham drove the ambulance within the speed limit. The plates were cloned from another vehicle operating on the other side of the city, so the ANPR cameras wouldn't flag it up as stolen. Dressed as he was in a green paramedic uniform, nothing looked out of place. The fact that he was a white man was why he'd been chosen to drive – the same as Ian who had driven the diversion car.

When they were a mile and a half from the target, Adham activated the lights and siren and put his foot down.

Atif looked at each of the men sitting on the floor of the stripped-out and now armoured ambulance. 'Ready?' he asked.

They all nodded and returned to their own thoughts.

'I said are you ready?'

'Ready!' they called out as one.

'Saeed and Hammad take your positions behind the shields. Waleed, Bilawal, behind them. You know how it's going to go down. They won't stop us, but when we break through the inner cordon we'll have seconds to deliver a decisive blow. The uniforms won't help us once we start shooting. Use those moments and pick your targets as the back doors open. Then kill anyone you see.'

The four men moved into position.

Atif took the lids off two boxes of fragmentation grenades, removed six and slid the boxes along the floor towards the bulletproof shields welded to the floor.

He called through to Adham. 'Don't forget to take your seat belt off. I don't want you stuck in the cab.'

'No chance,' replied Adham, as he waved his thanks to a young police constable who stepped aside to let them into the final road of the journey. 'Thirty seconds!'

The ambulance mounted the curb and smashed through the side of the checkpoint barriers. Adham slammed his foot to the floor and drove through the large open gates. He watched the confusion on the faces that he passed, before selecting neutral. He jumped out of his seat and into the back, allowing the ambulance to travel on under its own momentum.

Atif opened the back doors and threw two grenades. As he dived behind the cover of the shields, Waleed and Bilawal threw two more as Saeed and Hammad began firing. While more grenades exited the back of the ambulance, Adham reached into the cab and applied the handbrake.

Atif patted Waleed and Bilawal on the shoulders and opened the floor hatch. The two men dropped through the hole. Saeed and Hammad were firing aimed shots at the police personnel in open view of the back doors. The first rounds from the armed police began to hit the sides of the ambulance and then started to ricochet off the welded shield plates.

Atif took cover. 'Keep your heads down!'

The passenger window shattered behind him. Waleed and Bilawal began firing from their position beneath the vehicle, shooting left and right, slicing through any legs that they saw. Bursts of high-velocity rounds sent those left standing into cover. Adham reloaded his AK and fired a burst out of the back. The ambulance rocked as each of the tyres were blown out. The firing from under the vehicle stopped.

'They've killed Waleed and Bilawal – it's nearly time.'

The sound of gunfire outside increased in its intensity. Tom crawled back into the attic space. 'It's a fucking war zone down there. From where I was at the window I could see an ambulance getting the shit shot out of it.'

The room shook as Imran's team blew the shape charge to enter the conference building.

'Are you serious about breaking through there?' Harry asked.

'I am now,' said Gallagher. 'H, cover the hatch. Tom come and help me and Mark smash these bricks out.'

Imran had led the way through the hole into the attic space of the adjacent building. It took a few minutes to transfer the men and equipment through the small gap, as they hadn't been able to risk a bigger charge in such a small space. Then they had to drop through the hatchway into the corridor below. His ears were still ringing. They were all covered in dust.

'Baha, guard this entrance in case anyone comes through from above.'

Baha nodded, they all knew the plan – they'd gone through it enough times.

'Eisa and Cadi follow us as we clear each corridor. Draw the curtains across each end window and set the booby traps. Then join us on the first floor.'

Eisa and Cadi pulled their equipment from the pile of bags and stood to one side.

'The rest of you split into the two teams. Team One: Zeeshan, Syed, Salman, Yasir – clearing corridors with me. Team Two: Lufti, Tarif, Mahir, empty the offices as we go. Dekel work with them but stop on the second floor. Anyone in uniform, kill them. Move everyone else you find to the lecture theatre corridor. The delegates will have been told to stay in the room.'

* * *

Saeed and Hammad charged out of the back of the ambulance and were killed instantly by a team of black-clad men wearing helmets and respirators. Atif threw out the last of the grenades, nodded to Adham and followed them. He was dead before he could launch himself off the back step.

Adham was lying on the floor. He held the phone-detonator between his legs, underneath his plasticuffed hands. He was a white-skinned paramedic, a hostage. He saw the two SAS soldiers swing into view and smiled at them.

'Thank God,' he said.

Eight rounds struck him in the chest and head. The phone slipped harmlessly on to the floor of the ambulance.

* * *

Bannerman shouted above the noise to a passing police constable. 'Get those infernal things switched off. I think everyone is aware that we have a situation, don't you?' The SAS troop commander was only a foot away but the sirens were deafening. Bannerman turned back to the soldier. 'All of them?'

487

'Yes, sir, they're all dead. We've got our explosive specialist checking the vehicle over, ready for the bomb squad. It was a cheeky attack, if a bit pointless. Obviously, they weren't expecting us to be waiting in the bushes.'

'Quite,' said Bannerman. 'The building is locked down as per the plan. There are six plainclothes protection officers in there but no one else. The agreement was that no foreign agents were to be inside.'

'You'll be moving them out now?'

'Their own people are in a holding area down the road. The extraction teams are en route.' Bannerman saw John Kinsella striding towards him. 'No one makes a move until this lot is secured and we're happy there's no secondary threat.'

'Got it.'

'The extraction has to go by the numbers or Downing Street will be spitting. It's a mess but it isn't too messy. When you've finished with the ambulance, have your men strengthen the cordon some distance behind the Met boys and out of view of any news crews. The cordon's been thrown back another several hundred metres but that won't stop a creative cameraman getting a shot. Fortunately, the no-fly zone means that the Sky News chopper won't be buzzing overhead.'

'We'll move back to our cover positions. Don't worry, we shan't embarrass you.'

Bannerman smiled. 'No embarrassment Toby, you've done wonders as usual, but we need this to look as low-key as a terrorist attack in London can look.'

John Kinsella had stopped a few feet away and was looking at his watch.

'As the PM keeps saying,' Bannerman continued, waving the American over, 'Britain is open for business.'

'My team is ready, Sandy, what's the hold-up?' asked Kinsella.

'We're on plan,' said Bannerman. 'I need to get this lot tidied up to give you a clear path out. There are motorcycle outriders ready and waiting for your convoy.'

Kinsella held up his hand as a message came through his earpiece.

A police constable approached them, his face flushed. 'Sir, the Chief Super says to tell you shots have been heard in the building. We've lost comms with the officers inside.'

'Bollocks!' said Bannerman. 'Toby, with me. John, feel free.'

They reached the Chief Superintendent's command vehicle that had been brought in following the car bomb and waited as he finished a radio call.

'Matthew,' said Bannerman. 'You've met Toby Pereira. This is John Kinsella, CIA.'

489

The policeman nodded at the American and shook his hand.

'Sandy, bad news: the stairwells to the first floor are barricaded with office furniture. The corridor windows at the ends of all floors are covered and shots have been fired. We've got no comms with any of our people inside.'

'We stopped the attack,' said Bannerman, thinking aloud.

The soldier adjusted his weapon on its sling. 'We stopped an attack. It looks like the car bomb wasn't the main diversion – more of a diversionary diversion.'

Bannerman smoothed his hair. 'Yes, Toby, so it would seem. How the fuck did they get in?'

'That's for later,' said Kinsella. 'The question for now is what are you going to do now that they are?'

'There's something else I need to tell you,' said Bannerman, leading the American by the arm.

Gallagher smelt the familiar odour of a shape charge as they broke through the wall.

'We don't know what's beyond that hole – none of you signed up for this. This is as far as you go.'

'This is our natural environment,' Harry replied. 'This is the only thing any of us are really good at. Where else would we want to be?'

'Come on, boss,' said Mark. 'I haven't had this much fun in ages.'

Tom shuffled up to Gallagher. 'We'll follow you. Like you said we're less likely to get slotted if we move forward than if we take our chances back out there with the SAS.'

Gallagher looked at the faces of the three men. 'OK, we go. Let's get it done – then we'll find a decent pub to spend the rest of the day in.'

He checked the space ahead was clear and pulled Mark, Tom and then Harry through the gap, helping the latter with the equipment bags.

'We don't know who or what we're up against, so switch on,' he whispered, indicating the blasted brickwork ahead. 'Tom with me. H, Mark follow up behind. Let's break out the longs.'

Harry opened the packs containing the assault rifles. Each man took one and Harry handed out the full magazines.

Gallagher crawled forward with his rifle covering the hole. The area behind the blown-out masonry was the attic space of the building next door. Gallagher saw a square patch of light emanating from an open hatch in the floor. He signalled for Tom to hold his position and crawled through to the light.

Taking a small dentist mirror from the pocket containing his lock-picking kit, Gallagher eased forward and carefully scanned the corridor below. There was one man, armed with an AKS-74U, facing away from him. He held up his hand to hold Tom back, fitted the suppressor to his SIG Sauer, checked the mirror again and stopped. He couldn't risk anyone hearing a gun fire, even if it was silenced.

Tom crawled to help him, holding on to Gallagher's legs. The man in the corridor turned and walked under the hatch. Gallagher slid through and grabbed the man's head, snapping the neck in one fluid movement.

Tom pulled Gallagher back into the attic space.

Mark, Harry and Tom followed Gallagher as he dropped through the hatch, each assisting the man behind as they lowered themselves and their equipment to the floor below. Gallagher patted Harry on the shoulder as he saw his friend wince on impact.

The corridor was empty except for the corpse, whose two-way radio began to speak.

'We've got their comms,' said Gallagher re-attaching the earpiece cable to stop the noise. 'That's a start. Mark grab his jacket, weapon and shemagh.'

Imran's team had taken control of the lecture theatre. They'd killed four plain clothes police officers in a brief exchange of fire in the first floor corridor. The bodies lay where they'd fallen outside the room that ran most of the length of the building.

Imran stood on the stage behind the lectern, his AKS-74U slung across his back. In one hand he held a Llama

Comanche pistol, the Spanish copy of Smith and Wesson's .357 Magnum. In the other, he held a two-way radio.

The conference delegates were sitting in their seats, hands on heads. The various members of staff that his men had rounded up had been herded to a group of seats on the left, nearest the stage. Imran placed the radio on the lectern, followed by a mobile phone. He scanned the room. A man in his early thirties wearing a blue blazer and a striped tie averted his eyes.

Imran continued to look out at the rows of frightened faces. He signalled to Yasir, who was standing four steps up from the man in the blazer's seat. Yasir walked down the stairs and shot the man in back of the head. A woman to the right began to scream. Salman told her to stop but she'd lost control. He slapped her. She kept screaming and screamed louder.

'Get her up,' shouted Imran. 'Bring her here,' he said, pointing to the carpeted area in front of the stage.

Syed helped Salman pull the woman from her seat. She screamed with every step to the flat open area in front of the lecture theatre's seating. Imran waved his pistol to indicate where he wanted her. He knelt on the stage and spoke to the woman, who stopped screaming. Imran placed the four-inch barrel of the gun into her mouth. He spoke quietly to her again. She nodded.

'Help her back to her seat,' he said to Salman.

493

A wave of whispers rippled through the audience and grew into the sound of chatter.

'Silence!' shouted Imran. 'The next person to speak without me telling them will be shot.'

Yasir had rolled the body in the blazer over on the stairs. He held up a Glock pistol and a covert radio.

Imran pulled the lectern's microphone up a little so that it was level with his mouth without him stooping. 'Keep your hands on your heads,' said his voice from the room's speaker system.

'No name badge,' Yasir called.

'Check everyone in your section,' Imran said to his men.

Zeeshan pointed his AK at a woman in a black trouser suit and white blouse sitting four seats in, three rows up from where he stood. 'Where is your conference badge?'

'I must have dropped it during this morning's break for coffee.'

'Stand up,' said Zeeshan. 'Come here.'

She shuffled past the delegates sitting to her right, who awkwardly half stood to allow her passage. On the stairs, she made her decision and drew her Glock. Zeeshan fired a burst into her chest and the Glock was discharged harmlessly into the air above his head.

Out in the police command vehicle, the building's plans were laid out in front of them.

'Toby, how long before you can put a plan into action?' asked Bannerman.

'Ground floor entry is going to be difficult with the furniture barricades: we'd be fish in a barrel. The lecture theatre's fire exits both open out on to the stairs either side and it only has a row of small windows at near ceiling height. There is an option for entry through the corridor windows.'

Bannerman moved to allow Kinsella a better view.

'The corridor curtains are drawn and we don't know what's on the other side,' continued Pereira. 'So that's a no-go as far as a sensible course of action is concerned. Any delay when they know we're breaking in and they'll kill the hostages. Not to mention we could lose half of the entry teams to booby traps. There's access through the roof but we'll have to get the team up there without being spotted or heard.'

Bannerman nodded. 'I'd suggest we get them used to the sound of a helicopter by asking the TV choppers to buzz in – but, apart from the exclusion zone being in place, I don't want the terrorists to get a bird's eye view of our forces on News 24.'

'So, it depends on how quickly you want us to go in and how much of a risk you want us to take,' said Pereira.

Bannerman turned to Kinsella. 'We have no idea what's happening inside. The CCTV cameras have been disabled

495

and we can't get eyes in there as the terrorists control all the possible entry points. We've got an external wall but drilling through that, well, let's just say we shan't be.'

Kinsella beckoned Bannerman to follow him. 'If they kill those hostages and there's even a hint that they have Iranian backing,' he said in a whisper, 'you know what's going to happen. Trying to negotiate with Iran is going nowhere. The Iranian leadership would happily sacrifice half of their country's population to eliminate Israel. If this goes down, we'll be going to war within hours. And then, I promise you, the lid will come off and we'll all be screwed.'

A set of stairs linked the floors at each end of the corridor. Gallagher and Mark went left, sending Harry and Tom right. Through the glass of the fire exit leading to the second floor Gallagher could see an armed man wearing a red shemagh patrolling the corridor.

'We've reached the second floor,' said Harry in Gallagher's earpiece.

'One sentry with AK, walking your way,' Gallagher replied.

Two clicks.

'Stop.' Gallagher watched as the man pulled the stock of his weapon into his shoulder, aiming down the corridor. 'H, move away from the door.'

Two clicks.

The sentry continued to point the AK at the fire door. He knelt, stood, walked forward, knelt, stood and turned, lowering and raising the weapon at intervals.

'He's practising his drills,' said Gallagher.

Two clicks.

Gallagher turned to Mark. 'We can't risk having him behind us.'

Mark nodded as Gallagher used his mirror to check the man's position through the glass. The sentry had moved in their direction before turning to face the other fire door again.

Mark kept listening and looking down the stairwell below. Tom was doing the same thing on the west side.

'I'll drop him at the mid-way point,' whispered Gallagher. 'H, clear the corridor from your end and I'll meet you in the middle. Tom and Mark will keep the stairs covered.'

Two clicks.

Gallagher eased the door open. The man turned, dropping to one knee to bring his AK up. The stock hadn't reached his shoulder when Gallagher's rounds hit him in his chest and head. Harry came through the fire door at the other end of the corridor and began to clear the offices. Gallagher did the same and met Harry at the dead terrorist's body.

'There's a floor plan in the stairwell,' said Gallagher.

'Seen,' replied Harry.

'The floor below us contains the lecture theatres. Below that are the ground floor offices. Be ready for things to get busy. We'll stay in our pairs on each stairwell. Take it slow and steady.' He pulled off the man's jacket and shemagh and slung the AK over his back.

Gallagher rejoined Mark in the stairwell. 'How are you doing?' he whispered.

'I really haven't had this much fun in ages,' Mark replied with a boyish grin.

'Good, let's move.'

Harry heard the first-floor fire door shut below him. Tom froze, his assault rifle pointing towards the noise.

'Tango below, patrolling out to stairwell.'

The door opened and closed again.

'Tango returning to the corridor.'

Gallagher listened and held his position as the other sentry entered the stairwell on his side. He waited for the man to move back through the door.

'They can see each other,' he whispered. 'We'll need to take them simultaneously. Mark will get their attention. H, take your man with a pistol as he turns this way.'

Two clicks.

Gallagher watched as Mark laid his FNC rifle on the floor and adjusted the shemagh he'd wrapped around his head. Mark pulled the slung AK to his front and gripped the two-way radio that Gallagher placed in his free hand.

Gallagher nodded and held the fire door ajar after Mark had walked through. The sentry nearest their end turned. Mark waggled the radio out to the side at shoulder height indicating a problem. The terrorist reached for his own radio attached to his belt but then frowned and focused on the man who wasn't Baha.

Mark stepped to one side, revealing Gallagher in a low crouch behind him. Gallagher fired two silenced rounds and the man fell backwards. The man behind him hit the floor a second later and Gallagher saw Harry mirroring his firing position.

They dragged the bodies out to the stairwell as quietly as they could. Back in the corridor, Gallagher quickly took stock. On one side were two lecture theatres. On the other a larger one with two entrance doors, between which was a locked door bearing a small sign: PROJECTOR ROOM.

Harry and Tom checked the two smaller rooms, first looking into the interiors via the spyholes that were meant to prevent unnecessary disturbances to lectures. Gallagher used the spyhole in the door nearest to him and took in the scene unfolding in the bigger lecture theatre. Mark kept watch.

From his position, Gallagher had a good view of a large part of the room. Just inside, slightly to the left of the door, stood a man with an AK who was positioned behind the first set of sloping seats. The room was full of people sitting with their hands on their heads. He could see another armed man at the bottom of the aisle stairs. Behind this guard was the stage. One man was connecting a cable from a laptop on a small table to a video camera on a tripod. Another man paced behind a lectern gesticulating at seven hostages kneeling on the stage.

'Harry,' said Gallagher, taking out his lock-picking kit. 'Find the corridor lights and turn them off, will you?'

Harry nodded.

Gallagher began to pick the projector room lock, turning the barrel as Harry extinguished the lights. Inside the darkened room, Gallagher had a full view of the lecture theatre from behind the glass that allowed the equipment to project images to the stage below. The room's PA system was on and he could hear every word that the man on stage raved. He made a mental note of what he saw and then retreated back into the corridor.

'Bad?' asked Harry.

'Not good.'

'Plan?'

'Call the chaps in the white hats. Take up defensive positions. I'll be back in a minute.'

Gallagher entered one of the smaller lecture theatres and dialled Bannerman's number.

'I've got a bit of a situation, Owen. Can I call you back?'

'Sandy, I'm outside a lecture theatre full of hostages at the University of London. I'm hoping that it's the same situation.'

'I'm listening.'

'Twelve IC4 males accessed from adjacent building attic. Armed with AKS-74Us and various pistols. One dead top floor, one dead second floor, two dead first floor. Ground floor stairwells barricaded and booby-trapped, corridor windows and lecture theatre also rigged. The lecture theatre is full of hostages in their seats, except for seven on the stage. The ranting maniac in charge identified them as American and Israeli – looks like they were the panel addressing the conference. A total of eight men are positioned around the room.'

'We have Troop preparing. Explosives in the room?'

'Secured to the walls. There's something else on the stage. It looks technical: open metal case, cylindrical centrepiece, digital unit on the left.'

'We can have teams coming through from up top in a few minutes. Delay, harass, block, fix and channel if you have to, but don't engage.'

'No time, no choice. He's going to slot the panel members on camera. No need for him to hang around after that.'

'You're armed? Who's with you?'

'Yep, me plus three.'

'Christ, Owen, that's bad odds.'

'The only odds we have, unfortunately.'

'We'll kill the phone signal and shut down any internet access. We can't allow them to broadcast this madness. I'll send the teams in now. Wait as long as you can.'

'OK.'

'Good luck.'

Gallagher put the phone in his pocket and walked out of the room to brief Harry, Tom and Mark.

'Clear?'

They nodded.

'Remember, shoot fast and at the nose – don't fuck about.'

Bannerman explained the situation to Kinsella.

Kinsella massaged the bridge of his nose. 'Those memory sticks you had analysed, the circumstantial evidence you've gathered surrounding them, the Mossad guy, the woman from Six,' said the American. 'It's a Black Flag, you know it and I know it. We've been goaded into following a trail to Tehran. The Israelis have gone too far this time but it changes nothing. If those hostages die we're going to war. Not to mention that you're missing a dirty bomb that could be sitting in there, from what your man has reported.'

'I think even Mossad would draw the line at that but you're right, the public can never know it was an Israeli Black Flag operation.'

502

'You're damn right no one can know, it'd be a disaster. We have to keep public opinion with us in this war. We can't hand the enemy a propaganda victory like this. And you're forgetting your own people seem to be involved.'

'Believe me, John, I haven't forgotten.'

'Believe me, Sandy, we've tried a few operations like this and they can be very successful. Never against our allies or our own, though.'

Bannerman raised an eyebrow.

Kinsella ignored the implication. 'What are you going to do about your friend in there? How far does his involvement go?'

'Wrong place at the wrong time. If he lives, I'll see him through it.'

'If he lives and he stops this, I might offer him a job.'

'I doubt he'd take it, he's very Groucho when it comes to joining clubs,' said Bannerman as he turned. 'Toby! Be ready to brief me in two minutes.'

Imran picked up his radio. 'Baha, Dekel come down to the first floor and cover the stairwells. Eisa and Cadi hold your positions.'

Nothing.

'Baha, Dekel, respond.'

Nothing.

503

Imran paced over to a long canvas bag next to the lectern. Lufti had checked the video equipment was working correctly. It was time. He addressed the audience.

'We are now broadcasting to the world. We will show them what it means to fight for God.' Imran looked over at the Israeli and American delegates kneeling on the stage and pulled a gleaming sword from the bag. 'You are the first to die. The sword is the key to Paradise.' He looked at the radio in his hand. 'Baha, Dekel, respond.'

Nothing.

Urine pooled around a white-haired scientist's knees as frightened sobs were stifled in the audience. No one wanted to witness what was coming next, but no one wanted to join the men and women kneeling on the stage. There was always a chance. There was always hope.

Imran transmitted again. 'Eisa, go and check on Dekel and Baha. Cadi, hold your position. Acknowledge.'

The radio remained stubbornly silent.

'We lost the signal,' said Lufti.

Imran looked at the mobile phone resting on the ledge of the lectern. 'Tarif, go kick some sense into Eisa – tell him to check on the others.'

Tarif nodded as the left and right doors to the lecture theatre opened.

From the stage, Imran registered the men who had entered – the jackets, the AKs, the headscarves – and was about to launch a tirade against the sentries until his mind told him something was wrong. As the projector-room glass shattered he threw himself off the stage to the carpeted area below.

Harry and Tom fired from each side of the projector, hitting Syed and Salman who were standing on the stairs. Gallagher and Mark killed Tarif and Mahir who were nearest to each of the two doors. Zeeshan and Yasir returned fire from the area adjacent to the stage as Lufti followed Imran's lead and jumped into cover.

Gallagher and Mark crouched behind the top row of seats. The delegates were hiding as close to the ground as they could get. The Israelis and Americans on stage were trying to shelter in the alcove to the side.

'There are four at the front,' said Harry in Gallagher's earpiece. 'One to our right, three to the left.'

Tom fired a burst.

Gallagher took a breath. 'We need to stop anyone going near that case. Or any detonator. We've got to move quick.' He lifted his head above the backboard behind the seats, ducking back into position as rounds flew over his head.

Harry and Tom gave covering fire as Gallagher darted across the space at the top of the stairs to where Mark was waiting.

'What now, boss?'

'We haven't got time to fuck about. We need to kill these bastards and stop them blowing the room.'

505

Mark nodded and the team heard his voice in their earpieces. 'Cover me,' he said calmly.

Gallagher grabbed his sleeve but Mark yanked his arm away. 'For Kenny,' he said, turning and firing a burst down the stairs.

Harry and Tom fired aimed shots at the last known positions of the terrorists. Mark moved down the stairs in a low crouch, firing as he went. Yasir broke cover and shot him in the stomach allowing the burst to travel up Mark's chest and into his face.

Gallagher was six steps above where Mark toppled backwards. Tom hit Yasir in the head with two rounds. Harry fired at where he thought Zeeshan and Imran were hiding with Lufti.

As Gallagher thundered down the stairs his FNC jammed. Tom and Harry continued to lay down fire. Gallagher tossed the weapon to the side and pulled the slung AK from behind his back. Zeeshan emerged from his hiding position and took four rounds in the body from Gallagher's AK.

Imran bolted for the stage as Lufti stood to give covering fire. Gallagher stumbled and pitched forward as Harry and Tom both fired at Lufti before he could train his weapon on their falling friend.

Gallagher threw himself into an ungainly forward roll as he hit the bottom step and shot Lufti, who had made it into what he thought was cover.

Imran jumped on stage, ran to the lectern and held out his phone in triumph. He gripped one of the Israelis around the neck with his forearm, holding his Comanche pistol to her head.

'Now we die!' he shouted.

He pressed the speed dial number that had been pre-selected when he first entered the lecture theatre.

Nothing.

Gallagher had the man in his sights but didn't want to hit the hostage. 'It's over,' he shouted. 'Drop the weapon and step away from her.'

Imran looked at Gallagher, then at the phone and laughed before throwing the handset at him. 'It's over when I say it's over, *kuffar*.' He pulled the woman across the stage, heading for the metal case in a carefully slow crab-like manoeuvre.

Gallagher let the AK dangle from his chest on its sling and pulled out his SIG Sauer. He fired three times, hitting Imran in the thigh and shin.

Imran's legs buckled and he fell against the woman he was holding. He pushed her forward and fired past the hostage at Gallagher, killing a delegate who was trying to crawl away up the stairs. The woman jumped from the stage, curling up in a ball on the floor below.

Imran stared wildly at the case and dragged his leg. He could detonate the main bomb manually. As he threw himself at the centre of the stage, he turned his face to the side and saw Gallagher's pistol held in a two-handed grip.

Gallagher fired into the man's head until the SIG's magazine was empty.

Black-clad figures burst into the room shouting instructions that no one should move. Gallagher raised his hands and tossed the pistol. He placed his hands on his head and kneeled. He made no attempt to take off the slung AK and waited to be shot in the back. He heard Harry's voice at the top of the stairs calling out – identifying Gallagher as a friendly – and breathed again.

* * *

Almost an hour had passed before the SAS troopers led them out into the sunlight. Gallagher saw Bannerman approaching with a dark-haired SAS officer.

'Take those cuffs off him,' Bannerman said to the troopers either side of Gallagher. He indicated to Tom and Harry who were similarly flanked a few metres behind. 'And release those two men there.'

'Afternoon, Sandy,' said Gallagher, looking around at the area outside the university buildings. 'I'm afraid the mess inside is as bad as out here.' He rubbed his wrists now that they were free.

'Good to see you're in one piece, Owen.'

Gallagher turned and watched the stretchers coming out. The police were still evacuating the delegates with a team of paramedics and had started recovering the bodies of their colleagues. He stopped a policeman who was making notes. 'Which one is my friend?'

'Third one to come out of the door next,' said the sergeant.

Bannerman followed Gallagher, Harry and Tom. Gallagher pulled the blanket back, uncovering Mark Keane's shattered body and face.

Harry pulled the blanket back over Mark's head.

'I'm sorry, Owen,' said Bannerman.

Gallagher walked away.

* * *

The two detectives from the National Bureau of Criminal Investigation, a branch of Ireland's police force, *An Garda Síochána*, watched as the bodies were removed through the front door of the guest house near Fitzwilliam Street.

'What have we got?' the older man asked the ranking uniformed officer on the scene.

'Romanian male. We found his passport but no other forms of ID. There were several hundred Euros in the room but nothing else to go on. The second body is a young woman. Irish driving licence.'

'What happened?' asked the other detective.

509

'Looks like a professional hit: three in the head, you know they're dead.'

The older detective nodded and offered the two other men a pack of cigarettes. His NBCI colleague took one, while the other officer shook his head.

'That's pretty much all I can tell you at this stage, but that's why we notified you lot,' said the uniform. 'The forensics team will file a report and we're making enquiries door to door. We had a couple of gang-related murders last week, as you know.'

'So you think this is related to the turf war?' the detective with the cigarettes asked.

'Could be. There was a young Lithuanian shot dead in his bed in Bride Street last Thursday and the Romanian fella who was slotted in a house in Dorset Street at the weekend. Both were linked to gangs that are treading on local toes. Now we've got another dead Romanian with a bagful of Euros.'

'Has the male victim been in the country long?'

'Like I said, we're running the checks with his passport.'

The older detective blew out a long plume of smoke. 'Well, at least London has got all the bombs these days. This shouldn't worry the tourist board too much.'

* * *

510

Mofaz arrived at the private airfield in Oxfordshire in the embassy car. The chauffeur handed him his case. The rest of his effects would be forwarded later in the week. As he walked across the tarmac to the waiting Gulfstream G150, Mofaz glanced across the surrounding countryside. He wouldn't be back for a while. Perhaps he'd visit London again. He hoped so.

Perhaps he would return when he retired, visit old haunts and see the sights without looking over his shoulder quite so much.

For now, it was back to Tel Aviv. He'd been posted sideways. He'd have to ride out a small storm but the mission details were still secret and trails were obscured. His sponsors were satisfied with the part he'd played. If he kept his mouth shut and his head down, he'd regain his position in the promotion race within a couple of years. He had no regrets.

He entered the plane and nodded to the three operatives sitting in the group of four seats at the front of the cabin. The other occupant's head was bowed, his wrists cuffed, hands resting in his lap.

Mofaz looked to the rear of the cabin and selected one of the individual leather seats. As he drew level with the prisoner the man looked up. There was burning contempt in Ozi's eyes but the young fool knew better than to goad the men on the plane with angry and impotent words.

511

Mofaz slumped in his chosen seat. The pain in his shoulder was beginning to push through the painkilling effects of the drugs. Thankfully, the Gulfstream's seats were more than comfortable and he'd sleep for much of the flight. He was beginning to feel his age.

TWO WEEKS LATER

Tom had fallen asleep in the chair next to the bed. He tensed as he woke and scanned the room, remembering where he was. The shorter of the two nurses he'd spoken to that day – Alice – was tidying the flowers he'd brought for Connie. He'd arrived with a fresh bunch every day, but his sister had yet to see any of them. The IV drip at the canal had kept her alive but the sedative it contained had sent her into a coma.

'You should go home and rest. We'll call you if there's any change. These things take time, she's healing. The doctors are really optimistic, you know that.'

Tom stretched. 'Later. I want to be with her as much as I can.'

Alice filled the jug at Connie's beside with fresh water. He could feel the curiosity flowing off her. The staff had been told not to ask questions. But it was obvious that Connie had been through an ordeal and the armed police guards who'd stood outside her room for the first four days added to the mystery. This malnourished and initially hypothermic young woman in a medically-induced coma was certainly an enigma.

'Are you on duty tomorrow?' Tom asked.

'Day shift – why?'

'I'm going to be away for part of the day, I've got a funeral to go to. If she wakes up and I'm not here, tell her, will you?'

* * *

The rain had stopped by the time the mourners trooped from the church to gather at the open grave. Bannerman held back for the same reason he'd sat as far away from the pulpit as he could.

He watched as Gallagher, Harry, Tom and Frankie lowered the coffin on its straps. He'd offered to help with the funeral costs but Gallagher had insisted on paying for all of it.

As the vicar threw a handful of earth, Bannerman watched an old man wearing the scarlet coat of a Chelsea Pensioner hug Mark Keane's mother. He heard her crying change to a dreadful wailing.

Gallagher turned his ashen face and began to walk slowly away through the gravestones – a man alone, surrounded by his ghosts.

* * *

Rutherford pressed the intercom button and told Alexis Clark that he wasn't to be disturbed for at least an hour. He hadn't selected her on her looks – not that she wasn't a pretty young woman – but because she was a formidable gatekeeper.

He pushed back his chair and walked to the window. London was alive in the weak sunshine, going about its business as it had for two thousand years. The dust had settled outside and the dust was settling once again in the corridors of power. Rutherford had insulated himself and his political contacts well. Overall, they were pleased with how the operation had panned out. It had been somewhat messier than they'd envisaged but the result was the same: the UK and US governments were taking a harder line on Iran, in open support of the Israelis.

People had died, yes, but war meant damage. Nobody of note had been killed, after all – discounting the mayor, of course, but he'd been seen as a growing pain in the arse for some time. No, it had, on balance, worked out rather well.

The dirty bomb had been a shock. It hadn't been reported in the news. The delegates didn't know what it was and the terrorists were all dead. Everyone else involved had been debriefed with copies of the Official Secrets Act being waved in their faces. The Russians could not be embarrassed regarding the loss of the material. The Americans needed their support at the United Nations and now they were more likely to get it.

Flic Anderson was a problem, but she'd be keeping a low profile for a good while. She'd managed to leave the country. He hadn't been surprised to find out. There had been a possible sighting in south-west France but the trail had led nowhere. Anderson would pop up soon enough. When she did, there would be an Israeli kill team nearby. Neither Rutherford nor his contacts could risk her talking to anyone, particularly the CIA. Fortunately she wouldn't want to risk talking to them either, if she knew what was good for her.

He watched tourists on a river cruise waving at other tourists being bounced along the Thames in a RIB speedboat. London was business – that's what it did. The West End, the Georgian grandeur, the elitist echoes of the green squares, the great river: the lifeblood of a fetid but vibrant metropolis. London had always absorbed its shocks and always recovered quickly. That was something he had in common with this great powerhouse of a city. He smiled back at his reflection in the glass. Another thing he had in common with London was his ability to use the corruption of the great and the good for his own ends.

* * *

Flic Anderson was sitting on the balcony of the small villa that she had rented just outside the Moroccan town of Essaouira. She looked down on the pool and remembered the tiger named Hope swimming at the Baghdad zoo.

Getting out of Britain had been simple enough. She'd picked up a tail in Bayonne but had slipped the net. Getting back into the UK would be harder. She'd bide her time, build her contacts and formulate a plan. Not that she was in any hurry to head back to the rain. She needed some sun, some space and time to think. She needed time to channel her anger so her revenge would be cold in its brutal execution. She'd had confirmation that Alan the van man had delivered her crate to the storage unit in Hammersmith. The fees had been paid in advance. She had all the time that she needed.

Of course, she'd have to keep moving. The villa was rented for a fortnight but she'd be gone in a matter of days. Even though she'd dyed and cut her hair, changed her eye colour with lenses and was posing as an English teacher awaiting her friends, a lone woman would always elicit curiosity – wherever she was in the world. It wasn't a problem. She had money, half a dozen passports and a preternatural ability to sense danger.

She removed her sunglasses and walked into the shade of her bedroom. It was time for a swim, time to ease through the water like the tiger in the zoo, biding her time, waiting for an opportunity to show her strength with bloody tooth and claw.

* * *

517

Gallagher took a sip of wine, closed his newspaper and looked up.

'Owen, I just dropped by to say how terribly sorry I am again. I do feel awful about, well, you know.'

'Sit down Sandy; you're making the place look untidy.'

'How's Connie?'

'She's on the mend, apparently. She's out of the woods, according to the doctors, but still doesn't want to see me – which is understandable.'

'Tom and Harry?'

'Tom's calmer than I've ever seen him, but we won't be going on holiday together in the near future. Harry's busy trying to save his marriage.'

'And Mark's grandfather?'

'He's bearing up. I'm taking him out for a beer tomorrow with Harry, as it happens. What's the score with Parker?'

'He made a deal and headed off to Greece. His money will make him very welcome in that ailing economy. How about you?'

'What about me?' Gallagher asked. He topped up his glass. 'I still don't understand how our photos were kept out of the press, but it means we can all keep working.'

'My boss is a wily old fox and trusts his gut.'

'Good for him.'

Bannerman smoothed his hair. 'I'm still finding it hard to believe that Fluffy was involved in all that.'

'Fluffy?'

'Flic Anderson, it's what we called her at Oxford.'

'Fluffy?'

'An ironic moniker? You really are an oik sometimes, Gallagher.'

'I sometimes wonder if I missed out by not going to university, but then you open your mouth and the feeling passes.'

'All's well that ends well, though – right?' Bannerman looked out of the window as he spoke. Gallagher saw a melancholy nostalgia flash momentarily in the other man's eyes.

'No news on who she was working with?'

'Drawbridges have been raised. Meetings are being held behind closed doors, no entry for anyone below top-floor management. Of course, the Iranians are proclaiming their innocence to anyone who'll listen but there aren't many who will.'

'Any leads for finding her?'

'No, she's off the radar. She'll resurface, she'll have to.'

The room was quiet apart from the sound of Claire turning the pages of her fashion magazine behind the counter. Eve wasn't due on shift for another hour.

Gallagher sipped his wine and looked out beyond the corner towards the bustling Charing Cross Road.

Bannerman shifted uneasily in his seat and straightened his tie.

Gallagher folded his newspaper, coughed and indicated to Claire to bring another glass.

'So,' he said, looking back at Bannerman. 'Who do you want me to watch?'

jakemorrisauthor.com

Lightning Source UK Ltd.
Milton Keynes UK
UKOW04f1504090714

234825UK00002B/6/P